I Wanna Be - a Diamond … Someday!

◆

I Wanna Be - a Diamond ... Someday!

◆

Anton K. Vyborny

Order this book online at www.trafford.com
or email orders@trafford.com

Most Trafford titles are also available at major online book retailers.

Print information available on the last page.

ISBN: 978-1-4907-7442-8 (sc)
ISBN: 978-1-4907-7441-1 (e)

Trafford rev.   06/10/2016

North America & international
toll-free: 1 888 232 4444 (USA & Canada)
fax: 812 355 4082

Chapter one

Southside Johnnie's - a busy Montana bar - was loud with the late happy hour crowd. It could have been Billings, Bozeman, Butte or even Missoula, he'd been to all of them and had found solace at a friendly saloon in each place where he could take a seat either at the bar and find conversation or at a high-top table in a strategic corner where he could quietly observe all the activity and get lost in his thoughts. That was the usual way it went.

It was the middle of December the height of the Christmas season. The malls were packed with holiday shoppers as the merchants all stood by with their fingers crossed hoping that sales would beat the forecast. Climate change had arrived in Montana. It was so far the warmest December on record. Of course that didn't bother Geoff at all. Winter, cold weather and snow were all seasons and weather he could nicely do without, thank you.

After a few seconds the server approached his table - a pretty brunette with long hair that she had pulled back into a ponytail. Strands of wavy hair hung down along her cheeks framing her square jaw line that ended in a wide V- shape with a prominent dimpled chin. She was neatly dressed in a starched ribbed and pleated formal white blouse, string bowtie and black women's tuxedo pants. It all went well on her petite frame.

"Hi, welcome to Southside Johnnie's my name is Tara; I'll be serving you tonight," she said with a bright bubbly smile which lit up his table by the window. Her brilliant azure eyes sparkling in the subdued lighting.

"Nice to meet you Tara, I'm Geoff," he said.

"Will anyone be joining you?"

"No, Tara, it will just be me."

He ordered a glass of Merlot. She asked if he wanted to eat.

"Maybe later," he replied.

"Well, if you get hungry let me know, I'll bring a menu and explain our specials. I'll be right back with your wine."

She returned with his wine and met his eyes with a quick glance and a spontaneous easy smile. "Enjoy it, I'll check on you in a little while."

Maybe it was her looks, her personality, her mannerisms or a coalescence of all of those attributes that made him feel comfortable and gave him a sense of being appreciated or at least acknowledged as he glanced around the bar and allowed his thoughts to drift back to a time long ago –

<center>~~~　　　~~~　　　~~~</center>

Another Christmas, this one in Waikiki, Hawaii on the island of Oahu, where he was a young sailor sitting alone at the bar in a downtown club off Kalakaua Avenue. He was not in uniform of course. He had quickly learned that sailors back in those days were unwelcome guests in Waikiki, or for that matter near any military installation.

The sun was shining brightly through the open doorway to the street; the air heavy with the perfumed smell of the tropics just after the usual midday tropical squall. The bar was lively; although he was ignored by the crowd of revelers around him. He had given up trying to join in their celebration. He was alone with his memories of yesterday and his dreams for tomorrow. It was usually like this. Even this early in his adulthood it seemed the pattern for life was already set. Someday it would be different, he kept telling himself. But he didn't know when or even if, that someday would ever come. Deep down he really didn't believe it ever would. In the corner of his mind played the lament of a song verse over and over - *someday never comes.*

Years later whenever he felt like this he would just throw all his stuff in the bed of his truck and hit the interstate - move on to another address, another start. He would begin again - over and over until he got it right - if indeed he ever could.

~~~   ~~~   ~~~

Roused out of his reminiscence by the feeling of a soft hand resting on his shoulder, Tara came into his peripheral vision.

"You're awfully quiet Geoff, how are you doing... can I get you anything?"

"Oh I think I'm ready to have dinner Tara, any suggestions?"

"What do you have an appetite for... fish, meat, pasta or poultry?"

Before he could answer the host came hurrying over to the table and interrupted them.

"Tara, your husband's on the phone, he says it's urgent."

"Oh excuse me please, I... I'm sorry sir I really need to take this call," Tara said as she hurried away her bubbly countenance morphing into a frown of concern.

"I'm sorry about that sir, may I take your order?" the host asked.

"Thanks, but I can wait, I'm not in any hurry," he said.

A few minutes later Tara returned followed by another server, "Sir, this is Megan, I have to leave so she will be taking over for me. I'm very sorry; I hope you have a nice dinner." As she turned to leave a young man caught her in his arms.

"Honey, are you okay?" the young man asked her as an older man walked quickly up behind them. "Hey dad, thanks for coming," the young man said looking over Tara's shoulder at the man, "but it's probably better if we just go on alone. Can we catch up with you tomorrow?"

"Sure, son you two go on and give my regards," said the man as he absently glanced over in Geoff's direction. He began to turn and walk away but then stopped and turned for a second look staring hard at Geoff for a long moment; the furrows in his brow deepening with question.

3

Geoff sensed his stare and looked up making eye contact. As the seconds ticked off, layers of time slowly peeled away leaving a hint of recognition.

"Pardon me sir, you wouldn't by any chance happen to be Geoff McEwen?" the man asked as he approached the table.

"Yes sir I am... and you are? Oh for God's sake...," said Geoff as he recognized the voice and mentally connected it with a face and a name from the distant past. "Brian... Brian Wilkins! Geez...how the hell are you?" said Geoff jumping to his feet and thrusting out his hand.

"My, God buddy it's great to see you, you old son-of-a-bitch," said Brian grasping Geoff's hand in his old familiar crushing handshake.

Their handshake dissolved into a backslapping embrace.

"Still keeping in shape, I see. You're looking great," said Brian pulling a punch to Geoff's mid-section.

Geoff reacted instinctively grabbing his hand and retaliating with a similar shot to Brian's solar plexus. "You're in great shape yourself, you old fart. Geez, it's over 30 years; we said we were going to keep in touch. I guess I..."

"Hey buddy, I think we both just wanted to forget. How the hell have you been? Ever get flashbacks of the jungles?" asked Brian.

"Nah...you? Hey Brian, grab a seat! How's life after the teams?"

"Good... it's been good. Well you know... a lot of whiskey under the bridge, Geoff."

They sat down and began to put thirty years of life into perspective for each other. Geoff and Brian had been teammates attached to the same platoon with U.S. Navy SEAL Team One in Vietnam.

Brian liked Geoff; they had hit it off right away in the teams. They formed the perfect complement for each other. When Geoff was off on a tear Brian was there to haul him back to reality. When Brian had a wild hair up his butt Geoff could reason with him and cool things down. They were buddies for swimming and diving evolutions as well as tactical ground assault maneuvers. Geoff was open and straightforward. If he didn't like you, he didn't bother giving you any shit; he just walked away and left you alone. Never one to rain on a parade or try to stand out in a crowd on the beach he saved it all for when it really counted. When their platoon lost its point man Geoff stepped in and took over. He was good at it too. Brian attributed that to his quiet demeanor - still waters run deep. They had gotten through some hairy encounters without casualties. But neither Geoff nor Brian would take credit. They didn't need medals. Medals were for heroes. They were just teammates and everyone was better off because of that.

Brian had spent eleven years with the teams and had been attached to one of the last platoons to leave the Mekong Delta. After the teams left the country in the early seventies the usual disorder of standing down took over and a lot of the veterans walked away. Disenchantment with the execution of the war along with public antipathy fanned by large segments of the media left a bitter taste in their mouths. There were no heroes coming home from Vietnam. Nobody acknowledged a veteran and thanked them for their service.

Megan the server came over to check on them. "Hey...how are you guys doing, can I get you anything?"

"Yes, thank you, how about two shots of your top shelf tequila," said Brian. "You do still drink that old Mexican nectar?" he asked chuckling as he looked over at Geoff.

"It's still my drink of choice when I'm having more than one. Let's see yours was Beam and water as I recall."

"You got it covered buddy," said Brian, "although I have slowed down just a tad. It takes me two, sometimes three sessions to finish a bottle these days," he said with a raspy chuckle and a wide grin spreading across his weathered tanned face.

"Glad to hear that, you have to watch the old liver. You only have one," Geoff said with a chuckle.

"Yeah... I know," said Brian his lighthearted demeanor abruptly changing to a more somber mood as a serious expression flashed across his face.

Brian as well as Geoff had maintained his trim athletic build. They were both the same height, just a shade under six foot two. Obviously all the talk of excessive drinking was for the most part just male bravado. They both had been through two less than successful marriages.

"Speaking of vital organs, to change the subject a bit, did you happen to notice that young man I spoke with earlier?"

"You mean the one that walked off with my server?"

"Yeah, he's my son Chip from my first marriage. She's his wife Tara."

"She's a cutie, I guess he got his taste from his old man," said Geoff.

"Yeah, at least I had that much of an influence on him. They're the reason I'm here in Montana. I was settled in Florida but after Chip got married Tara didn't want to leave her family. Her dad's in very poor health. So I came out here to stay close. I've got a hell of a bit of irony for you… hold on to your seat Geoff because you're not going to believe this. You'd never guess it in a million years so I'll just go ahead and tell you - her dad is Frank Robbins. Does that name ring a bell?"

"Frank Robbins?" Geoff puzzled over the name for a minute. "Not Robbins, the CIA control operative in Cambodia, the one who wanted my ass on a platter, that one?" asked Geoff scowling in an expression of distaste at the memory.

"The very same buddy and I know how you must feel about him. Hell, even I would have taken him out back then if I had gotten the chance."

"The bastard pulled strings trying to get me court-martialed. Even changed some After Action reports redacting paragraphs from debriefs just to cover his own butt. Luckily time ran out on our deployment and I never heard any more," said Geoff.

"Didn't I warn you not to volunteer for any of those extra missions, especially the black stuff with the company?" asked Brian with a bit of a chuckle.

"Yeah, I should have listened. That sucker put paid to any thoughts I had of shipping over," said Geoff.

"Oh I heard he put out a lot of scuttlebutt about rules of engagement infractions, neutrality violations, even some bullshit allegations of war crimes – but it was all smoke, noise and no substance. I don't see how it would have gone very far," said Brian. "It was just a busted operation. Everyone who knew him back then knew he could be a real asshole."

"Sure, but the bastard even threatened to get State involved."

"He was posturing, that's all. If it had come down to that shit we would have invited him out on an op with the blessing of the CO. You know none of us would have stood by and allowed a teammate to get hung out to dry."

"Maybe not, but you can't fight the company, not back then...not now," said Geoff.

"It was more than just the agency, Geoff. CIA, Defense and State all had conflicting agendas in that crazy war. We got caught in the middle doing the devil's bidding."

"At least we got through it. Too many were less fortunate," replied Geoff.

"Yeah, but there's nothing you or I can do about that now buddy, you can't relive yesterdays. If you could you'd probably make the same choices and the same mistakes; if you did happen to change anything you and I might not be here today having this conversation."

"Geez, Brian you've really gotten philosophical. You never used to give a rat's ass about past choices or what the future might hold in store."

"Yeah, well I guess time changes people, mellows them. You know sometimes even an SOB like Frank can find God."

"Sure as long as he finds Him to his advantage."

"It's not like that, he's changed Geoff; he's a whole different person with a human side now. He's been married a long time, he has a wonderful daughter in Tara and now he's looking forward to becoming a granddad. Unfortunately, he might not get the chance. It turns out he's got a really serious medical condition – End Stage Renal Disease. He just suffered another complication this evening; that's why Chip came in to get Tara. They're heading over to the hospital see him. He needs a kidney transplant and time is running out. I tried to volunteer as a donor but I'm not the right blood type."

"Even so..."

"Now look, I know what you're going to say Geoff but he is, after all, Tara's dad and she's more like the daughter I wish I had then just an in-law. She's a sweetheart and a real daddy's girl and I think their very strong bond of love for each other is what brought about the sea change in him. I can't bear to see her or my son hurting and this has hit them awfully hard."

"Geez that's tough; it puts a whole different perspective on things."

"You can say that again. You got any kids Geoff?"

"No, my first ex couldn't have any and my second ex didn't want any."

"That's too bad, Geoff. Kids make it all worthwhile. If it weren't for Chip, I probably would have crossed over the bar by now."

"I've had my share of those moments too Brian but then my stubborn cynicism kicks in and I figure I'll just hang around and piss off some people. But getting back to Robbins, what's his blood type, anyway?"

"It's a rare one, AB negative. Not a lot of possible donors around with that type available for spare parts."

"Yeah well, you're looking at one", said Geoff.

"Whoa… you Geoff, you're AB negative?"

"Yes sir – now how's that for irony?"

"Geoff…oh geez…"

Chapter two

M uch later after they had closed the bar and he was back in his
room at the motel Geoff lay in bed tossing and turning and
futilely trying to silence the thoughts which were cascading through
the halls of his memory like a behind-schedule freight train screaming
down the tracks through the darkness of the cold night air. In his
mind a rerun of his recent past unwound like the film off a reel of a
bad b-movie.

~~~   ~~~   ~~~

Cheyenne Mountain in Colorado Springs loomed large - close
enough to reach out and touch. The day had been another fantastic
clear sunny Sunday although maybe twenty degrees cooler then
he would have liked. It was two weeks prior to the running of the
Kentucky Derby. Something about the thrill of the approaching derby
days along with the pleasant weather combined to instill a vibrant
feeling in his soul.

He had his favorite window seat for Sunday brunch at his favorite
downtown drinking establishment the Coldwater Canyon. It was a
brew-pub whose owners had had the good fortune, keen vision and
savoir faire to rescue an old derelict hotel building - which had been
destined to be razed to make room for a parking lot - and turn it into a

gold mine. It was a nice turn on an old folk rock classic verse - *they tore up paradise and put in a parking lot.* In this rendition they had torn up plans for a parking lot and built a little bit of paradise in a brew-pub. But it was much more than just a brew-pub, it had an enviable prime downtown location along with gourmet restaurant food, a gregarious friendly hard-working eager to please staff and an eclectic crowd that changed from night to night along with a hard core group of regulars all of which synergized to create a unique ambiance. There were no televisions on the ground floor which encouraged the social interaction of the crowd. The owners could be found most evenings sitting at the bar schmoozing the patrons and knew most of the regulars on a first name basis. It seemed as though time stood still and fortune smiled down on this little oasis in the turmoil of the times.

He had known a similar place once before - seventeen hundred or so miles east in Sea Girt, a small beach town on the New Jersey Shore. It was called the McKenzie Inn and had been the scene of many weekend afternoons and evenings after a day on the beach had parched his tonsils while he recovered from his first divorce. That was many lives ago.

After his second divorce he had headed west to pick up the pieces and build a new life. It had been a study in ambivalence as he crisscrossed the continent searching for whatever it was that even he could not define with clarity. Geoff's life or lives - as he liked to refer to them, since each address change seemed to be separate with no relation to those that came before or from those that would inexorably follow – had been an odyssey for longer than he could remember. Maybe it was his destiny or just something in his psyche that kept him moving from place to place in overlapping figures of eight or perhaps it was just one big figure of eight which he hadn't yet completed.

Colorado Springs had been an epiphany for him forcing his self-reflection into focus. When he came to the Springs he had found it comfortable maybe even home though deep down he knew it was temporary until life's vicissitudes would force him once again to throw all his belongings in the back of his pickup and ride on out to another new life. If it didn't fit in his pick-up it didn't travel. He suspected he was at heart a cowboy. Destined to ride the range from one roundup to the next – always looking at the horizon and never looking back at the gulches, divides, rivers and prairies in the dust of his past. That was as it should be he reasoned although if truth be known that was not how it was. He lived for his future but held on stubbornly to his past. He was painfully aware of his mistakes, missteps, shortcomings and the regrets that he wore as a burden weighing down his shoulders. But he had never intentionally hurt anyone.

Laramie Wyoming - a quiet unassuming cowboy town, a way station for freight trains hauling coal from the fields of Montana to the power plants of Texas - was situated on the high plains, the steppes of the west, and was home to the University of Wyoming.

He had always liked university towns. He was drawn to them probably by the exuberance of youth that filled the campuses and permeated the surrounding neighborhoods as well as the downtown shops, cafes, bars and eateries. He also had a deep attraction and admiration for cowboy towns; he identified with the romantic loneliness and the rough and tumble vagabond ways of life on the rodeo circuit immortalized in so many songs by Willie Nelson, Waylon Jennings, Johnny Cash and all the others.

Laramie to him was a cowboy town that shared the cosmopolitan aspect of a university town and thereby held a special fascination for him. He would come up here from Colorado Springs whenever he felt the need for a change of scenery; for an escape, to blow the stale air out of his life. It was a good place to sort things out and re-direct himself – get his shit together - as it were, in the common vernacular.

No he'd never been a rodeo cowboy. His only time on a horse - a weekend liberty with a Navy buddy – had been a disaster. They had stopped at a ranch on the way to Duluth, Minnesota. They rode the horses in their uniform whites. His horse sensed immediately that he was a greenhorn and decided to initiate him into horseback riding. At the far end of the riding pasture after several attempts at trying to knock him out of the saddle by trotting under low tree limbs his horse began to graze. He recalled his buddy's admonishment to not let a horse do that. So he finally smacked the rump of the horse with the reins while heeling it in the sides. Instantly the horse reared up and began a full gallop back to the barn. He held on, his butt crashing into the saddle exactly out of phase with the stride of his horse. By the time he made it back to the barn he had developed a full crop of butt blisters.

That was many lives ago. It often felt as though it was somebody else's life. His own life had devolved into a solitary one; whether by choice or chance he could never quite figure out. So the cowboy free spirit of loneliness had become his trusted companion.

In Laramie he had found another home at the Second St Saloon and Eatery. Well it wasn't really home in the true sense, just another safe port out of the storm of his life. It had been one continuous blow in his life for so long he had forgotten its origin. The town had become his comfortable way station; whether he was en route to Montana or heading west along the I-80 Interstate to California for another try at life on the sunshine coast. Lord, maybe he was a reincarnated seventeenth century cowboy drifter; sometimes he felt that old.

So when it ended, when he'd had his fill of bizarre encounters that passed for the romance of his life, and options became scarce Geoff threw all his shit - what there was of it - in the bed of his four-by and drove out of Dodge. Saying goodbye wasn't hard - no one cared so he didn't either. Just ride away and find another town off the interstate where he could make a stand and another try at finding a life.

He needed to get back up to Billings, Montana again someday - just for a while, to pick up where he'd left off back before the rains came. It had been raining long and hard in his life - but he was through it now and back alone. It was not that bad, he was comfortable alone. He was in good company when he was by himself. He could tumble with the wind.

I'm free. *Freedom's just another word for nothing left to lose* – as Kris Kristofferson had once written and sung in *Me & Bobby McGee*. Well you can't lose what you never had. Seattle might hold some promise - or hell north to Vancouver. He'd work it out - the decision - when the time came. Life would happen despite his plans so there was no urgent reason to forge any.

His ex-wife had called him a walking contradiction – partly truth and partly fiction. She was right though, that's who I am. Wherever I am, I want to be somewhere else. Life makes sense traveling on the interstate at 80 mph – when you stop it gets hopelessly confused. Dreams come apart in the cold gray dawn of reality.

He found himself heading south on the I-25 interstate. The night was dark. Once beyond the lights of any city the surrounding countryside was just mile after mile of suffocating darkness. A phrase suddenly popped into his mind; dredged up from somewhere in his past – Always begin a journey under the new moon. It is dark and there is no reflection - no second thoughts. Always go with your first choice, your first hunch; it's instinct, which is usually never wrong – it is after all, how we survive.

He didn't care much for 84 South the shortcut two-lane route from I-25 to Amarillo so he opted to continue south on the interstate clear to Albuquerque a city that made mile-high Denver seem like it was in a valley. Another trip east on I-40 to Amarillo didn't appeal to him at the moment, he had taken that route many too many times - so after a quick early dinner and a refuel in Albuquerque he was back out on the interstate and running south.

Out on the interstate his plans fell into focus. He always did his best thinking on the interstate. He had always promised himself he would check out Beale Street the next time he went through Memphis. He had no appointments and no time restrictions so that sounded like a nice distant objective. Now was as good a time as any - besides he didn't know when or even if there would be a next time.

The rain finally quit – or at least he had finally driven out of it. It had rained clear across Texas. He had taken I-25 down to its terminus at I-10 through to El Paso and continued on to the transition with I-20 which took him through the heart of Texas and such towns as Odessa, Midland and Abilene, to name just the ones whose names somehow stuck in his mind. He spent that night, a rainy one, in a motel in Abilene with no chance to look around for any of those pretty women who don't treat you mean - as mentioned in the lyrics of an old R&B song of that name as sung by George Hamilton IV.

Finally, when he hit Shreveport just across the border into Louisiana, the driving rain poured with such fury that he had to tailgate a semi to stay on the road. All he saw through torrents of water that his windshield wipers going full speed could not disperse were the taillights of the semi – four little flickering red spots dancing through a waterfall. He wondered how the driver managed to keep the rig on the road, but mused that as long as the semi was on the road, he'd be right there with him. He'd always had a lot of respect for long-haul drivers of 18-wheelers. He had taken many meals in truck stops and had some pleasant conversations and commiserations with a lot of professional truckers. Sometimes it was candid shared loneliness or other times sheer boredom for them.

But this rain was a torrential downpour; a bone-chilling, mind numbing, cold, windblown rain that penetrated right down to your soul. He was now more aware of the fact that he was alone. Of course he was always alone on these cross-country treks – fourteen, fifteen, sixteen – hell he'd lost count and records after twelve. It was like a fever. He needed to escape, to run from it all, the frustration, the loneliness. Or maybe it was a search – a search for a defining moment – to find himself, to find out who he was, what he believed in, what he stood for. The deceit, the games, the frustration, the humiliation experienced over so many years had taken its toll. He was a shell reacting to the trials and tribulations presented to him on a daily basis.

It'd been this way since the last days in Cambodia. The war for him had made sense – or at least he was comfortable with why he was there – unlike many of the other disenchanted troops. But after all he had volunteered.

He had gotten into it early – by May 1967 he was in country although it was not Vietnam – it was Cambodia. The trip over had taken them roughly three weeks more or less on a submarine cruising in some crazy zigzag pattern from San Diego to Pearl Harbor, to Kwajalein atoll where they transferred to another submarine that was staged there and continued on through Micronesia to Subic Bay in the Philippines and finally on through the Gulf of Thailand to the waters off the coast of Cambodia. For most of the trip they had cruised submerged.

The harsh sound of his windshield wipers scraping across the dry windshield brought him back to his current reality. He needed to stay alert to spot the junction sign for the route north to the I-30 interstate which would take him into Little Rock, Arkansas where he would transition onto I-40 for the final leg to Memphis.

It was late in the afternoon as he ran over the Mississippi River Bridge from Arkansas and saw the familiar *Tennessee Welcomes You* sign greeting him. In short order he was heading north along the Mississippi River on Riverside Drive, a right turn put him on Beale Street. He spotted a park-and-lock lot across from the Orpheum Theater with flat rates and pulled in and shut down his four-by.

He was here, right on Beale, all parked and ready to party. He headed east into the crowds past the police barrier that condoned off the main section of the Beale Street blues clubs and turned the street into a pedestrian mall. The sounds of the crowd and the music that drifted out of the many clubs were exhilarating. I think I'm gonna like it here, he mused to himself as an elated feeling of adventure took control and drove off the weariness from the long drive.

The green and blue neon of the sign caught his attention; The Delta Blues Café – a fitting name for a venue here on Beale Street. The smell of stale beer and smoke lingered by the open entrance as he walked in. Inside there were several patrons sitting at a long bar. It was an old structure, which appeared to date back probably to the late twenties, early thirties and Prohibition. He could just imagine the stories these walls could tell. There were several tables off to the side leaving a corridor that led back to four pool tables illuminated by dim hanging overhead lights. Two old black men played on one table while on another a twenty-something single practiced shots and tried to hustle a game from whoever took notice. Geoff took a seat at the bar.

"Yes sir, what can I get you," asked the barkeep, a distinguished looking black man with snow white hair, as he came over and placed a coaster down on the bar in front of him.

"Make it a Jack rocks, thank you."

Seconds later the barkeep set the drink down on the coaster, "Would you like anything else?"

"No, not right now thank you. Oh, by the way, do you have a blues band here at night?"

"Is this your first time on Beale Street?"

"Yes sir," said Geoff.

"Where are you from?"

"The interstate - I just drove in from Colorado."

"Ah," said the barkeep with a little up down nod of his head as though it somehow confirmed his intuition. "Well welcome to Beale Street sir, the capital of the blues. Down here we serve good barbecue, fine whiskey and great Blues until about five in the morning or as long as the crowd holds out. Musicians drop in for a drink, sit in for a set and jam and then move on. If it's Blues you're looking for, Colorado, you've found the right place."

As if on cue a gray-haired black man ambled in with a beat-up black horn case in his grip. Several patrons acknowledged him as Jackson. The words of an old country-blues song from another life ago ran through Geoff's mind. A song sung by Gene Watson, *The old man and his horn* - funny how the mind was able to dig way back in the archives and replay old memories as a response to some trigger.

The barkeep poured a tall neat Jack and brought it over to the table by the band platform where Jackson was limbering up the keys on his horn. Putting the horn to his lips, Jackson ran a riff or two and Lord Almighty it was the Blues. Geoff felt the hair stand up on the back of his neck, a shiver ran down his spine and his eyes lost focus and glazed over as he stared off in the distance.

~~~   ~~~   ~~~

I need someone - to lean on...you can lean on me.... the words of a Stones song ran over and over through the halls of his memory. That's all that was left. The Boulevard of Broken Dreams seemed as though it ran straight through the mélange that was his life.

Jack London Square, Oakland California - sitting in a nightclub sipping a glass of Chablis and people watching. The intervening years since the end of his time in service had gone by so fast with so little to distinguish one from another that they had become jumbled together in one endless bad recollection. The name of the club had long since escaped him but the evening was forever burned into his memory. It was a celebration of sorts for his successful completion of Systems Engineering training on his company's computer mainframe hardware product line. Feelings and emotions of the moment not the physical experience itself made it stick in his mind.

He had felt free - an awesome feeling of unencumbered euphoria - as if he were standing at the edge of a cliff looking out over the rest of his life. Anything was possible; there were no rules, no restrictions. It was his call; he was in the driver's seat.

He made another of his life-altering decisions that night. He had agonized over it for ten long years - half of those just unconsciously dealing with the circumstances, going through the motions, not really participating in life. He had felt like a spectator watching his own life through a glass window. He knew what he had to do, what he must do - although he dreaded the awful consequences, those that he knew were certain to follow, and those he could only conjure up in his worst fears and daydreams. But it was something he had to do for himself, for his own integrity. He had finally summoned the courage to take the step. His marriage was over; there was no use in holding onto what wasn't working for either of them. He needed to be free.

So when he died, they burned his bones – took the ashes and scattered them beneath this huge weeping willow on the banks of the Chattahoochee or maybe off the bridge over the Tallahatchie – yeah the one they wrote the song about. There were no songs about his life though; it was as if he had never existed. Even those whose lives he had touched in his journey along life's pathways had long ago given him up for dead. In the area hospitals another thirteen babies were born – three elderly patients expired from diabetes or complications thereof and time continued to add to the past. Life carried on without so much as a missed step or a hiccup. Lord, sometimes the awesome burden of insignificance was overpowering.

~~~　　　　~~~　　　　~~~

He came out of his reverie to find the barkeep watching him, "How you doing there Colorado; need that drink freshened?"

"Yeah, I guess I could use a fresh one."

The barkeep brought it over and set it down in front of him. "My name's Charles," he said extending his hand.

"I'm Geoff, nice to meet you Charles."

"Geoff, if you don't mind my saying - you look like a man with a lot of heavy thoughts."

Geoff gave a half-hearted chuckle, "Do I look that bad? It's just life I guess; sometimes it feels that if it were not for misery, pain and regrets I wouldn't have a life at all."

"I hear you man, I've been there too. Hang out for a while and let the music take it all out of you. There ain't nothing else. Sometimes you just got to let it out or it will eat you up inside. The sun's always going to shine tomorrow; you just need to get through the night."

A slow grin crept across the barkeep's face as he let out a soft chuckle and with a wink he wiped the bar rag over the bar and the rail in front. Motioning over towards Jackson with a nod of his head he said,

"Listen to my horn man, he's really good. You know sometimes it takes the Blues to chase away the Blues, that's really how it all started, that's what the Blues are all about."

The late afternoon passed quickly into the early evening. He ordered a steak sandwich for dinner and then decided that he needed to find a place to stay before it got too late. He paid the tab, left a generous tip and made his way back out onto Beale.

It was even livelier now. Couples and groups were going every which way, darting in and out of the cafes and bars and souvenir shops along both sides of the street. A cacophony of music bombarded him from all sides. He'd definitely have to return. There was much to explore and experience and lifetimes of music to hear.

Chapter three

It was Thursday - the tail end of the Memphis in May celebrations and early evening at the Delta Blues Café on Beale Street. The bar had begun to fill up - all the seats at the bar were taken. The tables were full of groups of four or more, oblivious to life outside their cozy immediate circle. A couple more musicians joined the band that had just come back from a short break. It seemed almost as though the musicians had materialized from some ethereal blues conservatory - they had either played together a great deal or they were each one a genius in his own rite. They played with complete abandon, each seemingly in their own world yet never stepping on another's part. The presentation of their music was seamless and once again it worked its magic on him.

His mind began to swim with scenarios of his past when Charles the barkeep put a fresh drink in front of him and bent over to advise him discreetly, "That's compliments of Amy – the pretty lady alone at the corner table."

Geoff cast a glance in the direction that the barkeep had indicated with his eyes and a slight nod of his head. She was looking his way. Their eyes met for an instant and he caught a slight smile as she turned her head away. He waited for what he felt to be an appropriate interval and then picked up his drink and made a roundabout approach to her table. Moving to her side he leaned over as he whispered discreetly,

"Pardon me miss, may I introduce myself?"

"Yes, please do," she said looking up at him with a pleasant smile.

"My name is Geoff, thank you for the drink, Amy."

She held eye contact as she answered, "You're welcome, Geoff. You looked like you could use another one."

"Wow, does it show from this far away?"

"Relax, Geoff, I'm probably a much better judge of body language and character than most. Please; have a seat if you'd like and tell me what it is that brings you to Memphis, to the Delta Blues Café, by yourself in such a pensive mood."

He pulled the seat out and sat down, theirs eyes locked for a long instant. Amy flashed a broad genuine smile, "Well, I'm waiting."

He felt as though he were eighteen and on his first date. "Amy, you're not only a good judge of body language and character but you have a real knack for control."

"Oh forgive me, Geoff, it's what I do, I ... well I asked you first."

"Ah - what do I do, where do I come from, where have I been, and who am I – really?"

"Yes, that's a fine start - in any order you'd like," she said with a matching mocking tone and a pleased chuckle. It felt like the start of a pleasant repartee. The ice, if there ever was any, had totally evaporated.

"Well it's a pretty convoluted story. Do you want the long or the short version?"

"Your call Geoff, tell me as little or as much as you're comfortable with."

"I drove here from Colorado a few days ago. Life just sort of dried up out west, at least for me, and I figured the Blues would be a great remedy for lonely, besides I'd always promised myself a trip to Beale Street."

"But you're not from Colorado?"

"You're right; I drove out there from Sarasota, Florida, where I'm not from either. Before Florida it was Raleigh, North Carolina; then Lexington, Kentucky; Mountain View, California; Reno, Nevada; Los Angeles; Silver Spring, Maryland; San Jose California..."

"It just goes on and on doesn't it Geoff? You haven't found it anywhere yet have you?"

"How do you know this, Amy?"

"It's in your eyes, something is haunting you."

"Okay, counselor, I think it's time you told me a little bit about yourself."

Amy was momentarily startled, but regained her composure in an instant.

"What has Chuck told you about me?"

"Chuck? I don't know any..."

"Chuck, the bartender - Did he tell you I was with the DA's office?"

Geoff put it all together rapidly and then chuckled, "Oh no, Amy, I used the label 'counselor' metaphorically. I'm not psychic and the barkeep didn't tell me a thing about you except that you had just bought me a drink. I didn't ask either because I'd much rather hear it from you. Anyway, the barkeep told me his name was Charles."

"It is, Geoff. It's just that most of us regulars know him as Chuck. I'm sorry I overreacted," Amy said as she reached out and touched his hand.

"No apology necessary Amy it was just a natural reaction especially from someone in your line of work. You're a very direct lady, I find that very attractive. You were about to tell me about yourself."

"Yes, well my life has been much more vanilla than yours Geoff; I was born and reared in Mississippi – Vicksburg. I went on to college at the University of Mississippi, 'Ole Miss' and then Tulane for law. After law school in New Orleans I just could not return to Vicksburg even though daddy had set me up with the leading corporate law firm there. But corporation law was just not for me. Maybe it was my outrage with crime or just my personal idealism but I wanted to make a difference. I wanted to see more convictions and less plea bargains. On the social side, I love the blues also - so there was only one place where I could put the two together and still be near my roots."

"So, how long have you been on the prosecution side?"

"Right from the beginning, after I passed the Bar I found out that Shelby County was looking to fill some district attorney slots. I applied; got hired and here I am - going on ten years this May. So where were you ten years ago?"

"Ah ha, are you by any chance another Casablanca fan?" asked Geoff.

"Oh, goodness, yes it's probably my favorite classic movie; I'm really quite a classic movie buff. I think the acting was so much more professional. Very little in the way of special effects and the scripts were mostly all written in socially acceptable English with very few if any off-color four-letter words."

"I agree Casablanca is my all-time favorite. I've got three copies, the original black and white, a colorized version and the 50th Anniversary edition stored away in Billings."

"Montana? You didn't mention that address."

"Well I haven't actually had an address there, yet - although I expect I will when I get back out west. I used to drive up to Billings for long weekends and weeks between contracts whenever Colorado Springs went stale on me and I felt the need to get away to clear my head."

"So, Geoff, why all the addresses - what is it that you're searching for... or trying to escape from?"

"Amy, as near as I can describe it – it's a feeling. Sometimes wherever I am I want... I need...to get away, to be someplace else. There must be a million lines in country songs written about that feeling.

Whenever I find a new place to settle in I try to assimilate into the local culture. I adopt it as my home until a string of bad experiences tells me it's time to move on. It seems like the longer I spend in one place the more mentally constipated I become. It takes a road-trip to relieve the mental stress, sort out the confusion and put my life back in perspective.

I've been called a walking contradiction – partly truth and partly fiction - by an ex-wife. I think she stole that line from a Kris Kristofferson song. Actually it's a characterization that I find rather fitting. I guess it's how I view myself.

I've also been told that I would make a stellar subject for a psychological dissertation - don't know as if I felt quite as charitable to that characterization. But you know Amy, at odd moments I do reflect on the lack of stability in my existence. It would be nice to find someone to hold onto. Someone to believe in me - believe in us."

"That's a universal desire of humankind...we all want to belong," she said looking deeply into his eyes.

"Yes I guess it is. To make a long story short, in my case I'm looking for someplace where my dreams can reconcile with reality and wondering if I'll run out of time before I find it. Sometimes it scares the hell out of me, at other times I'm reminded of a refrain from an old Bob Dylan song - *I was so much older then... I'm younger than that now.*"

Amy reached out and grasped his hand. "Geoff, you're a ship without a rudder in an uncharted sea - seeking a port that doesn't exist – it's the ultimate human tragedy. I think you see yourself mired in a lifetime of missed opportunities and failures and somehow always coming up just a little short - in your own mind. But you know Geoff, there are a lot of people in this world who appreciate candor, honesty and sensitivity - you are truly unique and very refreshing. I'm really glad to have met you and I'd truly welcome an opportunity to count you among my acquaintances."

Their eyes locked. Hers were understanding, soft and receptive - his honest, pensive and a bit sad. It was innocence; it was innocence lost. He leaned over closer to her shifting his focus between her eyes and her lips as if he were asking permission. She didn't pull back as he brushed her lips with a soft poignant kiss.

Amy leaned closer, her hand on his forearm as she whispered, "You have impeccable timing Geoff but I just hope we can take the time to get to know each other - I'd really like very much to get to know you on a personal level."

Geoff gazed deeply into her blue eyes. "I'd like that too Amy... I really would."

"Well then..."

"Say, I know it's awfully short notice, but do you think there's a chance we could start with brunch this Sunday?"

"Why I'd love to Geoff; do you have a place in mind or..."

"Hey, I think I'll need your help on that one, it's your town Amy. My choice would be someplace with lots of atmosphere, near the water - where we can have a leisurely brunch while we listen to classical music playing in the background."

"I know just the place Geoff; can I pick you up somewhere?"

"Well I wish you could but right now there's no address. I'm between motels at the moment. Why don't we just agree on a time and meet at the place, if you don't mind?"

"Well sure, we could do that… it's the Chez Louis Quatorze down on the river waterfront. I think you'll like it; it's the kind of place you just described. Say around twelve o'clock."

"Twelve it is Amy, and I'm sure I'll be impressed with the venue."

"Geoff, I hate to, but I really have to call it a night. I have a full calendar tomorrow. I've really enjoyed your company and our conversation."

"That's okay, Amy, I understand. Thank you again for the drink. I'm looking forward to Sunday; I just wish we could…"

"Geoff, if you don't have any plans for tomorrow afternoon, perhaps we could get together for a few drinks at happy hour and pick up where we left off this evening."

"That sounds great; I'd like that, Amy."

"So would I, there's a place called the Dixie Rose, it's in the financial district. Your typical professional crowd - lawyers, bankers and of course lots of salesmen. I'll probably get there between four and four-thirty but if I'm a little late, please don't leave – give me a little latitude. I will be there, I promise."

"It's a date, Amy, I'll be waiting for you even if I have to bring along my sleeping bag."

As they got up to leave he took her arm, "Amy may I walk you to your car?"

"Oh it's right outside - but sure, Geoff, I appreciate your gesture."

They walked out to her car, which was parked just beyond the police barrier at a yellow curb marked as a tow-away zone. Geoff caught her eye with feigned astonishment, "Hey, what's this counselor - perks, connections, graft, corruption?"

"Oh, stuff it Geoff," she said as she gave him a quick jab that just brushed his ribs. It's just Memphis showing some honest respect for one of its own."

"Yeah, a sucker puncher too," said Geoff as he rubbed his side in mock agony.

"Get in and quit making a scene, I'll drive you to your truck - it is a truck isn't it?"

"Yes it is; it's just up the street. Of course this is a one-way street and my truck is back in the other direction, but you can probably just flip a u-turn and get away with it."

"Keep it up Geoff …I'll let you walk," she said as sternly as she could manage before breaking into laughter.

When they got to the parking lot they turned towards each other and after a moment's awkward hesitation slipped into an easy embrace.

"You have made quite an impression on me lady; I'm really looking forward to tomorrow afternoon."

"So am I Geoff. You're very easy to be with. I feel as though we've known each other for a while instead of having just met. See you tomorrow, Geoff."

"Goodnight Amy, take care."

Chapter four

Traffic was heavy - it was the Friday rush hour. He found the Dixie Rose on a corner across from a public parking garage, so that's where he parked. It was about ten minutes to four, in his world - which was always fifteen minutes ahead of whatever time zone in which he happened to find himself.

The Dixie Rose had two entrances. The one he chose had large wooden double doors with a red rose-colored canopy above that extended out over the sidewalk. The top half of the doors had single pane windows with the word Dixie on the left window and Rose on the right window in gold lettering. Beneath the word Dixie were two crossed flagstaffs with the Stars and Stripes to the right of the Stars and Bars painted as though waving in the breeze. On the right window below the word Rose was a large painted red rose in full bloom. The entrance opened into a large lobby with a gift and sundries shop. Stained glass panes framed the entrance to the large oval bar with its two exterior walls of glass windows that provided a panoramic view of the downtown Memphis financial district. He took a seat at a hi-top with two seats where he could observe both entrances.

He ordered his signature drink - a tequila grapefruit, tall with a lime squeeze; he had switched to other cocktails depending on his mood and the venue especially on St. Paddy's Day and even drank red wine whenever he felt the need to become paranoid about his health, but his favorite remained tequila grapefruit. It was a drink he had first ordered as a young sailor stationed in Hawaii - back before he'd volunteered for duty in Vietnam.

He half understood why he had volunteered. Some of it was rebellion - he had not enjoyed Hawaii - it made him feel alien in his own country - even as hard as he tried to assimilate into the lifestyle. The other half he guessed was duty and patriotism. He had no problem with the American foreign policy of Communist containment. He had no use for those draft-dodging anti-war activists who didn't for the most part really understand the issues but just used it all as an excuse for hooligan behavior. Their daddies paid their expenses and bailed them out of the lockups, with such eloquent shock and denial as would have made Claude Rains' character Captain Renault of Casablanca proud – 'there must be some mistake, my innocent child wouldn't do that.'

The bar began to fill and still there was no sign of her. But it was early. Then a large party entered to an ovation of sorts. They were obviously regulars. He spotted Amy in the rear alongside a young weasel with his arm wrapped possessively around her shoulders. Geoff watched as her eyes quickly scanned the crowd and locked onto his. He looked away. An instant later she was at his table and he felt soft caressing fingers on the back of his neck. A pleasant fragrance of perfume greeted his olfactory senses.

Amy leaned over and whispered in his ear - "Good to see you Geoff, please don't misconstrue my colleague's actions. He hasn't been taught about harassment yet. Is this seat taken?" she asked rhetorically as she settled into it.

Geoff pushed back in his seat and affected his most pompous look as he said, "The jury is instructed to ignore the colleague."

"Thank you, your honor," she said with a chuckle.

Their eyes locked their faces inches apart. He leaned over closing the distance and brushed her lips lightly with a soft kiss. As he pulled back he felt her fingers running through the hair on the back of his neck. She took her turn and returned his kiss with a bit more passion than just a brush of his lips.

He looked deeply into her eyes for what seemed like endless seconds and then dropped all pretenses – "Amy, it's great to see you too and yes, I was a little deflated with your entrance but I'm over it now. Ever been married, counselor?"

"No, Geoff…I guess I've never found the time."

"Oh I don't know Amy; I think we all can find the time once we find the right person."

"You're right Geoff; I plead guilty to a platitude."

"Ah, well it was your first offense; I'm sure we can plea bargain and get you off with a suspended sentence and probation or maybe get the charge dropped."

"I'll throw myself on the mercy of the court Geoff," she said tossing her head back in laughter. It was genuine, not forced - an emotional release after a stressful day. She grabbed his forearm and squeezed, "Hey Geoff, I'm glad you could make it. I was really hoping to see you."

"And I was certainly hoping to see you again Amy, something told me to come to Memphis and I'm glad I listened. Maybe it's destiny."

"Maybe…how long do you plan on staying?"

"Well as usual I have no plans, I was just free-wheeling along the interstate and decided to indulge a desire I've always had to stop off and see the place. I guess I'll probably stay as long as Memphis wants me - as long as fate smiles down on me."

"What if you meet a lady whom you find devastatingly attractive and who seems to have a mutual attraction to you?" She caught him off guard. Here was a lady whom dared to be as candid as he was – a trait he found irresistible.

"Well at the risk of prematurely disclosing my hole card, let me just say that I would probably stay as long as that intelligent, refreshingly candid, breathtakingly gorgeous lady could countenance my presence."

"That could be a long time, cowboy," she countered with a wink and a wide smile as she gazed deeply into his eyes and rubbed her fingers along his forearm.

It was all he could stand. He could restrain his feelings no longer. He reached out and gathered her into his arms - she came willingly, slipping her hands around his neck. She brought her lips to his and they shared a few brief kisses settling back to look deeply into each other's eyes for a few seconds that seemed to linger much longer.

"Amy, I feel comfortable, very comfortable with you, like I've known you since high school – went to the prom together - then went our separate ways and now have returned to pick up where we left off."

"It feels the same way for me also, Geoff. But I think I've already told you that."

"Yes, you have, I just wanted to let you know the feeling is mutual."

"You know Geoff, it occurs to me that I know an awful lot about your inner feelings, yet I don't even know what it is you do as a vocation."

"Yeah, I guess it is kind of backwards - I haven't told you what I do or my birth-sign."

"Well, Geoff, I think we can dispense with the astrology - it's probably irrelevant at this juncture of our acquaintance. But what is it that you do for a livelihood?"

"I was a computer tech for more years than I care to remember - certainly more years than the duration of my interest or effectiveness plausibly even my competence if truth be known."

"Wow, Geoff, that's pretty self-deprecating - why are you so rough on yourself?"

"I guess I'm a little defensive, it doesn't hurt as much when I admit my own shortcomings. Most people I talk with who have never had a vocation in the computer field see only the glamour and overlook the constant pressure of pursuing state-of-the-art technology and the necessity to spend an entire career trying to avoid obsolescence while always watching over your shoulder for the next round of reorganizations, downsizing, mergers, acquisitions and outsourcing - all to appease the greed of the Wall Street sharks. When people lose jobs and careers for the sake of achieving a statistical increase in productivity and to assure the CEO's next million-dollar bonus the damn stocks go up as the ghouls of Wall Street profit off other's misfortunes."

"That sounds like an indictment against corporate America."

"Yeah it ought to be; unfortunately, it's one that'll never see justice served. Too many vested interests will just ensure the status quo."

"You can't fight the system Geoff; you have to find a way to make it work for you. So aside from management did you enjoy working with computers?"

"At first I did when it was an esoteric craft but once Silicon Valley and all the rest of its ilk in the industry turned it into just another commercial enterprise beholden to the bottom line I grew tired of constantly analyzing processes, procedures, data, code and systems and doing migrations, maintenance and upgrades."

"Wow, that sounds pretty technical and to me very tedious and boring," she said shaking her head.

"I like to create, to synthesize not tear down and analyze. I need to focus all my abilities on one specific problem and nail down the optimum solution rather than multitasking sixteen different problems simultaneously only to produce a half-baked product that winds up costing more because of required rework. I guess I just burned out on high-tech or at least computer clerking and info pushing."

"I don't think it was burnout as much as disillusionment, Geoff. I don't think it's who you were - who you are. Maybe you just grew out of it."

Geoff chuckled, "Amy, I think you have more insight into my persona than I do."

"It's what I do. My life's work is to try to figure out what motivates people. You've told me what you don't like to do and what you've done in the past, however you still haven't told me what you do now, in the present. Geoff, what is your story?"

"I'm a writer, an author Amy or at least that's what I've put on my business cards. It took a lot of years for me to feel confident enough in my own ability and to realize that I had the potential to scribble words on a sheet of paper that someone somewhere would care to spend the time to read. I finally quit procrastinating, pulled out all my old journals and edited my raw thoughts and ramblings into a coherent manuscript and tried to get published. When I finally succeeded, I found that it was worth the wait - worth the fight. All the insecurity and ambivalence faded."

"So what is it that drives you to change venues with such frequency? Is it a consequence of your writing, or is writing the benefactor from all this wandering, or maybe to couch it in more politically correct terms - this field research of social dynamics?"

"Hey, I like that definition I'll have to remember to use it. You know Amy, maybe writing does justify my nomadic existence, at least that's what I keep telling myself or maybe my wandering inspires my writing with a constant supply of new material."

"What have you got against putting down roots, Geoff?"

"Nothing, I'm not averse to commitment or making a stand. There is no simple answer, Amy. I can try to tell you why, but it will take more time than one or two simple conversations to make you understand. It's part of my psyche it's who I am. I'm an observer. I assimilate more empirically than I do from actual personal experience. In a lot of ways, I guess I'm more of a spectator than a participator in life. It's both a blessing and a curse. I think I learn more from other's mistakes, than I do from my own, since I seem to repeat my own mistakes over and over again."

"We all make mistakes Geoff - it's how we grow."

"You're right there Amy and I've certainly done a lot of growing in my life. Do you want to hear a little story about where I came from?"

"Yes I'd love to."

"When I was a young boy my family moved from Oak Park, Illinois the city where I was born, to a little rural town in northern Indiana. I was an outcast in my new school. I was ridiculed and taunted as a city-boy. It took me five very long years of misery and loneliness to feel accepted by my classmates, let alone make any kind of friends. By then it was too late, and we returned to my old hometown in metro Chicago.

It was only about one hundred thirty miles or so north of the rural town in Indiana but the pace of life and the teenage culture was light-years apart. I easily slipped back into the metro Chicago lifestyle, far easier than had been my adjustment to rural Indiana.

Then came high school and I had to make a choice between scholarship and popularity, at least in my mind, so of course I chose popularity forming a singing group with some friends I acquired very quickly back in Illinois in the shadow of Chicago.

Since I'd lost focus on my studies and consequently on what I wanted to pursue as a vocation I decided to postpone the decision and get my military obligation out of the way. Back in those days all guys eighteen and over had six years of obligated military duty to serve. Looking back on it I think it was a damn good system. Anyway, two weeks after high school graduation I was in US Navy boot camp at Great Lakes.

I guess something about Navy life stuck with me; maybe it's where I developed my habit or need to change addresses as often as I do. I've always felt that wherever I was, there was something more exciting going on someplace else. As we used to say in the Navy, the best duty station is the one you just left or the one to which you just got orders. To make a long story short Amy, in all my travels and through two marriages I just never found anyone who could love me as deeply, as sincerely and as unconditionally as I could love her."

"I can relate to that Geoff, there are an awful lot of disingenuous people in this world. But someday I think I want the long story. I enjoy listening to you. We haven't played any mind games, it's refreshing and I thank you for that."

"It's not my nature, Amy, I'm not a gamesman - it's nice to find someone in the single crowd who can appreciate that."

The young weasel from earlier rudely interrupted their intimacy. "Hey AJ, we're all going to the Skyline are you ready to go?"

"I'll pass Tom; I'll see you guys Monday."

"Ah come on we're going to make a night of it - you know the usual, a wild and crazy blowout. Come on AJ, I'll buy the first round."

"No thanks Tom, I said I'll see you Monday - have a nice weekend."

"Sure, okay - ciao baby, I'll give you a jingle in the AM."

As he left Amy turned to Geoff who was watching the exchange with an inquisitive look.

"Tom's a young buck with a tremendous ego problem exacerbated by his hormones."

"Forget it Amy, I recognize the type."

"Look Geoff, I don't want you to misunderstand, I don't want to derail anything before we even get to know each other."

"No explanation required - but if you insist," Geoff said as he gave her a wink.

Amy slid her hand around behind his neck and gently kneaded the muscles and then in one motion she closed the space to his lips with hers – soft, warm, innocent yet with a hint of desire and a promise of shared feelings. They lingered close, their lips moving back and forth against each other's sharing soft caressing kisses.

When they drew apart Geoff exhaled audibly – "Asked and answered counselor, explanation accepted, Amy."

"We had lunch a few times Geoff, as colleagues, now he considers that license for something more - although I've never encouraged him. I'm not into younger men."

"Amy I've seen his type more times than I care to recall. He's God's gift, trying to bed all the ladies who cross his path purely for their satisfaction - at least in his mind."

"I could not have paraphrased it any better, Geoff."

The bar was packed now - the bartenders surreptitiously increasing the volume of the background music until it was no longer just background. The crowd had to scream to be heard over the music and the cacophony of noise produced by the screams of others - it fed on itself to create the atmosphere of *where the action is.*

"Are you getting hungry?" asked Amy as she leaned close to Geoff's ear.

"Now that you mention it yes I am Amy; I would have said something earlier but I thought you might have plans - I didn't want to be presumptuous."

"I've cleared my calendar Geoff; this evening is ours - if you're so inclined."

"Well I'm feeling in a festive mood - I'm also hungry and there's nothing I'd like better than to monopolize your attentions for the rest of the evening," said Geoff.

"Great, let's take my car; I know the city so it will be easier."

"Yeah, especially since your car is probably right outside parked in a yellow tow-away zone."

"Don't start," she said faking a cross expression and stifling a laugh as they stood up.

He swept her into his arms in their first full embrace. They were perfect together. He could feel the firmness of her body pressing lightly against his. Her head snuggled into his neck, her lips on his neck maddeningly close to his ear.

"Umm maybe we should skip dinner Amy," he said his voice suddenly husky as he held her close and gently rubbed his fingertips along her back.

"No sailor, I'm hungry - let's go eat." She grabbed his hand very much in control and moved towards the exit.

"Whew, you are tough counselor; I'd not like to have you as an adversary."

"I can be tough, Geoff but I'm fair-minded never mean," she said with a wink as she slipped an arm around his waist.

The Castaway was down on the river. 'The best surf and turf this side of New Orleans and almost as Cajun'- was their boast. They got preferential treatment, Amy was obviously well known. Midway through the salad course the waiter brought over a Gin and Tonic. Placing it down in front of Amy, he bent over and whispered to her discretely.

She pushed it away saying, "Paul tell him to go ply his trade at the Cloud Nine." Moments later a less than sober lawyer type sauntered up - as best as his condition would allow - and rested his arms on their table.

"Hey, AJ just wanted to let you know - no hard feelings over the Hawkins' case, nice piece of work."

"Thanks for the complement Clayton but next time could you please use a little more discretion - I like my privacy when I'm with someone."

"Oh sorry, excuse me," he said with a shrug of his shoulder as he turned and shuffled away.

"Geoff, I'm sorry," she said squeezing his forearm.

"It's okay Amy, no apology necessary - you're in a high profile position and obviously very good at what you do, it comes with the territory."

"You're a sweetheart for understanding, Geoff - so different and refreshing from a lot of these southern good ole boys."

"Maybe you need to get away from all this, Amy."

"Oh, it's not so bad, they are not all like Clayton - he can be a real asshole sometimes."

The dinner came - the Shrimp Etouffee was superb. They dallied over a shared dessert, Almond Praline Supreme - the ice cream over a three-layer brownie of white and dark chocolate loaded with almond slivers, separated by crushed dark cacao and topped with hot semi-sweet fudge.

"We'll certainly get our chocolate fix tonight," said Geoff with a chuckle.

"Um hmm," she said as she scooped up the last spoonful of ice cream and offered it to Geoff. He waved it off but she playfully brought it back up to his lips in a gesture he really couldn't refuse. It smeared over his lips and ran down his chin but before he could wipe away the mess, Amy pressed her lips against his in a sultry sweet kiss until they both burst out in laughter. Stopping to wipe their mouths, they leaned into each other, their foreheads touching.

"Oh lord Amy; it's been a long time since I've had such a great time, since I've had such a strong feeling for someone."

"Geoff, I..."

"Amy, it's not something I say to all the women I date, it wasn't a line it..."

She cut him off; her hand was soft on his cheek. "I didn't think it was, Geoff, but maybe I am guilty of trying to analyze it. What I was trying to say - before you interrupted me, was that I'm having the same feelings as you are, and it's crazy - I'm usually a lot more level headed."

"Is it level-headedness or cynicism?"

"Geoff, have you ever considered a career in Law?"

"I wouldn't be any good - too honest and much too sensitive. Hey!" he exclaimed as Amy playfully drove an elbow into his ribs.

"What happened to courtroom decorum?" he asked rubbing his ribs and faking pain.

"There's a time for verbal argument and there's a time for physical intervention," she said her blue eyes wide as a self-satisfied smirk spread across her lips.

Their repartee was interrupted by the arrival of the waiter with the check. Geoff reached for his wallet - Amy stopped him.

"Please Geoff this is my treat - welcome to Memphis."

"Okay, thanks Amy, but this Sunday... please just forget your pocketbook."

"Sunday is a long way off," said Amy as she sipped her water.

"Yeah, it feels that way to me also."

"Where did you find a place to stay?"

"A motor hotel, one called the Majestic."

"Oh God, Geoff, that's a very seedy part of town."

"Well maybe it's seedy but it's also cheap and conveniently close-by which justifies the sub-standard accommodations."

"Cheap and convenient doesn't justify waking up dead. Maybe you ought to come home with me tonight and look for better accommodations in the morning. I do have a spare bedroom if that will make you feel more comfortable."

Chapter five

While Amy excused herself for a trip to the ladies room before they left Geoff sat there mulling over her offer for him to spend the night at her place. A little voice deep inside him kept warning him to beware of the potential for serious consequences should he give in to the temptation. If he was serious about this lady, he was about to repeat another mistake. His thoughts flashed back to another relationship with a lady a long time ago when he had allowed chemistry and biology to take over and rushed through the preliminary courting ritual and right to intimacy.

I was everything she was looking for in her man, at least that's what she had said at the time, he thought to himself. She had cautioned him to "go slow" – but he had dismissed that warning out of hand given how quickly the relationship had progressed from casual to serious. After a whirlwind romance of a month and a half her esteem for me had declined to less than snake-shit. She ended it as abruptly as it had begun. I really don't want to make that mistake again, not now. Not with Amy.

When she returned from the ladies' room Geoff broached the subject of his reluctance, "Look Amy, one night at the Majestic isn't going to kill me…"

"Forget it Geoff, I don't want to read about you in the police blotter. Case closed."

"Well okay, I'll take your advice and go find another place."

"It's probably a little late for that. Anyway, why are you stalling, is it because you don't want to come home with me?"

"Amy, there's nothing I would rather do, it's just that…"

"So what's your hang-up sailor? Let's weigh anchor, cast off, hoist the mainsail and catch the wind and let destiny take care of itself."

They left the restaurant and walked out into a cold Memphis drizzle that made the night unseasonably cooler than it should have been. As they walked to her car Geoff insisted that they retrieve his truck.

He followed her through the back streets of Memphis finally turning onto a wide street with a median lined with old oak, elm and fir trees. Her house was a single story brick bungalow situated on the corner of the main street and a cross street which dead-ended on her side. A full front porch with an overhanging green tiled roof had two large rectangular support pillars built halfway up with brick and topped by a heavy timber column on each corner. Two square pillars of the same design surrounded the three slate steps of the brick stairs. Stained glass panes framed the main double-door entrance and also the top and sides of the bow window of the living room.

Geoff was reminded of the houses he had seen and fell in love with in San Diego. The driveway took advantage of the corner property with an entrance from both streets. Thick shrubbery along the periphery of the driveway accorded privacy and exclusivity to the property. Amy led them in through the rear entrance of the house after they had parked in the attached carport.

The L-shaped kitchen was large, modernized and opened on both legs of the L through arches to a formal dining room with a wide graceful natural oak archway into the living room giving the whole floor plan a very spacious look and feel. On the other side of the living room through another oak archway was the small entrance foyer with guest closet, powder room and a hallway that led to the bedrooms and bath.

"Amy, this is a beautiful house. It's very deceiving much bigger inside than I would have guessed. It's the kind of house I've always dreamed of owning. We seem to share very similar tastes."

"I fell I love with it also, Geoff. My only complaint was the size of the bedroom closets. When I bought it there were three bedrooms, but I turned the third and smallest bedroom into an expansion to the master adding a full bath and more closet space."

"Wow that's quite an improvement. The only thing I would probably add for a crowning touch would be a Jacuzzi in the master bedroom."

"Oh I thought of that too and included it as part of the upgrade – a Jacuzzi with floor to ceiling mirrors on two sides, wait until you see it."

"Ahh, counselor, you and I really do have the same taste."

"Yes, we do seem to. Let's give it a test, how would you like to sip on a latte?"

"Hey that would go great right about now Amy - a latte, some blues and a little close time."

"Excellent, why don't you pick out something on my audio system Geoff, while I make the lattes?"

Ten minutes later when she came back into the living room with two large lattes on a tray Geoff was sitting there overwhelmed by the array of choices on her home theater system.

"Amy, maybe I'd better defer to you before I screw up something. I was thinking of some Kristofferson country blues, or maybe some smooth jazz. What are you in the mood for?"

"Ooh, that's a loaded question Geoff but really with all your technical experience I doubt that you could trash my system. Anyway I've got my CD Jukebox programmed and it sounds like program-five is just the ticket, let's give it a shot." She powered up the system and they settled down on the couch facing the fireplace with their lattes in hand.

"Amy, wouldn't a fire be great about now?"

"Oh Geoff, I was just thinking the same thing, would you do the honors?"

Geoff took two of the fire logs from the stack in the brass stand and lit them. He returned to the sofa and Amy slid her arm around him. As he turned his head to look into her eyes she closed the distance to his lips with hers and hesitated momentarily. Geoff looked deeply into her eyes and then to her willing and inviting lips. Focusing his eyes back to hers for a moment, he lightly brushed his lips against hers. Again their lips met and the kisses quickly turned passionate as their open mouths sort out each other's. It was passion, it was desire and it was love in its embryonic stage. They slipped their arms around each other in a long tender warm embrace. When they finally relaxed their embrace it was Geoff who first spoke. "Amy, I might not want to leave."

"I may not let you leave, Geoff."

"Well, when I wear out my welcome, please let me know."

"Oh, you'll know Geoff - if that contingency ever comes to pass - but hey we're getting way ahead of ourselves."

The evening slipped away into the wee hours of the morning and as the conversation waned the caressing and cuddling became more intense until Amy interrupted the mood with a proposition.

"Geoff I've got a new spare toothbrush you can use but I'm sorry I've got no jammies for you. Will that bother you?"

"I never wear them; I prefer to sleep in the buff."

"Even in the Colorado winter?"

"Yeah, I sleep that way year round, hot-blooded I guess."

"Have you ever slept on a futon?"

"I sure have Amy, for a whole lot of years. I had one back in Colorado. It just made a lot more sense for my bohemian lifestyle. When you move around as much as I do you learn to travel light and not collect a lot of baggage."

"Well I have a twin size not very comfortable futon in the spare bedroom. It's about like sleeping on this. Here let me show you," she said with a playful laugh as she slid forward and pushed him down to a prone position. "How does that feel, are you comfy, Geoff?"

With one motion he wrapped his arms around her and pulled her gently to him. She came willingly.

"Hmm, I am now, I could stay like this all night," he said as they smothered each other with tender kisses that lasted longer and grew more passionate with each succeeding one.

"I think we need to relocate. So what's your decision sailor, this couch, the futon or my queen size bed with a comfy air mattress?"

"No contest...I'll take the pretty lady with her queen-size air mattress," he said as he stood up, gathered her into his arms and carried her off to the master bedroom.

They slid between the sheets and into each other's arms in an easy caressing embrace. When they broke it was only to share some deep intimate kisses. They began to run their fingers softly over each other's body - touching, softly squeezing and caressing to the accompaniment of those pleasant sensual sounds that lovers make while discovering what pleases each other. Time stood still as their passion flowed then ebbed only to climb again higher than before in ever shorter cycles until reaching culmination. When the loving was finally over they lie still in each other's arms drinking in the afterglow of their lovemaking.

"Amy, I..."

"What is it Geoff? Is there something wrong?"

"No there's nothing wrong Amy, everything is wonderful. It's just that, well... I'm not looking for a one-night stand."

"If I thought you were you'd still be back on Beale street sailor."

"You know I'm really not checked into the Majestic that was just a ruse to..."

"According to my sources a man fitting your description with a truck just like yours was seen at the motel lobby of the Majestic."

"Geez, don't tell me you have active surveillance in all the seedy parts of town?"

"No, Geoff, you're just a terrible liar," she said breaking into laughter and pulling him closer to her.

"Touché, counselor," was all he could manage as he met her waiting lips with his. The kiss ended with playful wrestling interrupted by their laughter.

"I can't win against you, can I?"

"Don't even try, sailor."

"I could easily fall in love with you Amy," Geoff whispered, "I know it's way too premature to admit but hey, that's what I'm feeling and now that my immediate lust is satisfied I still have this very real warm and tender feeling for you."

"The feeling's mutual, Geoff," she whispered back as she snuggled close to him.

They drifted off into a serene unconsciousness - aware only of a deep warm contentment.

Early next morning when they awoke - still with their arms entwined it was Amy who first spoke. "Honey, I'm sorry, I really don't want to go but I have some errands that I need to get done. What do you think about a late lunch or an early dinner?"

"Amy, I want to be with you very badly right now, but my head tells me that you need some time, some space - why don't we just put things on hold until brunch tomorrow? I'll meet you there, at twelve o'clock like we agreed."

"Geoff…, you're not even going to pick me up," she said raising her eyebrows and pursing her lips in a coquettish pout.

"Well I just thought you might feel more comfortable and more in control of your circumstances. Besides I don't want you to feel smothered."

"Geoff, I have felt comfortable with you, with us, right from the first night when you came over to my table to introduce yourself - call it chemistry, compatibility or just incredible serendipity. And if I ever feel smothered I'll let you know…"

The gentle pressure of his lips against hers smothered her last words, if indeed there were any. Her mouth opened accepting his probing tongue and met it with her own. She slipped her hand behind his head and ran her fingers through his hair as their collective breathing quickened and became shallower. They paused after a minute or so looking deeply into each other's eyes.

After another long embrace he sighed saying, "Amy I'm sorry, I'm being selfish, I can't monopolize your time like this. You'll never get those errands done. I'll call for you tomorrow about twelve o'clock."

"Umm I'd already forgotten about my errands, but I really must get to them, and you need to go find a better place to stay. Maybe you should just come back and stay here."

"Oh please don't tempt me Amy, I think perhaps it's better if we took some time to get to know each other and let our feelings catch up to our libido."

"Oh now…that sounds like an agenda for a long term commitment."

"I've got the time if you have the desire and interest."

After another long intimate kiss and a caressing embrace that ended with them holding hands with their fingers entwined they finally parted. He just did not want to let loose of the flood of mutual feelings of the blossoming romance washing over them, but he understood that he must give her a chance to accommodate and sort out her thoughts and feelings.

Chapter six

Sunday for him dawned brightly and developed into a really gorgeous day - almost as if the positive energy given off by his new found relationship with Amy had influenced the weather system. And the weather always had a transformational effect on him which was manifest on his mental and emotional demeanor as well as his physical energy level. The sunny warm days of spring and summer could turn his dejection into euphoria.

Today was that kind of day; it had a pleasant rhapsodic feeling which took him back to the contented days of his childhood where even in his loneliness he found solace and serenity. It had been a big beautiful world back then that held so much promise for the future. Coupled with the exuberance of his youth to enhance its effect this promise made him feel as though he could go anywhere, do anything and succeed - succeed even beyond the bounds of his wildest imagination.

And for a few minutes he was back in the world of his childhood as he drove over to pick up Amy. The sight of a little old lady selling roses on the corner of the street caught his attention and broke his reminiscence. It was the perfect touch. He pulled over to the curb and bought six red roses - for love, six white roses - for honesty, and two yellow roses – for the promise of a safe return to each other's arms should they ever become separated.

The Chez Louis Quatorze, a large restaurant with banquet facilities, on the Mississippi River waterfront was magnificent. Situated on a ten-acre plot ensconced amidst a towering levee system for flood abatement it was built in the style of a large southern plantation manor with huge white columns across the front blended with the soft easy charm that reminded one of the mansions along St. Charles Avenue in the Garden District of New Orleans. Tall bald cypress trees draped with Spanish moss formed a natural canopy over the entrance drive leading to the guest portico and complimentary valet parking. A wrought-iron fence surrounded a courtyard to the right of the main entrance bounded on three sides by a cloister. In the center of the courtyard was a large granite and marble fountain. Brunch seating was inside in the Versailles Room or outside along widely spaced out tables of the cloister as well as under umbrellas scattered throughout the courtyard. They chose to sit out on the cloister which afforded more intimacy.

Amy looked gorgeous in a tastefully short clinging ivory satin dress with a plunging v-neckline into which she had added a flowery silk scarf. Cream stockings with ivory heeled slides to match her dress completed her ensemble. As soon as they settled into their seats a server approached.

"Good afternoon Madame and Monsieur may I bring you each a glass of champagne?" he asked with a slight bow as he proffered the menu.

"We would like to start with a bottle of Moet Chandon White Star Brut and I would also like coffee," said Geoff.

"Very good sir, and for Madame…will you be having coffee also?"

"Yes please, thank you," said Amy.

A combo of musicians made their way among the tables stopping to play requests and then moving on.

"Good afternoon, is there something we can play for you?" the lead musician asked as the combo approached their table.

"I would love to hear the Spring Concerto from Vivaldi's Four Seasons," said Geoff.

"Ah, a splendid choice sir, it is one of our favorites," having said that they launched into the first movement with all the aplomb of a chamber orchestra.

45

When they at last moved on Amy squeezed Geoff's forearm and leaned over whispering - "I really love that piece but I didn't think they would ever go away and I'm starving, let's eat."

They shared Belgian waffles made to order, French toast, Eggs Benedict, prawns, crayfish, pasta salad, fruit, veggies, thinly sliced rare roast beef, roast pork loin and broiled ham dallying over it for nearly three hours with many trips back up to the buffet tables. They even found room for dessert. Hazelnut dark-chocolate mousse brownies with a layer of white chocolate all topped off with French vanilla ice cream and hot caramel topping. Their server kept their cups filled with steaming coffee and refilled their champagne flutes as needed each time asking if everything was satisfactory.

They exuded an electric body language with constant eye contact, touching, whispering, winking, smiling and genuine laughter - they were obviously a couple deeply involved and oblivious to the outside world. After the brunch dishes were cleared there was dancing in the inside ballroom to a jazz combo.

"Amy you're a fantastic dancer; very smooth and light on your feet."

"It's because of you Geoff, you have a natural easy rhythm; you're very easy to follow."

"This is my idea of a perfect Sunday Amy, a fantastic brunch, terrific atmosphere, romantic dance music and the company of a very beautiful exciting and intelligent lady."

"Oh it is for me too Geoff; this is my favorite place in Memphis for brunch, but somehow today and here with you it feels even more special. I can't remember ever enjoying it quite so much."

After the dancing, they decided on a leisurely stroll along the stone walkway of the riverfront stopping frequently to smell the flowers or to gaze out at the incessant waves of the Mississippi. The sun was just beginning its descent into late afternoon lengthening the shadows, yet the air was still warm and fragrant with the blooms of early May. They strolled along, their arms wrapped around each other. Geoff gradually slowed the pace until they had come to a halt and he swept Amy into his arms and tenderly kissed her lips as they embraced. He had a very warm feeling of elation in his chest - he was falling for this lady - he needed her - he wanted her to love him the same way that he was beginning to love her - unconditionally.

"Oh Lord Amy, I just don't want this day to end."

"Um…I know; I feel the same way Geoff."

"What are you doing tomorrow?" Geoff asked as they walked back to the guest portico.

"Tomorrow…I…oh, it's Monday Geoff; it's one of my busiest and longest days. I have lots of case reviews and legal strategizing," she said stammering slightly in a suddenly guarded tone.

"You'll probably be ready for a break by noontime, maybe we can meet somewhere for a quick lunch," said Geoff.

"Oh…," she began with an uneasy laugh, "I'd really love to Geoff but I'll probably need to work straight through lunch and into the late hours. This whole week will be really hectic; I have to prepare for a very high profile case."

"Are you up for a drink at the bar before we leave?" Geoff asked pressing for just a little more time together.

"If you don't mind Geoff, I'd really like to make it an early evening, I…"

"Oh sure, I'm sorry I'm being a little clingy."

"It's not that Geoff, it's just that on Sunday evenings I like to relax in the Jacuzzi and turn in early so I'm ready for tomorrow. I know, I'm probably being a little selfish."

"No, no of course you're not, I understand. If anybody is being selfish it's me trying to monopolize all your time."

They retrieved his truck from valet parking and began the drive back to her place. The mood seemed to have changed; the conversation on the drive back was contrived at best. Geoff began to feel a little uneasy as his tension mounted. He did his best to dismiss it as just his over analysis and imagination. When they arrived at her house he walked her to the front door where they shared an embrace and a kiss. It felt strangely anticlimactic to Geoff and dampened his earlier feelings of euphoria. He began to feel a sense of foreboding not unlike rejection. Try as he might he couldn't make the feeling go away it was self-reinforcing and began to consume all his thoughts. All the preparation anticipation and hopes that this was the beginning of a shared romance began to slip through his fingers like the ephemeral pleasure of an ice cream sundae after consumption of the first few spoonsful.

He slept in late on Monday. When he did finally get up, he went out in search of an upscale coffee shop for a late breakfast. He hated to skip breakfast, it was his favorite meal. If by chance he did skip it, he found that he just could not function. His day just would not work.

He found a place called the Blue Plate Café and had a delicious three cheese Spanish omelet with a pot of steaming freshly brewed coffee. Along about the third cup his thoughts wandered back over the weekend. He tried to dismiss it all, knowing his damned wild imagination could spoil everything with a spin of expectancy that reality just could not match - at least not in his life.

He wanted desperately to call Amy - to hear her voice - to make plans to continue the development of their relationship, but he knew he must not. He had to give Amy some space. Familiarity would only breed contempt. Lord knows he had been taught that lesson over and over again. He did not want to go down the same primrose path with Amy. He needed to slow down and let her feelings catch up with his. He had a sense that she was special in his life. At least he hoped she would become his special someone - if he could only lose these lingering feelings of impending doom.

Was it all in his mind, would it really be different this time? Should he give this new dream romance time to come to fruition or was the ending already predestined?

"Would you like more coffee, sir?" his server was staring down at him with what he sensed was just a hint of impatience over his dalliance.

"Oh, no thank you, ma'am I think I'm all set."

"You have a nice day, sir."

"Thank you, you do the same ma'am."

Once back behind the wheel he found himself on the I-55 interstate heading south. There was comfort in old habits. He always hit the interstate when he had to do some serious thinking - to reorder his life - to sort it all out - make sense of it. It was only when he was moving at seventy-five mph that life made sense and he could see his next moves clearly. As soon as he stopped his life seemed to get hopelessly mired in confusion.

He began to wonder why Amy had come into his life. Was this just another build-up - another high mountain top from which to come crashing down into some abysmal pit to wallow in self-pity?

But what is life if you do not share it with someone? What is life if you cannot share it with someone? In the former instance it is lonely, in the latter it is tragic.

Do not under any circumstance succumb to this tragedy he told himself. Life is too great a gift to squander alone. To be able to share this gift with someone special serves only to elevate and increase its pleasure.

His thoughts began to wander back through past experiences. Bits of conversations from his past played over and over like worn out records. If only he had said... if only he had done... he could have, well no, maybe he should have...would it have made a difference...?

Stop it damn it. There's no life in a rearview mirror, just the dust of past poor choices that you are running away from. Always keep your eyes focused on the opportunity coming up in the windshield. Don't look back.

Move on! For once learn from your mistaken choices, damn it all.

He had promised himself it would not always be this way. Maybe he had lied to himself. He fervently hoped that he hadn't.

Chapter seven

He was miles into Mississippi, in the heart of the Delta Blues country when he exited the interstate at a place that just looked interesting - lonely desolate, a place where he could relax and sort out the confusion of his feelings. He passed a marker for Carroll County and wondered what life had been like down in these parts way back on the 3rd of June in the humid heat of 1953. Refrains from the country R&B song *Ode to Billy-Joe* as sung by Bobby Gentry began running through his mind.

As he rounded a curve and came up over a rise for a railroad overpass he spotted an old one-story farmhouse up ahead with a rusting tin roof and two large gables set back in a little clearing off on the left side of the road all by itself. It had a wooden front porch that wrapped around both sides. An old faded hand-painted sign - Dew Drop Inn - with a tilted martini glass and three drops dripping from it was mounted between the two gables.

He pulled into the small gravel lot on the side and climbed the two steps up to the side porch entrance. There were several wicker tables and chairs along the porch but they were all vacant at this hour of the day because of the heat. He walked around to the double screen door front entrance which opened into a foyer with two small tables under windows on each side of swinging louvered café doors leading to a large barroom done in rough-hewn pine. The bar had stools on three sides with an exit behind the bar that looked as though it led into the kitchen through another set of swinging louvered café doors.

The bar was not quite a third full with a couple of groups at the hitop tables. As he walked in most patrons looked over to see who it was, then turned back to their conversations when there was no recognition. He took a seat at the bar. The barkeep was neither young nor old but had an easy pleasant manner.

"How y'all doing today, sir?"

"Just fine thank you, sir - how about yourself?" he asked even though he had far too much on his mind to keep things light.

"Well I'd rather be off drinking a brew and holding a fishing pole, but this here would be a close second," said the barkeep with a twinkle in his clear blue-gray eyes. "What can I get for you, sir?"

"Make it a Jack Daniels rocks please."

When the barkeep returned with the drink he set it down on a coaster with a question. "You don't look like you're from around here sir. What brings you down to these parts?"

"Well I'm staying up in Memphis for a while but I just needed to take a drive out in the country and get my head straight."

"Memphis, you say, that's not just over the hill - it's about a hundred miles or so up the interstate."

"Yes sir, I enjoy long drives, it's a habit I picked up living out west in Colorado Springs. I'd often take a road trip up to Laramie, Wyoming and return on the same night which amounts to about a four-hundred-mile round trip."

"So what brought you to Memphis?"

"The Blues, I've heard it called the Capital of the Blues."

"Yes sir, up there on Beale Street they do play the Blues, but down here in the delta country we live the Blues. You can appreciate the difference?"

"Yes sir, I sure can. I'll bet you have some good blues players down here. By any chance can you recommend a local place down here with a good Blues band?"

"There's a place farther down into town called the Cotton Patch. They have a Blue Monday jam. I've got a few regulars that go down there all the time. If you'd like, I'll introduce you - it'd be better if you went there with a couple of the locals if you know what I mean."

"Ah, I understand."

"Down in these parts, if you're a stranger it tends to make some of the good ole boys a bit nervous - I don't put up with that stuff in here."

"Well I certainly would appreciate the introduction - my name's Geoff."

"Howdy Geoff, I'm Hank. Pete, Dan and Leroy ought to be along in the next half-hour or so."

"Well great that'll give me some time to grab a bite to eat. What do you recommend?"

"Well my wife's in the kitchen, she makes a killer Jambalaya."

"That sounds like the ticket, let's do it."

A few minutes later, Hank brought out a large bowl of steaming Jambalaya and some fresh corn bread - it all looked and smelled delicious. The first taste told him that he had found a little bit of heaven here in the delta country.

~~~   ~~~   ~~~

It was dark, pitch dark - late or early depending on your frame of reference - the moon was dark in its new phase. The stars were obscured by the overcast - all in all an excellent night for an undetected insertion. There was a warm humid foreboding off-shore breeze coming straight at them as they paddled their inflatable rubber dinghy towards the beach objective. The sea out around the submarine from which they had disembarked was as dark as black India ink with small choppy waves.

As they neared the beach the shore breakers increased in intensity and crescendo. Suddenly the dark tranquility of the night was shattered by the clatter of automatic weapons fire - AK's from their telltale signature. No visible muzzle flashes gave away the direction of the incoming rounds which walked their way out through the surf zone until they splashed barely ten meters off the bow of the boat. It was time to trim their profile a little. With a nod at each other they each quickly slipped over the gunwale disappearing into the surf - two of them keeping the boat tow rope between them. They breast stroked the remaining hundred meters or so towards the shore. It was a welcome diversion, taking their collective minds off the task at hand.

They were, each of them, dealing with their own fears, misgivings and apprehensions as they silently pushed on towards the beach.

It's strange how your whole life could flash before you in a crazy kaleidoscope of feelings, emotions, hopes and dreams, all fed by the adrenaline rush when survival was threatened. As if the story had to rush to conclusion or at least to a logical breaking point before the commercial break or the next and maybe the final chapter. He found himself thinking back to his first real date - it hadn't taken place until his senior year in high school just after he had obtained his driver's license. It was a Good Friday and he had felt so guilty about the impropriety that he had gone to see a movie classic with an obvious religious theme. She was his first flame. He had corresponded with her throughout his entire tour in the Navy until just prior to his separation when she had written him the news that she had gotten engaged to be married. His dream that they would pick up where they had left off when he returned to civilian life was shattered. It would become the norm for many of his future dreams as life unfolded contrary to his plans.

His thoughts were interrupted as they cleared the surf zone and their coral boots found the sandy bottom. They waded through the surf and broke for cover - a natural bunker formed by several downed palm trees - dragging the rubber boat quickly to a secure hiding place in the dense foliage. They spread out into a defensive perimeter and lay low listening for sounds of movement. There was nothing but the ceaseless crash of shore breakers attacking the beach then falling back to regroup with the next set to repeat the assault again over and over. It was the awesome tenacity of nature - humbling on one level yet inspiring on another.

After twenty minutes which seemed more like three hours Brave Cloud their lead petty officer was satisfied that there was no imminent attack and he assumed the point and signaled to move out as he slowly negotiated through the thick underbrush in slow careful steps to minimize any noise of movement. Geoff drew the third slot in their small column and moved out after allowing the proper interval. The butterflies in his stomach felt as though they were having a party. He forced himself to focus his senses on the sights and sounds of the night trying to establish his own feel for what was normal background noise. Anything over that threshold would trigger a heightened sense of alert.

They maintained sight-lines with their forward teammate to facilitate communication by hand signals as they moved silently in the direction of the last gunfire they heard which had stopped as suddenly as it began just before they made landfall. Even though their vision had adjusted to the low light conditions, the darkness of the night required them to adjust their interval closer than normal. As his own tension mounted he could feel little streams of sweat rolling down the center of his back.

After penetrating about one hundred fifty meters they crossed a trail running north-northeast. An easier route, but more exposed and now they would need to double their vigilance against ambush. Less than fifty meters onto this new trail Brave Cloud gave the signal to halt. Geoff froze in his tracks straining to discern any change in the background noise. All he could hear was the pounding of his heart in his ears.

A rustling sound in the dense foliage off to the left of the trail was the only warning. First two, then three more shadowy figures emerged noisily onto the trail not more than ten meters away beating the brush apart with their weapons. The element of surprise belonged to their squad as each stood frozen and silent in position with weapons at the ready. The five intruders were startled as they became aware of their adversaries and fumbled futilely trying to bring their weapons to bear – time clicked into slow motion. Brave Cloud initiated the close quarter firefight firing several rounds from his M-16 taking out the nearest two targets followed instantly by Jones from the number 2 slot with two bursts from his Stoner light-machine gun. Geoff, his number three slot completing the arc of the kill zone surrounding the five targets, squeezed off several quick rounds from his modified AR-15 a fraction of a second later taking out the last man standing. Each of them had swept his sector in the tight point blank range of fire. In less than five seconds, which seemed more like five minutes, the five intruders were dispatched. They quickly searched the bodies for identification or any sort of documents that might have intelligence value. Then recognition sank in, these bad guys were not Viet Cong/VC or North Vietnamese Regulars/PAVN, they were Chinese

Communists/ChiComs with Russian model AK-47s. They gathered up the few papers they found and sanitized the area removing the bodies and recovering spent brass. There was no time to bury them properly. They dragged them off into the heavy undergrowth just off the trail.

This was Cambodia; they were fifty to one hundred kilometers northwest of the border with Vietnam. Their mission would be in jeopardy of compromise if they didn't move quickly out of there and put some real estate between them and this confrontation. Five men would not be reporting back to their unit, whatever and wherever that was. They may not be missed for weeks, but then again maybe they would be – the papers they stripped away might hold a clue. It was time to boogie. They had another three hours by their estimate to travel to make the coordinates where they would establish the listening and observation post. The rest of the insertion passed uneventfully.

When they finally arrived at the assigned coordinates they setup a perimeter and Geoff donned his headset. The usual frequencies were quiet, strangely so. It was even money that Charlie had somehow gotten wind of their op and moved his whole operation – probably up to Laos. But that territory was the operational area of Army SpecOps and god-dammed inter-service rivalry would not allow for the sharing of intelligence. It was sometimes maddening - each unit developed its own intel and jealously guarded it. The justification, of course, was to avoid compromise, which was hard to argue against. It just made things more difficult and inefficient not to mention dangerous. The inactivity on the bandwidth and the heat of the approaching day began to take their toll and he caught himself daydreaming of other times, other places.

He had been attached to the team as a SOT, a special operations technician. He had joined them in Coronado California for SEAL basic indoctrination just prior to their deployment. He had had an intensive twelve-week regimen of physical conditioning, asymmetrical warfare arms and tactics, escape and evasion and survival training at Kaneohe Bay, Oahu, the Training Facility on Molokai and on the island of Maui at a Marine Corps jungle training command just prior to the trip back to the mainland – all part of what the U.S. Navy euphemistically called Temporary Additional Duty or TAD orders. He had volunteered for duty in Vietnam wanting but never expecting to be selected. It was strange how the Navy sometimes granted your wishes when they corresponded to the needs of the Navy.

When he had arrived at the Naval Amphibious Warfare command in Coronado he was impressed and in awe almost to the point of being overwhelmed. These guys had years of training, experience and conditioning on him. Brave Cloud had fought in the Korean Conflict as a member of a UDT team. And here he was a fleet electronics technician who only a few months earlier had been working on submarine communications since graduating Electronics Technician School at Great Lakes Naval Training Command. He did, however, have some special knowledge and experience on LORAN navigation equipment that figured into the classified part of this mission. Also his Top Secret clearance had been a highly desirable asset. The guys had accepted him as a teammate after an initial period of indoctrination that had really helped to buoy up his confidence. He had had ample opportunity to back out of the whole program but it would have meant being shipped back to Pearl with his tail between his legs. Besides he wasn't a quitter, no matter how tough the road got.

A tap on his shoulder brought him back to reality. Lieutenant Green was next to him moving his index finger in circles around his ear. It was their sign language for radio activity. He shook his head in the negative and the lieutenant slipped quietly away. Another hour went by and he reached back into his radio pouch and brought out the handset for the LORAN device he was field testing. He got a lock on two of the three signals he needed. He spent the next hour or so fiddling with different combinations of RF gain and antenna tuner settings and recording the results in his log. The rest of the day went by uneventfully.

As the darkness once again settled in Lieutenant Green passed the signal to prepare to extract. They retraced their route back to the beach with no further encounters and retrieved their rubber boat from its hiding place. The rendezvous with the submarine went off without a hitch. They swam out through the surf zone for about a quarter mile and then climbed into their rubber boat that they had been towing along. After about forty-five minutes of paddling they caught sight of the low silhouette of the CRAWFISH drifting slowly on the surface fifty meters off their port beam. Lieutenant Green exchanged signals using his flashlight with a green lens cover. Paddling over to the stern of the boat they climbed aboard and deflated their rubber boat stowing it away in the sail compartment. They entered through the conning tower hatch and climbed down the ladder to control where the skipper greeted them.

"Welcome back guys, Chuck's waiting for you in the galley."

"Aye aye, sir a steaming hot cup of coffee sounds great," they all said together.

Chuck was Lieutenant Charles Covington the Communications Officer of the boat cleared to Top Secret with cryptography and signals intel. They could relax and not mince words. Chuck had been a UDT teammate before opting for the better career ladder of submarines.

"Good Op, guys?" he asked as he passed around the coffee.

"Well interesting would be the operative word. The usual – no signs of Charlie, no radio traffic," said Lieutenant Green. "McEwen did get some solid fixes with our LORAN device that we'll have to verify against the charts. If they prove accurate enough it could turn into a viable locating device. We hope to be able to pinpoint a man's location down to a few meters within the entire theater of ops. It'll make search and rescue magnitudes more efficient and increase recovery rates."

"Nothing like technology, too bad it takes a war to bring out the best," said Chuck.

They didn't mention the firefight – that would have to wait for the debriefing after they filled out the after action reports known to the teams as Barn Dance cards.

The rest was history – well it all was – only parts of it replayed themselves in endless repetition in his mind whenever he wasn't focused on a task at hand. Would it ever be over for him? *I remember the night Clayton Delaney died* - the words and the melody of an old country song kept repeating over in his mind in maddening frequency. He could feel his anxiety building again.

~~~   ~~~   ~~~

The strains of a sad country song brought him out of his reverie – *nobody answered when I called your name* – the words, the melody the poignancy always got to him, formed a knot in his throat that made it hard to swallow. It passed in a moment with scarcely a twitch of his facial muscles. But it was enough. He wiped the sweat off his forehead. Hank was there with a quizzical look on his face.

"Is there something wrong with the jambalaya…a little too much Tabasco for you?"

"No…no, it's excellent; I guess that song on the jukebox just kind of brought back some old ghosts." After he said it he bit his lip and cursed himself silently under his breath. Damn, he had to quit displaying his feelings and treating his private life like an open book. Better to put on a façade and never admit to how you really feel inside. That was the way to play the game.

"Sometimes you just got to let it go," Hank said in a low voice over his shoulder as he moved away. Just then three guys walked in and took seats just to the left of his.

"Hi, fellas, what'll it be, the usual?" Hank called out as he set three cocktail glasses on the pouring mat.

"Howdy Hank, yes sir Beam and water around," said one of them.

The guy seated next to him glanced over at him, "How y'all doing sir – don't reckon I've seen you in here before."

"I haven't been here before sir, I just happened to be passing through…Geoff's the name."

Hank set the drinks down in front of them.

"Well I see you've already met," he said to Pete as he nodded over at Geoff.

Pete offered his hand and said, "Nice to meet you, sir, I'm Pete, this here is Dan and that's Leroy over on the far side."

Geoff got up and shook hands around exchanging pleasantries.

"How's the jambalaya tonight, Geoff?" asked Pete as he glanced over to see what Geoff was eating.

"Excellent, best I've had this side of New Orleans," said Geoff.

"Hank, order me a bowl of the jambalaya will you please," said Pete.

"Make that two please," said Leroy.

"Jambalaya sounds good…three please," said Dan.

"Geoff here was asking about some Blues bands. I mentioned the Cotton Patch and told him you guys are regulars over there and might be willing to show him around."

"Well sure we were just talking about maybe moseying on over there tonight, be glad to show you the place, right guys?" said Pete looking alternately at Dan and Leroy.

"Sounds good to me," said Dan – "he'd be a might safer with some friends."

"Aw, come on Dan," said Leroy, "the place ain't that bad anymore."

"Yeah, Leroy is right, it ain't like the old days," agreed Pete.

Hank brought out the jambalaya and the conversation switched to some local gossip. After a second round of drinks they decided it was time to head out.

The Cotton Patch an old brick textile mill that had been renovated after the mill closed down was in the run down section of downtown. It was a neighborhood typical of the locale of many Blues Bars – the last stop on the one-way train to despair and desperation - hell's half acre of lost souls.

The inside wall partitions ended at a height of eight feet to expose the twenty-foot ceiling. Electrical conduit ran to junction boxes from which hung large five bladed fans on long extensions. The ventilation ducts and sprinkler system were all exposed. A large antique L-shaped back bar stood off against the right wall as you walked in. The top surface of the bar was rough-hewn wood with about a half inch thick coating of epoxy resin. The bar rail matched the surface. A brass rail ran along the bottom of the bar as a foot rest. The immediate area around the bar had four-person hi-top tables. One step up and behind a railing were an assortment of doubles, quads and several large oval tables. Near the left wall across from the bar was the band platform.

They took seats at a hi-top just off the bar almost directly underneath a five bladed fan revolving slowly moving the air around and keeping the smoke away. Non-smoking sections hadn't yet arrived in this part of Mississippi. The bar was near full as were most of the hi-tops. As they ordered their drinks the lights beneath the fans dimmed and a combo of musicians took up their instruments on the platform. This first combo featured a bass player, a Dobro player, another acoustic guitar and one snare drum with brushes. They launched into their cover of *Down Home Blues*. A few couples got up to dance. This one particular couple caught Geoff's attention. It was hard to see in the dim lighting but something about the way she moved and her features, as best he could make them out at this distance, were familiar. They danced well together, like they knew each other rather intimately. When the song ended the couple went back to their seats - a party of four at a table behind the railing. Could it be? Geoff tried to drive the crazy thoughts away dismissing them as just his overactive imagination.

"Geoff, you're awfully quiet. What do you think of our little hideaway?" asked Pete.

"This is my kind of place, Pete. Good atmosphere, great music…"

"Some good looking women too, but you have to be careful." said Dan.

"Careful?" asked Geoff with a quizzical look on his face.

"Dan means you have to know who's with whom, or you can get yourself into a nasty confrontation." said Leroy.

"Relax guys; I'm not looking for women, just want to listen to some good blues and sip some old whiskey."

Geoff looked around to see the lady that he had noticed dancing get up and walk across the bar room apparently, he supposed, to visit the ladies room. As she walked around to the far end of the bar the lights revealed her features clearly to him. He felt a shock to his senses as adrenaline kicked in, a sudden lump in his throat and an unsettling sensation in his stomach. He didn't hear himself inhale but it was audible to the others. They glanced over in the direction of his stare.

"You have good taste there Geoff," said Pete. "She's a looker."

"Smart too, that's Amy Johnson. She's a hot-shot prosecutor for the District Attorney's office up in Memphis. Definitely on the fast track career-wise," said Dan.

"Amy's a Mississippi gal, Vicksburg," said Pete. "Powerful family, her dad's a Mississippi state senator. Leroy here even got to know her dad," he said with a chuckle.

"Yeah, from the wrong end of a shotgun," said Dan with a deep belly laugh.

"Ah come on guys, that was a long time ago," said Leroy. "He wasn't even a senator back then."

"I take it she comes here often then?" said Geoff.

"We see her here quite often. Always with Tom Reilly another up-and-comer from the Memphis DA's office," said Pete. "He's got daddy's approval, so I guess she's spoken for."

Geoff's head was swimming. He'd heard enough, he didn't need to hear any more of the sordid details. "Hey guys, I hate to have to leave so soon but I've got some early errands I need to take care of up in Memphis tomorrow and it's a long trip back. I think I need to head on out. Thanks a lot for your hospitality, I really enjoyed it. I'll remember this place and maybe get back here someday."

"Take it easy on the interstate, Geoff. The Mississippi State Patrol is usually out in force at night with radar," said Pete.

"Thanks for the warning; I'll keep it in mind. Gentlemen, you all have a good evening."

He decided to visit the men's room before the long trip back. As he approached the door of the men's room the ladies room door swung open and out walked Amy.

"Geoff! Wha...what are you doing here?"

"I might ask you the same question Amy. Pretty high profile case you're working on there."

"What are you talking about?"

"It was going to be a long day, you said, 'No time for lunch, probably burn the midnight oil' – yeah sure, at the Cotton Patch snuggling up with your boy toy."

"It...it's not what you think it is," she said still being defensive.

"Oh, is this field work or just keeping in touch with the good ole boys?"

"Look, I don't have to justify my actions where they don't concern you Geoff."

"No, of course not, I just thought there was something special developing between us. How foolish of me. I see I was just taken in by your expert courtroom theatrics."

"Just a minute there, cowboy, are you so insecure that you had to follow me around or are you stalking me?" she asked in a particularly ugly tone, all pretense of decorum gone her eyes on fire as though she were doing a summation in court.

"Don't flatter yourself. So long counselor, have a nice life."

Chapter eight

S o when Memphis went sour he threw all his stuff in the bed of his trusty 4-by and got back out on the interstate heading south on the I-55. He thought briefly about stopping in New Orleans but he needed the ocean right now. He needed to watch the waves crashing endlessly onto the beach climbing inexorably higher with each set until the invisible force of the tide brought their advance to a halt and began to chase them back down to their lowest ebb only to have them begin their assault anew and recover their ground six hours hence. The tenacity of the ocean refreshed him by its example. It cleansed all the frustration, pain and misery from his soul. It convinced him to go on, to not allow life to beat him into submission.

He transitioned from I-55 south to the I-12 bypass which would lead to the eastbound I-10 heading for Jacksonville where he'd catch I-95 for the short trip south to St Augustine.

He began to get hungry and remembered an outrageous make-your-own omelet that he'd gotten at a pancake house just off I-12 in Covington Louisiana on one of his past cross-country trips.

That wasn't too far ahead. Let's see if he could remember the exit.

Twenty minutes later he was seated in the non-smoking section of Bobbi-Lynn's Pancake Emporium. He had the uncanny ability to make a wrong turn two thousand miles into a road trip and then repeat it on another trip several months or even years later – over and over again. He guessed that meant he had never learned from his mistakes. Well what the hell, in his next life he'd be perfect.

He ordered the omelet loaded with Jack, Swiss and Provolone cheese, green and red bell peppers, mushrooms, black olives, ham, chili with beans, lots of jalapenos and extra salsa. Sourdough toast and a steaming cup of coffee completed his order to the server who just shook her head in amazement.

"Um umm, honey, are you going to eat all that?"

"I'm on my way to Jacksonville; I need something to keep me going"

"Um hmm, well in that case I'd better brew some fresh coffee, I suspect you'll want more than one cup, I'll bring you a carafe when it's ready."

"Umm fresh brewed, that sounds great, thank you miss."

The omelet was fantastic, as good as he remembered. In this crazy world of wholesale change for the sake of change it was refreshing to find some things unchanged.

Forty minutes later he was back out on the interstate. He had dawdled a little longer than he'd planned but what the hell he had no schedule to keep. As he passed signs for Biloxi and Gulfport he remembered another port-of-call; a place called Burma Road a casual concept café and bar not far off the interstate or maybe it was on the business loop. Another place to indulge his fantasies or maybe if he were lucky to strike up a conversation and make another shallow acquaintance. He made a mental note to stop in there on his next swing back out this way.

By the time he got to Pensacola he was suddenly tired. Maybe it was the climate change of the panhandle. He decided to take the prudent decision and call it a night so he drove out to Pensacola Beach to find a motel.

The next morning, he was up early and jogging on the beach; the sand felt good squeaking beneath the pounding of his heels as his lungs filled with the fresh breeze blowing in off the water. After a quick shower, check-out and breakfast he was back out on the interstate running east once more. He made excellent time to Tallahassee; traffic was light and moving at the speed limit and better, he probably wouldn't need fuel until Jacksonville which at this rate would be a little after noon.

About eleven thirty he transitioned onto Interstate 295 which would put him on Interstate 95 just north of St Augustine; he was making even better time than he had figured. Less than an hour later he had exited Interstate 95 and was heading east to pick up A1A towards the beaches. Once on A1A he headed south, crossed over the Bridge of Lions and followed it through Anastasia Park and on down along the shore to St Augustine Beach.

As he drove slowly along the beach route he spotted another old relic from his past that jogged his memory. Robbie's Refuge a restaurant built on stilts. It had a deck built on its flat roof with an overhang that summoned to mind images of the flight deck on an aircraft carrier. A lower deck shaded by the upper deck ran around the outside of the main bar on the first floor which was twelve feet off the ground. He decided that it warranted a stop for lunch where he could maybe get a recommendation for local accommodations that were a bit out of the mainstream of the usual hotels and motels.

"Hi honey, what'll it be today?" the lady barkeep, a gorgeous blonde, inquired as he took a seat at the first floor bar after climbing up the winding wooden stairway.

It was just as comfortable and friendly as he remembered from his last visit whenever that was. There was a good crowd sitting at tables as well as along the opposite and adjacent sides of the rectangular bar. The inside walls of the bar were highly varnished planks of pine hung with all kinds of old fishing gear; nets with conch, starfish and other assorted seashells and cork floats all of which gave it a very nautical character.

"A cold draft sounds good."

"We have two for one specials on Coors Light."

"That'll do, oh and a menu too please."

She came back with the brew and a cardboard menu. He looked it over and spotted a turkey club. Reuben sandwiches, Turkey Clubs and French Dips made his world go round he mused as he put the menu down.

"What looks good to you, sweetie?"

"The Turkey Club, no mayo with mustard instead of thousand. Also may I substitute some fruit instead of the fries?"

"Ah…oh sure we've probably got some wormy apples and black bananas in the back."

"Aw…hey, Lana don't you go chasing away the paying customers," said a young guy sitting across the bar.

"Oh shut up, Pete, I'll cut you off," she said over her shoulder.

"There goes the free music; I'll start charging for my services now."

"Charging! Pete you're lucky we don't charge you for the exposure, otherwise you'd be out on the pier picking for what people throw in your hat."

"That was cold Lana; I deserve more respect than that."

"I'm sorry sir," she said stifling a laugh and ignoring Pete as she turned her attention back to Geoff, "Pete's a regular here. We all love him and he knows it, but you can't let him take advantage. I'm just joking about the fruit. Would you like a pickle with your club or jalapeños?"

"No contest, the Mexican peppers."

"Great, I'll have that for you in a flash."

He sat there sipping his beer when Pete came over. "Excuse me sir, I didn't mean to butt into your business, I just like giving Lana shit, my name's Pete."

"Howdy Pete, I didn't mind, I enjoyed it; it adds to the homey atmosphere, I'm Geoff nice to meet you."

"You don't look like a tourist; are you from St Augustine?"

"You're half right I'm not a tourist at least not in the strict sense but I'm not a local either. I just drove in from out west to spend a little time on the water."

"Well then, welcome to St Augustine, if I can be of any assistance this is where you'll find me."

"Hey maybe you can; you wouldn't happen to know of anyone looking to rent out a boat with sleeping facilities and access to marina services?"

"It turns out I do, my buddy's old man, Jack Schreid, is an agent out at the marina; I'm sure he can fix you up. I think I may have one of his cards. Yeah, here it is," he said pulling a weather beaten card from his wallet. "Just tell him Pete Townshend referred you."

"Pete Townshend, eh? Damn, you've aged remarkably well."

"Yeah, that's my real name; I get a lot of mileage goofing on people sometimes."

"Well thanks a lot Pete; I'll give him a call. Let me buy you a beer or whatever you're drinking."

"Hey, thanks I never refuse a drink. Stick around if you can I start playing at four."

Lana was back with his food and Pete went back to his seat to let him eat. Geoff ordered a beer for Pete and dug into his food. The Turkey was fresh, not the usual turkey roll. It was a real gourmet club sandwich. He had another beer and checked his watch; it was just after two-thirty. He got his tab and got up to leave as Pete looked over.

"Got to run Pete, I want to go check on that boat; I'll be back later."

"I'll be here, most likely, thanks for the brew," said Pete.

Geoff went back out to his truck and retrieved his cell phone. He punched in the number from the business card; it rang twice and then cut over to another number and rang again.

"*Hello, Jack Schreid,*" said a voice at the other end.

"Hello, Jack my name is Geoff; I was told by Pete Townshend that you may be able to find me a boat rental with sleeping facilities and marina access."

"*I'm sure I can fix you up. Come on down to my office I'm heading there now. Do you know the Channel House Marina?*"

"Well I just got in town; I'm not too familiar with St Augustine."

"*Where are you now?*"

"I'm over at Robbie's Refuge, that's where I met Pete."

"*Oh, of course, he's a fixture there, great guitar player. Hey I'm heading over in that direction I can swing by there and pick you up or you can follow me.*"

"That's sounds great, I'll wait for you here, I'm in a gray GMC 4-by with Colorado tags."

"*Ok Geoff, give me about ten minutes.*"

In a few minutes a black Jeep Wrangler with the top down pulled up in front of Geoff's truck. The driver waved him over. Geoff got out and walked over to the Jeep.

"Jack Schreid," said the driver, a man about the same age as himself as he held out his hand, "I assume you are Geoff."

"Yes, I am."

"Hop in we can take my Jeep; I'm coming back here afterwards anyway."

"So what kind of rental are you looking for?" asked Jack as Geoff climbed in and they drove away.

"I'm really just looking for a boat to bunk in on the water. I'm a little tired of motels. Nothing fancy, I probably won't even be taking it out unless I get a wild hair up my butt."

"Hell you can bunk in an old derelict, but you don't strike me as the type. If you want something that'll be a pleasant change from a boring motel room, complete with galley, head and shower facilities, something that's also seaworthy so that if you do decide to take it out you have that option then I can help you out."

"Maybe I was being a bit too nonchalant; a galley, head and shower facilities certainly would be my first choice if I could find something like that."

"In that case I think I might have just the ticket. It's got really nice appointments; it's owned by a Canadian couple who only come down occasionally for a short visit in late October. They've asked me to rent it out for some extra income if I find the right party. How many are there in your party?"

"It's a party of one; just me."

"Well if you hang out with Pete at Robbie's you won't be playing solitaire very long especially with this boat. He's got fans, women and groupies from Daytona, Fort Lauderdale and Miami driving up to hang out with him; I'm sure he'll introduce you around. What brings you all the way to the east coast of Florida from Colorado, if I may ask?"

"The water, Jack; I just needed to get back to the ocean. I've spent some time in the Navy and got used its effect on me. I'm also using the trip as research for my writing."

"Oh, you're an author, what have you gotten published?"

"Mostly free-lance stuff, but one day I'm hoping to put my book out there."

"I've heard that's a great feeling, especially if you're not some totally jaded celebrity," said Jack.

"It will be for me; sort of the capstone of a long journey."

They arrived down at the marina and Jack pulled past several rows of docks until he got to a more remote section. He parked and they got out and walked down to the gated entry. Once inside they walked the length of the pier down to a floating dock where a single boat was tied up.

"It's a thirty-nine foot Catalina cruiser one of the early ones they produced but it's been maintained and even upgraded beautifully," Jack said as they climbed aboard and walked aft on the teak weather deck to the cockpit. "You can have meals right here in the cockpit; it has a folding leaf table and plenty of seating. Let's go below I'll show you the salon, galley and cabins."

They entered through the cockpit hatch and stepped into the salon.

"Just look at the size of this salon Geoff; you've got the full use of the twelve-foot beam. The galley here has a large refrigerator/freezer with top and side access, three-burner stainless steel stove and over the counter microwave. The starboard dinette over there can convert to a single berth or settee."

"Hey now, this is first class," said Geoff with a soft whistle as he looked around.

They walked through the forward bulkhead hatch to the guest cabin which was bright and airy and featured a double berth with innerspring mattress.

"Certainly not like anything we had in the Navy," said Geoff as he looked over at the bunk.

"Hold on, let's go back aft to the master cabin, I saved the best for last, check this out Geoff."

The master stateroom had a huge full beam athwart ship berth that was over eight feet long, two hanging lockers, built-in cedar lined drawers and large storage bins. Adjacent to the master cabin was a two compartment head with enclosed shower stall and bi-fold door.

"We provide all the sheets, towels, linens, galley utensils, pots, pans, dinnerware and silverware. You've got a complete package here. I'll even throw in a complementary bottle of champagne. What do you think, Geoff?"

"It's a beautiful boat, Jack; it's a lot more spacious than I expected I'd see from topside and it's in excellent shape, it looks to be in showroom condition."

"Yeah these boats can be deceiving. They are very well crafted. And this boat has been lovingly maintained. If you're interested, we can go back to my office and work out the details."

"I'm very interested Jack, it's a gorgeous vessel, quite a bit fancier than I thought I'd find available."

"Well, you look like a mature responsible guy, Geoff. I wouldn't have brought you out to see this if I didn't think you would respect the property."

They went back to the office and Geoff filled out some paperwork and left a refundable security deposit and cleaning deposit along with rental for a month. He got a card key that fit the dock gate and marina Laundromat along with the keys to the boat.

"How's your seamanship, Geoff?"

"It's probably a little rusty, well… make that quite a bit rusty."

"No problem, my son Jason has his Coast Guard master's license. I can get him to give you an orientation cruise. Since I've still got a lot of influence with him we'll just include it at no extra charge as part of the rental."

"That's an offer I'd be a fool to refuse."

"Fine, just let me know when you're ready and I'll arrange it. Hey, it's just about four o'clock, time for happy hour. There's a nice bar and restaurant here at the marina but Robbie's has more action if you know what I mean. Oh before we go let me make a call to my cleaning crew and get them to give it a quick once over and make sure it's inventoried and ready for you. Give them about an hour or so and you can move your stuff in."

Chapter nine

Fifteen minutes later Jack and Geoff were back in the parking lot of Robbie's. It was now much more crowded than before. The upper deck was rail to rail with twenty-somethings and those that were still trying to hold on to that designation. Most were in swim wear with sunglasses and visors - baggie surfer trunks for the guys and string bikinis for the gals appeared to be the overwhelmingly favored attire. They found a couple seats at the inside bar.

"First one's on me Geoff, after that you're on your own."

"Hi guys what'll it be...hey you're back; I guess you liked that turkey club," said Lana looking over at Geoff and flashing a bright smile.

"Yes I did, it was excellent, I'll have a Coors Light," said Geoff.

"Make that two," said Jack. "Lana, have you met Geoff?"

"Well yeah sort of, he was in earlier for a couple and a sandwich, he got to meet Pete. You know how that goes. Don't mind us Geoff we're all like family here. Nice to meet you," she said extending her hand.

"You can plan on seeing Geoff around here a lot; he just rented out Bobby McAllister's boat," said Jack.

"Ooh, nice boat. You can take me out for a cruise sometime," Lana said with a wink.

"Yeah, like your old man will let that happen."

"Oh hush up Jack; he'll be at the track."

"Don't do it Geoff, this she-wolf is trouble," said Jack.

"Pardon…Moi, trouble," Lana said glancing at them and fluttering her eyelashes as she poured two iced mugs of beer from the tap.

"Hey, there's my son Jason. Hey Jas, have you got a minute?"

A tall tanned young man in his late twenties with sandy blond hair and gray eyes came over. "Hi, dad what's up?"

"Jason this is Geoff. He just rented out Bobby McAllister's boat."

"Nice. How are you doing Geoff, you're going to really enjoy that boat with its internal mast and electric winch system. It sails itself."

"He says his seamanship skills aren't quite what they used to be, I told him you could take him out for a refresher."

"Sure, be glad to, you'll need a little orientation on the equipment and cockpit instrumentation anyway. Let's see tomorrow is out but how about Wednesday?"

"That will work fine for me," said Geoff, "I'll leave the day open so whatever time is good for you is fine with me."

"I like to go out early; I'll be over there Wednesday morning about eight-thirty or is that too early for you?"

"Eighty-thirty is fine with me I'll be up on deck and all set to cast off the mooring lines," said Geoff.

"Good, give me about fifteen minutes either way. Catch you later, I'm going to go check out the upper deck," said Jason.

Pete was sitting on a chair on the band platform strumming his acoustic guitar over an amplifier just loud enough to be heard over the din if you focused on it yet not loud enough to overwhelm the conversations. He was picking a rhythm and blues number. Geoff went over and stuck a couple of bills in the tip jar, getting an acknowledging nod from Pete. After a few more numbers Pete took his break and made his way over to say hi.

"How's it going Jack, did you get Geoff here fixed up with a place to sleep?" asked Pete.

"Better than that, he rented out Bobby McAllister's boat; Jason even volunteered to take him out for a shakedown cruise," said Jack.

"Hey now, that's a real babe magnet. I'll have to talk to Jason and see if we can't put together a fun cruise for the weekend, we'll supply the cold beer and hot women."

"There you go Geoff, I warned you about Pete here. He throws away more women than most guys meet."

"Ah now Jack, I'm not that wild anymore; I've settled down to one or two a week with maybe a couple of fresh ones for the weekends."

"Geez, Pete you've got to tone that down," said Jack. "Women aren't sushi, you've got to be sensitive these days, right Geoff."

"Don't ask me, I haven't figured them out yet; but you can't argue with success, if the approach works why change."

"How are you gentlemen doing over here? And I use that term loosely, except for you Geoff," said Lana as she came over to check on their drinks.

"Hey ask Lana her opinion," said Jack.

"Forget it guys, I won't be drawn into your male sexist discussions. Be careful Geoff, these people will warp your brain," said Lana.

"I'll have one more Lana then I need to hit the road," said Jack.

"Make that three more with one for me and one for Pete, if you have time Pete," said Geoff. "And put them on my tab please, thanks Lana."

"Hey thank you Geoff, I always have time for a brew-ski," said Pete.

Jason came down from the upper deck and walked over to join them.

"PT what's up my man?" he asked as he high-fived Pete.

"Slow afternoon, how's the crowd topside?" asked Pete.

"Young stuff, got to be a lot of bogus ID's up there."

"Hey Lana, who's on the bar upstairs?" asked Pete.

"It's the new guy, Jared; Why?"

"Jas, says it looks like an underage crowd up there, so I thought I'd ask. I need to protect my gig."

"Oh, I thought you were bucking for a manager's slot. It'd be a cut in pay for you if you were - no more gratuities," said Lana over her shoulder as she poured two mugs of beer.

"Geez if I were to take a cut in pay, I'd be paying the house to play here."

"Whine, whine, whine…isn't it time for your next set or are you playing twenty and breaking forty," said Lana all the while tending to her customers.

"Lana if you weren't a really pretty lady I'd..."

"Well I am a lady, but I can still kick your butt."

"Whew, you guys really go at it don't you." said Geoff.

"She's got a thing for me," said Pete.

"In your wild wet dreams playboy, go play with your guitar."

"Ouch," said Geoff.

"See Geoff, aren't you glad you found this place, it's like a soap opera," said Jason who had been sitting back taking it all in. "Hey Pete I have to run, catch you later dude. Geoff, I'll see you Wednesday if not before."

"Hey Jas, before you go dude; what are you doing this Saturday?" asked Pete.

"Nothing, I guess just recovering from Friday night."

"Well I thought we could get a few babes together and go for a party cruise on Geoff's boat; you know, give him an introduction to the St Augustine social scene. What do you think Geoff are you up for that or is Saturday too far off to plan?"

"Bring it on, I'm ready for anything you can come up with; I should be a skilled Bosun by the weekend given the master instructor I've got," said Geoff. "What do you think Jason?"

"I'd be surprised if you weren't, but I'll be there just to keep you out of trouble if the need should arise," said Jason. "We can talk more about it Wednesday. I've got to run guys."

"Later dude," said Pete.

"Take it easy Jason," said Geoff.

Pete got up to start his next set and Lana came over to clean up the bar.

"How are you doing? What happened - all your new friends desert you already?"

"Yeah I do that to people sometimes, but I don't think I'll be here much longer either. I need to get down to the boat and get things all squared away and maybe lay in some foodstuff for breakfast. But before I go I think I'll get a bite to eat," he said as he scanned the bar menu for some light dinner. He ordered a bowl of conch chowder and the seared tuna platter.

"Can I get you another beer?" asked Lana as she brought out his couch chowder.

"No, I think I'll switch to a tall Tequila grapefruit with a lime squeeze. I just can't drink beer all night; I'm not that much of a beer drinker." About fifteen minutes later Lana was back with his dinner. The bar crowd had thinned out. Half the tables surrounding the bar were now empty. People were leaving, drifting off to pick up their lives elsewhere or going home to flop in front of the television until they fell asleep after consuming bags of pretzels, chips, ice cream pops and the whole assortment of addictive TV junk food that supports the snack food industry to say nothing of doctors trying desperately to get them to change their lifestyles.

"You're awfully quiet," Lana said as she brought over a silverware setup.

"I usually get that way when there's no one left to talk with, it's a bad habit I've developed, I guess."

"So where are you from?" Lana asked taking advantage of slack time for some customer relations.

"You mean originally?"

"We can start there, if you like."

"I was reared in Oak Park, Illinois - just outside Chicago many lives ago. Since then I've traveled through every state except Alaska; even lived for a while in about eleven of them."

"Which one is your favorite?"

"Whichever one I happen to be in at the moment; when that's no longer the case I hop back on the interstate and find another address."

"Oh, excuse me for a minute, I've got a customer."

"So what makes you move around so much?" Lana asked as she came back.

"It's a guy thing I think; I've been that way since my divorce. The Aussie aborigines have a word for it; they call it a walkabout, except in my case I think my drive-about has gone on much longer."

"Do you have any kids?"

"Married twice, divorced twice, no kids."

"Would you have liked to have had kids?"

"Oh yeah, sure, it'd be a great legacy. I could become a granddad. That's got to be a wonderful time in life. What about you Lana, are you a Florida native?"

"Oh, yes, I grew up in Fort Walton Beach, do you know where that is?"

"Oh yeah, I've been through there quite a number of times."

"I went to Florida State for almost three years but then money became a problem so I dropped out. I hope to go back and finish up someday," she said with a chuckle raising her eyebrows and giving a little shrug of her shoulder.

Lana was blonde with really, in Geoff's opinion, gorgeous blue eyes - probably about five foot eight with the slender physique and tawny complexion of a surfer. She had a perpetual smile that could turn to a devilish pout and a self-satisfied chuckle that would break out into easy laughter.

"I take it you're married?" asked Geoff.

"Well… yes, I am but on paper only; it's still legal but that's going to change soon, but please don't spread that around."

"You have my word, Lana; I know how these things can be. Besides I don't know anyone well enough to gossip. Do you have any kids?"

"No, thank goodness, I won't have any ties with him after it's over. Hey I better let you eat, enjoy it."

She came back after he was through eating to ask if he wanted anything else.

"No thanks Lana, I'm ready to settle up."

"You're going to love that boat, Geoff and the Channel House Marina is real classy," she said as she brought over his tab. "There's a restaurant with a cozy bar over there called the Eight Bells. I go there sometimes when I need to escape. You should check it out."

"Maybe I'll catch you there sometime," he said as he got up to leave.

"Maybe; have a good night Geoff," she said with a smile and a quick wink.

"Um hmm, you too Lana."

Chapter ten

Geoff drove back to the marina full of anticipation. He was eager to see how his latest choice of accommodations would pan out. He parked in the same remote section they had used earlier and walked down to the gated entry to try his cardkey. It worked on the first try, so far so good he thought to himself as he walked down the length of the pier to the floating dock. As he climbed down the few steps to the dock he noticed the name of the boat on the stern – *Cowgirl got the blues*. I'll bet there's a really interesting story behind that name. I'll have to ask Jack about that sometime he said under his breath as he climbed aboard and went below to check things out.

He checked out the storage bins in the master and guest cabins and took a quick inspection of the galley supplies. In the galley he found dinnerware, glassware, silverware, placemats, pots, pans, a filter basket with filters that fit over the mouth of a one-liter carafe to use as a pour-over coffee maker and even a two-slice toaster - in short everything he could possibly need for as long as he chose to stay. And true to his word Jack had arranged for a bottle of Moet Champagne now chilling in the reefer.

In the berthing spaces he found extra sheets and pillows stowed neatly in the storage bins. The master and guest berths had already been made-up. Everything was freshly cleaned. He was impressed; they had done a very thorough job. He had a feeling this was going to work out very well. It never ceased to amaze him what you could accomplish connecting with the guys in a bar. It was a lesson he had learned from his dad, very early in his youth but fortunately he hadn't learned to share his dad's penchant for imbibing to extreme, at least not on a habitual basis.

He made a run to the local food store he had passed on the way in and picked up supplies for breakfast and lots of fresh fruit. After he'd gotten it all stowed away he spent some time transferring his clothes in from the truck and stowing them in the master stateroom. Then he went up on deck to the cockpit and stretched out on the seats to watch the last rays of the receding day slowly turn from red-orange to red and then to deep purple. The dockside lights came on as nightfall finally claimed its victory over the receding daylight. A myriad of lights now became visible across the marina which reflected as a dancing mosaic on the ripples of the ebbing tide.

It was quiet and peaceful with only a very light breeze, just enough to keep the air fresh. The gentle motion of the boat had suddenly made him sleepy. He stayed for a few more minutes and then got up and went below to turn in.

The early morning sun blinking through the porthole caught his eye as the boat rocked on the morning high tide. He had had a great night's sleep, hadn't woken up at all. The salt air had worked its magic - he felt really refreshed with an appetite to match. He pulled on a pair of shorts and went topside along the weather deck to the bow. He stood there looking around listening to the cry of the seagulls and watching the pelicans glide over the water and suddenly drop down into the waves to trap their breakfast prey. There was a fresh breeze and a cloudless sky promising the gift of a gorgeous day ahead.

He went back below to hustle up some breakfast. The main entrée was always the same when he was making it; oatmeal - it was quick, easy and healthy to boot. He sliced up a granny apple and a banana and put on some water to heat up for the coffee. When the preparations were completed he decided he would have his first breakfast up on deck in the cockpit. He ate his oatmeal slowly savoring his first cup of coffee with breakfast and then had two more cups as he sat there surveying his surroundings and letting his thoughts wander.

This was a good decision, renting this boat. It felt comfortable. He began to think about what tomorrow would bring when he went sailing with Jason.

It had been a long time since he had been out sailing. When he separated from Navy active duty he had stayed in San Diego. He took a job as a second shift electronics technician with one of the local defense contractors. He used his veteran's education benefits to take courses at San Diego State and found he had some natural aptitude for computers and programming. On the weekends he spent time down at the marina doing odd jobs and became fast friends with several boat owners who introduced him to the basics of sailing.

After getting his bachelor's degree in three years going year round at San Diego State he headed up to San Francisco and wound up in Silicon Valley settling into what for him became the grind of high-tech. He couldn't afford his own boat so sailing took a back burner to what he thought would be his road to success in the computer industry.

Instead he got upsized, downsized, reorganized, spun-off, consolidated, merged, acquired, relocated, laid-off, furloughed and otherwise disenchanted with an industry that worked twenty-four-seven-365 way before that jargon was coined by the talking heads.

The computer industry just chewed up workers until they lost their individualism and spit them out on a refuse pile of industrial waste like so much contaminated nuclear waste to be buried in the caverns and forgotten. When a corporation's personnel costs became a detriment to the steady escalation of executive compensation and rewards they moved off-shore to strip-mine for cheaper resources.

But that was all many lives ago. He had come to terms with it long ago. There was nothing to be gained by revisiting a bad career choice. Now that he had the time and freedom, perhaps it was time to return to sailing.

He had never mastered the challenge of sailing upwind as close into the wind as possible known as close-hauled in seamanship. It required a technique known to sailors as feathering which called for focus and patience tacking back and forth in a zigzag pattern alternately heading up or sailing into the wind until the sails would luff or flutter then falling off or sailing away from the wind until the sails fill and then repeating the process.

Whenever he had to sail upwind he opted more often than not to use auxiliary engine power. Patience it seemed was not his strong suit.

Just thinking about it made him start to get anxious to get back into it. Well daydreaming about tomorrow's adventure wouldn't get today's chores done. He needed to get some laundry done, check out the marina facilities and get some more food supplies so he could have his meals aboard. That should give him some quality time to get in some writing, something he'd been neglecting lately.

The next morning after his second night of refreshing sleep aboard the boat he was just getting through his second cup of coffee when he spotted Jason coming down the dock.

"Good morning Jason, nice day for a sail."

"Yeah it looks primo out today; the marine forecast is good too, steady light offshore breeze, a little chop, all in all a good day to be sailing."

"I've got some coffee made but it's decafe. If you need something stronger it'll have to be a coke."

"I need the caffeine, I'll go with the coke," said Jason.

"You know my dad used to tell me that whenever he couldn't break a bolt apart that he would just pour a little coke on it and let it set for a few minutes and then he was able to easily twist it right off," said Geoff.

"Ha, yeah I've heard that too, that's why I always make it a practice to chase the coke with a few beers so those carbs balance everything out." Geoff went below and got a coke and brought it back topside to the cockpit. Then they took a bow to stern inspection tour with Jason pointing out all the features that made this particular boat a skippers dream to sail.

"So Geoff let me get an idea of what your experience has been, when was the last time you were out sailing?"

"That would be just before I left San Diego probably twenty-five years ago, but I did manage to get keelboat certified with some Coast Guard seamanship courses."

"Oh really, great, so you have been through the regimen. It comes back easier than you think; the old bicycle cliché applies, once you've learned you never really forget. Let's go over some of the finer points that you might have forgotten or any that might have changed."

They reviewed the nautical rules of the road and right of way, hierarchy of power, collision avoidance and capsizes - both how to prevent them as well as recovering from them. Jason stressed that avoiding a collision took precedence over strictly obeying the rules. Jason was thorough he alternately quizzed and coached him along. The more they talked the more nautical terms came back to Geoff. After a little over an hour Jason was satisfied and Geoff felt confident that here was a guy who could definitely teach him something.

"Well sailor, what do you say, let's cast off the lines and get underway," said Jason. "Do you feel comfortable taking her out?"

"As long as you're here, Jason I don't think you'll let me screw up too badly."

"Good, let's do it."

Jason stood by as Geoff fired up the auxiliary engine; they cast off the mooring lines and Geoff eased it away from the dock. Once they had cleared the entrance to the marina Jason had him kill the engine and they switched over to wind powered sailing. The electric winch system and the internal genoa halyards made hoisting the sails child's play. Jason coached him through the entire spectrum of three hundred sixty degrees of points of sail.

They started out running downwind and jibed on a port tack, to broad reach, through beam reach and on to close reach. Then Jason had him reverse the process and return to running downwind and then jib on a starboard tack, through broad reach, to beam reach and on to close reach. They sailed close hauled on a starboard tack heading up - or into the wind - until the sails began to flutter or luff and then they executed a maneuver called falling off - or heading away from the wind - to allow the sails to fill.

For the final maneuver Jason had him take it all the way through the irons - or straight upwind - to stall the boat in the water showing him how to recover to sail close hauled on a port or starboard tack. To Geoff, out on the water, it was all much more fun and challenging than it sounds.

He was working hard but gradually he began to feel his feathering technique improving to the point where he felt the same exhilaration he had felt on snow skis when he became accomplished at close parallel turns. Jason sensing Geoff's growing confidence was sitting back with a grin admiring the progress of his student.

"One last drill, Geoff; COB or crew overboard." Jason took the boat's floatation device and threw it overboard. Then he coached Geoff on the proper procedure to maneuver on a close reach to the leeward side of the floatation device and retrieve it from the windward side of the boat.

"You're outstanding Geoff; either a very quick study or you have been sandbagging on your experience," said Jason coming over with a high five. They had been out on the water almost four hours. "The only thing you're lacking now is rough sea sailing in strong winds and big waves. And that'll have to wait for another day when we get those conditions, but you have definitely gotten the basics down, now you just need sailing time."

"Jason I'm about ready for some chow. Do you have time to join me, I'll buy?"

"I'm ready, let's go up to the Eight Bells they have a good luncheon menu and its right here in the marina."

With the wind blowing offshore Geoff lowered the jib and mainsail and brought the auxiliary engine back online. Twenty minutes later they were tied up at the dock. As they were walking over to the restaurant Jason brought up the topic of the weekend.

"Geoff, are you okay with the fun cruise on Saturday? I mean Pete can be a little pushy at times."

"I'm fine with it; I'm actually looking forward to it."

"Don't get me wrong, I love the guy and I don't think he means to be that way but he is very gregarious by nature and sometimes it strikes people as moving in and taking charge."

"Well if it weren't for Pete we wouldn't be having this conversation. He's the one who referred me to your dad, and I'm sure glad he did. Really good guitar man too I might add."

"Yeah, he's good people got a good heart too; he'll make you feel like an old friend twenty minutes after you meet him. So I'm sure we'll have a good time, let's hope for good weather."

Chapter eleven

Friday Geoff went back to Robbie's for happy hour. The week had flown by for him. He had gone sailing again on Thursday although this time by himself to get some more practice and increase his confidence on the drills Jason had taken him through. There had been an onshore breeze as he was returning but he hadn't felt comfortable yet coming in to port under sail so he had docked under auxiliary power. This morning he had taken the boat over to marina services for fueling and had gotten the holding tank emptied and the fresh water tanks topped off. After that he held a stem to stern field day scouring everything. He was ready for the weekend and anticipating a big party.

There was a good crowd at the bar by the time he got there. Pete was already into his first set. Geoff caught his eye and Pete nodded in recognition as he took a seat at the bar.

"Hey stranger," said Lana as she came over to take his order, "I haven't seen you all week, I thought you might have sailed away somewhere."

"Well I have been out sailing and getting my sea legs back, but I guess the week just slipped by getting everything shipshape and settling into life on a boat."

"Hmm, I think I'm jealous. So what's it going to be a draft or tequila grapefruit?"

"I'll go with the tequila, it's Friday." As he looked around the bar his gaze settled on three attractive ladies sitting on the opposite side near the band platform, two blondes with a brunette in the middle, her long hair the color of dark chestnut.

Both blondes were chatting away while the brunette was mostly listening and nonchalantly scanning the bar crowd. The blonde on the left got up and went over to Pete after he had finished his song. She had a short conversation with him and then returned to the bar. When she sat down she let her eyes slowly scan the crowd. Her gaze settled on Geoff and their eyes locked for a fraction of a second then she leaned over saying something to the other two. Now the other two looked over in his direction and then they all huddled close and began to talk back and forth.

Girl talk, he thought to himself. He didn't want to get caught staring so he picked up a menu that was lying nearby. When curiosity got the best of him and he looked up again just one blonde and the brunette were there glancing his way as they talked between themselves.

He sensed her approach a fraction of a second before his peripheral vision caught sight of the blonde, whom had just spoken with Pete, walking up beside him.

"Excuse me, you're Geoff aren't you?"

"Yes, I am… and you are?"

"I'm Stefanie, Pete's girlfriend. He asked me to come over and introduce myself. We are supposed to go out sailing with you tomorrow. Come on over and meet the others and hang out with us."

He grabbed his drink and followed her over to the other side.

"Girls this is Geoff, our captain for tomorrow; Geoff this is Allison and Jennifer."

"Hi… Allison, Jennifer, nice meeting you," he said gently clasping each of their hands in turn. "Oh and Stefanie, thanks for the vote of confidence in my boating skills but as for captaincy I'll probably be more the first mate rather than the skipper. I'll defer to Jason as the acting skipper - with his experience and credentials - he's certainly more deserving of that distinction. Besides he promised to keep me out of trouble."

"Oh I don't know about that, Jason told me he was pretty impressed with your boat handling when you guys were out Wednesday," said Allison.

"Well he's being gracious, but I'm confident we'll have a nice time tomorrow," said Geoff, "as long as the weather cooperates."

"The last forecast I saw predicted a gorgeous weekend so I think we'll luck out," said Jennifer flashing a bright smile.

"Allison, when is Jason supposed to be here?" asked Stefanie.

"He should be here anytime now, he said he had to take care of a few things at the office before he left but that was over an hour ago."

"So what do you do for a living Geoff?" asked Jennifer.

"I'm a free-lance writer – a bit of a nomadic one I must admit but I like to think that all the traveling is part of my journey to fame and fortune. What about yourselves, ladies, how do you occupy your time?"

"We work in the airline industry as flight attendants," said Stefanie.

"We're based out of Atlanta," said Allison "Stef and I do the corridor to New York, Boston and sometimes Chicago. Jenni here, the lucky stiff, gets the long layovers to Dallas, Denver and Los Angeles."

"Seniority has its perks," said Jennifer with a smirk and a shrug of her shoulder.

"All of six months, you call that seniority?" said Allison.

"Hey, I worked very hard over those six months."

"Now don't fight girls, let's make a good impression on Geoff," said Stefanie.

"We're just teasing Geoff we actually get along fantastically well together. We share a place down here in St Augustine to call home when we're not on flight," said Jennifer.

"I've always thought of the airline industry as an ideal career - really exciting, especially with all the travel," said Geoff.

"It is in the beginning, but like a lot of careers it gets routine and becomes a job. The perks like free travel are nice but the sacrifice in pay can get tough," said Allison.

"Add to that the schedule and the possibility of getting called out when you're not expecting it and it can be pretty hard to have a life outside of your career," said Stefanie.

"But we make the best of it, and besides it was our choice, no one twisted our arms," said Jennifer.

"That's our Jenni, always accentuate the positive," said Allison.

"Yeah, and always be ready for the next adventure, she keeps us constantly in the fast lane," said Stefanie rolling her eyes and shaking her head.

"Oh hush, don't give Geoff the wrong impression of me," said Jennifer.

Jason came through the door and walked over, "Hi ladies, hey Geoff; looks like you found the pack, or more probably they found you."

"Truth be known the real credit goes to Pete, he pointed me out to Stefanie here and she made the introductions," said Geoff.

"Of course, old Pete the matchmaker, it's what he does best," said Jason.

"Hey, hey come on buddy don't go spreading rumors," said Pete as he walked over to pick up on the last bit of conversation.

"Why don't we get a table, so we can get something to eat," said Jason.

Notwithstanding the crowd, Pete used his influence and they got a table reserved for staff and special guests. They ordered two pitchers of Margaritas and a plate of steamed mussels in hot marinara and a pizza. Pete had to wolf down his share in order to get back to the bandstand for his next set. It was a good crowd and he didn't want to let anyone think he'd quit for the evening. Stefanie finished her pizza and went over to take a seat on the band platform with Pete to play the tambourine. Jason and Allison took off somewhere leaving just Jennifer and Geoff and time for them to get to know each other.

"Well Jennifer, it looks like it's up to you and me to finish the rest of the pizza and 'Rita's," said Geoff.

"Oh please, call me Jenni; all my friends do. We are going to be friends, aren't we?" she asked rhetorically with a wink and a sexy smile. She switched seats and sat down beside him topping off their glasses from the pitcher.

Geoff raised his glass in a toast, "Here's to the promise of a new friendship." They clicked glasses and drank together.

"I feel like a few bites of pizza but I can't finish a whole slice, want to share a slice with me?" she asked as she put a slice on her plate.

"Sure, sharing is fun. I'm pretty full myself, but I can go a few bites."

She brought the slice up to his mouth watching as he took a bite. Then she took a bite and put it down on her plate. Her brilliant chestnut brown hair was neck length in the back and a little shorter on the sides which let part of her ears peek out. She was wearing a really complementary subtle fragrance.

"Jenni you have gorgeous green eyes," he said as their eyes met close up.

Oh, thank you Geoff, so do you I see. Us green-eyed people need to stick together," she said with a wink and a chuckle.

Pete had started playing a slow blues number and a few couples were dancing. "Oh, I love this song can we dance?" she asked as she grasped his arm.

They got up and she slid closely into his arms as they fell into an easy slow waltz step. She followed him expertly almost as though they had been partners for a long time. She seemed very relaxed in his arms. "Oh Geoff, you're a wonderful dancer; you've got a really smooth rhythm that's so easy to follow," she said emphasizing the word 'so' in a soft easy drawl.

"I guess it takes one to know one, you're an excellent partner."

When the song was over Jennifer went over to talk with Stefanie and they got up and went off to the ladies' room. A few minutes later when they came out they walked over to the table and Stefanie cut a hunk off the last slice of pizza.

"Geoff, I hope you don't mind if we get a late start tomorrow, maybe around one o'clock in the afternoon? We all usually sleep in late on the weekends when we're not on flight," said Stefanie between bites of the pizza.

"One o'clock is fine with me; I'll probably sleep in late myself."

"Why don't you give me your cell phone number so I can play den-mother to get the whole gang together and we'll meet you down on the boat?"

They traded numbers and Stefanie said goodnight.

"Geoff can I get a ride back to my place with you?" asked Jennifer when they were once again alone. "I'll probably be spending the night all by my lonesome. Allison's away somewhere with Jason and Stef is spending the night over Pete's place."

"Certainly, Jenni; are you ready to go now or do you want to hang out here for a bit yet?"

"Oh I think we can just disappear, let's go."

Jennifer directed him to a nicely landscaped house just one street over from the beach road. The landscaping was mature so the house was probably thirty years or more old, but it had been well maintained.

"Come on in," said Jennifer grabbing hold of his arm. "I'll give you the ten cent tour."

The inside had been upgraded with an open kitchen and living room, a master suite with bath and two smaller bedrooms which shared a large full bath with a shower, tub and Jacuzzi. In the front of the house was a den with a double door.

"Nice place," said Geoff as they completed the tour and walked back out to the living room.

"Thanks, the landlord lives out of state somewhere so we just deal with the management company. They are really nice and haven't increased the rent since we've been here going on three years. Maybe they figure that with three single professional women who are away a lot of the time there will be less wear and tear."

"I'm sure that's a big consideration," said Geoff.

She led him over to the oversized couch and they sat down. "Can I get you anything to drink? We have all the mix for margaritas if you want to stick with that or..."

"Actually I'm ready for some coffee or just water; I've had enough to drink."

"Coffee sounds good, but it'll have to be decaffeinated at this time of night or I won't get to sleep," said Jennifer.

"That's fine with me, I usually drink decafe anyway."

Jennifer got up and put on the coffee carrying on the conversation as she did.

"It's my two weeks for the master suite. We take turns, although Stef has been spending most of her time over at Pete's place."

"I'm surprised that such a drop-dead gorgeous gal like you is not occupied like your housemates on a night like this?"

"It's the down side of all the extended layovers; I've also been stuck in Dallas during bad ice storms and in Denver when it snows heavily. Sometimes the flight from Los Angeles gets canceled because of conditions in Dallas or Denver so I'm stuck out on the coast. It makes it difficult to keep a relationship going unless I want to be a part-time girlfriend to someone who is sleeping around with the next available squeeze."

"I know what you mean. With all my traveling I sometimes wonder if I'll ever be lucky enough to find the right lady to settle down with and grow old together."

"Umm, speaking of that, my dream is to one day settle down in a big house with a wraparound porch, a swing and a hammock all set way back on several acres of land with a front yard of mature live oak trees covered in Spanish moss," she said coming over to the couch. She settled down on the couch sitting close to him with her legs drawn up under her.

"I couldn't have painted that picture any better myself Jenni, you and I share the same kind of romantic dream." He turned to look at her and their eyes held contact. He glanced down at her lips, slightly open and then back to her eyes which were watching him intently.

In a moment the mutual unspoken invitation was answered as they each split the distance between them and their lips brushed and met in a soft easy kiss. After the first kiss ended Jennifer moved closer and slid her hand around his neck running her fingers through his hair and shifting her glance from his eyes to his lips and back. The second kiss lasted longer and grew more intimate than the first. When it ended she was resting her head on his shoulder and running the back of her fingers gently over his cheek and chin.

"Geoff... I don't want to spend the night alone. Now please don't misunderstand or judge me, it's just that being alone gives me the creeps. I also believe in serendipity and I like to live life to the fullest in the current moment. Nobody is guaranteed tomorrow so let's hold on to the present – tonight, and make the most of it."

"Jenni, I have no argument there. I couldn't have stated my case any better. I might be a lot of things but I'm definitely not judgmental.

I also find independent ladies - especially very attractive ones with lots of initiative - absolutely exciting and irresistible."

"Oh thank you, sweetie...we are going to have a wonderful time together. Goodness I forgot about the coffee. Let's have some and then you can join me in a shower, if you'd like. It's getting past my bedtime," she said staring deeply into his eyes as she brought her lips to his for another kiss.

Chapter twelve

Whether it was the sunlight peeping through the closed blinds that caught his eye or the soft caress of her fingers running through the hair on his chest that triggered his sense of feeling…he awoke to see Jennifer with her chin resting on the hand of her propped up right arm watching him, her green eyes sparkling in the morning sun. The fragrance of her body tantalized his nostrils and made him wild with desire.

"Good morning Geoff, did you sleep well?" she asked while leaning over to kiss his cheek.

"Good morning Jenni," he said as he gathered her into his arms. She came easily. "I slept very well, thank you, and you?"

"Um hmm, wonderful; I guess I was a little horny last night. I hope I didn't leave you with the wrong impression," she said leaning over again and brushing his lips with hers in a soft kiss.

"Hey, we agreed there would be no judgments. Besides if truth be told I probably needed you more than you wanted me."

"Let's just call it mutually horny then," she said with a sexy laugh.

"Ah yes, agreed!"

She ran her hands over his chest. He kissed her softly. She kissed him back softly at first and then more passionately with parted lips, her tongue darting out to seek his. Their fingers moved over each other in gentle caressing patterns. They traded moans of satisfaction as each in turn kissed and caressed the other. Then they gave in to their mounting passion and sexual desire and made love slowly savoring the ebb and flow of their mutual pleasure. When they finished they stayed close embracing and basking in the afterglow, neither one wanting to break the spell.

"Ohhh, yes, that's the way I want to wake up every day for the rest of my life," she said as she planted soft kisses on his lips.

"Umm, now that's a life I would love to share."

Her cell phone rang in the other room, momentarily interrupting the mood.

"Oh shoot, I left it on the coffee table. I need to answer it, it might be important, I'm sorry."

She kissed him one more time and slid out from under the sheet partially covering them. Geoff followed her with his eyes as she got up to go retrieve her cell phone admiring the soft curves of her naked charms.

"Good morning Jenni; did you sleep well? I didn't wake you did I?"

"Hi Stef, no… you didn't wake me and yes, I slept very well, thanks. I always sleep well… especially when I don't sleep alone."

"Oh! … I'm not interrupting anything am I?"

"No, your timing was golden. If you had called ten minutes ago I wouldn't have answered."

"So, tell me about him? Anyone I know?"

"You introduced him to me last night."

"Oh my Goodness Jenni, you do work fast, how do you do it?"

"It's just chemistry Stef, if the feeling is right - go for it hon."

"Well I thought you two made a nice couple last night on the dance floor. You seemed to be really in natural rhythm with each other."

"Oh that we are Stef, he brings natural rhythm to everything he does."

"Oh really; are we talking sex here Jenni?"

"What else, it's the best barometer I know. He's definitely on my short list of best lovers."

"Umm…ah… will you two be able to make it by one o'clock? It's almost eleven-thirty now."

"Um…yeah, we may have to take a cold shower but we'll be there."

"You go girl; we'll have to talk more later… see ya."

"Ciao!"

Jennifer came back to bed and slipped in beside Geoff.

"Umm warm me up lover; it's chilly without your arms around me. That was Stef she called wanting to know if we can make it by one o'clock."

"Did you tell her to postpone it an hour or so?"

"No, of course not; we have to go."

"But that was before last night, and this morning."

"Are you still horny baby? I told her we might have to take a cold shower."

"That might not be enough."

"Tsk...Geoff! You really are horny. C'mon lover let's go take a shower," she said as she grabbed his wrist in a firm grasp and pulled him out of bed with her. They took a shower - a long shower, soaping each other up and rinsing each other, touching, cuddling, kissing, caressing and hugging until finally they gave in once more to their mutual desire.

Stefanie and Pete were standing on the dock waiting when Geoff and Jennifer finally got there about quarter after one.

"Guess the cold shower didn't work, huh?" said Stefanie with a conspiratorial chuckle.

"Aha, see Geoff, I was right; it should have been cold water," said Jennifer feigning privacy with her hand by her mouth yet still speaking loudly enough to be heard by Stefanie and Pete.

"Well it probably would not have worked anyway; it'll take more than just cold water to cool me down around you Jenni," said Geoff as he slid his arm around her waist and drew her close to him.

"Oh-oh, better watch him, Jenni he sounds like he still has his motor running in high gear," said Stefanie.

"Umm hmm and it's not some under-sized small-block we're talking either honey," said Jennifer.

"Jenni!" Stefanie said with mock embarrassment.

Jennifer winked at Geoff who was standing there lost for words and just rolling his eyes. She slipped her arms around his neck and pressed her body against his kissing him lightly on the jaw line just above his neck.

Jason and Allison came walking up holding each other around the waist. Ali had on a red windbreaker over her white bikini top. White shorts and white deck shoes completed her outfit. Both Stefanie and Jennifer also had on windbreakers over their yellow bikini tops with matching shorts and blue deck shoes to match their windbreakers. The guys all wore t-shirts, shorts and deck shoes.

"I hope everyone brought their appetite; I planned on a little brunch before we weigh anchor," said Geoff as they climbed aboard *Cowgirl got the blues.*

"Oh I do love this boat; I could live on this with no problem," said Jennifer.

"Is that a suggestion? Are you angling for an invitation?" whispered Stefanie, although it came out louder than a whisper.

"Oh hush girl, I was just voicing my strong admiration for this gorgeous boat. And I really like the name on the stern. Geoff, do you know the story behind the name of this boat?"

"No, I'm sorry I don't. I've been meaning to ask Jack about it but I just haven't gotten around to it," said Geoff.

"Well as I heard it from my dad," said Jason, "Bobby McAllister was married to a real sweetheart from Calgary, Canada. She was a rodeo champion up there. They lived up there for a while until he convinced her to relocate and try life in Florida. She got homesick almost immediately. So he bought this boat and had it completely refurbished for her birthday trying to convince her to stay. But it didn't work. Finally, he reluctantly gave her back her freedom and she returned to Calgary. He hasn't sailed on it since - spends a lot of nights over at the Eight Bells here in the marina just knocking them down."

"Oh, that's so sad. I hate to hear stories like that," said Stefanie.

"Yeah, it's definitely a downer I'm sorry I asked," said Jennifer.

"Hey now, let's not dwell on the minefields of life. I've got some champagne let's get the party going," said Geoff as he disappeared below to retrieve a bottle from the galley.

"I'll go hunt up some glasses," said Jennifer as she went below. She brought back six flutes, Geoff poured the champagne and they sat around the cockpit table toasting the day and sipping the bubbly.

They finished the first bottle and were working on a second when Jennifer got up and said, "Okay girls let's assemble in the galley for meal prep before we all get blitzed."

Geoff showed them where he had stowed the groceries and offered his assistance. They shooed him out of the galley and took over. In less than forty-five minutes they were serving brunch below at the galley table.

The menu consisted of scrambled eggs with provolone cheese, grilled grouper, breakfast fillets and fresh cut fruit all prepared and served with the perfection and efficiency of years of experience as flight attendants. They cracked open another bottle of champagne along with a container of orange juice and mixed mimosas. A steaming carafe of coffee made the rounds as the final touch. After they finished they brought the coffee up on deck where Geoff and Jason made ready to get underway.

Geoff was at the helm as they eased away from the dock and made their way through the marina to the open water of the bay. It was a gorgeous day with a bright blue sky and a steady breeze that promised an excellent day of recreational sailing.

As the day grew warmer the ladies doffed their shorts and windbreakers and lounged in their bikinis soaking up the sun. Allison and Jennifer were each about five feet nine. Stefanie was maybe an inch or so shorter but had a more athletic figure and more prominent bust which was very evident in her bikini top.

Allison seemed to be the reserved co-ed type probably really intelligent and no doubt even more gorgeous and sexy wearing oversize glasses. Jennifer, well he hadn't quite figured her out yet. He could easily get very attached to her, especially after their romantic interlude of last night and this morning.

He also hadn't figured out the reason for his current run of good fortune. His romantic miscue in Memphis began to feel like another life from his distant past.

Geoff, Jason and Pete took turns spelling each other on the helm. Whenever Jason took the helm there was a noticeable increase in speed. The sails stayed full regardless of the wind shifts as Jason showcased his experience and professional skills with sail trim. It wasn't that he intentionally meant to outdo or grandstand; it was just very competent master sailing skill that seemed natural for him. He was good and it showed without being showy.

As the early afternoon passed into the late afternoon Jennifer and Stefanie went below to prepare some sandwiches. Geoff and Pete stayed up on deck sipping on their beer. Allison was teasing with Jason who had the helm. After Pete relieved Jason on the helm Jason picked her up, lifted her over his shoulder and carried her below to the accompaniment of her playful yelps and barely token resistance.

"Hey guys are you ready for a sandwich?" asked Stefanie as she turned around and spotted Jason heading for the forward cabin with Allison draped over his shoulder laughing, giggling and squealing as he came through the galley.

"Ah thanks Stef, but I think we'll pass and get one later. We have a more pressing urge at the moment if you know what I mean," said Jason.

"Uh... yeah, I guess all that sun, wind and salt water had a huge effect on your libidos," Stefanie said with a mischievous chuckle.

"Tsk Stef!" said Jennifer in mock astonishment.

"Just a normal reaction for a young healthy couple hon, I'm getting a little horny myself. I think I'll go seduce Pete as soon as I have my sandwich. Don't tell me you haven't given it a thought Jen," said Stefanie with raised eyebrows and a shrug of her shoulder.

"Oh but I have and by the way the master cabin is reserved Stef, you'll just have to wait your turn for the forward one," said Jennifer glancing over at her with a self-satisfied smirk.

"Didn't you guys get enough last night and this morning?" asked Stefanie laughing wickedly.

"Stef there are three things you can never get enough of in this world - money, fun and great sex. I'll probably never get all the money I want but the fun and great sex will make up for it quite nicely," said Jennifer fluttering her eyelids.

"Shoot I'm not going to wait around for Allison and Jason to finish up in the forward berth I'll just go seduce Pete topside. If we have to we'll use the cushions in the cockpit, nothing like a little cockpit sex," said Stefanie.

"Um hmm at sea-level or seven miles high get it where you can. I guess that's why we are such good friends Stef. We think alike!" said Jennifer.

"Yeah…c'mon girl let's go topside and sexually harass the guys," said Stefanie with a lascivious chuckle and a mischievous wink as she stripped off her top.

"YEEHAH Stefanie! Go for it girl," Jennifer shouted as she doffed her own top and followed her girlfriend topside.

Chapter thirteen

D ays later - well it seemed like days, but in reality more than a month had already passed. It was late afternoon and Geoff was lying on the bunk in the master cabin staring absentmindedly at nothing. His eyes like the thoughts running through his head focused on nothing for more than a few seconds before moving on to another image as another fragment of memory crossed his mind.

Jennifer had stayed down on the boat with him that night after the weekend sailing party with Stefanie, Pete, Allison and Jason. Hell she had damn near moved in with him bringing down several changes of outfits and stowing them in the master cabin. Not that he was complaining of course, it was easy getting used to having her around. And it was nice.

They had breakfasts and dinners together, had gone sailing a few times and spent passionate nights falling asleep in each other's arms exhausted from their lovemaking. She had warned him that she could get a call at any time and might have to fly off on short notice. But all her warning just bounced off his consciousness to be discarded in the next moment of their romantic rapture. He was comfortable with her and yes he was getting very deeply attached to her.

Then it came. Late one evening as they were sipping champagne up on deck celebrating being with each other her cell phone rang. She took the call and immediately got up and walked away as she began speaking hesitating between words until she got better reception or maybe it was for privacy until she got out of earshot.

Several minutes, long minutes for him, she came back to announce with an air of insouciance, "Geoff I have to go off on an extended layover. I'll be in Dallas for a couple of days and then fly on to Denver. After that they need someone to fly the Denver-Los Angeles route. I could be gone… a few weeks or so."

"Well it's not like it's your choice," he said trying hard to be understanding even though it was just words and not his true feelings. "You have to do what they're paying you for. I'm going to miss you Jen, a lot. I've really developed deep feelings for you and I've been hoping that what we have together will develop into a long, lasting relationship. Maybe even…"

She had cut him off, cut him off expertly. She cradled his face in her hands and smothered his lips with a long sensual kiss. "I'm going to miss you too baby, more than you know. But it won't be any longer than necessary, I promise," she said in a soft sexy whisper.

"You'll call me regularly?"

"Um hmm, as soon as I get situated, think positive this may be good for our relationship – give us a little breather to sort out our feelings."

Lord, he had to lighten up. He was showing too much of his hand. "I'm sorry Jen; I guess I let my foolish insecurity take control there for a second. Look I'll be here for you when you get back, just please give me a call every once in a while and let me know how things are going."

"I will Geoff. And you be good, don't go picking up anybody at Robbie's. I'll ask Stef and Allison both to keep an eye on you."

They shared a long hug and some tender kisses.

"Geoff, it's getting late and I need to get up very early tomorrow so I think it's best if I pack my things and spend the night back at the apartment. That way I won't disturb you when I leave and also I can get away quicker if you know what I mean."

Geoff wanted to make love with her, wanted her right then but he knew the timing was all wrong. She had already slipped back into her persona as Jennifer the Flight Attendant.

Now thinking back, he wished he had handled it a little better, no damn it, a whole lot better. They had had an awkward drive back to the apartment. She was the career conscious women; he was excess baggage - just holding on, clutching tightly hungry for her attention - but he felt the unmistakable tug of her beginning to emotionally detach from their relationship.

She had called from Dallas the next day to let him know she had gotten there safely and then again from Denver a few days later. They were quick calls – obligatory - to check in. She said she didn't know any more than she had already told him.

After more than a week without any communication he called her cell phone but only got her voice mail.

A few days later she called but it was a quick curt conversation. There weren't any personal strokes to comfort his ego it was all business. They had her on a very busy schedule. She didn't know how long she would be out there; she was just taking things one day at a time. She'd let him know if anything changed.

Well there was nothing to be gained by dwelling on past things he couldn't change. He finally convinced himself that he needed to get out, get off the boat, be somewhere around people. So he took a quick shower and headed out for Robbie's his mood slightly elevated by his choice of destination.

He took a seat at the bar. It was quiet for a Wednesday evening; he guessed that most of the happy-hour crowd had already departed to prepare for tomorrow's workday.

"Good evening sir, what would you like?" said the bartender, a new one he hadn't seen before, as he came over with a wine glass that he was polishing.

"Oh, uh, where's Lana tonight?" Geoff asked surprised by a new face.

"Lana's off tonight, I'm filling in - my name's Steve."

"How are you doing Steve, I'm Geoff. Make it a tequila grapefruit tall with a lime squeeze."

"Do you want that double tall?"

"No...single tall is fine."

Steve went over to the other station to make the drink. Geoff looked around at the bandstand which was vacant and dark. "Hey where's Pete, the guitar man?" Geoff asked when Steve came back with the drink.

"He took off early."

Geoff was suddenly feeling alone, deserted, his forlorn deflated mood of earlier began to regain control. With no one to talk with he finished the drink faster than he usually did. Steve was back to ask if he wanted a refill.

"Would you like another round sir," said Steve when Geoff's glass was not quite three quarters empty."

"Yeah, one more I think and that'll do it."

He finished that one quickly also, paid the tab and walked back out to his truck. Something made him pick up the cell phone. He always left it in the truck when he went into a bar or restaurant. He didn't need to be talking on the phone when he was drinking or eating. It was his time for himself. The world could wait until he finished.

There was one missed call; he recognized the number as Jennifer's cell phone. He punched in the number and waited for the connection feeling himself getting a little tense and wondering why. It rang a few times and then got forwarded to voicemail.

"Hey Jen, it's Geoff, sorry I missed your call, hon. I'll be waiting if you can please call back. Love ya, bye"

He was nearly back to the marina when his cell phone rang. He recognized the caller-id number as Jennifer's.

"Hi Jenni, how are you doing honey…and where are you?" he said trying to sound nonchalant and positive but he was tentative at best and aware of the rise in pitch of his voice. He hoped it wasn't obvious to Jennifer.

"Oh I'm fine Geoff, I'm on layover in LA… how are you?"

"I'm missing you a whole lot Jen, but outside of that I'm doing okay. So what's up, when do you think you'll get back?"

"Uh, that's sort of up in the air. The attendant I'm replacing is on long-term disability and they don't know when or if she'll return."

"Well are they looking for someone to replace her permanently. I mean this is just temporary with you, right?"

"Geoff, things are very tight in the airline industry these days. Any attrition they experience is good for the bottom line. So I don't know… umm."

"Gee, Jen, I… I was hoping to hear some good news, like maybe a definite date for your return."

"Geoff…I… I've been thinking…about us…I…uh, well I'm sort of a … well I'm really a free spirit. It was nice the time we had together, I really enjoyed it but I…I've kind of moved on."

Geoff felt a sharp stab in his solar plexus as a cold dose of reality set in. He could feel the beads of sweat forming under his eyelids. Well you're still perfect guy. Can't win for losing! Damn, damn, dammit all to hell he cursed to himself. He exhaled dejectedly.

"Whew…so Jen, I…I guess this is how the story ends."

"Geoff, I'm sorry, truly I am. I let things get too heavy too soon."

"Yeah, well I think we can skip the post-mortem on a dead horse. Look Jen, I wish you well, take care of yourself."

"You too Geoff, I'll always remember our good times together."

"Yeah Jen, I…I guess I'll do the same."

"Goodbye Geoff."

"Bye Jen."

He closed the cell phone and tossed it aside as he pulled into the parking area for the marina. As he killed the engine the flood of emotions came cascading down to smother him with a sickening sensation.

Rejection, he never got used to it; he probably never would. Hurt, pain, regrets…what could I have done better…what if I had said this then or done something else there. No damn it, let it alone, it's over, done, dead. She has already moved on, don't be a fool. For once in your life learn the lesson and take it to heart.

He headed over to the Eight Bells his safe port in a storm. He was working on his second tequila grapefruit when he felt a soft hand rubbing his shoulder, smelled the delicate fragrance of perfume and heard a familiar voice from behind.

"Hi Geoff, how are you doing?"

"Lana, hey now…it's great seeing you, lady, you've really made my night," he said turning around to face her. "I was over at Robbie's earlier looking for you, but they said you were off and Pete had already left. I felt deserted. Here, please… have a seat; may I buy you a drink? How have you been?"

She looked splendid and super sexy in an off-white silk sun dress with green lattice work and large golden sunflowers. Straps from the gathered waist ran up over her breasts and behind her neck to form the halter top with a neckline that plunged revealing her curves and afforded the perception that she likely wasn't wearing a…ah now easy, he wasn't supposed to notice that she was foundationally unencumbered up top. Or at least not get caught noticing.

If you did get caught glancing a few inches below their chin you risked being labeled a sexist male chauvinist or worse a pervert and received a look that would freeze dry ice. Unfortunately, women wouldn't accept the argument that it was just the male way of complimenting their feminine charms or appreciating their sexually alluring attire. Of course he finally had to admit to himself… trying to rationalize it wouldn't fly. There was no excuse for behavior that women found offensive and no justification for male chauvinism in polite society. Real men, gentlemen, had to rein in their proclivity to sexually objectify women and learn to respect a woman like a lady. At least he was a work in progress in that regard. In his next life he'd be perfect, for now he'd plead the inability of the weaker male gender to overcome basic carnal instincts.

Her blonde hair was fastened up off her neck – in the sexy way ladies did that - with strands of hair cascading down framing her face. She had on long dangling earrings, a killer tan and was wearing a fragrance that was absolutely aphrodisiacal.

Geoff motioned for the bartender and Lana ordered her usual.

"I had my court date today for my big D," she said in a soft resigned and slightly dejected voice.

"Oh boy that's always a downer, are you okay Lana?"

"I don't know Geoff, I think I just want to put it behind me and move on."

"Did you go dressed like that," he asked with raised eyebrows and a big grin as he let his eyes wander slowly over the allure of her femininity.

"Oh goodness no, I was much more conservative. Do you like my new outfit? I bought it as a consolation gift to myself."

"On any other good looking woman it would be terrific enough but on you Lana it's sensational. You look singularly gorgeous tonight."

"Ohh thank you Geoff, you're such a sweetie."

"So how did your day in court go? Do you want to talk about it?"

"You've been through it. It's never fun. There are all the ambivalent feelings to deal with. Should I have tried harder? I really did want it to work. And maybe a little apprehension about where do I go from here."

"Oh yes, the old familiar phantoms of a busted relationship, they have been a fairly constant part of my existence. But you'll get through it Lana, it takes time but the sun does come back out, the images fade away in the rearview and the puddles dry up after the rainstorm."

The bartender brought over her drink a Chambord Martini.

"Umm thanks Geoff I needed this," she said holding up her glass to clink his for a toast.

"To better days and longer nights to get through it all," said Geoff as he tapped her glass with his.

"I'm so glad I ran into you Geoff; it really has lifted my spirits."

"So am I Lana, believe me the feeling is mutual. It's kind of a coincidence; I just ended a relationship today also, although nothing quite as deep as yours."

"Oh...anyone I know?"

"I've been seeing Jennifer Coulter, I'm sure you know her, she's friends with Stefanie and Allison - actually they all work together as flight attendants."

"Oh yes, I know them well, especially Jennifer."

"She called up from Los Angeles tonight to tell me to take a hike, have a nice life and don't look for her in it."

"Ohh...I'm sorry...I could have saved you some heartache Geoff. She has a reputation of being very capricious and quite a bit of a flirt. I think it is probably for the best that it's over quickly. You don't need to lose a lot of sleep over her."

"Hmm, yeah I always forget about the female grapevine and with you being a barkeeper to boot...I guess I should have checked her out with you."

"Always trust your bartender," she said rubbing his thigh just above the knee and giving a little squeeze.

He turned his head to face her and their eyes locked contact. Geoff felt the electricity and glanced down at her lips which were slightly parted and seemed to be beckoning for a kiss. He went for it. She didn't back away, just tilted her head and brought her lips to his. It was a quick kiss but full of promise of something more.

"Ooh that was such a nice sweet kiss. I was hoping you'd get my message," she said.

"It was a tender moment; I just went on instinct."

"You have good instincts then," she said with a sexy wink.

"You send clear messages."

"Let's not sit here and get blitzed Geoff. Are you in the mood for a walk on the pier, it's a nice night for it and there's a gorgeous full moon out tonight."

"Great idea, Lana I couldn't dream of a better ending to a trying day."

They finished their drinks and headed out. The night air had cooled considerably.

"Ooh it's gotten a little chilly. Put your arm around me baby, keep me warm," she whispered as she drew near him and slipped her arm around his waist.

They walked along the pier looking out over the water with the light of the moon's reflection shimmering along its surface exuding a peaceful pleasant feeling. From several boats the dim lights of the cabins added their reflections in a dance across the water.

"Where are you tied up?"

"I'm in that last row. Hey, you haven't seen my boat yet. C'mon I'll give you a tour."

They got down to the boat which was gently rocking on the incoming tide. Even with the lights along the pier, shadows danced along the deck. Lana hesitated. Geoff swept her up gently in his arms and agilely climbed aboard.

"Ooh you do that so well, I'll bet you're a great sailor. Were you ever in the Navy?"

"Yeah many lives ago; someday when you have a lot of time to kill I'll tell you about it."

They went below and he gave her a tour through the salon, galley and forward cabin and then they went back aft to the master stateroom.

"Oh this is really plush I never expected it to be so large and comfy looking. I do love this boat. You have to take me out sailing."

"Whenever you have the time, I'll be here. This is my home address right now. Hey…I've got some champagne, how about sharing it with me topside; we can continue the celebration of our mutual new freedom and the first night of the rest of our lives."

"Ooh – champagne, moonlight and a good looking man, how can I refuse?"

"Okay, lend a hand mate; the ice is in the reefer, the bucket is in that locker under the sink, the glasses are in the locker over the washboard. I'll pop the bubbly."

"Aye, aye sir," she said with a mock salute as she broke up laughing.

They carried the glasses, ice bucket and champagne topside and settled onto the bench in the cockpit at the small folding table.

"Here's to both our former spouses and to having the freedom to seek our own happiness, whatever and wherever it might be," said Geoff.

"And with whomever it pleases us to share it with," she said gazing deeply into his eyes.

They sat wrapped in each other's arms slowly sipping champagne. With each sip they snuggled a little closer sharing soft kisses and gentle caresses. They had finished nearly half the bottle without much conversation but some things are better just left to instinct.

Her mood turned a little pensive, "All I wanted was to feel loved and to share in the happiness and security of a good marriage. But that was all over by the end of the honeymoon."

"Religion tells us that marriage is made in heaven. Unfortunately, wisdom shows us that a lot of those we get into down here just don't stand muster," said Geoff.

"You know I never cheated on my ex, even after he moved away from the house. I was afraid to take a chance, afraid that he would do something abusive, even though it was okay for him to whore around with whomever he pleased."

"That's all in the past now, Lana; he has no control over you now."

"Um hmm, today is my independence day, and tonight is the beginning of my celebration. Geoff… I don't want to sleep alone tonight, it's been a long time and life is too short; I want to make love starting tonight and every day for the rest of my life. Are you ready and willing to indulge a new divorcee and share my celebration of independence?"

"Lana, I've been ready and more than willing since the first second you walked up to me tonight. Why don't we retire to the master cabin and finish off this bottle in comfort while we begin the celebration of our new lives and put the past behind us."

Chapter fourteen

The rays of the early morning sun shone through the porthole over his head and danced on the far bulkhead. He glanced down at Lana lying naked on her back next to him. She was still sleeping, her head resting on his left arm just above the elbow. He slowly shifted the focus of his gaze admiring the curves of her firm athletic body, which compared well with one of a surfer or competition beach volleyball star. Her well defined firm breasts rose and fell with her breathing in serene harmony with the gentle rocking of the boat's hull against the morning tide. Her sculpted right thigh bent at the knee rested against his left thigh with the ankle tucked under her left knee. She was definitely the inspiration for whom someone had coined the currently popular cliché drop-dead gorgeous; the waves of her thick naturally blonde hair were still nearly perfectly groomed. She wore it in a style that was still long enough to put up, yet short enough to show her neckline her ears and her prominent angular jaw line all of which made her devastatingly attractive, in his opinion. He realized he had a preference for short hair styles like hers on women. Rather than hide them it showcased their delicate features.

As he admired the charms of this pretty lady from his vantage where she wasn't able to watch him watching her, he reflected on how only weeks ago he would never have allowed himself the absurd liberty to indulge in the fantasy he was now living. What was seemingly inconceivable then was now, through an incredible change in his fortune, reality. Would it be a permanent change or just an ephemeral tease?

They had made love until very early in the morning and then had fallen asleep totally satiated and mutually exhausted from their passion. He ached to gather her up in his arms and smother her with kisses over her entire body.

Her eyelids began to flutter and she stirred as she awoke and made a sleepy-eyed survey of his nakedness and then of hers.

"Oh Geoff, did we really do what I think we did last night?"

"You're not having morning after lover's remorse on me now, are you?"

"Um mm, no - No remorse no regrets; It was wonderful. A release I needed badly after years of frustration," she said as she ran her fingers lightly over his chest.

"It was wonderful for me too Lana, I'm hoping it was just a terrific prologue to something deeper and more meaningful."

She leaned over and kissed him warmly on the lips her breasts brushing softly across his chest teasing him to instant arousal.

"Umm...we can talk later; we're both naked, let's not waste the moment," she said in a husky voice as she kissed him again and ran her fingers lightly and slowly down the hair on his chest tracing little figures of eight.

His desire elevated rapidly but he held back wanting to prolong the enjoyment of foreplay. They kissed and cuddled, caressed and fondled until their mutual desire grew to fever pitch.

"Um baby...let me ride topside," she said in a voice hoarse with passion as she swung her leg over to straddle him.

He nuzzled her breasts with his nose and ran his tongue over her hard nipples. She rose up on her knees arched her back and mounted him moaning softly as she took him deeply inside her. Then she bent forward and rested her breasts on his chest while she tenderly planted kisses all over his face and neck. He responded in kind kissing her face neck and ears and running his fingers lightly down her back as they lay still for a few moments savoring the feeling of intimacy. They fell into a slow easy rhythm and let their passions rise thrilling to each other's moans of satisfaction.

After a few minutes Lana picked up the rhythm her breathing coming in short shallow gasps that matched her quickening short thrusts and louder moans. And then she slowed the pace teasing him with her control. Once more she quickened the pace only to once again slow down driving him wild with desire.

She cradled his face with her hands, "Please don't close your eyes or look away baby I want to share this with you with our eyes wide open," she said in a passionate hoarse whisper. Then she moved her face close to his and closed the distance between their slightly parted lips to share a long deep sensuous kiss.

She began the intimate dance of love once more until they reached the summit of mutual loss of control and time stood still as together they each journeyed into their separate ecstasy still gazing deeply into each other's wide open eyes.

"Oh Lana, I love…," Geoff was half-conscious of his voice as the words tumbled out.

Lana smothered his mouth with hers driving her tongue fiercely inside against his. Then she collapsed on his chest nibbling on his neck as her heartbeat slowed and her breathing returned to normal. He caressed the back of her thighs, the cheeks of her derriere and slowly moved up the small of her back. He ran his fingers lightly over her spine and gently rubbed her shoulders.

"Oh, that feels wonderful, you do that so well."

He could feel the weight of her body gradually increase as she relaxed. Her eyes blinked closed and she dozed off with her head on his chest. Geoff ran his nose lightly through her hair and along her cheek deeply inhaling the sweet fragrance of her. He was on the edge of blinking off himself when she opened her eyes.

"Oh goodness, I don't want to but I have to get up. Geoff, what time is it?"

"Oh let's see, it's… almost nine-thirty," Geoff said glancing over at the travel alarm on the bulkhead ledge.

"Shoot, I have to be in work by eleven to open, and I need to get home, shower and change into my work clothes. Now where'd I throw my panties…I hate wearing yesterday's soiled undies but I didn't bring a change and I can't go without. I didn't allow for the good fortune of our little rendezvous."

She found them on the console on top of her dress and quickly pulled them on and slipped into her dress. "Gotta go," she said as she rummaged through her purse pulled out a card wrote a number on the back and handed it to him. "That's my cell phone; please... call me later when you get a chance, see ya." She gave him a quick hug and a kiss on the cheek then turned and headed out the hatch.

"Don't work too hard, catch you later," It was all he could manage before she was gone. He wanted to send her off with a real passionate hug and kiss but he knew she was in a hurry.

He sprawled back down on the bunk and lay there trying to collect his thoughts. He didn't want to let go of the feelings. He wished that he could stop time, set the clock back to a few hours earlier and then experience it all over - again and again like a movie on a DVD. But life wasn't a movie and it wasn't captured on a DVD that you could replay at will to relive the good times over and over until you wore it out or grew tired of them and tossed it aside or discarded it. Lana was as strong and independent as Jennifer had been. Damn...he was so attracted to independent ladies... but sadly they seemed to be his nemesis.

He took a shower made a quick breakfast and brought it topside to the cockpit. His thoughts flashed back to late last night and another beginning. Would this be real or was it just another shallow tease. And if so how many more would he have to go through before he found someone whom he could hold onto - who wanted to hold onto him as much as he wanted to hold onto her.

"Hey, Geoff" a voice from the dock made him look over to see Jason standing there.

"Hey Jas, how you doing...what are you up to down here."

"I heard about Jennifer, I wanted to come down and see how you were doing?"

"Wow, good news travels fast, huh? Come on aboard and sit for a spell. I've got a beer if you want one."

"No, but I'll take a cup of coffee if you have any left."

"It's still just decafe."

"That's fine it'll keep me healthy."

Geoff poured the coffee into the extra cup he'd absentmindedly brought up with his breakfast.

"I should have warned you Geoff, Jennifer's a barracuda and she can be a bit fickle; I hope you didn't get too burned."

"Ah, easy come easy go I guess…it's just that I didn't see it coming…got sort of blindsided."

"Allison tells me that's her specialty she'd rather be the dumper than the dumpee…always in control."

"Yeah, well what goes around comes around… every dog has its day, but hey…I don't wish her any ill wind."

"That's a good attitude. Talking about wind, I've been watching the long range weather forecasts. There may be a front coming in the next day or so that'll bring some weather and high seas. If you're up for it, you and I can go out for a check ride in rough conditions."

"That would be great; it should take care of any deficiencies in my seamanship."

"You don't have any deficiencies Geoff, you just need some more time on the helm and you can teach this stuff."

"Yeah, right, I'll leave the instructing to the pros."

"Well, I've got to run and get some errands done, I'll give you a call if the forecast pans out and we can make some plans. Thanks for the coffee…later Geoff."

"Take it easy Jas."

Geoff watched him disappear up the dock as he drained his coffee then took the dishes below and gathered up the laundry to make a run over to the Laundromat at ship services. During the wash cycle he came back and washed, dried and stowed the dishes. Once the clothes were in the dryer he came back and swept and swabbed the galley. That left just topside to field day.

By the time he'd gotten everything shipshape to his satisfaction it was almost quarter to four. As soon as the busy work was complete indecision set in. Should he call Lana, or just go up to Robbie's and see her.

Well if he went up there he really couldn't talk with her privately like he wanted to. It was too public and he didn't want to discuss personal issues with her in work. Besides he was sure she'd appreciate the discretion. No he would definitely call her.

He wanted to see her, he wanted to hold her in his arms; he needed to feel her body against his and smell the sweet fragrance of her. But would she want to see him again so soon after last night and this morning?

Damn it was happy hour now, she would be busy, no time to talk. She might even be upset if he called her now. She might not even answer. She was working for tips and good tips came with good customer service, she didn't have time for idle talk. Good tips also came for flirting, for making the guys feel special, like she was interested in them. There'd be guys hitting on her that she had to keep interested. She was a free lady now; would she make them keep their distance or...

It was five fifteen, time was crawling. It seemed like it always did when you were trying to kill it. But when you were on the borderline of being late for an appointment it flew by. He had to wait until after happy hour when the bar crowd would slow down.

After another half hour he had worked himself into frenzy and finally could wait no longer. He punched in her number; it rang twice and she picked up.

"Hello."

"Hi Lana, it's Geoff; how's it going?"

"Oh, hi Geoff, uh...look I'm in the weeds right now, a big crowd just came in. I should be getting off at eight. I'll give you a call then, okay?"

"Okay, I'll be..."

"Thanks Geoff, bye."

"Bye," he said into a dead connection.

He went below and sprawled out on the bunk with his cell phone on the ledge. It was loud enough to wake him if he fell asleep - he was a very light sleeper.

He did fall asleep. It didn't wake him.

He awoke with a start and looked over at the travel alarm. The light from the full moon was shining brightly through the porthole it was 2210 hours, ten after ten in the civilian world. He grabbed the cell phone and checked for missed calls...there were none.

Chapter fifteen

He was in that neither state: neither fully awake nor soundly sleeping – maybe it was his subconscious handing over command to his consciousness. A fragmentary scene played out in chilling vividness and on some level of consciousness he struggled to determine if this was a real experience or a dream.

In the scene a hostile looking male figure in a trench coat was standing in a lighted vestibule pounding menacingly on the glass paned French doors barely eight feet in front of him. He watched as the intruder reached down forced the lock and threw open the door in what seemed to him as only a mere second. The man jumped inside the room now only a few feet away and leveled a shotgun at him scowling wickedly. Geoff stared without emotion at the point blank double barrels and then at the contorted evil sneer on the man's face as he waited for the inevitable. Then as abruptly as the man had entered he grimaced, jerked his head to the right and lowered the weapon… the scene faded as Geoff awoke in a rush of adrenaline with a ringing in his ears.

Was it a dream or was he awake? He struggled to open his eyes and when they finally obeyed his command the master cabin came into focus. He grabbed for his cell phone by instinct.

"Hello?"

"Hi, Geoff it's me, Lana."

"Lana, Hi…uh"

"Geoff I'm sorry I didn't call last night; I got really slammed right after you called. I didn't get off until eleven o'clock. I was going to call but I figured it was too late."

"It's never too late Lana, you could call me at 0'dark thirty and I would still be thrilled to hear your voice."

"Ohh…, I'm sorry; next time I promise I'll call, okay?" She paused for a moment and then continued, *"Hey listen I'm off tomorrow maybe we can have breakfast."*

"That'd be nice. Why not come on down to the boat and we can cook up something together."

There was an awkward pause on her end and Geoff sensed the unspoken reluctance and quickly added, "Or if you want we can just go out that's probably easier. Why work on your day off?"

"They serve breakfast on the patio at Eight Bells, maybe we can meet there."

"Sure, that'll work fine for me; oh by the way what are you doing after work today?" After he said it he bit his tongue. Easy there guy you're getting a bit too pushy his inner voice cautioned him.

"I'm working late today; I'll be closing"

"Oh okay, then I guess I'll see you tomorrow morning – How does ten o'clock sound."

"That's good for me."

"Great, I'll be waiting for you have a good day Lana and don't work too hard."

"Oh I won't, see you tomorrow Geoff, bye."

Geoff closed the phone and threw it back on the ledge. A conflicted mood was descending over him. He looked out the porthole to see an overcast sky and became aware of the increased movement of the boat and the sound of the straining mooring lines. The weather seemed to be in sync with his life. His cell phone rang.

"Hello"

"Hey, Geoff - Jason, I've been trying to get in touch with you. There's a bit of a storm brewing. Are you up for a little rough weather sailing?"

"Gosh, yes, nothing would please me more."

"Great, give me about twenty minutes and I'll be down there."

"I'll be waiting."

"Good I'll see you in a bit."

In twenty minutes or so Jason was on the dock. By then the weather had deteriorated with the wind speed picking up to a strong breeze or about twenty-five knots. Once on board Jason tuned the radio to the marine weather station to get the latest forecast. Small craft warnings had been set. Off in the distance the ominous gathering black clouds and lightening on the horizon met an angry sea churning with whitecaps. The weather would be turning nasty.

"On second thought Geoff I don't think it's a good idea to head out in these conditions. It's gotten a bit more intense than I thought it would. Now with the lightening, prudence says we just ride it out in port, what do you think?"

"I agree no sense getting ourselves into a situation where we could wind up giving the Coast Guard more work to do, I'm sure they'll have their hands full looking out for others with more confidence than their level of skill warrants. I think I'll head up to the Eight Bells and see if I can get a late breakfast omelet," said Geoff. "You care to join?"

"That sounds good, I think I will, I've got nothing planned since I had blocked out this time for sailing and besides I skipped breakfast this morning."

Breakfast was served until 1100 Hours No exceptions read the menu and it was nearly quarter to twelve.

Well there were always exceptions; you just had to create the right ones. You started by getting on the right side of the server. Of course it always helped if the server was a lady. They lucked out. Laura was very receptive to their conniving ways and they got two made to order three cheese and chili omelets with hot salsa and jalapeños.

Laura had just served the omelets and refilled their coffee when an older gentleman came in and waved at Jason.

"That's Bobby McAllister, do you mind if I invite him over to the table?"

"No, not at all, I'm living on his boat it'd be nice to meet him."

"Hey Bobby, come join us," Jason called out as he got closer.

"Well sure thing thanks, I hate eating alone."

"Bobby this is Geoff; he is the gentleman who is renting out your boat."

"Geoff, this is Bobby McAllister, he's the owner of the *Cowgirl*."

"It's a pleasure Geoff."

"Nice meeting you, sir, that is one fine boat you have there, she handles like a dream, pretty much sails herself."

"Thank you I'm glad it rented out to someone who can really appreciate it. Jason here tells me you are a pretty decent sailor."

"Well he probably exaggerates but I am beginning to get my sea-legs back."

"Then you've done a lot of sailing before?" asked Bobby.

"Yes, quite a bit. After I left the Navy I stayed down in San Diego for several years. I got my keelboat certification and was going to get a commercial skipper's ticket but my plans got shelved when I went back to Chicago for a visit."

"What did you do in the Navy?"

"I was an Electronics Technician until Vietnam came along; after I volunteered for duty in Vietnam I got some retraining as a Special Operations Technician."

"Then the adventure began, right?"

"Oh yeah, I was young and bulletproof with a top secret clearance and life shifted into overdrive; it was a heady time."

"How long did you spend in the Navy?"

"Six years, I was going to ship over but some unfortunate experiences changed my mind, so I decided I'd get out and set the world on fire."

"How did that go?"

"Just when you think you have life by the tail roles get reversed and you find yourself on the other end of the leash."

"Yes, I know the feeling. I spent twenty years in the Navy myself. I was Communications Officer on the submarine Dragonfly."

"No kidding, I worked on Dragonfly when I was stationed at the Pearl Harbor Submarine Base."

"Small world, isn't it Geoff? I was in line for Exec but we had some misfortunes on a Westpac deployment and I was the scapegoat. It all blew over but it still had broken my confidence as well as having left a stain in my service jacket. I left the Navy after that tour."

"What did you do after that?"

"I had a stroke of luck that turned my fortunes around one hundred-eighty degrees. I took a local discharge in Hawaii and went to work for this advertising exec I had met in Ewa Beach, Oahu. I made a ton of money and never looked back. Eventually I went back to the mainland and opened my own ad shop in Newport Beach."

"I don't mean to interrupt, but while you two old salts trade sea stories I need to get back to work," said Jason with a chuckle.

"Oh I didn't mean to cut you out of the conversation, Jason," said Bobby.

"No apologies please; I'm glad I introduced you two, but I do have to get some things done. I'll see you both later. Geoff I'll keep a weather eye out for some good challenging sailing conditions...without the gales and lightening."

"Take it easy Jason," said Bobby.

"I'll be ready Jas, just give me a call." said Geoff.

"Well Geoff do you have any plans for the rest of this afternoon," asked Bobby after Jason had left.

"No...nothing pressing at the moment."

"Good, then let's continue this at the bar I'll buy you a round."

"You twisted my arm."

"You know I might be interested in selling the *Cowgirl*, of course it would have to be to someone whom I knew could handle her and also appreciate her...someone like you. Would you be interested?"

"Bobby, she's a sweet boat but boats have anchors. I'm afraid I'm too much of a vagabond to make a commitment like that."

"I guess I can understand that; have you ever been married Geoff?"

"Yes, married twice and divorced twice... working on number three if I can find her."

"Heh, heh yeah, you'll find her when you're not looking. If you keep looking you'll never find her. I've been married three times. My first wife died too early, my second wife should have been like my first, and *Cowgirl* is the namesake for my third former wife. I'll be working on my fourth if I ever get over her. It gets tougher the older you get."

"Amen to that," said Geoff.

They traded buying rounds till the late afternoon. Bobby had to leave for an engagement while he was still reasonable sober. Geoff stayed on and decided that dinner would be the chopped steak special. He was nearly through his dinner when his cell phone rang.

Damn why'd I bring that fool thing in here he said under his breath as he glanced at the Caller ID. It was Lana's number and he felt an uptick in his mood. His imagination kicked in with hasty plans if she was getting off early. And for one of those rare occasions he violated his own prohibition and answered the call.

"Hey, Lana what's up?"

"Hi, Geoff, uh... about tomorrow, I can't...I have to go out of town early to the panhandle to take care of some family business. Soo...can I take a rain check on that breakfast."

"Huh...Oh yeah, sure, sure Lana; you do what you have to do. Uh, how long do you think you'll be gone?"

"Oh, I...I'm not really sure yet Geoff. Our family gets crazy sometimes. My sister is coming in from Oklahoma and my two brothers from Texas will also be there. We're spread all over the map; we hardly ever get together anymore, so..., uh..."

"Listen have fun with your family, I guess I'll see you when you get back then...?"

"Yeah, I'll give you a call as soon as I get back."

"Good, so then... have a safe trip, uh... I'll be thinking about you Lana. I'll miss you."

"Umm, okay Geoff, take care... bye."

He reminded himself that this was precisely why he never made plans as he closed the phone and ordered another round.

Chapter sixteen

The rhythmic sound of the waves slapping against the hull in combination with the gentle undulation of the morning tide rocking the boat with a slow lethargic motion, the groan and creak of the superstructure and the sound of the seagulls scavenging their breakfast, all synergized to impress themselves upon his unconsciousness waking him from another fitful night of sleep.

He rubbed the crud away from the corners of his eyes. Looking out the porthole he could see the horizon, pale yellow – turning orange then red-orange as the new day announced its arrival. From someplace came the wonderful aroma of fresh brewed coffee. A fresh breeze cleansed away the stale odor of the pier.

He became aware of a dull throb dancing around in his head – but it was nowhere near as bad as he deserved. It had been another night of drinking to forget and since he couldn't remember what it was he was trying to forget it had obviously worked – well that was a bit of self-denial, he knew exactly what it was he needed to forget. He slowly pulled himself up into a sitting position and threw his legs over the side of the bunk. Rising slowly to his full height he tested his balance and negotiated the few steps to the galley sink. He ran some water and splashed it on his face. Wiping off his face, he changed his tee shirt for a clean one and pulled on his windbreaker. It was time to go see about some breakfast, his favorite meal of the day. He could skip lunch and sometimes dinner when he was drinking, but never breakfast. They were getting to know him as a regular at the Eight Bells.

He had been on a binge since that other night, when the hell ever that was. It was the night Lana had called up to postpone the inevitable end of what he had thought could be the beginning of a relationship – the one he had been looking for…waiting on for so long. It was nearly within his grasp. He lunged at it. It was his, and then it was gone, smoke and mirrors - another mirage disappearing on the cold hard plain of reality.

Perhaps it was time to put St Augustine in his rear-view mirror. It had been the usual rodeo – the pleasant anticipation of a new life, another chance to get things right. But like all the others before it there followed the full speed run down the straightaway and the inevitable crash and burn after the second turn as reality once again came up short of expectations first with Jennifer and then with Lana. He had been dumped back to back in one week. Geez, that had to be some kind of a record, even for him. Post-mortems of life were useless; as Bogart was rumored to have said as a favorite remark - *you pay your money and you take your chances.*

He spent the rest of the day holding a field-day on the *Cowgirl* and then called Jack Schreid to advise that he was terminating the rental. He would forfeit the remainder of the month's rental; that was okay with him. It was a small price to pay for the good times he had enjoyed. Jack tried to talk him into finishing out the month but his mind was set on leaving. He would stay the night so that he could leave early tomorrow morning or as early as he could get his butt up. He spent the evening at Robbie's saying goodbye to those whose acquaintance had made this stopover a little bit of paradise for him. Pete even dedicated a song for him during his last set that brought a lump to his throat.

"This here's a song for a friend of mine. I only got to know him for a few short months but the memories we made will last a lifetime. We had some good times, didn't we my friend. Sorry to see you go, you'll be missed but I understand that sometimes moving on means leaving. Just know that wherever you go and wherever you are you'll always have a friend back here in St. Augustine," said Pete as he introduced the song. He played and sang his cover of *A Pirate Looks at Forty* an old Jimmy Buffett number and one of Geoff's favorites.

Geoff was up the next morning at sunrise to pack his truck. It took longer than he had patience for but when it was finally done he went over to the Eight Bells for one last breakfast. He was going to miss this place just like he missed all the places where he had taken refuge from the storms of his life. He recognized the old familiar feelings of ambivalence as he sat eating breakfast. He had come to welcome them as a normal part of his life. They meant he was still in the game, still calling the shots, still free to be whatever the hell he thought it was he should be.

He headed south on A1A and then changed his mind. He needed the interstate, needed to blow out some of the clutter of cobwebs distracting his thoughts. So he headed inland and got on I-95 heading south. Just under four hours later he saw the exit signs for Boca Raton. He had been there before, it was time to pay another visit and see what had changed. He exited and headed east back out to the beach. When he reached A1A he headed south.

There it was the Tidewater Café a comfortable art-deco restaurant and lounge right on the intra-coastal waterway in Boca. It was like finding an old friend, one he could rely on to be there and accept him unconditionally with no questions. It was nice to be able to travel across thousands of miles, years later and still find remnants from past lives. It lent a pleasing sense of continuity to his world.

He took a seat at a hi-top, in the lounge of course. He had brought in his steno pad intending to do a bit of scribbling. The picture windows afforded an excellent view of the yachts of the idle rich and those attempting that impression. It was a warm, sunny lazy Sunday and with nothing on his mind save memories of other times and places – he felt a quiet peaceful contentment or maybe it was he had finally mastered denial. Classical music played counterpoint to the large screen TV which was tuned to a football game with the volume muted.

Football, already! Then he realized it was, after all, early September and this was the opening weekend of football season. Where had the summer gone?

"Hi, my name is Sherri, welcome to the Tidewater. We have specials on Wings, Nachos and Baby-back Ribs, two for one drafts and well drinks. What can I get you?"

"I'd like a tequila grapefruit tall with a lime squeeze and I think I'll have the ribs. But I'm going to need a really hot spicy sauce, do you have one?"

"If you like hot and spicy we have a killer sauce that you'll probably like. The ribs also come with a side of coleslaw and French fries is that okay?"

"May I substitute something for the fries?"

"Black beans and rice?"

"That sounds delicious, that'll work."

"Great, I'll be right back with your drink."

Denver was beating Oakland 16-0 in the 2nd quarter with less than 4 minutes remaining until halftime. He began watching it but the focus of his thoughts kept straying.

Strains of an old Dean Martin song kept playing on a jukebox somewhere in the caverns of his memory. *I don't want a room full of roses – I just want my arms around you.* He began to mentally relive his experiences of the last few months. It was getting difficult to sort it all out – everything seemed to flow together. In his mind's eye he saw Amy. He remembered her sitting at the table in the Delta Blues Café the first night they met. He fast-forwarded his mental memory tape to the night at the Dixie Rose.

Sherri interrupted his reverie with his drink order. "I'll have your ribs in just a few minutes, okay?"

"That's fine; I'm not in a hurry."

The grapefruit juice was fresh squeezed; he took a long sip as his thoughts drifted back to the Dixie Rose.

It seemed so long ago – almost like another life, well to his way of thinking it was another life. He had allowed himself to relax his guard and fantasize mutual feelings of a future together. It had of course all been smoke. He had, in spite of himself, repeated another mistake. He had gotten too comfortable, maybe even too complacent and began to listen to his heart. It reminded him of a lawyer who had once advised him as he had sold his home after his second divorce –*Always follow your head, your heart will get you in trouble.*

With Amy it had again gotten too intense too fast. Not for him, but probably for her – as with all the others in his recent string of heartaches. He could count Jennifer in there amongst his broken dreams.

Maybe they had tired of the lack of challenge. It seems they all wanted someone exciting, wild, dangerous... not domesticated and predictable. Most found someone, usually the wrong someone and wound up in a unilateral relationship or worse - abused and battered or in the extreme - dead. Couldn't they learn from each other's mistakes? Well he hadn't – maybe they couldn't either.

Maybe his theory of nice people and users traveling through life on perpendicular paths was true after all. It seems that all the good people, the *givers* in this world travel along life's pathways parallel to each other – just as the *users, takers* and *gamesmen* all travel on their parallel paths, which run perpendicular to the former. The result of course being that all the good people the *givers* only intersect and meet the *users, takers and gamesmen* while these rapscallions only come across and exploit decent people. It was the curse of humanity: to the lions go the sacrificial lambs.

In Lana's case she was testing her new found freedom and going through that wild and crazy post-divorce stage. She needed time to get her feet back on the ground. He unfortunately was just the first of a string of love-toys she would have to work her way through before she settled down, if indeed she ever did. Did she use him or did she just freak out with the prospect of a premature commitment? Had he expected too much, or pushed too hard? Ah hell, maybe he had used her to get over Jennifer grasping like a drowning man trying to get hold of anything he could to sustain himself. One fantastic night and one morning and it was all over.

"Here we go honey, sorry for the wait. I bought you another drink to make up for it. Let me know when you're ready for it and I'll bring it over."

"Well hey, thank you very much Sherri, I appreciate that." The ribs were excellent, very lean and meaty and well done the way he liked them and the sauce had a nice zing. The black beans and rice were delicious; it all went down well.

He finished his meal and was enjoying his drink when two guys from a large party that had just come in began pushing the two remaining vacant hi-tops together. They commandeered a few extra seats from the bar but were still short of seats and table space. Geoff motioned to one of the guys looking around for a solution.

"You're welcome to use this table if you like; I can retire to the bar."

"Ah, you don't have to do that sir," he said.

"It's okay; I don't mind; it looks like you guys have a big party enjoy yourselves."

"Thank you, sir, thank you very much."

He took a seat at the bar. Sherri wiped down the tables and took the drink orders and then she came up to him.

"That was very sweet of you," she said patting him lightly on the back. You have another drink coming from them, I'll tell the bartender. I'll close out your check and bring it here."

"I did it for the karma; a former father-in-law of mine once told me that if you do good deeds you'll get good things in return. I could sure use some good things in my life."

"Well I hope it all works out for you," she said with a wink as she walked off.

He began to jot a few lines down and quickly got absorbed in his writing when an attractive young woman took a place at the bar one seat over to his right. She had a small three by five spiral notepad into which she began to write profusely. People were always asking him what he was writing whenever he was sitting at a bar scribbling. It was amusing sometimes. Some people became very paranoid that he was taking notes about them. He decided it was time to turn the tables.

He waited until she had taken a break and then asked, "What are you writing?"

"Oh just some notes to myself."

"You seem to be writing quite profusely for such a small pad, why not use a steno pad. I'm never without mine and sometimes get a lot accomplished as I sit in a bar and daydream or just people watch."

"No this is fine. What about you? What are you writing?"

"I'm just scribbling some scenes that I might use as seeds for a book I hope to one day get published."

"I had a complete book on my computer, all ready to be published. It was this great story about crows."

"Are you talking about Crows - as in the tribesmen of the Native-American Crow Nation?"

"No, not the Indians, it was about the birds. There was this one crow that always saw these other birds migrating south and it made him curious. He talked to them about their travels and they always had these wild stories to tell. It made him jealous. One day he decided to tag along with them. The rest of the story is about his trip and experiences all through the eyes of a bird. It was a wonderful story, but my computer crashed and I lost the whole thing. I can never hope to rewrite it."

"But didn't you back-up your hard drive or at least print off some of your manuscript?"

"Do you know how it feels to lose a large part of your intellectual property? It's devastating. So what's your book about?"

"It's essentially a human interest story. The main character is searching for his defining moment and hoping that love comes along with it while second guessing himself and living in the past with regrets and what ifs."

"Is it autobiographical?"

"Geez, I hope not, at least I don't think I'm quite in such bad shape. Of course they say write what you know. So I would have to say in all honesty that there probably is some of me in there."

"There seems to be a lot of sickness going around in the male gender. It starts at a very early age. I've heard about little boys in fifth to seventh or eighth grade standing on trash containers peeing on little girls. Some kind of sick macho thing at that young age, it's no wonder there is no respect for women in this country. Men just lie all the time, like my ex-husband. He cheated on me but swore he never had sex. So I called his girlfriend and asked her specifically what they had done. She told me they just had mutual oral intimacy. But that wasn't sex? You men all lie so much you begin to believe your own sick stories. I'm from Canada and I thought it was bad up there but you American men take the prize."

"Oh what part of Canada are you from?"

"The eastern part."

"Oh, where in the east?"

"Nova Scotia"

"Where in Nova Scotia?"

"Halifax"

"Ahh, I've been there, a very pretty and friendly city as I remember. I took a road trip up through the Maritime Provinces after getting laid off from work in Colorado. I drove to New Brunswick to visit the Moosehead Brewery, one of my favorite brews and then continued all the way out to Halifax and had a great time visiting some of the pubs and listening to Celtic folk bands."

"Yes it is pretty, I used to enjoy it but it has changed so much. That's why I left to come down here and see for myself what this country is about. Boy that was a mistake."

"Really...I'm sorry."

"I've been interviewed twice by the CIA. They are hounding me to renounce my Canadian citizenship and join them. When I refused they threatened to harass me if I don't agree to come to work for them. There's so much corruption here in this country, it's pathetic. Your government lies to you and you people just ignore it. How can you support such an imperialistic, interventionist, illegitimate and corrupt government?"

"Whoa...where did you get such a distorted opinion of the United States?"

Changing the subject abruptly and getting agitated she asked, "Are you always by yourself?"

"Well I..."

"Don't you have family or close friends?"

"Umm..."

"All you men are alike; you just want tits and ass. It's all physical with you. Once the physical attraction is gone you throw away the fucking marriage."

He was going to interrupt her but he thought better of it and just listened.

She continued, "I went down to the local strip club here in town and they asked if I wanted a job. I asked them why they thought I was looking for a job. They told me that women usually come in during the afternoon for interviews. Then I asked them if they would hire me if I was looking. And they told me, 'absolutely honey, on the spot, you are one hot babe.' I told them to shove their job; that I'm just here doing research on fucking sick male habits."

There was no point in rebutting any of her ranting litanies of grievances he just sat there incredulous at what he was hearing. The bartender was even avoiding them until Geoff glanced over and caught his attention.

"How are you doing on that drink, you still have another one coming," he said to Geoff.

"I'm ready, you can bring it now."

"How about you miss, can I get you anything?"

"No, no I'm fucking out of here," she said in a wild ranting voice as she got up and stormed off.

"I should have told her to leave a half hour ago," the bartender said shaking his head. "What the hell is her problem?"

"I guess she's going through the anger phase of post-divorce recovery."

"Well then she needs to get some serious therapy. You can't throw bricks at the entire male gender and tear down the country - especially if you're not a citizen or even a resident - and expect not to alienate a whole lot of people."

"We're a great country we protect those rights for everyone," said Geoff with a shrug as he went back to his writing.

When he next took a break and looked around the bar had quieted down considerably. There was just him and another couple sitting at the other end of the bar. A few tables were still occupied but even the large party had departed.

It was the usual transition time between crowds that all bars go through. If you've ever sat in a bar long enough - as he had on not a few occasions - you began to recognize the pattern.

It was probably time for him to take his leave also. He got the tab and headed out deciding to drive the beach route north.

A little over two hours later he found himself in Vero Beach and not in the mood to drive any farther so it was time to look for a motel for the night. He drove north on A1A until he found his usual no-frills bunkhouse, he didn't need fancy for one night, just a rack with clean sheets.

The motel was on the opposite side of the highway from a quiet strip of beach which had lots of vegetation separating it from the highway and an access path that wound down to the water. It would make an excellent spot for his morning jog.

He'd get an early start in the morning and shoot back up to Daytona and maybe check out a local beach up there that he had learned about from a biker who he had met in a bar back in Laramie.

Chapter seventeen

The sun ran once more behind the clouds and each time in the newly emerging shade the temperature noticeably cooled. A warm moderate breeze kicked up and a gust of wind blew the loose sand off the dunes to cover his blanket and cooler with a fine dusting of grit. This was a secluded part of Daytona, yet unspoiled by the sea of high-rise hotels and clutter of the more renowned parts. It was the last refuge for the locals who came to enjoy it for its charm and not to pollute or exploit it.

But it wouldn't be long before this last little bit of heaven was sacrificed to the greed of the developers to assuage their endless appetite for their five cars, three boats and a plane. Their highly leveraged lifestyles only fed their frenzied pursuit of more choice real estate to develop or plunder as the case may be.

No he wasn't a tree hugger, he understood the necessity for progress; he supported it, but there had to be some mitigation of unrestrained development to achieve a balance upon which we could all agree.

It was late in the season, yet at the same time nearly the start of the next which would bring another influx of tourists to this year round destination resort. Most families and couples had other plans and except for a few surf-casting fishermen he was nearly alone with his thoughts.

Well he was alone. They certainly weren't intruding. It suited his mood just fine. He welcomed the quiet times with which to reflect upon who he was, where he was, where he had been, where he was going and where he hoped to go. He liked to use these quiet times to put his life into perspective and to try to determine a direction for the future.

Ah, but to hell with agendas and plans – they were, at least in his life, a blueprint for frustration and failure – far better to just deal with life spontaneously. When things slowed down and all the spice seemed to have dissipated, well that was probably a sign that he had overstayed his welcome and had become a too familiar face. So it was time to move on and seek another refuge – another venue where he could resume his search with renewed spirit. It was, after all, who he was.

Would it ever end? Did he really want it to? Sometimes yes, he answered to himself, he wanted it over with all his heart and soul – at other times, maybe even most times - he was just too mentally exhausted to give a damn. Ten thousand drinks in a thousand bars in a hundred cities – it all became the same. The conversations, the shallow acquaintances and his bad choices all began to melt into a mélange of boredom, loneliness and desperation – the mosaic of his life.

He shifted his gaze out at the sets of waves assaulting the shoreline. He was always impressed by the tenacity of the tides, which at least in this epoch had neither a beginning nor any discernible end.

As he scanned the shoreline to his right, off in the distance a large plume of blowing sand caught his attention. As the plume closed the distance to where he sat, the small blot at the front of the cloud morphed into the shape of a Jeep Wrangler with open cab, roll bars and huge balloon tires. It slowed down enough as it passed to reveal a lady in shorts, a bikini top and a sun visor headband over her long blonde hair behind the wheel. She looked his way and waved, but continued on. As he followed her trail down the beach with his eyes, he saw her slow down still more and swing around in a wide arc heading back towards him. She pulled up and stopped about ten yards away, shut it down, got out and walked over towards his blanket.

As she approached within earshot he called out to her, "Nice day for 4-wheelin."

"Yeah, I love this beach without all the tourists."

"I know what you mean."

"Are you by yourself?" she asked stopping at his blanket.

"Yeah I am, how about you?"

"Well I am now, my ex-boyfriend's in a body bag under the cargo net in the back," she said raising her eyebrows affecting a self-satisfied whimsical expression and adding a little chuckle as an easy smile crept across her lips.

"Well that's one way to win an argument."

"Ah, a great sense of humor, I like that in guys," she said as she winked and flashed a bright smile revealing brilliantly white perfect teeth.

"I'll remember that, I'd hate to wind up bouncing around in the back of your buggy in a rubber sack."

"Mind if I sit down?"

"Oh geez, I'm sorry, forgive my rudeness. Here, let me scoot over and make some room on the blanket."

"My name's Sondra," she said offering her hand.

"Hi Sondra, I'm Geoff," he said taking her hand and holding it for a few seconds. "Nice to make your acquaintance, are you in a hurry to bury the bones or can you hang out awhile, spend some time and have a little conversation."

"Oh, I can kill some time; these bags are pretty odor proof."

"Um, level with me Sondra… you didn't really croak your ex now, did you?"

"Well no Geoff, but I should have – he is such a jerk."

"Do you need to get something off your chest or do you just want to forget about it and move on?"

She sat down and began to fix her hair into a ponytail as she turned to him. "Let's forget about him and move on. I see you have Colorado tags – you're a long way from home."

"That's not my home; it's just the last place I came from."

"What brought you to Florida?"

"The water - I missed the salt air, the majesty of the ocean and the tides."

"Why not California?"

"I chased my California Dream up and down that state Sondra. I searched all over, lived in North County San Diego, San Fernando Valley, the LA basin, San Gabriel Valley and the place they euphemistically call Silicon Valley. I guess I grew jaded of spoiled children and the *he who dies with the most toys wins* lifestyle."

"What do you do Geoff that allows you to go wherever your fancy strikes you?"

"It's not so much what I do as it is who I am. I like to think of myself as a free spirit. A lot of other people probably see me as a nomad, a drifter, tumbleweed, rolling stone, bohemian, vagabond or maybe even a gypsy – take your pick."

"Wow, Geoff you sound pretty self-deprecating, I'm not here to judge you. And who cares what other people think, they don't pay your bills."

"Thanks Sondra, sorry if I sounded a little self-disparaging but it's easier to stomach if it's my own observation."

"Oh hey now you're getting defensive on me. Are you a seeker, are you searching for something?" she asked seeming honestly intrigued as she folded her arms over the tops of her bent knees and locked her eyes on his waiting for his answer.

"I don't know, sometimes I think a big part of my search is to escape from myself. Or maybe I just need to find the right lady and settle down, someone to keep me company as we grow old together… my soul mate. I really hope to find her one day. I'd like to believe that there is a possibility that she exists."

"I'm sure she does Geoff. You're a very attractive man. You shouldn't have a problem. You probably have a whole bunch of girlfriends."

"Yeah, maybe in some parallel universe but in this one my social life is a bit sparse."

"You still haven't told me what you do for a living."

"I had a career once as a computer tech working with IBM mainframes until the fun and job satisfaction slowly faded. When I began my career I felt, I think, like an artist must feel. A completed program was like a work of art that I had lived with for a while. Over the years those feelings were replaced by the tedium of just pushing out more code. The next project became just like the prior one with a different name. Eventually I got stuck fixing other's mistakes and updating bad code while the less skilled moved on to other more cutting edge applications."

"It sounds like you were caught up in the infamous corporate grind."

"Yes when I stopped to analyze my situation I realized I was. Then one day I realized my skills had become obsolete. The natural progression of a high-tech career is entry-level trainee, code drone, senior guru and then after a bunch of reorgs, mergers and acquisitions and staff reductions the job offers dwindle to independent contracting. As a contractor no one was willing to invest in upgrading my skills. Recruiters and their client companies just wanted to use whatever I knew until it wouldn't suit their bottom line any more. I couldn't self-finance upgrading my skills with the escalating cost of computer education which had specialized into expensive curriculums targeting corporate clients, or maybe I just couldn't find the incentive and motivation – so I walked away from it all."

"Then how did you pay your bills?"

"My mom passed away and left me with enough money to pay off my credit debt – then I sold my house, threw all my stuff in the back of my pick-up and got back out on the interstate. Now I do free-lance writing and maybe an odd contract here or there when I get lucky."

"Do you like living on the edge?"

"Well I think it's what I do best – I thrive on change and my itinerant lifestyle allows for a constant supply of new challenge and the luxury of never becoming bored with life."

"What about lonely, don't you ever get lonely?" she asked as she shifted position stretching out her legs leaning back and extending her arms behind her to support her upper body with the palms of her hands.

"Ah, Sondra, that's another story altogether, it comes with the territory."

"Well how do you deal with it?"

"Denial…I fight it all the way until I realize it's hopeless and then I usually just hit the interstate and drive until I figure out the next place to stop and make a stand. But enough of me and mine, tell me a little about yourself – what do you do, Sondra?"

"I own a boutique here in downtown Daytona."

"How's business?"

"Really competitive, but I get by."

"What kind of merchandise do you retail?"

"I sell swimming apparel, sportswear, tees, lingerie, and intimate apparel like Victoria Secret – I try to specialize in some fashions and sizes the large mall shops don't carry, it's the only way to beat them. We used to do fashion shows at business lunches back when they were trendy, but most of the guys tried to solicit the girls and I just grew tired of the tasteless comments."

"I can understand that, there are an awful lot of assholes out there."

"Oh goodness yes, I could write a book about all the characters I've met. Hey Geoff, I was just on my way to the Channel House. If you're hungry they have fantastic seafood and a great menu featuring a whole range of choices from assorted entrées to casual items like mussels, crabs, clams and grouper sandwiches – would you like to tag along, I'd love to hear more of your story."

"Sure Sondra, I'd love to, besides you've just whet my appetite - thanks for the invite."

"Well let me warn you though, I'm a regular there and there are some real jerks at the bar – it's becoming a magnet for a lot of macho bullshit."

"Thanks for the warning but it shouldn't be a problem. I passed sandbox 101 with flying colors. I usually get along with most people one way or the other."

They took her Jeep and left Geoff's pickup on the beach deciding it was safe since high tide had already crested and it was a good thirty meters from any tide pools. Entering through the dining room door – at Sondra's request to avoid the regular bar crowd – they got seated in the rear by a window overlooking the channel which was part of the Intracoastal Waterway. It was still early so the dining room was less than half full.

As they looked over the menu Sondra grasped Geoff's left forearm – "Oh Geoff, let's do crabs."

"That sounds great to me Sondra, with a pitcher of brew to wash it all down." They ordered a half-dozen of the large crabs and a pitcher of the local micro-brew.

"Are you a crab aficionado Geoff?"

"Well my second ex finally convinced me to try them, but it wasn't until after we were already divorced so I'm sure you can refine my novice techniques."

"Well hey, if anyone can - with my credentials - I certainly can. I'm originally from the Chesapeake Bay area. I grew up catching and eating crabs."

She rubbed his forearm and gave it a squeeze for emphasis. Geoff was lost in attraction to her eyes – the beautiful emerald green enhanced by her suntan – when she made eye contact and locked his stare with hers as a broad smile crept slowly across her lips. He caught himself staring intermittently at her eyes, her smile, her teeth, her whole face; he exhaled audibly feeling a little foolish.

"What is it?" she asked, with a tilt of her head, a quizzical look and a sexy chuckle. "Why are you staring so hard, do I have seaweed or something stuck between my teeth?" She laughed playfully and gave his arm another squeeze.

"Pardon me for staring Sondra; you are just very easy on the eyes. I know that probably sounds trite and like a line but it really is just an honest impression. And please, I don't mean to be sexist."

"Oh thank you Geoff, I've heard it before, but I still enjoy the complement."

"Sondra - wow that name sounds so formal."

"My close friends call me Sonni – you can too, if you like."

"Thanks – Sonni, what can you tell me about your personal life without getting too personal."

"I've been married twice also. The first lasted less than a year – the second almost four years. My first ex-husband was a closet druggie when I met him. After we were married it all came out. He spent the whole honeymoon high and wanted me to do drugs with him. I tried to get him to go to rehab but he wanted no part of that so we parted company. My second ex liked his family, especially his mom more than me."

"It doesn't sound like there were any children."

"No thank goodness, I took all the right precautions since I really didn't see a future in either relationship and I don't like the single parent lifestyle. I'm still looking for the right father type when I decide to settle down. I've got time although I'll hit the big four-o at the end of this year so my biological clock is ticking but it's not so loud that I can't ignore it for a while."

"So how long have you been in the boutique business?"

"Let's see, oh goodness it's going on four years already. It doesn't seem that long."

"Time has a way of slipping away from you and the demands of life seem to require more and more of your time as you get older," he said.

"Yes, that's certainly true in my case. The boutique is a cover for my beach persona; my real career is as a marine biologist at the Institute for Oceanography in Daytona."

"Really, now that's impressive – what are your background credentials?"

"I earned my master's from UCSD and I'm currently working on my PhD at the University of Florida."

"Hey now Sonni, I'm really impressed, I feel like a real fool for that comment about spoiled children in California – it's a generalization and just like most generalizations pretty shallow."

"Forget it Geoff, it doesn't apply to me so it didn't register, besides I've encountered my share of that type out there. That's probably why I'm content to be back here on the East Coast."

The food server brought out a pitcher of blond micro-brew; it was the lightest one on the menu.

"I thought we would stick to the light brews," Geoff said reaching for her glass to pour the first round – "don't want to overpower the taste buds and spoil the taste of the crabs."

"Light's fine with me Geoff, I'm not much of a beer drinker I prefer drinking wine or champagne. My favorite drink is mimosas with brunch."

"Mimosas…well no kidding, Sonni you and I would make a perfect couple – that's my preferred brunch drink also."

The server brought out a steaming tray of crabs and asked if there was anything else they required.

"No, I think we are set for a while, thanks," said Geoff.

"Well enjoy, I'll check on you later," said the server stuffing his pad into his server's apron and hurrying off to his next table.

They started on the crabs, Sonni giving him some helpful coaching when he seemed a little hesitant about his next maneuver. The conversation, what little there was, switched to the crabs. Sonni spoke up just as they were each finishing their last crab.

"So what's in your future, Geoff – if you don't mind my asking?"

"I'm an open book Sonni, I don't mind at all. You know I've read somewhere that life is what happens when you plan something else, so I've really given up on planning things. It cuts down on the disappointment of spoiled plans."

"Oh come on Geoff, think positive."

"Well I have thought a lot about going back to school for graduate work, just can't seem to settle on any one discipline. I seem to vacillate between a Master's in English, Political Science or Geopolitics or International Relations. Sometimes when the mood strikes me I think about Philosophy. None of which is particularly vocational. I guess I'm not very materialistic."

"Education doesn't have to be about materialism. It can give you a broader perspective and more appreciation for life."

"Oh I definitely agree. If I could develop my own interdisciplinary degree it would probably be Geo-Political Economics with some Philosophy thrown in for grounding. The closest curriculum I've found to fit my various interests is a program at Tulane."

"Hey, now that's not a bad school – can't beat the location", said Sonni.

"Ahh yes, New Orleans – I need to return there someday. There is something spiritual about that town that touches deep down to the depths of my soul."

"Oh, I know, I love New Orleans also Geoff, but I'd like to find someone with whom I can share all the feelings – I think it brings another whole dimension to the experience."

"Yeah, I know what you're talking about. I get the same feeling at times. Of course at other times for lack of a better choice I am comfortable just being solitary. In all the trips I've taken to New

Orleans I've somehow always wound up going alone, probably because I usually decide to go on the spur of the moment."

"Perhaps you need to find someone who shares your sense of adventure."

"Definitely and it's not like I haven't been looking. I just haven't been fortunate enough to find that special someone. So I console myself that I am more open to new experiences when I'm alone. It can be good and bad, happy and sad, outrageous or egregious – sometimes all at once like during Mardi Gras which to me is the ultimate paradox."

"I still think I'd rather share it with someone," she said wrinkling her nose.

"I would if I could; maybe unrequited love is the foundation for the feeling of spirituality that it holds for me. Sometimes I feel as though I've been single for so long that I doubt I'd be good company for anyone anymore."

"Oh please, stop... you seem to be very sensitive Geoff, maybe too much. I think perhaps you expect too much of yourself. So you set yourself up for failure. And when it happens you think that life has really let you down."

"Yeah Sonni, I know - I've got a terminal case of the 'feeling sorry for myself blues'."

"No, Geoff that's not what I meant, please don't take it that way, I'm not being judgmental and I don't know you well enough to understand where you're coming from or all that you have been through. I just think you're a little too tough on yourself. You strike me as someone who is worth getting to know. I know I'd welcome a chance to get to know you," she said as she reached out her hand and ran her fingers softly over his forearm with her wide open eyes looking deeply into his.

"Sonni, I'm looking for... I really need to find... a lady with whom I can relate; someone to bring out...no, to demand my best qualities. I want to be able share my feelings and my dreams yet I don't want to be patronized – I just want to find someone who can believe in me – believe in us."

"And I would like to find that same kind of man Geoff, we seem to share the same sense of romantic idealism in our choice of relationships."

"Well hey Sonni, at the risk of being sorry for making another premature commitment, if you're willing to take a chance and you have no plans for the next hundred years or so, I think we could build a wonderful future together."

"Whoa Geoff, you sound like you've been reading my personal dating profile. I've never really believed in destiny but maybe I need to reconsider. I'm really glad to have found you on the beach this afternoon and to have had the nerve to stop and say hello. I don't usually go up to strange men but something about our encounter felt different."

"Sonni, I'm not much of a leader and I'm certainly not a follower, but if you're not intimidated by the unknown and care to hang in there alongside me for a while maybe we can weather the storms together. I won't promise forever but I can promise that I'll be there for as long as you want me around," he said as he reached out and took her hands in his.

"I'm willing to take that chance Geoff, as long as we can take our time and really get to be friends. I won't compromise my priorities – I'm not looking for a whirlwind romance," she said looking deeply into his eyes.

"Neither am I Sonni, I'm willing to invest the time to build a foundation of friendship that I hope will blossom into a lasting relationship."

The server returned to ask if they would like anything else.

"I'm fine," Sonni said, "Unless you want anything."

"No I think we can settle up," Geoff said as he proffered his credit card. As the server left to total the check Geoff turned his attention back to Sonni. "Thanks for inviting me Sonni, the crabs were excellent but the best part was the conversation, sharing your time and company and the hint of a promise of a future together. I really enjoyed being with you."

"You're welcome Geoff, and I really enjoyed your company also, but I didn't mean for you to pick up the tab."

"Please don't be offended Sonni, I guess I'm just old school about some things."

"I appreciate it Geoff, thank you. It's my treat next time," she said with a determined look and an easy chuckle as she reached over and squeezed his forearm.

"Sonni, do you have any plans for the rest of the evening…maybe we could hang out awhile, perhaps find someplace with a live band."

"Oh I'd love to Geoff, but I really intended to make this an early night – I need to get home and get some research done. But tomorrow is Friday and I have no plans. There is a place just down the strip - it has a long name, the Surfside Saloon and Eating Emporium but the locals just call it the SEE - they have a Blues band on Fridays starting at happy hour that plays until closing. Do you like Blues, Geoff?"

"Oh yeah…that's my first choice in music. Can I pick you up or shall we just meet there?"

"I'll be on campus tomorrow and also running errands around town, I don't know, it's probably easier to just meet there. Is four-thirty give or take okay? It starts to get crowded early on Fridays."

"Four-thirty it is then, I'll get us a table," said Geoff.

The waiter came back with the credit receipt and bid them a goodnight. They left using the same door they had come in avoiding the bar crowd, which had grown quite loud now that happy hour was in full swing. Sonni drove him back to his truck and stopped beside it.

"Thanks for the fun evening Geoff, I'll see you tomorrow night," she said as she leaned towards him.

The body language was right, the look in her eyes inviting. He took a chance and took her in his arms. She came willingly and they shared a lingering easy hug. He fought back the urge to kiss her.

"Sonni, I'm so glad we met and I'm really looking forward to tomorrow."

"I am too Geoff, see you then."

"Don't study too hard," he said as he let her go. He climbed out and she waved and drove away.

Chapter eighteen

Alone again...the old familiar feeling of melancholy once again paid its visit. It was always like this after some positive personal interaction. After the high dissipated he always felt a huge letdown. Would there ever come a time when it didn't have to end, when the sharing and the caring would go on. He hoped so, as he had so many times before and he hoped that this time it would be different from all the busted relationships of his past which had ended too soon.

He found a quiet little motel about a quarter mile beyond the Surfside SEE on the opposite side and decided it would do. He just didn't feel like doing anything else so he checked in for the night. The television was an old black and white but the room was clean and had been converted to non-smoking. He took a quick shower and then hit the sheets. Within minutes he had dozed off.

He awoke the next morning just after sunrise feeling really refreshed. Feels like a great day for a jog on the beach, he thought to himself. He dug out his trusty old cutoffs and headed out the door.

After a short drive farther down the strip he found a deserted parking area just off the beach. No gates, no signs, no meters, no attendants, just a gravel parking lot with grass and weeds growing up through the sparse gravel. He jogged down towards the water and did a few stretching exercises as a fresh steady breeze blew in from the water. The smell of the salty ocean air filling his lungs was exhilarating. It was always great to get back to the ocean. The waves, the sand, the gulls and all the other seabirds served to relieve the turmoil swirling inside him allowing him to refocus and put his life back into perspective. He began an easy pace along the water's edge heading back north and let his mind wander. Fifteen minutes into his jog he was passing the parking lot of the Surfside SEE. He jogged on for another five minutes and then turned around for the return trip. The twenty-minute return was spent daydreaming about the upcoming evening.

Once back at the motel he shaved, showered and set out to find a place for breakfast. Off on a side lot next to a strip mall he found a small café surrounded by sand and dune grass. A wide wooden gangplank running over a storm drainage trench with side rails of thick rope hanging between stanchions covered in braided rope work led to the front entrance. Half buried in a sand dune to the right of the gangplank was a rusted old sea anchor lying on its side with one fluke buried up to the crown. Rusting links of anchor chain attached to the ring at the top and twisted around the shank running down to the throat at the bottom of the anchor. Piles of assorted seashells and pebbles mixed with the sand and dune grass as landscaping. An old weather-beaten sign proclaimed 'Capt'n Jack's Neptune Café and boasted - Best chow on the strip Mess hours 0400-2000.'

Okay...let's check out the captain's mess deck, he chuckled to himself. The inside like the outside had a very nautical motif. The walls were covered in a mural of seascapes and coastal scenes. A deep blue ceiling with white flecks gave the impression of stars in a clear evening sky.

A fishing net strung along the ceiling by the long convex-shaped counter contained an assortment of seashells, cork and various other flotsam. The counter had sand and seashells buried beneath thick coats of clear acrylic with a laminated rope running along the outer edge of the surface. There was counter seating in canvas-backed captain's hi-chairs for twelve.

He took a seat at the counter to the left of two other couples and after a quick glance at the breakfast menu written on a chalk board against the wall ordered the creamed beef on biscuit, a side of oatmeal, some stewed prunes and coffee. He had a sense of pleasant anticipation as he pondered the upcoming activities of the day. But today he was probably going to just kick back and waste the hours until it was time for the rendezvous with Sonni at the SEE.

He caught himself fantasizing about the evening and chastised himself for being foolish and for conjuring up expectations and therefore bad karma. Of course he didn't know if he believed that, but then with all the strange twists in his life he suspected that he probably should. His reverie was interrupted by the server refilling his coffee for the third time.

"Will there be anything else, sir?"

"No thank you, breakfast was excellent, my complements to the Captain."

He paid the tab leaving a generous tip. As he walked back out to his truck he decided on a return to the motel to see if he could catch some television news reports. Once he got back and turned on the set he quickly learned what he had suspected at first glance last night – no cable.

The local stations carrying the morning talk shows had already transitioned to mundane commentary with uninteresting guests babbling vaingloriously about their personal accomplishments. Maybe a drive would kill some time.

It was a gorgeous day, bright and sunny with a nearly cloudless sky and temperature warming up as he headed back south along the strip. Once he got past the still deserted parking area, the site of his early morning jog, it was just dunes on both sides of the road.

About a mile or so farther down the road ran over a causeway bridge connecting back with the mainland and merged into a two-lane highway. He chose the northbound lanes heading towards the main business area. He passed office buildings interspersed with commercial properties and the usual luncheon spots supported by all the commercial activity. Then the speed limit reduced as he neared the heart of downtown. There was more pedestrian traffic and the blocks were shorter.

Just up ahead was a wide open expanse of manicured lush green lawn in a park setting with mature cypress trees covered in Spanish moss providing a thick shady canopy. Three one-way streets with slate sidewalks on both sides surrounded the center park providing ingress and egress from the main street. Set back from the sidewalk opposite the park stood several important looking buildings, which he assumed to be the municipal government as he identified first the Court House and then City Hall with an adjacent parking garage, a Fire Station and a large Post Office. Another of the buildings, a large modern one with sweeping expanses of smoked glass panels, housed the public library.

Bookstores and libraries topped his list of places to spend time... lots of time. As he pulled into the parking lot he reminded himself that he hadn't scribbled anything down in his ubiquitous steno pads for a while. Now was as good a time as any to catch up on his writing. He reached into the back and grabbed his latest steno pad.

Entering the library, he and walked past the checkout and reference desks and found some tables spaced out between the book stacks. He had written only a few paragraphs before his focus faded into daydreams. It was always easier for him to write at a bar while sipping a drink and watching the interaction of the crowd. A hand on his shoulder brought him back to reality.

"Hi Geoff, this is a pleasant surprise!"

It was Sonni, leaning over his shoulder, her cheek close to his, speaking in a low voice.

"Sonni, hey the pleasure is all mine; you're the last person I expected to see here, I thought you were going to be on campus," he whispered back.

"I did go there for some appointments but the campus library was really crowded so I decided I'd check out a few of the collections over here. For a public library they have a very good reference section, especially in Marine Biology. Are we still on for tonight at the SEE?"

"You bet...I'm ready for it right now Sonni," Geoff replied as he tilted back his chair arching his back in a stretch and turned to wink at her.

"Umm...don't tempt me Geoff, it wouldn't take much, I'd love go with you but I've still got some more errands to run. They shouldn't take too long, but I need to get them done. So I guess I'll see you there in about an hour or an hour and a half."

"Hop to it then lady, don't waste time, go on get out of here," he said in a teasing voice as he shooed her away.

He went back to his writing for a few more paragraphs and then surrendered to his unfocused thoughts and packed it in. He browsed for a while in the section on new releases in non-fiction.

He glanced at his watch. It was ten minutes later than when he had glanced at it in what felt to him like a half hour ago. Time was standing still – he was anticipating tonight. He had told himself to live in the moment but it wasn't working. When all else fails go for a drive he told himself.

He left the library and retrieved his truck and drove around aimlessly trying to concentrate on the scenery until he finally gave in and headed back to the motel where he sprawled out on the bed expecting to kill another half hour or so.

He awoke with a start and looked at his watch. It was quarter to five. Damn he had done it again – slept through the intermission clean into the feature – and if he didn't get his butt moving there might not be a feature. He took a quick shower and drove over to the SEE consoling himself that at least he had been fortunate to pick a motel close by.

The parking lot was already crowded but he managed to create a space. Once inside he found the bar buzzing with the after work crowd letting loose from a long work week. A quick panoramic scan of the bar convinced him that she wasn't here inside. He made his way through the crowd towards two open French doors that led to an outside deck where a guitar man was just setting up his amp and speakers.

A large gazebo with a thatched overhanging roof served as a tiki-bar. It had seating in wicker chairs along three of its sides. Several whirling ceiling fans hung over the inside of the structure circulating the air to keep the bar staff and patrons cool and comfortable. He spotted Sonni sitting on the far end. As he made his way over she saw him and waved. When he got there she stood up with pursed lips and reached out for a hug. He responded to her invitation with a quick easy kiss and gathered her in his arms.

"Umm, hi... sorry I'm late Sonni, I went back to the motel to kill some time and dozed off; I hope I didn't keep you waiting too long."

"Oh no, I only got here about ten minutes ago; I was afraid I was the one who was going to be late, so it worked out okay. I was saving a seat here for you but it got taken," she said looking over with displeasure at the man sitting to her left. The man glanced over from his drink to look at her and then quickly up at Geoff.

"Oh, I was just leaving, here you can have the seat," he said as he picked up his drink and moved hastily away.

"Thank you," she said rather icily.

"Was there a problem, Sonni?" asked Geoff looking at her and sensing the agitation in the tone of her voice.

"Oh just the usual jerk, I was sitting here with my pocketbook on the seat and he came along and wouldn't take my word for it that I had reserved it for someone. Then he began to hit on me."

"Are you okay, do I need to go have a talk with him?"

"Nah, forget him let's just enjoy ourselves."

"So, did you get all your errands finished?" he asked changing the subject.

"Uh huh, they took a little longer than I had anticipated but yes, they are all finished so I've got a long free weekend. I don't have to be anywhere until Tuesday."

"Great maybe I can help you fill in the time if you're so inclined."

"Umm yeah, maybe... actually I was kind of counting on it," she said as she playfully leaned over and gave him a hug.

"Oh a decisive demanding lady who knows what she wants; I like that. This should be a very delightful weekend. Shall we start off with dinner?"

"Um hmm, I already put us in for a table; I felt confident I could convince you to have dinner with me."

"Sonni, right now there's not much that you couldn't convince me to do."

"Ohh, is that carte blanche? – you'd better watch out, I could get used to that."

"Go right ahead get used to it; I'll give you all the time you need to make the adjustment."

"You know Geoff it almost feels as if there is something paranormal going on with us. I mean we met on the beach by chance and then today at the library neither of us could have known that the other would be there."

"Maybe its synchronicity or destiny pulling us together," said Geoff.

"Or just fortunate happenstance," said Sonni

"Whatever, I'm okay with it, as long as it continues," he said as he put his arm around her and drew her close.

"Umm me too," she said leaning in to him with her face close to his and her eyes locked on his.

The message was sent and received; Geoff brushed her lips with a light kiss. Sonni responded in kind and they sat there silently lost in each other's eyes for long seconds.

They had just ordered fresh drinks when the table pager lit up in the side pocket of her pocketbook. The inside dining room was quieter and more intimate than the bar. Large picture windows on three sides overlooked the beach. The evening special was broiled grouper with a rice pilaf and fresh steamed asparagus. So they went with the special.

After dessert and a latte, they went back to the bar to catch the blues band. They managed to get a table with the changeover from the happy hour crowd to the blues lovers. They danced a few numbers of the first set and then decided on a walk on the beach.

Although the sun had already set there was a gorgeous red glow in the western sky. They each slipped out of their shoes and Geoff eased his arm around her shoulders. Sonni responded by slipping her arm around his waist. They strolled along slowly, their footsteps sinking into the sand while they watched the red glow of the sky fade to pink, then to pale yellow, then to cream as it reflected off the few scattered clouds. The cream colored sky turned to pewter as the evening gave way to the night.

Almost as if on cue they both stopped and slipped into a close embrace. Sonni ran her fingers over the back of Geoff's neck and through his hair. Their lips met in a long tender kiss broken by a slight pause to gaze into each other's eyes then followed by another deeper kiss. Sonni's tongue gently probed Geoff's lips until he opened them to accept. He returned the gesture pulling her body closer. She didn't resist. The firm athletic fitness of her body against his felt wonderful. She was probably about five foot nine and fit perfectly in his arms. Geoff spoke first when they finally broke off the embrace and resumed their stroll.

"Sonni do you have any pressing errands for tomorrow and Sunday?"

"No, Geoff; why, what do you have in mind?"

"I was thinking of a little weekend getaway, a road trip to Key West. I'd like to reacquaint myself with the place and I'd love to have you along to share it with me."

"Ohhh that sounds like fun."

"Of course, I realize it's quite early in our relationship to be going off together, so if you have any apprehension at all or think we should postpone it a bit until we get to know each other better, I'll understand."

"Yes it is kind of quick Geoff, but I might not get another free weekend for a while. I really have to start knuckling down and finish my dissertation so I can complete my doctorate before I'm too old to put it to use. Besides I'm a big girl now, accountable for my own actions and I can take care of myself. I'm also a pretty good judge of character and you're easy to get to know."

"Yeah, that's me an open book, no hidden agendas, pretty shallow, huh?"

"Oh I don't think so Geoff, I think you are much more complex than you let on, but I really do trust you and I feel very comfortable with you. So no more discussion, I'll trust my women's intuition…let's go for it. I've got an evening dress I've been dying to wear, just haven't had the right occasion. Can we go dressy on Saturday night?"

"Absolutely, dressy it is for Saturday evening. We are going to have a fantastic time Sonni, I promise I won't betray your trust or your intuition."

"Although on second thought maybe I'll bring along my nine millimeter with a couple extra clips. I do have a permit to carry," said Sonni raising her eyebrows mischievously.

"Oh Lord, I forgot about your former boyfriend in the body bag in the back of your Jeep."

"I'm only goofing Geoff, I don't own a gun," she said as she stopped and gave him a quick kiss on the cheek.

Chapter nineteen

Geoff was up early Saturday to get in his morning jog. They had agreed to get an early start and stop off to get breakfast. Her place was a few blocks in from a main road in a nice quiet neighborhood of single family homes. He parked in the driveway and went up to the front entrance. Sonni answered the bell immediately.

"Good morning Geoff," she said with an effervescent smile that he found instantly irresistible as she gave him a sweet kiss and a hug.

"Umm what a nice greeting, good morning sunshine, you look like a million dollars Sonni."

She was dressed in white shorts and a flowery blue silk top with one of those elastic necklines that could be worn either over or off the shoulders depending on how sexually provocative one wanted to be.

"I love mornings, especially when I'm going on a trip with someone special. C'mon in and make yourself at home Geoff, I'll just be a minute. Get yourself a drink if you'd like, I've got all kinds of juice in the fridge," she said her voice bubbling with enthusiasm.

Beyond the foyer the living room seemed larger than the outside of the house would allow. It had an archway to a Florida room and another archway into a spacious kitchen which also joined the opposite end of the Florida room as a dining area. On the opposite side was another archway leading to a hall and the bedrooms and bathroom. Geoff went into the Florida room and took a seat on a large comfy sofa which had a view of the pond that ran along behind the house as well as the neighbors' houses on either side giving the backyard the expansive look of a golf course since there were no fences between the properties.

Sonni checked her answering machine and then made several calls leaving messages where she could be reached. In ten minutes they were on their way.

They stopped at a local pancake house for breakfast and were back out on the road in about a half hour. Five minutes later they were on the southbound I-95 interstate on-ramp merging into traffic which was surprisingly light. After a few minutes in the interstate fast-lane Sonni broke the silence.

"Where were you in Colorado?"

"The Springs, Colorado Springs."

"Oh, I've been there, although it was a long time ago. My Dad was Army, but I was a little girl. I don't remember much about it."

"Ah yes, there are a lot of Army types out there – Army, Air Force and even, believe it or not, Navy. It's a very military town with active duty, reserves, and retired. A friend out there told me that it was once on the list of the ten best places for women to meet eligible bachelors. In a lot of the bars out there the mix was three or four guys for every gal and that was when the Army was out on deployment."

"So that's why you're here in Florida?"

"Yes, it's a habit of mine – whenever I get frustrated, bored, bummed or burned out I just hit the interstate and drive until my head clears."

"So what were you doing in the Springs?"

"It's a rather convoluted story, I moved to the Florida west coast from the research triangle of North Carolina. I stayed for a while but then left Florida to find a place where people worked at jobs other than in the service sector supporting the tourism industry. I wound up in Colorado Springs by way of Reno, Nevada; Laramie, Wyoming and Denver, Colorado. I landed a few contracts in the computer field but then it all turned into smoke and mirrors. Colorado is a gorgeous state but its only drawback, in my mind, is that it lacks a beachfront with tidal water. So after I had played out all my aces I decided it was time to move on or maybe back – so here I am; I thought I'd give the east coast another go."

"You really do move around a lot, huh?"

"Yeah, I guess I live my life in a pattern of figure eights. I just keep crossing back over venues from the past again and again until I get it right. What about you, Sonni? How long was your dad in the Army?"

"He was a thirty-year career man. Besides Colorado, we spent time in North Carolina, Kentucky, Kansas, Hawaii, South Korea and Germany. Then he went on some Special Forces operations which of course we didn't get to go on."

"So you've been around the block a bit also?"

"Yes, and now I'm ready to settle down, but not until after I finish my doctorate."

It was early afternoon as they neared Key Largo, traffic had been light most of the way down except for driving through Miami where it got a little heavier but they still had made excellent time.

"Hey, Sonni, are you in the mood for some clam chowder? I know this neat place on the beach with excellent Manhattan style," he said as they passed through the first cross streets of the key.

"That sounds great Geoff, right about now my buns could use a little break, and a stretch would be really welcome."

"Oh goodness I'm sorry Sonni," he said rather sheepishly. "I can be a real robot behind the wheel. It comes from spending so much time driving alone. Look, anytime you need or want to take a break, please just sound off."

"Oh I will, I'm fine driving long distance but riding in the right seat gets me bored."

A few minutes later they pulled into the parking lot of Jonathan's Landing. A pier ran out from the beach with slips where pleasure boats could moor while dining at the restaurant. A few steps up and a short walk to the end of the pier through the delightful aroma of cooking seafood brought them to the door of this two-story restaurant with a green tiled mansard roof, weathered cedar shingles on the sides and blue awnings over large picture windows. The windows afforded a complete panoramic view of the pier, beach and the Intracoastal Waterway. As they walked along the pier Sonni slipped her arm around his waist and slowed their pace almost to a halt.

"Is there something wrong? Did you forget something in the truck?" Geoff asked as he looked at her.

"No… I just need a kiss," she said as she slipped her other arm around him in an easy embrace. As their eyes locked contact their lips met in a tender kiss.

When they broke off to continue on to the restaurant, he whispered softly in her ear, "Wow lady, what was that about?"

"I just had the urge and thought you might want one too, I know I did," she said with a shrug of her shoulder, a wink of her eye and a bright smile.

"I love your urges Sonni, don't ever ignore them," he said as he gave her arm a gentle squeeze.

"You're a sweetie, Geoff."

"Heh, it takes one to call one, as we used to say in kids' games," he said smiling and winking back. They walked the rest of the way to the restaurant entrance holding hands, swinging their arms like kids and laughing at themselves. Once inside they approached the hostess stand and made a request for something with a view of the water. They were seated immediately at a window table overlooking the sound, which was part of the Intracoastal Waterway.

Geoff picked up the wine list and scanned it over quickly. "Sonni, are you in the mood for some champagne?"

"Ohhh, yes Geoff, that sounds great; I'm always in the mood for champagne," Sonni said looking up quickly from the menu.

"Ah, great – you know, this could be the start of a really compatible relationship."

"Oh I hope so Geoff, I would really like that for us. I'm so tired of deceit, arguments and discontent."

"I'd like it for us too Sonni, it's been a long time."

"For me too, Geoff, I've been concentrating so much on my degree that I've neglected any sort of social life."

The server approached their table and introduced himself taking their drink order. Geoff ordered a bottle of Moet White Star brut. Once it was open and poured they shared a toast – to good company, a great atmosphere, the adventure of life and a promise of something more neither one could quite yet verbalize but both craved deep within their hearts.

They each ordered a crabmeat cocktail and a large bowl of Manhattan clam chowder. The chowder came out first and it was every bit as good as he remembered - on a road trip down from Sarasota on his way to Key West for New Year's Eve – many lives ago.

The mood was right and the atmosphere very comforting with no sense of urgency forced on them. The combination produced a very pleasant sense of well-being. Time ceased to matter. Their conversation was the easy unforced flow of a couple still getting familiar with each other yet very comfortable in each other's company. Caught up in the ambiance of it all they were both reluctant to let it go.

Geoff finally broke the spell, "Sonni I could stay here all afternoon, I'm really enjoying it, but we really do need to get back on the road."

"Umm hmm, this was so nice and relaxing but I'm also excited to get to Key West."

Geoff paid the tab and after they made their last restroom stops they strolled arm in arm back out to the truck.

"We still have about two hours' drive ahead of us and Key West is problematical for accommodations without reservations," Geoff said as they pulled out of the parking lot.

"You didn't make reservations?" she said fluttering her eyes in mock consternation.

"It was a spontaneous decision, I'm sure we'll find something Sonni, don't worry."

"Leave it to me I'll get us some rooms," she said with a mischievous laugh as she tugged the neckline of her top down below her shoulders exposing a little cleavage.

"Hey now lady just how am I supposed to keep my eyes on the road and concentrate on driving with you distracting me like this?"

"Oh you haven't seen distraction yet," she said in a coquettish tone as she tugged her top down to only inches above her elbows exposing still more cleavage.

"Okay, O...K, let's see how far you go Sonni," said Geoff shrugging with feigned detachment as he glanced between her and the road.

She waited until his eyes were intent on the road and then tugged her top down quickly flashing her breasts and covering up before he turned his head. The second time she flashed he caught her and she squealed quickly covering up. He eased the truck to a stop off the highway and gathered her gently in his arms. He stared deeply into her eyes as his brought his lips to hers for a long passionate kiss. Then he began to plant kisses on her cheek, her chin and her neck slowly moving down to her chest. She squealed as he nuzzled her cleavage.

"Oh, oooh Geoff, okay…Geoff oh baby stop, honey… I won't tease you anymore…I promise…Stop before you get me so horny we can't…"

He brought his face back up to hers and tenderly kissed her lips. "Sonni, you are driving me wild."

"And you are making me crazy. C'mon baby drive, let's get to Key West already so we can play."

From Key Largo down through the rest of the keys the causeway traffic was light which enabled them to make good time.

"It's funny how the miles seem longer when you are looking forward to arriving at a destination and the anticipation is building," she said as the miles rolled on.

"Yes, I know what you mean. The shame of it is oftentimes we fantasize to such extreme that the reality is a letdown, or at least mundane. It is the curse of imagination but it's the only drawback that I know of – fantasy is still the cheapest way to travel."

"Well maybe we can turn some fantasy into reality this weekend," she said with a wide smile and sexy chuckle as she reached over and gave his thigh a squeeze.

"Oh…I think my fantasies are already becoming reality," he said taking her hand in his and kissing it.

They made the city limits of Key West a little before five in the late afternoon. Continuing on to the old town they tried the first large major chain motel that they saw figuring that the cheaper places would be all booked up. As it turned out the very friendly front desk clerk had neglected to put up the 'No Vacancy' sign but had just minutes before gotten a call from the innkeeper of the Hacienda del Fuego advising he had a vacancy because of a late cancellation. The Hacienda innkeeper had even mentioned a possible discount. Geoff seized the opportunity and offered his credit card to reserve the room in response to the desk clerk's offer to call ahead.

The vacancy they lucked into was a few blocks off Duval in a very exclusive looking Spanish hacienda. It was set way back from the street through a walled courtyard with tall old live oak trees cloaked in layers of Spanish moss. A lighted cobblestone pathway led from the covered parking between the trees up to the entranceway through an arched portico.

The walk up the pathway with Sonni's soft delicate hand in his grasp filled him with a euphoric feeling in anticipation of what he hoped would be the beginning of the fulfillment of his dreams. They walked through the door into a large richly appointed dark oak trimmed lobby with a cobalt blue ceramic tiled floor. Plush tan leathered seating surrounded several round low tables behind a fountain. An archway led to a small intimate bar. Sonni took it all in and caught her breath.

"Oh Geoff, this place has to be very expensive. Maybe we should just keep looking," she whispered.

"I think you're probably right, but while we're here let's just hear what they have to offer, I have a good feeling about this place." He gave her hand a squeeze as they exchanged glances. The discount indeed did bring it down to only slightly extravagant.

"We'll take it. I don't think we can find anything comparable," said Geoff.

"You won't be disappointed, senor – I am positive."

Once they opened the double door of the suite on the third floor and looked inside any feelings of hesitation and misgiving faded. As they crossed the threshold Sonni exclaimed,

"Oh goodness, Geoff... this is fabulous – it looks like a honeymoon suite."

Hold that thought, an old cliché flashed instinctively though his mind. He discarded it out of hand not wanting to sound fatuous and superficial. "Yes Sonni, it certainly does – it even feels like one to me."

The living room was tastefully furnished with a sofa, loveseat, coffee table and side chair. A home theater setup and wet bar completed the atmosphere for a fantastic romantic getaway. French doors opened onto a balcony that extended around the corner to the spacious bedroom. In the bedroom was a Jacuzzi built against a floor to ceiling mirror. Off to one side of the Jacuzzi was a tiled open shower. On the other side was a mirrored dressing area, double clothes closet and the door to the bathroom with the usual tub and shower. Behind a louvered privacy door was a low one-piece commode and accompanying bidet. In a word, it was the essence of intimacy. A warm humid breeze gently stirred the lace curtains over the open French doors of the bedroom leading out onto the balcony.

Sonni was all over the suite, touching and checking things out. She opened the cooler behind the wet bar and squealed.

"Oooh look a bottle of Moet Brut and some Swiss chocolates. How does sipping champagne, munching chocolates and cuddling up on the couch with an old classic movie playing for background sound to you, Geoff?"

"Sounds like heaven Sonni, especially cuddling with you - absolute heaven."

"You open the champagne," she said handing him the bottle, "I'll go order the movie."

They settled down on the sofa, the movie came on and the champagne went down easy between bites of chocolates after a toast to *here and now*. The cuddling grew more tender and intimate and as their passion rose the kisses became more intense and lingered longer.

"Geoff," Sonni said in a seductively purring tone of voice as she looked deeply into his eyes, "Let's take a shower and finish the rest of the champagne in the Jacuzzi."

"Umm, just when I thought it couldn't get any better it just got better," he said.

"Oh just wait…it can still get better, a whole lot better," Sonni said with a sexy wink as she disappeared into the bathroom.

He started the water filling the Jacuzzi. When Sonni emerged from the bathroom, he audibly caught his breath at the sight of her. He tried to speak but his words came out in stammering confusion… "Sonni! Oh wow… whoa, uhh, I mean…" Sonni's completely nude slender well-tanned body showing only very skimpy tan lines was the essence of vibrancy and fitness with well sculpted muscle and soft curves over her torso, thighs and calves. Her well defined firm breasts were in perfect proportion to her trim athletic body, not oversize and obviously natural.

"Geoff, you're not ready yet! Come on baby, get naked and come take a shower with me," she ordered in a feigned chastising tone. "C'mon… last one in is a rotten egg."

Sonni stepped into the open shower and turned on the water. In seconds he was stepping into the shower behind her. She grabbed his arm and pulled him close to her under the spray. When they were both thoroughly wet Sonni slipped her arms around his neck and pressed her body firmly against his. Her open mouth met his in a passionate deep wet kiss. They soaped each other between embraces, rinsed off, quickly toweled off and walked hand in hand to the Jacuzzi where he had the champagne bucket and glasses on the rail. Geoff switched on the jets and they settled into the warm bubbling water.

"Ready for some champagne, Sonni?" he asked as he wrapped his arms around her and gently kissed her waiting lips.

"Umm hmm, yes, champagne and lots of kisses," Sonni said as their open mouths found each other's in another long lingering kiss.

"A toast, to the beginning of a great new relationship, may it withstand the test of time," he said.

"I hope so Geoff, I really do."

"So do I Sonni, with all my heart." The relaxing heat and bubbles of the Jacuzzi combined with the cool crisp taste of the champagne worked to erase any lingering inhibitions. The kisses grew more passionate and their tongues danced with increasing intensity while their hands caressed each other. They laughed and giggled – totally caught up in each other's desire and passion.

"Honey maybe we should relocate to the bed," he said in a whisper hoarse with passion. Sonni responded by climbing onto his lap straddling him. She showered his face and neck with kisses.

"Geoff, baby, I…I don't think I can wait any longer." It came out in a hoarse stammer between shallow heavy breaths. Sonni arched her back, caught her breath and moaned softly involuntarily shuddering as he initiated their lovemaking. Their eyes widened and locked in wonder and passion. Their breathing became shallow and rapid. He brushed her forehead cheeks and chin with soft tender kisses then smothered her lips with passionate yet gentle kisses. He ran his lips along her jawbone down her neck to her collarbone and continued down her chest nuzzling between her breasts and planting soft kisses on her erect nipples. They began the slow undulations of love accompanied with mutual soft moans of pleasure. As their mutual passion mounted their rhythm increased as did their heartbeats and breathing. Perspiration formed a soft sheen on her lowed eyelids. Sonni began to quiver, her breathing coming now as shallow pants in time with the rhythm of their bodies.

With her eyes tightly shut she let out a staccato shriek as she arched her back and drove hard grinding against him. Time stood still as the climax of their lovemaking washed over them together and yet separately, each in their own world of ecstasy. Sonni slumped against his chest in exhaustion. He gently rubbed her back and softly kissed her hair. With their remaining energy dissipated by the frenzy of their lovemaking, they embraced tenderly as their breathing slowly returned to normal.

The surrender to exhaustion was complete as Sonni looked up at him and softly whispered, "Umm, take me to bed, honey, I'm so sleepy."

He gently picked her up and climbed out of the Jacuzzi. Sonni grabbed the towels as he carried her over to the bed. He gently toweled her off, interrupting the procedure often to plant soft kisses on strategic erogenous parts of her body.

After he quickly toweled himself off, he pulled back the bedclothes and they collapsed in each other's arms surrounded by pillows.

"I love you, Sonni," he whispered as he gave her the last kiss of the evening. "Umm, love you too baby," she managed in a soft sleepy whisper that trailed off as sleep overtook her. They slept soundly snuggling together.

Chapter twenty

An old familiar sound from long ago stirred him from a deep sleep. Somewhere off in the distance a rooster began crowing to greet the new day. The sound took him back briefly to the five years of his boyhood he had spent in rural northern Indiana. The reminiscence was an ephemeral peaceful feeling he could never completely grasp and hold on to in his consciousness and always in an instant it faded away.

Back in the reality of the present it was ungodly early; the gray light of the new day was fighting to dispel the darkness. It wasn't yet winning. He glanced over at Sonni beside him. She was snuggled up with her legs drawn up and her back against him. Her breathing was slow and regular. He wanted to reach over and caress her, hug her, smother her with kisses but he held back not wanting to wake her up. She was still sound asleep and the perfect picture of peacefulness. So he lay there quietly close enough to smell the fragrance of her body. How did women always manage to smell so good he wondered? Her aroma was intoxicating to him.

He shut out the rest of the world and just focused on her. Would she be the one...would this time be different? *'Que sera sera'*...whatever will be will be – the poignant words of an old song from his boyhood came back to him. He allowed his thoughts to drift out of focus and dozed off.

He was awakened some time later not by a familiar sound but this time by the tactile stimulus of soft fingers running through the hair on his chest. He opened his eyes to see Sonni smiling at him.

"Oh did I wake you up, I'm sorry," she said very disingenuously with an impish grin. "But as long as you're awake, I want a kiss," she said with feigned audaciousness as she bent over him allowing her breasts to lightly brush against his chest as she pressed her open lips over his, her tongue gently probing until he responded in kind.

She moved her fingers slowly over his chest along his stomach and down to his thighs. Then softly kneading his quadriceps she now began moving her hand slowly higher gently brushing her fingers lightly over him coaxing him to peak arousal.

Geoff gathered her in his arms and she slipped her leg over his straddling him while at the same time taking him inside her. Time stood still as they lay there quietly looking deeply into each other's eyes savoring the feeling of intimacy. Then their lips met and they exchanged kisses that grew more passionate and hungry as their bodies slowly undulated in the sensuous rhythm of love. Their moans of satisfaction mounted to a crescendo as their mutual climax washed over them. Afterwards they lay there in silence savoring the fading feeling as Geoff ran his fingers lightly over the back of her thighs, her derriere and up the small of her back.

"Eak…," she squealed and shuddered involuntary as his fingers set off her ticklish reflex. Then in a fit of giggles she snuggled up against him planting soft kisses and a few playful nibbles along his neck.

"Umm, good morning, honey. That's the way I want to wake-up for the rest of my life," Geoff said running his fingers through the back of her hair.

"Good morning, baby. I hope you don't mind aggressive lovers."

"Sonni you can aggress me like that anytime, every day, all day long."

"I can get really horny in the morning when I wake up next to the right guy. And when I'm really horny I like to take the initiative and ride on top. I suppose it's the rodeo cowgirl in me."

"Did you ever ride rodeo?"

"Yes, I used to rodeo in western Maryland so I'm really good in the saddle – I can ride with the best of them."

"You can say that again lady, as they say in rodeo 'that was a great ride cowboy'."

"We could get pretty wild and raunchy back in those days – our mantra used to be 'Save a horse, ride the cowboy...YEEHAH!' I saw that on a bumper sticker once. I thought about getting it but decided it might attract the wrong attention."

"Daddies don't let your daughters grow up to be cowgirls...make 'em be librarians, schoolmarms and such...," Geoff parodied in a bad off-key baritone.

"Hey forget you... chauvinist, the days of barefoot and pregnant are over," she said feigning an assertive feminist tone.

"Aw, I'm sorry; I was just getting into the cowboy thing," he said with a disingenuous chuckle.

"I know, I can already read you like a book and you needn't apologize so quickly...I'm not that fragile, I won't break if you tease me. I'll just tease you worse in return," she said planting soft light kisses on his lips. As she tried to back off he held her tight. She resisted weakly for a few seconds and then surrendered to a long passionate kiss.

"I'll remember that...I don't ever need to apologize to Sonni."

"Hold on now... I didn't say that; you still have to treat me special."

"Okay I can see I'm not going to win this repartee. Look now that we've gotten the blood pumping I guess we can skip the morning PT," he said as he ran his fingers softly over her upper arms and shoulders. "Maybe we should just relax in bed and canoodle some more."

"Nothing doing, Geoff... C'mon get up. Let's go for a jog on the beach."

"You really want to? We skipped dinner last night aren't you hungry?"

"We've already satisfied my most important hunger this morning at least for now so let's take time out for a jog and work up an appetite for a big breakfast. Then we can stroll down Duval and come back for an early afternoon siesta."

"Something tells me you don't have sleeping in mind."

"Shoot, you read my mind, am I that transparent?"

"No, not at all, we are just on the same wavelength, I love you Sonni."

"Umm... love you too, baby. C'mon let's take a shower and get going."

It was about quarter to eight when they got down to South Beach and began their jog toward Smathers Beach. The sun had been up awhile but the air was still cool on the beach with a breeze coming in off the Atlantic. They jogged for about fifteen minutes and then turned back.

Once they got back to South Beach they decided to have breakfast on the outside beach patio of Seashells Cantina and Raw Bar under a giant awning. They ordered a pitcher of water to re-hydrate themselves and mimosas and coffee to drink along with their entrées of eggs Benedict and a Belgian waffle that they split between them. After they finished the meal they ordered another mimosa each and more coffee.

"This is absolutely perfect, Geoff – I'm so glad I suggested making this trip."

Geoff looked over at her with raised eyebrows and an amazed expression.

"Well okay, maybe you might have suggested it, but I convinced you to go for it. You were ready to weasel out with some lame prudish excuse about it being too premature in our relationship," she said smirking and goading him between chuckles.

"Hey now Sonni, that's not quite how I recall the conversation," he said playing it straight.

"You're wrong," she said trying to keep a straight face but failing as she broke out into easy laughter, "Oh forget it Geoff, I'm just being a brat," she said still chuckling as she leaned over and kissed him softly near his ear. "I feel so comfortable with you it makes me crazy. I guess it brings out the zany in me, I really am enjoying our time together."

"I am too Sonni, I especially enjoy sharing it with a crazy flashing rodeo cowgirl."

They paid the tab and went back to the hotel to shower and change and then went back out to Duval Street. On a walking tour they visited the Harry S. Truman Little White House Museum and the Hemingway House and then browsed the art galleries along Duval. They spent almost two hours at the aquarium where Sonni was in her element. She filled in explanations for Geoff after the tour guide finished his monologue at each attraction. As she expanded on one of his presentations the guide overhearing her turned to listen and then came walking over.

"Excuse me miss, you seem to have quite a lot of knowledge about all this. I'm curious; may I ask what you do for a living?"

"I'm a Marine Biologist at the Institute for Oceanography up in Daytona."

"Ah…um, well okay," he said in a chastised tone of voice. "Listen if I make any glaring errors please feel free to correct me. It'll be a learning experience for me."

"Oh, I think you're doing fine I just added a few mundane details."

After leaving the aquarium they walked out to the harbor end of Duval and checked out the Dock of the Gulf a large resort they had seen in brochures in the lobby of the Hacienda. They found a sumptuous restaurant - the Boat House - in the complex and decided to make reservations for a late evening dinner.

Then it was off to check out Margaritaville for some libations and a light lunch. When they got there the place was quiet, just the usual tourists who came in expecting to see Jimmy Buffett in person hanging out at the bar or maybe strumming his six-string. Hell, he was married with family and had his fingers in so many pies he didn't have time to schmooze down in Margaritaville in Key West. But the music was there and with it all the memories it evoked.

Almost as soon as they walked in and took a window seat where they could watch the passing crowds Jimmy's *Pirate Looks at Forty* came on the sound system.

"Ah, one of my favorite Buffett tunes."

"Oh that's such a sad song it's sort of a lament on life."

"It does kind of bring out the melancholy Sonni; all the missed opportunities and those I let slip away. I'm always reminded of the old German saying: *We get too soon old and too late smart.*"

"See, like I said it's a sad song. But you know today is tomorrow's yesterday Geoff, so if you resolve to make the most of the current moment there won't be any regrets in the future."

"Um hmm, you're certainly right about that. There is definitely no future in the past. Anyway, getting back to the present and looking into the future a bit, you mentioned you were working on your PhD. How far along are you in your studies Sonni?"

The server interrupted to get their order, the signature margaritas and two Caesar salads with shrimp.

"I'm ABD Geoff…oh excuse the academic acronym, I mean I've finished all my coursework and I'm researching my dissertation. I took dissertation a couple of semesters ago and had my topic approved by the committee and my Advisor, so now I'm researching the current literature in my area of interest. I've really just started to scratch the surface, but already I can see the real challenge will be to keep a narrow focus and resist the temptation to range far and wide."

"I'm familiar with the acronym. I had a conversation once with a server working tables in a favorite restaurant of mine in Palo Alto, California a long time ago. He mentioned to me that he was ABD, all but Dissertation as he explained. But he had put it on the shelf and was no longer actively making progress. I think it's a real shame to go so far, invest all that time and treasure, do all that work then leave it unfinished and not get the reward you've earned and so richly deserve."

"That's for sure Geoff, but sometimes it's unavoidable. I think it's probably like writing a book, sometimes life gets in the way and your priorities change."

"Amen, to that Sonni, I'm afraid I have to plead guilty to some of that. I've been thinking and talking about going back to school for graduate study probably since I finished my undergraduate studies but it's still an unfulfilled goal."

"Oh Geoff you should go back and get your PhD – misery loves company."

"Hey, now Sonni, you don't look all that miserable."

"No, I'm really not Geoff; life has been good to me I have nothing to complain about."

"Well if truth be known, I don't either except for possibly my own procrastination and maybe not putting out the extra effort to take advantage of all the opportunities that I've had and recognizing those that I didn't think were there. But despite all that I've done pretty well. Maybe it is that regrets are part of the baggage of wisdom."

"Everybody has some regrets Geoff; if they don't have, then I think they are very narcissistic self-serving and insensitive to their interaction with others. And you're definitely not in that category. So lighten up, stop second guessing yourself and being so self-critical."

"You're right Sonni; it's a bad habit I've gotten into."

"Oh I'm sorry Geoff I don't mean to be preachy. Hey, I think it's time we headed back to the room for our siesta, are you ready?"

"You read my mind Sonni, let's go!"

They paid the tab and headed out.

Chapter twenty-one

That night at dinner they watched the big red globe of the sun as it seemed to sink into the waters of the Gulf while waiting for their table on the Sunset Deck at the Boat House. They had gotten there early so that they could watch the sunset. It scorched a brilliant red path in the water as its reflection on the waves gave the effect of setting them ablaze and then slowly it disappeared beneath the surface of the water over the far horizon. The western sky was left riddled with streams of pink lighting up the scattered puffs of clouds like pink cotton candy.

Off in the distance they could hear the strains of bagpipe music coming from the pier as the Key West sunset celebration shifted into high gear.

Just after dusk they were seated by the windows overlooking the now dark waters of the Gulf. Sonni looked terrific in a cobalt blue silk and taffeta evening dress with spaghetti straps and strapped slides with medium heels. Geoff was dressed in vanilla dress slacks with a fitted dark blue flowered silk shirt he wore outside his slacks. Tan leather tasseled loafers which he wore sans socks completed his outfit.

"Shall we do champagne again, or would you prefer a change?" asked Geoff.

"I don't need a change unless you do."

"No reason to change what works for us, champagne it is," said Geoff.

"We'll have a bottle of the Moet Brut please," Geoff said to the server standing there waiting for their drink order. The server was back shortly with a bottle of Moet along with an assistant to set up the stand for the ice bucket. Expertly uncorking the champagne without the slightest bit of spill the server poured a sample for Geoff. After Geoff nodded his approval, the server filled their flutes and stowed the bottle in the bucket.

"Enjoy the champagne, I'll give you some time to look over our menu, I'll be back in a few minutes to take your order."

After ten minutes or so the server returned to take their order. They ordered crab cakes and the conch chowder for their appetizers and a Caesar salad followed by an entrée of fresh lobster tail and chateaubriand with black beans and rice and a side of mixed vegetables.

Another assistant brought a basket of assorted bread and rolls and filled their water glasses. The server returned with the crab cakes and chowder. Then after a proper interval he brought their salad in small cold glass bowls. The entrée was not served until their appetizer and salad plates had been cleared. Each course was served at a deliberately relaxed pace that allowed for maximum enjoyment of each course and time for conversation throughout the meal.

Halfway through their meal a reggae band began with a tribute to Bob Marley.

"Whew, I'm stuffed. I can't believe I finished all that. But it was so good," said Sonni when they had finished eating and the busman came over to remove their plates. As soon as he finished cleaning up their server wheeled over the dessert cart with an overwhelming variety of diet busters.

"I hope you left a little room for dessert, everything looks delicious," said Geoff.

"Um hmm but I think we'll have to run an extra half mile tomorrow after all this."

They settled on the Cacao Praline Soufflé along with the obligatory Key Lime Pie. Café con Leche and a snifter of Remy XO cognac for each of them completed their dessert course. After they had finished dessert the server insisted that they stay at their table.

"It's good for digestion, just sit back relax, dance, enjoy the music and the atmosphere," he had said with a deep jovial laugh.

They danced a few numbers and then the lure of a walk on the beach overcame them and they slipped away into the night. A gigantic Harvest moon was rising in the nearly cloudless sky as they shuffled along the beach at the water's edge. It seemed near enough to reach out and touch. A faint cool breeze blew in off the water.

"This is so perfect Geoff, it's like a dream. It's going to be awfully hard to have to leave it and go back to reality tomorrow."

"Forget tomorrow Sonni we still have tonight. Remember what you told me? Let's make the most of the moment." They stopped and nuzzled trading soft kisses with each other. "I feel like the luckiest guy in the USA," he said holding her close.

"And I'm the luckiest gal in the whole world."

"Okay, then I suspect that I'm the luckiest guy in the whole galaxy," he said laughing as he said it.

"You're not going to win…I'm the luckiest gal in the whole universe," she said with a chuckle.

"Whew, I guess we are a pretty fortunate couple. Did you know that if you make a wish on a Harvest moon it will come true before the next Blue moon?"

"Geoff, are you making that up?"

"Sonni, you're a doubter. I'll bet you don't believe in tooth fairies or serendipity either."

"Oh but I do and especially synchronicity. Don't you remember how we met on a beach and then planned this trip on a beach? And now here we are again on another beach. It's almost as if the beach and the water have drawn us inexorably together."

"That's a great observation Sonni, it seems that way to me also. What made you come up to me on the beach that first afternoon?"

"You really want to know?"

"Um hmm, that's why I asked."

"When I first saw your truck I thought that you were a friend of mine. Then when I got closer I realized you weren't him. But I saw your Colorado tags and I just thought I'd make a friendly impression on a visitor. Besides I liked what I saw."

"So the whole thing was mistaken identity," he said faking a dejected look.

"Well honestly that's how it started but after we started talking we seemed to hit it off and I was intrigued. So I thought I'd invite you to join me and hang out awhile and now I'm glad I took a chance. I usually follow my women's intuition and it's rarely ever wrong. Now it's your turn. What did you think about me?"

"I didn't know what to think. You waved and I looked around and didn't see anyone else near me that you could be waving to but then you kept going. When you turned around and came back, I thought maybe you were with the beach patrol and were coming over to give me shit about something. Then you came up with the body bag thing and your kinky sense of humor just bowled me over. So in my mind I was wishing that I would be so lucky as to get to know you. When you asked me to go to the Channel House with you I figured I was on a roll. Once I found out that not only are you gorgeous with a quick wild sense of humor but you're also very intelligent and educated to boot I thought I must be dreaming - you made a huge impression on me Sonni."

"You know, a lot of guys are intimidated by my education and degrees. I guess they feel they won't get the upper hand."

"I love intelligent, independent ladies, especially attractive ones. I can admire them without feeling like I have to protect them from the world. And I don't need control over them. All I'm looking for is a friend and a partner or if I'm really lucky and find someone special a soul mate."

"It doesn't sound like you have any hang-ups with commitment."

"No hang-ups. I'm ready Sonni, with the right lady I'm ready and willing."

"Hmm speaking of ready, I'm ready for the Jacuzzi. We still have time to stop off and get a bottle of champagne."

They stopped at a liquor shop with a window advertisement of champagne on ice and bought a bottle of Moet and some dark chocolate with almonds and headed back to the hotel. It was like turning the clock back to the night before except this time they skipped the movie and went straight to the Jacuzzi.

This time the affection was even more intense. They were getting accustomed to pleasing each other. It took a while to finish the champagne they were too busy cuddling. They fed each other chocolates and entwined their arms while they sipped their champagne. When Geoff poured the last of the champagne into their flutes they toasted Key West.

"I want you baby, but not here in the Jacuzzi. Let's make love in bed until we fall asleep in each other's arms," Sonni said as they finished their last sip of the champagne.

They quickly toweled off and slipped between the sheets into each other's warm embrace. After about fifteen minutes or so they had kicked the top sheet off and cuddled naked touching, caressing and kissing each other in all the erogenous zones they knew and then discovered new ones as they went along. When they could no longer hold out they surrendered to their desires and slowly made love changing and trying different positions as their excitement grew to fever pitch and the explosions of sexual ecstasy took control.

They finished off with soft passionate kisses. "Um I'm not finished yet baby, I still want more," she whispered hoarsely as she kissed his ear and neck. She nibbled on his neck. "Oops, ohhhh Geoff I'm sorry, I think I'm going to leave a mark, baby."

"It'll be my brand, honey. Leave all the marks you want." Geoff reached over and gently drew her on top of him, slowly caressing her as their arousal began anew.

Sonni was more intense this time. When she finally gave in to her desire she arched her back and drove hard against him as she moaned in satisfaction. Starting out maddeningly slow at first and then gradually quickening the pace yet still keeping perfect rhythm with him until her control slipped away and she surrendered to the pent up excitement of the sensuous feelings coursing through her. Together they climbed the stairway of sexual rhapsody until it totally overwhelmed their collective senses.

She collapsed gently into his arms. "Umm...hold me, hold me tight, baby."

Geoff ran his fingers softly over and down her back, over her derriere and down along the back of her thighs. He felt the weight of her body gradually increase as she relaxed and fell asleep in his arms.

Sometime during the night, he felt her slide off him and pull the sheet up over them. They awoke together as the early morning light streamed in through the shutters of the French doors.

"Good morning honey, did you sleep well?" he asked as they wrapped their arms around each other.

"Um hmm, how about you?" she asked as they exchanged kisses.

"Like a baby after you wore me out last night," he said.

"Hey, who wore whom out? I was so exhausted after we made love that I fell asleep on you, I'm sorry. I woke up in the middle of the night and I was still on top of you. I hope I wasn't too heavy for you."

"Not at all, your warm naked body was as light as a feather, I hope mine was as comfortable to you as yours was to me."

"Umm it was until your stiff member poking into my ribs woke me up. I was going to take advantage of it but I didn't want to wake you."

"Wake me next time honey, please... making love with you always takes precedence over a few extra winks of sleep," he said brushing his fingertips lightly over her shoulders and arms. She restrained his hand when he got to her breasts.

"Umm, what time is check-out, Mister Horny?"

"Not until one o'clock."

"Oh great we have plenty of time."

"Umm hmm and I know just how we can use it," he said pulling her close and kissing her neck and shoulders.

"Noooo," she said drawing it out coquettishly. "We can go for a jog on the beach, have a big breakfast and then get back here for a shower and pack up."

"My but aren't you efficient, you've got it all planned out. Did you ever take courses in Industrial Engineering, you know - time and motion stuff?"

"No, of course not, as a scientist and a businesswoman I'm just naturally well organized and time conscious. Today is a travel day after all. Let's go – up and at 'em," she said as she picked up the pillow and playfully pounded him with it.

"Now you begin to sound and act like my old Drill Instructor."

"Come on," she said grabbing hold of his arm and pulling him along with her to the shower.

They got wet and soaped each other up and rinsed off. Geoff started to get amorous but she coyly held him off.

"Now Geoff if you start something we're going to run out of time."

They went back down to South Beach and ran the same route as the day before. Then they went back to the beach raw bar where they had eaten the day before. After another big breakfast they went back to the room to shower and pack up.

Once they were finished packing Sonni's mood seemed to shift. "Oh my goodness, this has been such a fantastic weekend that I neglected to check my voice mail," she said in a somber voice.

"It'll still be there when you get home, why not wait to deal with things then?"

"Oh I can't Geoff; I need to keep in contact, I have some crucial issues in my life that I'm trying to resolve."

"Anything I can help with?"

"I …I'm sorry, I would really rather not discuss it right now if you don't mind. I'm not trying to shut you out Geoff, I just don't want to burden you with my problems."

"Oh no, that's okay, I understand. I don't want to butt into your personal life, at least not without an invite."

She retrieved her cell phone and punched in the number for her voice mail. Then with a frown on her face she disappeared into the bathroom and closed the door. When she came back out about fifteen minutes later Geoff was lying on the bed absentmindedly surfing the television channels.

"Geoff we need to get moving, I'm going to shower in here so we don't get distracted, if you know what I mean."

Geoff checked to make certain they had packed everything then sat down to wait for Sonni. This time she came out about a half hour later dressed in white shorts and a full cut flowery silk top in a gorgeous fuchsia.

"Wow, Sonni, you look fantastic. That top is a knockout."

"Oh thanks, Geoff – glad you like it."

Geoff had finished dressing and had on beige shorts and an olive green short sleeve Henley.

"You look great too. That shirt really brings out the green in your eyes, Geoff."

"Can I have a hug?" he asked.

"Umm hmm but just a little one," Sonni said holding out her arms.

"I love you, honey."

"Umm, me too...Geoff, please don't get me started. I know how you are and I know me also. We have a long drive ahead and I would like...I need to get back early."

Geoff's sensitivity kicked in, he was perplexed. Was it his imagination or was Sonni pushing away? She seemed to be preoccupied with getting back – or was it getting away from him. Was this the beginning of his old nemesis - lover's remorse?

She was focused on tomorrow. The intimacy of the weekend had somehow slipped into the past or gotten derailed by the technology of voice mail. He tried to put it out of his mind but it began to nag him and his wild imagination began to conjure up fatalistic scenarios of denouement.

They loaded up his truck and Geoff went into the office to drop off the key and check out.

"You're all set. Have a safe trip back to Daytona," the innkeeper said as he glanced at the address in their file. "Come see us again soon."

"Thank you, I sure hope I get the chance."

"You say that as if you don't believe it."

"I don't know what to believe right now."

"Your lady friend, she is very beautiful, very attractive. You make a nice couple."

"That's what I thought."

"Do you love her?"

"Yes."

"Does she love you?"

"I don't know."

"Ah, amigo… these things take time. An old saying - if you love someone set them free. If they return they are yours. If not… they never were."

"I've done that too many times. None of them have returned."

"Give her time, don't push her. You cannot change what is in her heart; you can only show her what is in yours."

"I wish I had your faith and patience."

"If it is to be, then one day your hearts will dance together… then and for all eternity. Vaya con Dios, mi amigo."

"Thank you my friend and may God bless you too."

Chapter twenty-two

Key West was like a honeymoon she had said but the return trip to Daytona felt like a recurring nightmare for Geoff. There were long periods of awkward silence. He tried to engage her in small talk but it was as if a curtain had come down between them. She had erected a barrier, a stone wall that he just could not breech no matter how he tried.

"Hey Sonni you're pretty quiet, are you getting tired?"

"No, I'm fine."

"Are you getting hungry, do you want to stop and get a bite."

"No, not really - I need to get home."

He could feel the tension mounting until it was almost thick enough to cut with a knife. He began to resign to his own frustration. Just as it seemed his life had presumably turned a corner the same old quagmire lay dead ahead. It had taken the wind from his sails. He was becalmed once again heading into a sea of heartache.

The silence became deafening until at last Sonni smashed it with her delivery of a broadside he knew was coming but hoped with every ounce of his being that it was just his crazy negative imagination getting in the way.

"Geoff, I think we need a time out."

The words he was prepared for still hit him like a shot in the solar plexus. It took his wind away. There was the old familiar physical pain in the pit of his stomach.

"And...?" he asked. "Is there anything else you want to say to justify your unilateral decision or is this just a brush-off?" His words were blurted out and after he said them he wished that he could take them back or at least had used more diplomacy.

"It...it's not like that, I'm not brushing you off Geoff. I like you, a lot...well even more than that - I have very deep feelings for you. It has nothing to do with you, it's me. It's just that everything between us has developed a lot quicker than I had anticipated and I feel like I'm out of control. I had a really wonderful time this weekend, maybe too wonderful. Please don't misunderstand. I... I just, well I think we just need some time off, I know I do. I need to catch my breath and sort out my feelings. And more importantly I need to settle some pressing personal business."

"I'm sorry I never meant to push, Sonni – I thought our feelings for each other were mutual."

"Oh they are, Geoff, it's just that the timing is all wrong, I'm not ready yet to make a commitment."

"Well time is one of my long suites Sonni. I'll back off and give you all the time you need if it will make you more comfortable. As long as I know I'm still the leading candidate for your affections."

"Thanks, Geoff, I appreciate that, I knew you'd understand."

"Oh I understand, all right. I'm just getting a little motion sickness from these constant roller-coaster relationships."

Sonni reached out and stroked the back of his neck. "I'm sorry... are you okay, Geoff?"

"Yeah, umm...yes Sonni, I'm fine," he said as he kept his eyes riveted straight ahead at the road. He just couldn't look her in the eyes. His grip tightened on the steering wheel and he hoped she didn't see his knuckles turning white.

The rest of the drive back was agony for him. He had once again fallen into the same trap. He had played his cards too soon - galloped when he should have been trotting.

It was the curse of his nature. *No matter how much you work out, how well you eat, how good your lifestyle – you cannot overcome your genetics and heredity* a doctor had once told him. Maybe that also applied to emotions he mused.

When they got back to her house they unpacked his truck methodically, the only communication focused on the task at hand. A shallow kiss and a lingering embrace left a poignant aftertaste.

"Call me during the week Geoff, please. I care a lot about you."

"I care about you too, Sonni...a whole lot."

It - whatever it was – was over.

On the way back to his motel Geoff stopped off at a liquor store and bought a liter of tequila a half gallon jar of cold grapefruit juice and a bag of ice. They had a promotion with a display of pint glasses embossed with NFL team logos. He picked out one with the San Francisco Forty-Niners. He had followed them back in the playing days of Joe Montana.

Back in his motel room he turned on the television and found an old classic movie just starting. That would do for background noise. He poured a double shot of tequila over ice and cut it with the grapefruit juice. Some lime would sure be nice but this would do. He pulled the bedcovers down, stripped off his clothes and collapsed on the bed with both pillows under his head and the drink on the nightstand. He stared at the television not really watching it.

He thought back over the last few months. Amy in Memphis, Jennifer and Lana in St Augustine and now it seemed like Sonni in Daytona was slated to join the others in his ignominious gallery of relationships that could-have-been or should-have-been. Damn, if only he had used more finesse.

He was on his fifth double tequila when the movie ended. But since there was still plenty of grapefruit juice left he couldn't let that go to waste. Besides he was just beginning to numb his feelings of inadequacy.

Sometime later after several more rounds of tequila when he could no longer focus on anything he fell asleep or maybe it was into unconsciousness.

~~~   ~~~   ~~~

And then came the rain…slowly at first, as if with hesitation and then suddenly with renewed force and vigor until the giant droplets beat a mad crescendo on the tin roofs of the compound.

Stripes of tracer rounds parted the tall grass outside the perimeter. Exploding mortar rounds added their thunder to the din. The pitch dark sky lit up with exploding star shells. The dance of death had begun once more.

Shadowy figures illuminated suddenly in the deadly aerial fireworks darted here and there seeking advantage, safety and shelter from the onslaught. The sweet fragrance of the surrounding plants and vegetation and the surreal beauty of thousands of flashes in the night sky were accompanied by the pungent odor of cordite and ground shaking concussions as barrage after barrage of explosive ordinance rained down mercilessly. As always the excruciating screams of the wounded and dying filled the humid night air with the ultimate horrendous counterpoint to the oncoming silence of death - horrific death. In an instant life is violently snuffed out. A living, breathing, thinking, feeling human is ripped asunder extirpated and rendered just another corpse - detritus to be stuffed into a body bag.

Somewhere, someone will grieve. Someone's life or maybe many lives will become a little emptier. Time will of course heal the wounds, but not the scars, they will remain forever. Time will certainly not cleanse the memories or fill the void left by the unfulfilled promise of a full life which will never come to fruition. The next generation and those that follow will suffer the loss of diversity to the gene pool. There is no way to know what might have been. The future will take a different fork forever changed.

The rage in him subsided as suddenly as it had overwhelmed him. The images of aerial phosphorescence, exploding star shells and rockets illuminating the tall grass of the jungle clearing like a surreal sea of doom faded out to black. The horrible spine chilling screams piercing the blackness of the moonless night ceased their macabre serenade. His labored breathing and racing heart settled down to the relative evenness of a shallow slumber – more like surrender to exhaustion.

He awoke – as he always did after one of these nightmares - in a fit of convulsions and a feeling of nausea which consumed him until the violent spasms of retching completed their course and he lay cold and shivering in the damp sweaty sheets.

'Alberta, Alberta – where you been so long...Alberta, Alberta ....' a refrain from an old Eric Clapton blues tune ran through his mind.

He swung his legs off the edge of the bed and with a bolt rose to his full height. With one motion he stripped the bed and threw the balled up sheets into the corner. On the way to the bathroom he paused briefly and grabbed the television remote to toggle on the television and channel surf for some news. Finding none he turned it off and tossed the remote back on the dresser in disgust. He had to know what day it was – what was going on.

The long shower felt good. He just stood there letting the water cascade over his head and face until he had figured out what he needed to do. First order of business was some PT and a jog on the beach. Then he'd check out of here, go have breakfast and find a new place with at least color television and cable news.

He went back to his old parking spot down along the strip. Today he jogged for forty-five minutes punishing himself before turning around for the return leg to his truck. Afterwards with the sweat pouring out of him he felt tired but exhilarated. He took another quick shower back at the motel and then checked out and headed off to Capt'n Jack's. A little routine was good for the soul he reasoned – you didn't have to think about it, it just became automatic.

In the opposite direction maybe a half mile from the SEE he found another motel. This was more upscale with a restaurant next door. The rooms were situated inside a veranda which ran throughout the whole complex. His room had a thirty-inch color television inside an entertainment cabinet and a king-size bed. There was the usual assortment of HBO, pay-for-view movie placards and a binder with local attractions, places to eat and entertainment venues.

After he had listened to the news on ABC, CNN and FOX and sampled several other network offerings he decided to spend some time back in the library. Once he got there he kept checking the aisles looking around expecting, hoping to see Sonni but after a few hours gave up and returned to the motel room to check out their selection of eateries.

That was the way the week went by. He was marking time, spectating not really participating. On his way to breakfast Friday morning his cell phone rang.

"Hello"

"Geoff… hi it's Sonni."

"Hey hello Sonni, I was just about to call you," he said lying a little. "How are you?"

"I'm okay Geoff, I…I thought you'd call. When you didn't I got a little worried about you."

"I'm a big boy, Sonni – I can take care of myself," he bit his tongue after he said it angry with himself for showing his feelings sardonically.

Sonni brushed it off.

"Geoff I know it's awfully short notice but I wanted to invite you over for dinner tonight. Are you doing anything?"

Geoff's mood lightened. "Oh no…nothing, I'm free. I'd love to come over for dinner. What can I bring?"

"Just bring yourself. How does Italian sound?"

"Italian is fine with me. I'll bring a bottle of Chianti"

"Ooh that sounds good. Try to be here for seven. You can come a little earlier if you like but I might still be cooking."

"Okay Sonni, I'll see you then, have a good day."

"You too Geoff, I'll see you tonight, bye."

Geoff closed the phone. He was ecstatic. Breakfast tasted the best it had for the entire week. He had a better appetite, stayed longer and had a few more cups of coffee savoring a pleasant feeling of anticipation.

Chapter twenty-three

The day could not go by quick enough for him. He caught himself fantasizing scenarios for the evening. He tried to force them from his thoughts but each time they rematerialized with another variation on the same theme - She had had a change of heart; She missed him immensely couldn't get him out of her mind; She realized that they were meant for each other and she could commit to him and still get her PhD with his love and support.

He waited until six thirty to go out and get the wine along with a dozen long stem red roses. Twenty-five minutes or so later he was parking in her driveway.

She answered the bell dressed in white shorts and a flowery green scoop neck top in a shade that emphasized the green of her eyes. Her blonde hair was up in a pony-tail in the back with strands coming down along her ears. She looked a little tanner than when he'd seen her last.

"Wow Sonni, you look terrific. Looks like you got a little sun," he said handing her the roses and putting the wine down.

"I've been working on the beach doing a survey. Oh roses, that's so nice! How thoughtful, you don't give up, huh sweetie? They are gorgeous, I really do appreciate them, thank you Geoff," she said giving him a nice hug. They shared a kiss – not a deep passionate one but one with promise.

"You have great timing Geoff; I just finished with all the prep. I need you to come help set the table." She had some light classical music playing in the background.

They set the table together, Geoff opened the wine and let it breathe and then they sat down to an appetizer of shrimp cocktail. Geoff poured the wine and offered a toast.

"Here's to a pretty, intelligent, sophisticated lady whom I was very fortunate to meet and hope to get to know better and better for a long time to come."

"Umm, thank you you're such a sweetie, Geoff; what am I going to do with you."

"If you need some suggestions, feel free to ask."

"We need to eat before the pasta cools and gets all stuck together."

The next course was a tossed garden salad with Italian vinaigrette dressing. Then Sonni brought out the main course veal parmesan in a chunky red sauce of tomatoes, herbs, spices, garlic and basil with asparagus and broccoli on the side.

"Sonni, this veal is excellent. And the sauce is one of the best I've ever had," he said after the first few bites. "How did you find the time to prepare all this?"

"I cheated a little; my mom came over last night and helped with the sauce. Everything else I got done this afternoon."

"You, amaze me Sonni, you are good at everything you do."

"I'm just driven I guess, kind of a perfectionist. I got that from my dad. He became a head chef for a large restaurant in Annapolis after his stint in the Army."

"Do your folks live nearby?"

"Yes, they live right here in Daytona. They moved down here right after I returned from San Diego after my second divorce."

"It must be nice having family close by."

"Yeah it is, we are pretty close. I get to see them for all the holidays and sometimes on weekends I'll pop in over there."

"What about brothers or sisters, do you have any?"

"Just one sister, she's married and lives out in Montana – Billings or Bozeman I get them confused. She's a professor at Montana State."

"Ah, then it's probably Bozeman. That's where their main campus is located," said Geoff.

"I do need to get out there and visit, but it'll have to wait until after I get finished with my PhD."

"I've promised myself a return trip to Billings one day, maybe we can go out there together," Geoff said.

Sonni didn't respond leaving Geoff feeling foolish and a little dejected.

When they had finished the main course Sonni asked, "Are you ready for dessert now or do you want to wait a bit?"

"I'm ready whenever you are, what do we have for dessert?"

"Fresh Bing cherries and French vanilla ice cream. Let's have it now. I'll make some coffee also."

She ladled out two servings of cherries from a colander and added a big scoop of ice cream. "Be careful, the cherries still have pits."

"How come, you mean you couldn't take the pits out?" he said with a pretense of complaint as he chuckled wryly."

"Oh don't be a baby."

He was glad to hear that. They had been far too serious over this meal. He needed to break the mood and inject a little levity.

Sonni poured the coffee and sat down to begin eating her dessert. She nibbled on a spoonful of ice cream as she silently watched him. Then all at once she blurted out,

"Geoff I…I think I might be pregnant," she paused and then continued, "I guess we should have been using condoms. I'm not ready for a baby yet, I don't know…what are we going to do?"

It was a bombshell out of the blue. This could be good or bad. Was she looking to him for support or pushing away?

"Sonni how sure are you that you might be pregnant?"

"I should have gotten my period by now. I'm almost a week late."

"You know lots of things can cause that. Are you always regular?"

"I know that Geoff but it's not in my history. I'm never late; I'm either on time or a day or so early. And we did have a lot of sex."

The cold clinical characterization of their love-making as sex, leaped out at him feeling like a sucker punch.

"Sonni all I can say is we'll just have to wait and see what develops. But I don't think you should jump to conclusions until after you've seen your gynecologist and get solid confirmation."

"Well what if I am?"

"Well to be cold and clinical, then you'll have a choice to make... either have the baby or terminate."

"I don't think I can go through having an abortion."

"Then you have a second choice...either put the baby up for adoption or keep it."

"And if I want to keep it?"

"Then you can either rear it as a single mom, or better yet marry me and we can rear our daughter together in a happy loving home."

"And how do you know it would be a girl?"

"Men's intuition – if she were even less than half as good-looking as you I'd have a real fight on my hands to keep the boys away."

"Oh Geoff... be serious please, what do you think I should do?"

"I think you should marry me; I love you Sonni."

"But I can't marry you Geoff, at least not yet - I'm not ready to get married again. I've got to settle some personal issues first and I need to get my PhD - I promised myself."

There it was the objection he needed to overcome.

"Look Sonni, I think we are getting way ahead of the situation. We need to cross the bridges when we get to them."

"Oh you're right Geoff; it's just that...oh, I don't know. Maybe I'm being selfish."

"Forget that notion Sonni. Right now you have a lot on your plate. I can see that. All you can do is take things one day at a time and deal with them. I'll support you one hundred ten percent in anything you do."

He wanted to grab her in his arms, to hold her tight and make her understand that he would not let anything or anyone hurt her. But he knew he was powerless, just a bystander who could observe but if he got involved would only complicate matters. He had already played his aces...it was up to her.

"Some dinner... huh? I'm sorry Geoff, if I spoiled it for you. I just didn't know how else to tell you. I didn't want to just blurt it out over the phone."

"The dinner was fantastic; I enjoyed everything but especially your company. And thank you, thank you very much for sharing your confidence in person. Things will work out Sonni. And they'll work out for the best, they always do. Come on lady, let's get these dishes cleaned up and square away the galley."

He rinsed the dishes and she loaded them into the dishwasher while he scrubbed the pots. In a little over half hour they had the kitchen and dining room all cleaned and straightened out.

"Wow that was quick Geoff, thanks a lot for helping."

"Teamwork always beats individual enterprise in anything. Hey it's still early, do you feel like maybe taking in a movie?"

"Why don't we just stay here and watch something. I've got a bunch of old movies that I love and haven't watched in a while. Do you like old classics?"

"Oh yes, I sure do. What have you got?"

"Take a look in the cabinet and pick out something you like."

Geoff walked over opened the cabinet and rummaged through the selections. He spotted a DVD of Sabrina the original version with Humphrey Bogart and Audrey Hepburn – it was still sealed.

"How about this?" he said holding up the case.

"Ohh that's one of my favorites - I found it in DVD and haven't gotten around to watching it yet."

"It's always better when you watch it with someone," he said.

"Geoff I have a bottle of Chardonnay do you feel like an after dinner drink?"

"That would be perfect; it'll complement the movie."

"Here you go, open it for me please, I'll get some glasses."

Geoff poured the wine and they sat down on the couch to watch the movie. Sonni at last was close beside him.

"Do you know any French Geoff?"

"I had two years in high school. I remember just enough to get me in trouble which I did once long ago on a business trip to Paris."

Audrey Hepburn was singing La Vie En Rose. "Ooh that song has such a poignant sound. I wish I knew the words," Sonni said.

"It's one of my favorite songs, I've heard the English transliteration but I don't think it does justice to the original colloquial French version by Edith Piaf which has a haunting tragic quality. It seems to mirror the tragedy of her life. One of the main verses was transliterated loosely to *If you give your heart and soul to me, then life will always be like living with rose colored glasses.*"

"That's really sweet. We should be so lucky," she said.

"Yeah…the tragedy in the classic sense is the oftentimes unrequited nature of love given the caprice of life itself," said Geoff.

"Ooh now that is poignant."

"It's just my subjective interpretation; maybe I need a pair of those rose colored glasses."

The movie ended with Lionel and Sabrina together on a ship bound for Paris. There had been some emotional scenes about relationships but it all worked out in the end and as in so many of the old Hollywood classics they presumably lived happily ever after.

"I love these old classics, even if they are a little Pollyannaish," said Sonni.

"So do I Sonni, they broke the mold on those old pictures with the lion's share of trash that passes for blockbuster entertainment these days."

Sonni stifled a yawn. "Oh goodness, I'm sorry. It's not your company, Geoff. I've just been on an emotional roller coaster this week. I'm really pooped out."

"I guess it is getting late. I'd better be shoving off. Sonni look - please call me and keep me advised. If there is anything I can do to help… anything at all, or if you need to talk, please give me a call, anytime. You're not alone in this."

"Thanks Geoff, I will, I promise."

"I love you Sonni and I'll be there for you. You just have to let me."

"I know Geoff… I know, I love you too."

Chapter twenty-four

He spent the weekend and the following week taking long runs on the beach. He had settled into a routine. Up at first light or a little before, stretching, push-ups, sit-ups, abdominal crunches, leg-ups and then a one and one half hour run on the beach. He thought about joining a health club but dismissed the idea because of his tenuous situation here in Daytona.

Right after the beach run he would shower and have breakfast at Capt'n Jack's. They knew him now by name and had his order which never changed already started when they saw him pull into the parking lot. After breakfast on the good days he'd work a few hours on his writing. If he lost focus it was time to head back out to the beach for another run. On those days he'd have a turkey sub sandwich to hold him until dinner.

On Thursday he had finished his morning jog and was pulling into the motel parking lot when his cell phone rang. It was Sonni's number.

"Good morning Sonni, how are you doing today?"

"Good morning Geoff, I'm doing marvelous. How are you doing?"

"I'm doing fine. You sound really perky today."

"Oh I am, I have some great news…I got it, I got my period. I am sooo relieved."

"That's great, fantastic Sonni, your life is back to normal. I'm very happy for you."

"Oh goodness yes Geoff I am so happy, you have no idea."

"Why don't we go out for dinner somewhere and celebrate Sonni, are you doing anything tomorrow evening?"

"Oh I've got to work late Friday. I'll be up in Jacksonville. But Saturday I'm free."

"Well why don't you come jogging on the beach with me Saturday morning and we can plan out a mutually agreeable agenda?"

"Okay where can I meet you?"

"I'm staying at the Grande Daytona Motor-Hotel on the strip next to Trattoria Italia."

"Oh yes, I know the place. I've been to the restaurant. They have great lasagna."

"Let's try for around oh-seven-thirty."

"That's good, I'll see you then."

"Have a great day Sonni."

"Oh I will Geoff you do the same, bye."

"I love you Sonni," he said into the ether. She had already terminated the connection.

His new high from the prospect of seeing Sonni again lasted for a day. On Friday afternoon as he was going out for dinner he noticed a missed call on his cell phone. He rarely carried the thing around, usually just left in his truck. He'd missed some calls that way but if they were important either they would call back or he would. And with cell phones there was always voice mail. He didn't need to be in constant communication with the world. The voice message was from Sonni,

"Hi Geoff…about tomorrow, Can I have a rain check? I'm going to be stuck up here in Jacksonville over the weekend. Sorry."

He listened to the message a couple of times letting it sink in. He should have seen that coming he told himself. Just chalk it up to lessons not learned. He should have given her more time.

Of course maybe he was jumping to conclusions. Perhaps she really was working the weekend up in Jacksonville. She hadn't ever lied to him before, why would she start now?

He decided he wanted to dine somewhere by the water. He needed to watch the waves and drown his disappointment in libations. It might be a good night to take a taxi and leave the driving to the pros. So he went back to the room and called a local taxi.

A half hour later he was at the Channel House. He was seated at a table by a window where he could watch the boats sailing up the Intracoastal. It was in the same area where he and Sonni had sat on their first night together. Maybe it was even the same table. He hadn't taken note of the exact table that night; he'd been too engrossed in Sonni's company.

He ordered steamed mussels on the half shell in a spicy marinara and the grouper platter. Drinks for happy hour were two for one so he got two chilled beer mugs of tequila grapefruit with a lime squeeze.

In short order the server brought out the steamed mussels along with a basket of warm Italian bread. The mussels and the sauce were excellent. He had finished them off along with a mug of tequila grapefruit and was munching on the bread crusts and downing his second mug when the server returned with the grouper platter.

"I guess you liked the mussels?" she said chuckling as she picked up the plate of clean shells without a trace of sauce left.

"They were excellent, miss...just excellent."

"Can I get you anything else?"

"Give me about five minutes and you can bring another round of drinks."

"You got it, sweetie."

He was halfway through the grouper platter and on his fourth mug of tequila grapefruit when he heard a commotion at the other end. He looked up to see a group of six people coming in from the bar and being shown to a large round table down at the other end. His eyes picked up a familiar face that his brain did not register immediately. He looked up again to verify his first impression.

It was her, damn. It was Sonni with some young dude; their arms entwined both laughing as they took a seat with the others.

He finished his grouper although it had lost all the taste it had only a few moments earlier. Now it was just something to swallow and wash down with his drink. He glanced over at the table a few more times but they were all engaged in their own world, oblivious to anyone else and besides his table was far enough away that he wouldn't be obvious unless one was scanning the tables.

When his server came back to check on him he asked for the tab. As he left his table he walked slowly towards the bar glancing at Sonni and pausing deliberately until their eyes locked for an instant and he saw her reaction. He gave a slight nod of his head then shifted his eyes away and continued on through the archway to the bar.

He thought about leaving. If he had his truck he probably would have left. But he decided on another round. Let's just see how this plays out, he thought to himself. He found a seat at the bar and ordered a round.

"Did you have dinner tonight in the dining room?" the bartender a pretty petite blonde asked.

"Yes, I did, why do you ask?"

"That's an unusual drink; I've never served one before until tonight. And tonight I served a bunch on the dining room service bar. Does it have a name?"

"I call it a Chihuahua," he said.

"Why, yes of course, it would have to be, it's a Greyhound with tequila."

"Well hey…you're a very insightful barkeeper. I also like to call it a poor man's Margarita…similar taste but not as sweet and less expensive."

"I'll remember that, enjoy it, I'll keep it filled for you," she said with a chuckle.

"Geoff" A familiar voice called out his name. He turned around to see Sonni.

"Didn't you get my message?"

"Yes, I did. You said you were stuck up in Jacksonville and would be working up there over the weekend."

"That was my first message. I called again later and said that the weekend work had been canceled. And that if you wanted to reschedule we could do that."

"I never got any other message Sonni, except for the one you just sent me in there."

"No…no I called and left a message on your cell phone."

"There was none Sonni."

"Then I must have punched up the wrong number – someone has a strange message on their voice mail."

"Well, Okay. So you're back in town. Will I see you tomorrow?"

"Geoff, I…I've made other plans. When I didn't hear back from you I figured you weren't interested or you had other plans."

"Hey now Sonni how could you possibly come to that conclusion. Haven't I made it obvious enough that I'm in love with you? And now I see you tonight getting cozy with somebody else."

"He's just one of those regulars from here that I told you about," she said as the young man walked up behind her.

"Hey babe, what's up? You said you were going to the ladies' room. And who the hell are you?" he asked looking crossly at Geoff. "Are you trying to steal my girl?"

"I'm not your girl, Keith," Sonni said moving closer to Geoff.

"Come on, let's get back to the party," he said grabbing Sonni and pulling her away.

"Stop it Keith, I be back in a minute."

"You're coming back now," he said grabbing her around the waist.

"Leave me alone," she said a loud voice as she forced him away.

"Don't give me a hard time, bitch," he said lashing out and smacking her in the face.

Geoff jumped to his feet and lunged at him grabbing his arm in a lightening quick arm twist and joint lock wrenching it violently behind him which brought a scream of agony and in one motion he swept his legs slamming him down on his knees. "Son, you never hit a lady, not ever - but especially not when I'm around and I happen to know the lady."

"Ahh, you're breaking my arm, you bastard."

"You're lucky I didn't rip it out of the socket and stick it up your butt. I'm just getting started; your head will be next."

"Hey, hey…what's going on here?" security said running over.

"This creep just struck this lady who happens to be a friend of mine. I'm giving him a little hands-on remedial education on social graces and proper respect for a lady," said Geoff.

The security guard looked over at Sonni who was rubbing her cheek, "Did he strike you miss?"

"I…I'm okay."

"Hey Randy I saw it all," said the man sitting next to Geoff. "This here gentleman and the lady were talking and this punk came over and got real obnoxious to him, then grabbed her and when she pushed him away he smacked her across the face."

"Get on your feet, you're out of here. Let's go get your tab settled," said security as he hauled Keith up off his knees and roughly dragged him away by the arm.

Geoff drew close to Sonni. "Are you all right?" he asked in a low voice.

"Yes, Geoff. But I…I think I'm going to need a ride home tonight."

"We'll have to cab it over to my place and pick up my truck. Are you ready to call it a night?"

"I just have to say goodnight to some friends, I'll be right back."

Geoff sat back down. "Thanks for your corroboration my friend, for a few minutes there I thought I'd be shown the door also," he said to the man sitting to his left.

"Don't mention it. I've seen that punk in here a lot before. He's a troublemaker. I never could understand what she sees in him, she's way too attractive for a low-life jerk like that."

"You've seen them together here before?"

"Yeah, a few times, he always seems to treat her like a piece of property, if you know what I mean."

"Who knows what attracts women, if I did I'd write a book and get rich," said Geoff.

"I'll be looking for that book, if you ever get it figured out. Maybe then I can find me a nice woman, settle down and quit hanging out in bars."

"Amen to that brother."

Sonni came back to the bar and Geoff paid his tab and asked the bartender to call for a cab.

"It was nice talking with you, sir, you have a good night," Geoff said to the man.

"Thank you, sir, you do the same."

They rode the cab in silence back to Geoff's motel. Once they were in his truck and back out on the road Geoff broke the silence, "So who is that guy, Sonni?"

"You remember the first night we met on the beach?"

"Yeah, how can I forget?"

"Um, well he's the ex-boyfriend in the body bag I was joking about."

"Too bad it wasn't for real then."

"Yeah, I can't seem to get rid of him. He doesn't consider himself my ex; he still thinks he can control me."

"Maybe you need to give him a clear unambiguous message."

"It's more complicated than that Geoff, it's a long story."

"I've got the time, if you want to share it with me."

"We only dated for about a month. But when I told him I didn't want to see him anymore he refused to accept it. He kept coming around even though I threatened to call the police a few times."

"Maybe you should have followed through and called them."

"He told me if I didn't go out with him that he would go to the police with evidence he has to implicate me in a drug ring he claims was going on at my boutique along with prostitution."

"There's no way he could do that, is there?"

"Geoff it's a reputable business but it's one that is always suspect. I have no control over what my girls do on their own time. As a businesswoman I can't fire people without just cause. It's very hard finding good help, especially at the wage I can afford to pay. If I have clear evidence against one of my girls, I'll remind her of my standards of conduct for employees and put her on probation. If she doesn't straighten out she's terminated but it all has to be documented."

"Sonni, my sense is he's a pretty unsavory type. Why would the police believe him?"

"Geoff it's common knowledge that the police use a lot of unsavory types as informants. It just takes an overzealous vice detective along with a cooperating prosecutor trying to make a name for themselves and they can trash my reputation and the good will I've built up in my business and I'll lose a significant part of my customer base. And I need that income stream from the boutique to help pay my student loans, living expenses and home maintenance."

"Geez, do you think it would come down to something like that?"

"I can't take the chance that I might jeopardize my business with the scandal of a police bust and all the attendant gossip even if it's later cleared. The damage to my good will and reputation won't go away. People are slow to change their initial impressions. It might even have a negative impact on the value when I try to sell it - that is if I'd even be left with a business to sell."

"So this bastard is holding this as leverage over your head, blackmailing you to try to keep a hold on you like some kind of chattel."

"That's why I'm so driven to complete my PhD. Once I get that piece of paper I can command a much higher salary. Then I can sell the boutique, easily pay off my student loans and start a new life somewhere else."

"In the mean time you have to dance in his saloon."

"Yeah, but at least I get to choose the music."

"Damn, I wish I could do something to help."

"You can't Geoff. There's nothing you can do. I got myself into it; I'll have to get myself out of it."

"What about legal recourse."

"I don't have any. There's no hard evidence of either criminal or civil wrongdoing. It's all hearsay except for maybe that slap this evening. Besides I can't afford it, I think it would be throwing good money away at a bad situation. If I bide my time maybe he will hang himself legally and disappear. At any rate I just need to concentrate on my dissertation and get my PhD."

"Whew! It sounds like you've touched all the bases; it has to be awfully frustrating."

"Yes I have considered all the angles and it is frustrating, I've been at it a long time. It's just going to take patience for a while longer."

"So where do I fit in, if anywhere Sonni?"

"Geoff I'm juggling too many things as it is. At this point I really just need a good friend to lean on if you can stand that role."

"Well to be honest, I was hoping for a much bigger part in your life."

"I know, Geoff. You've made your feelings crystal clear and I thank you for that. It's refreshing to meet someone who doesn't play games."

"But no matter how hard I lobby you won't budge – no chance for a promotion?"

"Geoff I love you as a person, as a friend… a very intimate friend but it can't be more at this point in my life. The timing is wrong. Please understand."

"I can't stand by and watch you get abused by this jerk - I won't."

"I know I saw that tonight and I thank you for that but you can't confront him either. That would only complicate the situation for me. And you might get yourself into something that you'll regret."

"I'd regret nothing in regards to your safety and well-being."

"I know Geoff," she said taking hold of his forearm and gently squeezing while looking deeply into his eyes with a look that made him ache for her. "But I don't want you to get into jeopardy because of me. I care about you way too much...I mean that with all my heart. Please, just stay out of it Geoff... for me."

"What about after this is all over, after you've gotten your PhD and rearranged your life?"

"I can't predict the future Geoff but perhaps one day I might surprise you and show up on your doorstep and then maybe we can pick up where we left off."

"And if not, we'll always have Key West," he said wryly. "But I'll take Key West over Paris any day."

"Oh so would I Geoff, as long as I could be there with you."

They had been sitting in her driveway for the last ten minutes or so. Geoff reached over and gathered her in his arms. She slipped her arms around his neck running her fingers gently through the hair on the back of his head and kneading the tight muscles of his neck.

"I won't say goodbye Sonni," he said. "I'll just say so long... see you at the next rodeo." Their lips met for a long passionate kiss that felt every bit like those of long ago in Key West and yet somehow held an unspoken promise for the future...wherever and whenever that was.

Chapter twenty-five

G eoff agonized over the situation he once again found himself in - wondering why he usually managed to get to the dance only to wind up watching the lady of his dreams waltz away leaving him with a sick empty feeling in his gut.

He needed to give Sonni some time to get her life together and the space in which to do it. Pushing her any harder would only alienate her feelings for him. At least that's what the conventional wisdom of relationships dictated. And lord knows he had had more than his share of personal experience to back up that premise.

Well he wouldn't be able to do that from her backyard. He knew himself all too well. There was nothing left to do but get back out on the interstate and drive until the raw feelings turned numb with time.

Heading north on I-95 up the east coast of Florida he took the familiar ramp onto westbound I-10. The east had once again receded in his favor as a place to find contentment. As the miles rolled by he had to acknowledge the familiar gnawing feelings of inadequacy, regret and emptiness but he chalked them up to just another payment on the price of freedom and his inviolable grasp of personal integrity. He would be who he was. He would remain in the final analysis true to himself – if the people of this world saw things counter to his inclinations well that was their right, it mattered not to him. He had paid his own way and would exit at the time and place that pleased him. He was through trying to please the others.

'Alberta, Alberta where you been so long? ...ain't had no lovin in a very long time' – the familiar refrain of Eric Clapton's rendition cascaded through the passageways of his consciousness. It was good company. It beat a soothing counterpoint to his solitary condition. It also passed the time.

As he passed the familiar signs for Eglin Air Force Base he once again reflected on his feelings of honor, courage and commitment. Oftentimes he wished he had made the Navy his career. Separation and discharge at times felt like a divorce. When he hit Pensacola he had to stop. They were the fly-boys, a different breed but still Navy blue.

The Hanger Deck restaurant and lounge was right off the causeway at the east end of the beach. It had a huge patio set in amongst a circle of palm trees with umbrella tables interspaced with potted plants. It was surrounded on two sides by a covered patio with a thatched roof and large overhead fans to circulate the air and keep it cooler than the outside patio. The covered patio featured a large oval bar and more tables. Two sets of French doors led inside, which was much cooler than outside, to a more formal dining area with a large trapezoid shaped bar.

He took a seat at the outside bar so he could feel the fresh breeze coming in off the gulf. Looking over at the back bar the bottle of Maker's Mark caught his eye. It brought back a stream of memories - all good - giving him a peaceful easy contented feeling. His mind wandered back over scenarios of past choices he had made while traveling along his chosen forks on the highways of life. There was nothing he could do about them now. He was here at this time and place by virtue of the composite sum of his past choices. Many of them - perhaps even the majority - he reluctantly admitted to himself had been less than optimal. But he was here and still in the rodeo – that was some kind of consolation.

Life is a rodeo – you spend a lifetime like a bull-rider struggling for your eight seconds of happiness on the big stage. Or perhaps it is Five-card Stud – you get to play the hand you're dealt, and run, fold or walk away. Oftentimes there is an awful lot of standing water and stones in the road. It's like a walk through a minefield with one difference – you can survive a minefield but you can never survive life…in the end it will kill you.

The bartender very efficiently served up his usual request for tequila grapefruit topping it off with two lime slices and Geoff began to record his thoughts on his ubiquitous steno pad. He had a lot of thoughts, heavy ones. It was therapy; it helped him cope or maybe just helped pass his solitary moments between fantasies of grandeur. There was a sparse crowd. That was good, it allowed for better concentration. It also increased his imagination to fill the void of social interaction.

He had lost track of time and wasn't aware of her taking a seat next to his. A tin cigarette case resounded as it was set down on the bar. Seconds later a companion lighter was nosily set down alongside the case accompanied by the exasperated and artificial sound of a throat being cleared.

He glanced over in the direction of the interruption only to lock eyes with an attractive blonde. Her petulant scowl instantly morphed into a pout.

"Oh you are alive, I was ready to call the paramedics," she said raising her eyebrows a little as she looked over at him her eyes darting between his pad and his face until finally fixing her gaze intently on his eyes. She was dressed or nearly dressed, depending on your sensibility, in a low-cut cream colored silk sundress with spaghetti straps over her bare shoulders that revealed a lot of well-tanned cleavage. A slit up the side of the dress exposed a likewise well-tanned athletic looking leg including a good bit of her very shapely thigh.

"Pardon me; I guess I was really engrossed in my writing. I didn't see you take a seat."

"What are you writing, that's so important?"

"My next million-seller, I hope."

"Really, what's it about?"

"I'm being facetious; it's just some raw stream of consciousness that I might someday be able to salvage as scenes in a novel."

"So you're a writer?"

"Yes, that's how I like to think of myself on my good days."

"Is there anything else?"

"No, no you are right, of course – every day is a gift."

"You say that as if you don't believe it."

"I only believe what I can embrace."

"Oh...I like that; is that some sort of suggestion?"

"My name is Geoff, and yours?"

"Vicki Lynn or just Vicki for short whichever suits you I'm not particular."

"I'll call you Vicki only because I'm lazy, but I do like the Lynn part. It's a pretty name for a very pretty lady."

"Stop it, you're embarrassing me."

"Sorry Vicki, I really didn't mean to, but somehow I don't believe you embarrass that easily."

"You weren't always a writer, what did you do before?"

"Is it that obvious?"

"Women's intuition."

"You're scaring me."

"Come on, come clean."

"Okay, okay... I am heir to the Tabasco fortune."

"So, you're from Louisiana?"

"Of course, my great granddaddy was the first to swim Lake Pontchartrain with his hands tied behind his back."

"Really! Well my granddad was the first to jump from the Royal Gorge Bridge in Colorado wearing bungee cord suspenders on his lederhosen."

"Then we have a lot in common, ancestors with great athleticism."

"Either that or their grandchildren are great bullshit throwers," she said rubbing her shoulder against his.

"I stand by my story."

"I'm not surprised; it's a man thing isn't it?"

"Are you having a bad time with some guy, and you've decided to take it out on me?" he asked with mock annoyance.

"Oh double entendre I like that."

"It was unintentional."

"Um hmm, so then it was a Freudian slip?"

"Vicki did you come over here just to beat me up?"

"Oh no sweetie, I just like to give back what I get. But if I told you that you have a nice body would that make you feel better?" she asked with a whimsical look.

"Geez Vicki, I'm trying hard to figure you out but it's a bit like playing blind man's bluff and so far you're beating the pants off me."

"There you go with another sexual inference. You really are horny, huh?"

"Vicki you play a tough game."

"Relax honey. Don't tell me you can't handle a little pursuit."

"Well I think I do better as the pursuer than as the pursued," he said.

"I like to reverse roles on my conquests, it's a nice challenge, "she said as she sipped her drink.

"So far you're giving a stellar performance," he said.

"Oh thank you for that. So will you be having dinner with me?" she asked.

"Only if you ask me nicely," he said now beginning to enjoy the verbal duel.

"I think I just did," she said reaching over and stroking his thigh.

"Vicki, I would be delighted to accompany you to dinner."

"Great, I'll go reserve a table for us." She got up and went off to the hostess stand. He followed her with his eyes taking in her slim hips and well-toned calves enhanced by the heeled slides she wore. She was back in a flash.

"I asked for a window seat with a water view. They said it should be about twenty minutes. Do you like the water, Geoff?"

"Um hmm, that's one of the reasons I came here it has a very soothing effect on me."

"Oh it does for me too. I love being by the water, living by the water and most of all making love by the water."

"Yes I ah, I definitely agree with you. We must be cut from the same cloth," said Geoff.

"Ooh now that's kinky, I like that. I can dress in your clothes and you can dress in mine."

"Umm... I think you misinterpreted something in that old cliché."

"Oh sweetie come on you are a bit inhibited now aren't you? That's okay, we'll work on that."

The hostess came over to show them to their table which was inside. As they followed the hostess to the table Vicki slipped her arm around Geoff's waist and drew him close. "Keep me warm, baby it's so cold in here my nipples are getting hard and sticking out," she said in a low voice as she moved her face close and nuzzled his neck.

Geoff put his arm around her shoulder and held her close, "Always ready to accommodate a lady in distress."

The table was in a secluded cluster behind a partition of greenery and a small fountain that had a series of miniature cascading waterfalls. They were the only ones seated in that section. Vicki slid into the semi-circular booth and pulled Geoff close next to her. She took his hand and placed it on her upper thigh.

"See how cold I am; look I've even got goose bumps on my legs. Ooh your hands are nice and warm. Rub my thigh baby and warm me up."

"What shall we have to drink, wine or maybe champagne?" asked Geoff.

"Let's skip the alcohol and stay sober, making love is so much better sober, don't you agree?"

"I won't argue against that."

"Some men are so dense when it comes to good sex. If they would just lay off the booze they wouldn't have problems," she said stroking his thigh.

"Um hmm, I think that's a commonly known but usually ignored fact."

The soup was lobster bisque; it was thick and piping hot. For an entrée they had Halibut Steak broiled with rice and fresh asparagus. They ordered a pot of green tea and sipped it throughout the meal.

For dessert they shared a bowl of fresh fruit. When they had nearly finished the fruit Vicki speared her fork into the last slice of orange and brought it up to Geoff's lips. As soon as he had accepted it she slid her hand around his neck drawing his face to her waiting lips. It was a passionate sensual and very erotic kiss. It had the intended effect on him as her other hand rubbed his thigh and then moved over to settle lightly on his crotch. He could feel himself getting aroused as they broke off.

"You are going to spend the night with me aren't you Geoff?" she asked in a soft seductive voice as she looked deeply in his eyes while she probed his crotch with her fingers.

"Uh…Vicki, that's an offer that my body won't let my head refuse right now even if my head wanted to."

"Mmm, yes I can tell that, c'mon baby, let's get out of here," she said as she gave his thigh a firm squeeze.

Chapter twenty-six

G eoff followed her Mercedes in his GMC four-by-four with a combination of guarded anticipation and gnawing apprehension bombarding his thoughts as he mentally reviewed the interaction of the afternoon and early evening.

He hadn't really asked the right questions, didn't really know anything substantive about this very sensual and attractive woman who had so far seduced him while he in turn had offered not even token resistance.

It was out of character for him even given his recent string of romantic misadventures. But he trusted his instincts and knew they would kick in when and if the situation warranted.

She turned down a beach access road and took it all the way to the end. Her house a very modern looking beach house similar to those one would find in Malibu, California was raised on steel stilts on a bluff overlooking but just off the beach. It would take a storm surge of probably over forty or fifty feet he estimated to threaten her decking which ran around the entire perimeter of the house. It had a large front deck with passageways wide enough for chairs on either side leading to the rear deck. Both the front and rear decks had retractable awnings over double sets of French doors.

"You've got a really gorgeous place here," said Geoff as they started up the oversize stairway to the deck.

"Thank you; it's my play pen… the real love of my life."

They went inside to a large foyer with a cathedral ceiling and a spiral staircase that led to the loft bedrooms. The lower level was an open plan which including the foyer featured a large kitchen with a cooking island complete with built in grill and a counter-top dining area. A formal dining cluster and surrounding living room with double doors leading to a study completed the lower floor plan. A huge flat-panel home theater system was the focal point of the living area along with two outsized couches and a love seat. A large low oval mahogany coffee table shaped like an artist's palette on dual pedestal legs set between the couches.

"Make yourself comfortable Geoff. I've got a pretty eclectic selection of wine in the fridge, pick out something we can sip on, I'll be right back," she said as she disappeared upstairs.

Geoff selected white Bordeaux and began searching the cabinets for two wine glasses and a cork remover. He found them naturally in the last place he looked along with the corkscrew in the drawer below. He was just opening the wine when Vicki quietly slipped behind him and wrapped her arms around him. He was immediately aware of a pleasant scent of lilac.

"That fragrance smells marvelous on you Vicki."

"Thank you Geoff, I'm glad you like it. It's one of my favorite," she said running her hands over his chest. "Oh Bordeaux, an excellent choice, I would have chosen the same," she said still holding on and looking around him. "Here let me help with the glasses. There's an ice bucket in the lower cabinet just to the left of the sink." She let her hands slide off and Geoff turned around and caught his breath as he took in his first look at her since she had come downstairs.

"Oowwweee Vicki, that outfit is… oh my goodness, you are going to drive me erotically mad."

She had on a lavender lace halter baby doll with matching garter belt and string bikini bottoms. The allure of her long slender legs was enhanced by white thigh high stockings and matching strapped slides with heels. He ran his eyes slowly over her admiring her near nakedness.

"C'mon baby, go get the ice bucket bring it on over to the couch and play with me."

Geoff filled the ice bucket about halfway with ice and some cold water, took a hand towel from a closet and walked over to the couch.

"House rules for male guests - nothing but boxers allowed on my couch; you'll have to strip off some laundry baby," she said in a seductively sexy voice.

He obliged feeling a bit strange and began wondering if he was getting into some kind of a kinky bondage situation. But he tried to force it out of his mind as he poured the wine.

"Ooh…you have a nice hard body, I like that in my lovers," she said running her fingers over his deltoids, across his latissimi dorsi and pectorals and down his abdomen. "Let's have a toast," she said raising her glass… "Here's to good living, good loving and hot sex."

They clinked glasses and took a sip of wine with Vicki staring intensely at him from over the rim of her glass. She was definitely in her element, in control and enjoying every minute of it almost like some sort of dominatrix. The thought flashed through his mind making him feel a bit unsettled.

"Vicki, what line of work are you in that allows for such a sumptuous living."

"I'm into Real Estate as a realtor and investor, but why do you ask now? We have more important things to discover about each other."

"I just like to add a little dimension to enhance the experience."

"Are you married Geoff?"

"No, not anymore, I've been there twice but it didn't last. What about you?"

"I'm married, at least on paper. We have a very open relationship. He does whomever he wants and I do the same. Ha, ha sometimes we both do it together in the same room and then switch partners."

"Ah…Okay, I think that…that's probably a bit more than I needed to know."

"Ohhhh, does it freak you out that I'm bisexual?"

"Uh…no, not at all, well maybe that he, uh…your husband is. I mean I can understand two women getting together but I'm sorry the thought of two guys leaves me cold."

"Oh phooey, you need to explore your sexuality."

"I'm well aware of my sexuality, Vicki, it doesn't include men."

"How sad Geoff that's a very narrow sexual orientation."

"Well I'm very catholic in a lot of ways but my sex life is staunchly parochial."

"Oh honey… we need to get you to relax so we can enjoy ourselves."

She got up and went over to the entertainment cabinet powered up the system and slipped a DVD into the recorder. A title flashed on the screen *Virgin Sorority Girls give it up for Alpha Mau Omega*. From a drawer next to the cabinet she took out an electric blue four by six by three-inch-deep tin with hand painted Asian designs on the cover and sides along with a rolled up linen napkin. She brought them over to the table and put them down between them and eased into his lap as the first scene came on. She took a sip of wine from his glass and then brought it to his lips holding it while he sipped.

The scene in the video showed a young coed dancing on a bar in a sorority house and removing an item of her clothing after each song until she was naked. Then she was joined by a guy dressed in just low-rise boxer briefs and they gyrated and ground their bodies together. Finally, they disappeared upstairs and another coed took their place.

Vicki slipped the straps of her baby doll down over her arms and let the top fall down around her waist exposing her firm breasts with hard nipples. She buried his face in her cleavage squeezing her breasts over his face. Then she smothered his mouth with her open mouth sucking his lips and flicking her tongue into his mouth.

"Baby, come on don't be so stiff. Let's have some fun," she said as she slipped off his lap and reached over to take the cover off the tin. "Here, I've got something that will loosen you up."

Inside the cover was a black velvet pouch holding a mirror that she took out and placed on the linen napkin on the table. Then she opened the wax paper wrapping beneath to reveal what Geoff suspected he'd see - the illicit white powder of what he guessed was cocaine.

"Whoa hold on, Vicki…you're way out of my league lady, I don't mess with that stuff and I don't feel comfortable around anyone who does."

"Oh baby come on, I can take you places you've never been. It's a whole new world. You just have to relax and let it happen. We can fuck until dawn; you'll get off so far you may not find your way back."

"Yeah that's what bothers me among other things."

"What's bothering you, baby, tell mommy? Let me take you inside me and fuck your brains into mush."

In the scene on the screen a guy was on top having rough intercourse with a coed who clearly was not enjoying the experience. A towel under her buttocks was spattered with drops of blood. The sick exploitation and putative rape was repugnant to him.

"Vicki I don't have the right – hell nobody has the right - to tell you how to live your life as long as it doesn't impinge on anyone else's rights. And I'm going to try really hard not to be judgmental but it's obvious to me that you and I come from two different worlds. We have some serious compatibility problems that defy reconciliation."

Geoff stood up, retrieved his jeans and slipped them on.

"Oh come on baby, you're not going to leave me here all horny now are you?"

"Thanks for your company this afternoon and evening Vicki, it was enjoyable as far as we went but now it's taken an ominous twist that I just can't countenance. It's time for me to take my leave."

"What a pity, we could have had some really outrageous sex."

"We'll never know now, will we? Look, don't bother to get up Vicki, I can let myself out; goodnight and goodbye Vicki," he said as he slipped on his docksides which he had left in the foyer by the door. As he walked out the door he closed it behind him and never looked back.

In short order Geoff was back out on the I-10 interstate once again heading west. He tried to block all thoughts from his mind and concentrated on the traffic. It was just about twenty-one thirty hours early enough to get in several hours of driving then stop in time to still get a good night's sleep. He began to curse himself for his earlier stupidity of not paying attention to the signs and bailing out of a bad situation before it became totally bizarre. Okay so he was a little slow on the uptake but he had come to his senses in time, just chalk it up to...ahhhhh damn just forget about it.

He turned on the radio and scanned the stations and caught sound bites of the current crop of country rap music. He wasn't in the mood for that. Still scanning, he finally found a blues station and left it on.

The miles flew by and he began to see signs for Mobile Alabama. He remembered his promise to himself to visit New Orleans on his next swing through but it would be probably after midnight by the time he made it there.

So let's just get a place in around Mobile and rack out early and make it to NO fresh tomorrow, he thought to himself. He drove past several more exits until he found some signs for the cheap motels that you find convenient to the interstate. The first place he checked out had a vacancy so he took it and shut down for the night.

Chapter twenty-seven

The next day dawned a little later than Geoff had anticipated the night before. I guess the body just needed some additional sleep to recover mentally as well as emotionally, he mused. Anyway it didn't matter; he had no schedule, no appointments to keep nor any deadlines to meet. So after his morning PT and shower he searched out a place for breakfast. He looked through the usual advertisements in the motel room and a flyer caught his eye. A place called the Breakfast Gourmet opened at four o'clock in the morning and served until two in the afternoon. Perfect...now if he could only find it.

It turned out to be on the service road but on the eastbound side of the interstate and the ubiquitous orange construction cones made for the usual detour from hell. But once he got there it was well worth the aggravation. The menu was almost the size of a magazine replete with short vignettes about the history of the different varieties of breakfast entrees. They had all the cereals – both cold and hot, pancakes and waffles in twenty-seven varieties, eight variations on French toast, and eggs in any style – fried, boiled or poached with of course the specialties like omelets, benedicts, hashes and creamed beef along with assorted breakfast meats of beef, ham, pork and poultry. Then there were the breakfast rolls, the muffins and pastry section with even five different flavors of brioche. It was rare to find a restaurant where anyone even knew what a brioche was let alone to have several choices of them on the menu. Different varieties of specialty coffees and teas and even champagne for those so inclined rounded out the very comprehensive menu.

Geoff took his time ordering and of course ordered more than he could finish because he wanted to sample as many of the items as he could and because in the morning his eyes could always grasp more than his stomach could hold. But he did himself proud. He was finishing his second large latte which came in a pint glass and munching on his second brioche as the server came by to check on him.

"Oh my goodness, bless your appetite. How do you eat all that and stay so skinny?"

"It must be the genes."

"Really, well you have to let me know where I can buy a pair of them," she said laughing. "Can I get you anything else today, maybe something to go…if you manage to get hungry by tonight?"

"You are in a jovial mood this morning, aren't you?" he said laughing pleasantly.

"I always am, I enjoy meeting people, it's interesting, and I like what I do."

"That's the secret to happiness they say, just keep smiling no matter what."

"Oh I do, and it works, my cheerfulness rubs off on a lot of people."

"You have a nice day, Suzanne he said reading her name-tag."

"Thanks, honey, you do the same. Come back and see us again."

He had spent an hour and a half at breakfast but it had totally replenished his spirit. It was time to hit the interstate. The Crescent City was calling him.

New Orleans had always been a catharsis for him. He remembered his first trip to Mardi Gras following a painful second divorce. It was happy - it was sad, it was good - it was bad, it was beautiful – it was ugly…a study in contradictions. Maybe that was why it had become his chosen city. It was who he was; it captured the bohemian essence of his soul. From the I-10 interstate he merged onto I-12 so he could take the causeway. There was something spiritual about New Orleans that he felt as he drove across the Pontchartrain Causeway. He needed to be here when he needed to heal. And so it was again this time.

He got a room off Airline - beneath the causeway, it advertised hourly rates. The registration window sported half-inch iron bars. The clerk was friendly, if a little surprised by his request for three nights with an option to extend. She gave him the keys to three rooms to make his choice.

The room he chose had heavy burgundy velvet drapes on a double rod over yellowed lace sheers. It was a sentimental reminder of simpler more romantic times back before the need for iron bars over windows. The room exuded the atmosphere of a brothel, not that he had first-hand experience from a visit to one or at least would ever admit to it. There was a shade underneath the curtains that pulled down to block out most of the daylight. That was important since it was always daylight by the time he managed to overcome the attraction of Bourbon Street and crawl back to the quieter confines of his room to crash and gain a few hours of sleep only to repeat the cycle again later that day until he could no longer discern the day of the week. New Orleans for him was a non-stop party.

He drove around reacquainting himself with all the places he'd seen on his past sojourns to the Crescent City. He spent several hours on St Charles taking the streetcar from South Carrollton to Canal Street and then on the return trip getting off near Copeland's where he stopped for a late lunch-early dinner. It was not even carnival, but it was still a party. To him New Orleans was a town where you could relax, let your hair down and get as crazy as your own inhibitions would allow. It cleansed the spirit. You laughed at yourself in admonishment vowing never again to take yourself so seriously. It was like a shot of the elixir of life – a renewal, a reminder that in the grand scheme of the universe you are but a grain of sand for an instant of time.

He remembered a little coffee shop he had found in Metairie on a prior visit to Mardi Gras. They served great lattes and had fresh brioche. He managed to find it again and made a mental note to make it his place for breakfast.

High on his agenda was a visit to Club 747 on Bourbon Street to see if his favorite pianist was still there. He had made the acquaintance of Al Boudreaux several years ago when he had gone down to New Orleans to celebrate his jubilee birthday. Back then Mr. Boudreaux was close to ninety but still of strong voice, amazingly limber on the keyboard and yes, still a ladies' man - one of the stellar last talents of a fading generation. It had been a memorable evening back then. He was surrounded by strangers but felt as though he were among old friends. It was great to be alive and experience these times. They were too few and too far apart.

It was still light out when he got to Club 747. From the street he could recognize the strains of Al's unmistakable keyboarding and his distinctive vocal accompaniment. As he entered he glanced over at Al sitting at the keyboard. Al looked up and gave him a nod of recognition as he took a bar-stool nearby. This was going to be a special afternoon. As soon as there was a break between songs he approached the piano with a 10-spot.

"Mr. Boudreaux, no special requests sir, just keep jamming the blues, I'll leave the choice to your discretion."

Al looked up from the keyboard, "I don't remember names son but I remember faces. You've been in here before."

"Yes I have, thank you, sir. I don't know how you can recall one face out of the thousands you must see. I've caught your performance several times and have one of your CDs."

"Ahh, I remember the people who appreciate my music," said Al with a chuckle as he took a sip of his drink.

"Oh I'm sure everyone appreciates it but not everyone shows it. Too many people are in too much of a hurry to stop and enjoy life's special moments."

"That's the secret of a long rich life – live every hour as if it were your last," Al said with a grin and a deep chuckle as he began to massage the keys.

"Amen, Mr. Boudreaux."

The afternoon passed too swiftly into evening. Al played his last set and graciously accepted a drink, a Johnnie Walker Black as Geoff remembered, before he began to break down his gear and pack up for another day.

As Geoff stepped back out onto Bourbon St. the night was alive with the sounds of laughter and merriment. Music from the clubs spilled out onto the street as he passed each place.

It was rock, it was jazz, it was blues, it was zydeco – the sounds all blended together in a pleasing cacophony along with the sidewalk entrepreneurs to produce the synergy that was the magic of Bourbon Street and made it arguably the soul of the Big Easy.

"Hey, I'll bet I can tell you where you got them docksides?" a street vendor called out to him.

"Yeah, I'm sure you can," he yelled back over his shoulder as he kept walking. The rest of the evening passed into oblivion with no real conversation at the several bars he visited. It was like this more times than not – just throw away nights where he felt invisible, isolated from all forms of human contact.

Sometimes he welcomed the solitude, tonight he needed to interact. He wanted the stimulation of a conversation with anyone about anything. He just wanted to escape from the prison of his own thoughts and the attendant rehash of past experience with the inevitable constant mental stream of what-ifs. Life would happen for him sooner or later, although oftentimes he wondered if he shouldn't push harder – take a hand in his own destiny. The old bromide of *everything comes to those whom wait* was wearing thin. He was living proof of the adage *he who hesitates is lost*.

The night had degenerated into an inner battle with his old demons. He wouldn't win, it was unproductive – it was time to call it a wrap. On the way back to his truck, which was parked on Carondelet, he chanced upon one of the ladies of Bourbon St. – or maybe her purview was the entire French Quarter. She caught his eye and fell in step with his pace.

"You look like you have a lot on your mind."

"Yeah, a bit," he said.

"Why don't you buy me a drink and we'll talk about it."

"Sure, why not."

"I know a place just a block over, they have billiards. Maybe we can shoot a game?" she said.

"Sure, I'm up for some pool," he said.

It was the usual dark bar of the French Quarter – smelling of smoke and stale beer with three pool tables and an assortment of video machines off to the side. He got some drinks and change for the pool table. They played a few racks and then she suggested 9-Ball for five bucks a rack.

"Okay, I'll go a couple racks," he said without really thinking about it. He was forty bucks in the hole before he knew what hit him. "Lady, you are some good hustler," he heard himself blurt out.

"I just got lucky honey I'll give you a chance to even it up – how about double or nothing?"

"Well sure, can't quit now," as soon as the words came out he knew for sure he'd regret them. To his surprise, he won – it was easy, maybe too easy.

"Well there goes the rent money. Me and my baby will be back out on the street again," she said with a dejected look at him. "Look, I really need the money – even twenty bucks would help out a lot."

He reached into his pocket and withdrew his wallet. He pulled out a c-note and said he'd need to get change.

She gave him a sideways glance, "Oh honey, you carrying too much cash for the quarter. Look, take it all out of your wallet and stick it in another pocket – put it in your inside coat pocket. C'mon let's get out of here," she whispered nudging him towards the door.

Back out on the side street he recognized the pick before it sprung. Two dudes were arguing loudly by a car parked at the curb with its door wide open.

"Oh, Damn, left my lighter back there," he said as he quickly spun around and strode swiftly away fighting temptation to break into a run which would call attention to himself but quick enough to slip away and back into the crowd surging back onto Bourbon Street. Lessons once learned the hard way are not easily forgotten. Still he cursed himself for getting into the situation in the first place.

As he walked towards Canal St. a sudden craving for fresh pizza came over him. He wondered if Luigi's was still there. He began to get a little discouraged as the blocks passed with just t-shirt shops. He'd get his hopes up at each new intersection only to be disappointed again. Just as his desperation level was reaching its peak the sumptuous smell of fresh tomatoes, pepperoni, sausage, peppers and jalapeños drifted his way. There it was – his safe harbor in a storm. He was downing his second slice when this young woman - well really young actually, she looked young enough to be his daughter – interrupted his meal.

"That looks so good; may I have a bite of your pizza mister?"

"Oh, sure," he said, a little too surprised to refuse.

She took a large bite and as he watched her she gulped it down as if it were her first meal of the day.

"May I have another bite?" she asked.

"Look, why don't I just buy you a slice? What would you like on it?"

"Oh no thank you, please I…I'm sorry to have bothered you."

"Hey, I'm not bothered and I insist. You look pretty hungry."

"Well, okay, I'll have the same as you had."

He bought her a drink to wash it down.

"Thank you, you're so nice. You're a sweet man. Are you by yourself?"

"Yeah, it's a bad habit I picked up a long time ago. What about you?"

"I'm by myself also, do you live around here?"

"No, I'm just passing through, staying at a local motel."

"Would you like some company for tonight?"

"I, uh…"

"Mister I'm not a hooker or anything; I just need a place to stay for tonight."

"Look, how do you know I'm not some deranged serial killer or rapist?"

"My women's intuition, tells me I can trust you."

"Hasn't your intuition ever been wrong?"

"I can take care of myself."

"My name's Geoff, what's yours?"

"Danielle."

"Okay, Danielle, you've got a place to crash. Let's get out of here."

The sun was beginning to rise and the delivery trucks were out in force replenishing for the next day's business as he drove slowly through the narrow streets until he got to the Airline on-ramp. Once on Airline it was a straight shot to his 4-star accommodations.

"It's nothing special Danielle, but I didn't expect I'd be entertaining any company. Why don't you take the bed; I'll sleep over here on the couch."

"Geoff, you're so kind, but I don't want to put you out."

"No, please that's just the way it's got to be. I'll be fine."

It was almost one o'clock in the afternoon when he opened his eyes and looked over to see her still sleeping all curled up in the covers. He shaved and took a quick shower, dressing in the bathroom. When he came out he found her beginning to stir.

"Good morning Danielle or actually good afternoon. Did you have enough sleep?"

"It was great, Geoff, much more than I usually get."

"I'm going out to fuel up my truck. You can get cleaned up and dressed in some privacy and then we can go hunt up some breakfast when I get back if you'd care to join me. I'll wait for you outside."

"Thanks, I'd like that I can be ready in about fifteen minutes."

"Take your time, there's no hurry Danielle. I probably won't get back for a half hour."

He pulled back into the motel parking lot about twenty-five minutes later to find her waiting for him. She had a fresh scrubbed look with a clear complexion that didn't need makeup. Her natural blonde hair was tied up in a ponytail with strands of hair framing her face.

"What are you up for, a big meal or something light?" he asked as she climbed into the passenger seat.

"I'm not a big eater when I first get up, but it's up to you Geoff."

They went to his Metairie coffee shop and had lattes and brioche.

"Danielle, if you don't mind my asking, where's home?"

"I don't mind; I, at least, owe you the courtesy of a reply. I was born and reared in Beaumont, Texas."

"How was life growing up in Texas?"

"Oh my life was great until mom died. Our family life died with her. My dad grew remote and changed after he got remarried and didn't have time anymore for me or my younger sister. He was totally absorbed in work and his new wife. My step-mom was a real witch who didn't want us as friends or step-daughters."

"That had to be devastating to be alienated by a cruel woman moving in to monopolize the affections of your dad after the tragic loss of your mom, how did you handle that?"

"I tried to play mom for my sister as best I could, but I guess I wasn't good enough. After I graduated high school she got in with the wrong crowd and wound up overdosing on ecstasy at a rave."

"Oh Danielle I am so sorry," Geoff said wincing at what he'd just heard.

"That's when I left home, five years ago."

"Where did you go, what did you do?"

"I went to Austin for a while and got a job as a waitress. Then I met a guy who promised me the world but turned out to be a pimp who just wanted to add me to his stable. So off I went to Dallas and then Fort Worth. I got so tired of users and takers one night I just got drunk and thumbed a ride on an eighteen-wheeler heading to Florida. The driver pulled into a truck stop in Baton Rouge and told me it was time for me to pay for my ride."

"Geez, those kinds of predator slime balls are all over these days."

"Yeah they are, but this one met his match. I scratched his face, gouged his eye with my thumb jumped out of his truck and ran into the C-store. Then I caught a ride to New Orleans with this young couple I met in the restaurant."

She recited it all showing almost no emotion. It was obvious that she had been de-sensitized by it all.

"Girl you are something else. Life has visited tragedy on you and knocked you down in so many ways and yet you just get back up on your feet and keep fighting. I'm awed by your resilience and tenacity."

"I get that from my mom. She survived breast cancer, then developed cervical cancer and came through a hysterectomy with flying colors only to learn they hadn't gotten it all. It spread to her liver and pancreas. She had radiation and chemo and came home weighing eighty-seven pounds. The cancer never killed her, pneumonia did."

"Whew, oh my God, Danielle I..., I'm sorry to have made you recount all that tragedy." Swallowing hard to clear the lump in his throat he reached across the table and held her two hands in his slowly shaking his head marveling at her courage.

"It's okay Geoff; I think I needed to hear myself talk about it more than you needed to hear it, she said as her eyes welled up with tears. Maybe it will get me back on track."

"Danielle, are you okay?"

"Yeah…I am now, it gets easier the more I talk about it, thanks for listening."

"Let's get out of here and get some air."

They drove over to the garden district and Geoff suggested a stroll through the Tulane campus.

"The last time I was here I was looking for the graduate admissions office," he said as they walked along the open quad of the campus along St. Charles. "I wanted to enroll in their master's degree program in Political Economics."

"It doesn't sound like you did, why not?"

"I guess life got in the way. I shelved that project just like so many others before and since. I read somewhere that *life is what happens when you plan something else.*"

"Maybe you didn't want it badly enough."

"Wow…that's an amazingly astute observation for someone your age."

"I'm sorry, I didn't mean any disrespect."

"It's okay; I'm not offended, not in the least. It's actually refreshing to get called to account. So what's your plan for the rest of your life, Danielle?"

"Oh, oh, now it's my turn in the barrel. You remind me of my dad. I haven't thought about my dad in a long time. Telling you my life story kind of brought back a lot of memories. Maybe it's time I went back to Beaumont and tried to reconnect with him, if he's still there."

"Hey now, that'd be a great start, Danielle; time heals a lot of differences. I'm sure he's worried about you and missing you a whole lot right now."

"Yeah, maybe; I need to find a way to make it happen. I don't want to chance hitchhiking anymore."

"That's not a problem, Danielle; if you don't mind a long drive in my truck I'd be happy to take you back to Beaumont."

"Geoff, please, you've done so much for me already; you have been like my old dad, the one who was married to my mom. I don't want to take advantage."

"Thanks for the compliment. I would love to have had a daughter like you; and no you're not taking advantage. I'll be getting as much out of seeing you turn your life around as I hope you will."

"Are you sure it's not out of your way?"

"Not at all, I'm heading west; I'd welcome your company."

"Thanks, Geoff, you really are an angel."

"Well I don't know about that, I'll settle for just a guy who doesn't want to see a pretty young woman, who has had more than her share of grief, hurt anymore. Let's go retrieve your stuff get your clothes laundered, maybe shop for some new outfits and have dinner at Copeland's. We also probably ought to find better accommodations here on the avenue."

She had some things stored in a locker at the bus terminal. They did the laundry then found a discount ladies' boutique and got her some new traveling clothes. Geoff checked out of the airline motel and found a two room suite at the Hotel Villa d'Orleans.

It was eight-thirty in the evening by the time they finished all the errands and sat down to dinner at Copeland's. Geoff ordered some champagne.

"Here's to Beaumont Texas, and a new start on the rest of your life Danielle," he said raising his glass.

"Geoff, you truly are an amazing man; how will I ever repay you for all you have done for me."

"My reward will be watching you get your life back together. I really believe that things happen for a reason Danielle, and you are long overdue for some good fortune. I'm glad I was somehow chosen to play even a small part."

Chapter twenty-eight

I t's about two hundred sixty miles from New Orleans to Beaumont
Texas give or take a few crow miles, which comes out to about a
four hour drive more or less depending on how much you want to
bend the speed limit and how many stops you make for snacks, drinks,
restroom breaks and gas. By the time they finished packing, checked
out and had breakfast it was nearly straight up noon when they hit the
interstate heading west.

They had lingered over dinner the night before, even having
dessert. The champagne had a relaxing effect and Danielle's pleasant
southeast Texas drawl had become a little more pronounced.

She had worked as a candy-striper at the local hospital in
Beaumont as a teenager after her mother had gotten sick so she could
be near and spend more time with her. She was gifted in academics
and had made the honor roll throughout her entire time in high school
and had gotten inducted into the national honor society. She had spent
the summer before her senior year taking care of her mom at home
after her mom's latest bout with cancer and the radiation and chemo
treatments.

At the end of the summer a week before the beginning of her first
senior semester her dad had allowed her and her sister Tammy to take
the bus to Galveston to visit their favorite aunt as a consolation for
their summer of care giving. That weekend her dad had called with

the grim news that mom was in the hospital with pneumonia and not doing well. They hurried back as fast as they could.

They got to the hospital twenty minutes too late. A priest had intervened to allow them to see mom one last time. Afterwards they had flown into a rage at their dad because he hadn't called them sooner.

"My dad looked crushed, his shoulders were bent over and he just sat there and took our verbal tirade. 'She was always so strong,' he said. 'She had beaten all the odds, won all the battles. I didn't think this would get her either. I was wrong. I'm sorry guys,' and then he got up and went inside their bedroom and shut the door. I still remember the hurt expression on his face and the faraway look in his eyes as he listened to us.

After that we didn't see much of him. I think his closing the bedroom door that night was symbolic of him shutting us out of his life. He began working long late hours and started dating someone from work. They were married almost a year after my high school graduation."

"How did you get along with your step mom?"

"We didn't… really, she was only interested in being daddy's wife; she didn't seem to want any part of being our step mom."

Danielle had tried, she said, as hard as she could to be a role model for her sister Tammy even though her sister's talents were more artistic and less academic than hers. But the need for her sister to belong and the influence of peer pressure had proven stronger than family ties.

"Tammy began to get remote and we grew apart. She began resenting my replacement as her authority figure and rebelled. She got in with a wild clique at school and started going to a lot of late night parties and sleepovers and hung out until the wee hours. Sometimes she would be gone for days, God only knows where.

Then early one Sunday morning the county sheriff came to our house to advise us that my sister had been taken to the hospital after she was found comatose at one of the popular teen rave nightspots. She had ingested a large amount of ecstasy and had been declared brain dead. She was on life support while the hospital evaluated whether she was a candidate for organ donation. None of her friends ever came by to pay their respects, visit or share any details so we only knew what the police told us."

Geoff listened in silence growing sadder by the moment as the realization that he had no answer for her pain sank into to his consciousness. He struggled mentally to find the words to give her some comfort and renewed hope for the future.

When she had finished her story he looked at her in silence for a minute struggling to compose himself and told her simply, "Look, Danielle take my cell phone number and keep it with you, always. Call me - please, anytime for anything you need or if you just need to talk. I promise you I will be there to listen and help, no matter what time of day, night or day of the week."

At breakfast Danielle had bounced back to her seemingly carefree self. But once they were back underway on the interstate she withdrew a little. Geoff could sense some tension beginning to mount. They had already passed Baton Rouge before she finally broke the silence.

"Geoff, I'm getting freaked out. I don't think I can go through with this. I…I'm sorry I got you involved."

"Danielle, relax. Take it easy! I'm not going to dump you anywhere you don't want to be. We can go drive by your old house, visit your old neighborhood, maybe your old high school, and the downtown shops. I think you'll enjoy seeing what has changed after five years. If I'm wrong, I'll drive you back to New Orleans or anyplace else you want to go."

"What if my dad doesn't want to see me, or doesn't even want to remember me?"

"Then he'd be going against his human nature as a father. I can't speak from experience but all the father daughter relationships I've seen or heard about have always been positive. I'm betting he would give the world to hear your voice again and have a chance to reestablish a relationship that he let slip away."

"Maybe, but…"

"Young lady, I think you have put it off long enough. You need to at least try. We'll find a place to relax a bit and then when you're ready you can try to call him."

"Do you think he'll talk to me and not slam the phone down?"

"If you were my daughter whom I hadn't seen in over five years and you one day gave me a call it would be a dream come true. I'm betting it'll be the same for him."

"You're not going to let me out of it are you?"

"You've come this far in the process don't stop now, just make a phone call Danielle, that's all I'm asking. If it doesn't work out, at least you will have tried. That's all you can do. That's all anyone can ask. You owe it to him, but you owe it to yourself even more."

"Oh you're right… you're right, of course Geoff. I'm sorry for being such a wimp."

"Stop it Danielle, you're far from a wimp. I have seen nothing but a very tenacious resilient young lady. It takes a lot of selfless courage to reach out and try to mend fences. I'm betting on you honey."

"Geoff, you are the best friend I have right now. I'm so lucky to have met you, even if it all started with a bite of pizza."

"Hey, I'm getting just as big a kick out of having met you. I'm beginning to feel necessary again."

The miles and time flew by. They stopped in Lake Charles for a break and a bite to eat. The remainder of the drive to Beaumont went just as fast. Danielle seemed comfortable to let the chips fall where they might. Geoff was content to let it all pan out swallowing any private random thoughts of misgiving which he was determined to keep to himself.

When they arrived in Beaumont they drove around as Danielle pointed out all the landmarks she could recall along with the significance of them in her life.

"Take the exit for the downtown business center. Hang a right at the next signal. There it is! That's my old high school. It still looks the same as it did when I was going there. Well, maybe the trees are a little taller and there are a few more fences and shrubs."

They drove by slowly and Danielle spotted another landmark – "Oh my goodness! …hey, Digby's is still there. It was my first part time job back in high school. I worked the snack bar."

Farther down the road another memory came back, "Over there's the Laundromat where I did my laundry after I left home."

They made a left onto a boulevard at Danielle's direction.

"And there's Fouquet's, it still looks the same. I went there on my first date. Over there is our local theater. The balcony was known as the passion pit for the underclassmen. By junior year most everyone had their driver's license and we all became far too mature - we thought - to go to indoor movies. Drive-ins were the rage and didn't have ushers to chaperone."

"Unless I miss my guess, it sounds like you're enjoying this little home coming trip," said Geoff with a chuckle.

"Oh my goodness... yes, I really am; I didn't think I'd missed it this much. It's only been five years."

"Well five years at your age is a long time."

They passed an upscale extended stay motel that advertised suites.

"Well what do you say; shall we get a place and set up a command center for your reunion efforts?"

"Geoff, I feel like I'm imposing on you. You've done so much for me already."

"I'm doing it for me as much as for you. I want to see you through this. I won't feel like I've done enough until I see you and your dad together again."

"Well, we may not get back together."

"That may very well turn out to be the case Danielle. You can only control your side of the reconciliation but at least you will have tried. Regardless of the outcome you will have shown respect, integrity and courage in making the attempt. What I'm trying to say is do it for your dad but most of all just do it for yourself. Will you do that?"

"Yes Geoff, I will."

They turned around and drove back to the extended stay motel. They got a rather nice suite with two rooms and a kitchenette fully equipped with dishwasher, refrigerator, stove top and microwave. It also had a fairly complete supply of china, glasses and silverware.

"All the comforts of home," said Geoff. "Let's settle in and figure out what we want to do for dinner."

"How about a takeout pizza with some beer," said Danielle?

"Just the ticket, you read my mind," said Geoff. You check the yellow pages and order us a loaded pizza - your choice as long as it at least has pepperoni, black olives, green peppers, mushrooms, jalapeños, lots of sauce and uh...extra cheese."

"Hmm what's left for choice? But that's okay it's fine with me; we seem to have the same taste in pizza," she said with a pleasant laugh.

"Great, I'll go make a beer run. Do you have a favorite?"

"I'll drink whatever you like."

Chapter twenty-nine

Geoff returned to the motel with the beer about twenty minutes later. As he walked in from the parking lot he saw a parked car with a lighted pizza sign on its roof. When he got to their cluster he saw the room door ajar. It was the only thing he disliked about this place – there was access directly to the rooms from the parking lot instead of to an inside secured hallway which he would have preferred. He felt the old familiar pangs of apprehension as he burst through the doorway anticipating but ready for the worst only to find the pizza delivery man in an animated conversation with Danielle. The body language told him they were old friends.

"What the...," said the delivery man as he quickly stood up startled from Geoff's quick entrance.

"Oh excuse me, I saw the door ajar and it triggered an alert, I guess my old instincts just kicked in," said Geoff.

"Geoff, this is Steve Allison, a high school classmate of mine. Steve this is Geoff McEwen. He's the reason I'm back in town. He's a real keeper," said Danielle.

"Yeah Steve, I keep 'er out of trouble. Or at least I'm trying to," said Geoff extending his hand. "Good to meet you Steve sorry if I startled you."

"Nice to meet you, sir, Danie here tells me you're a writer."

"Yes I am, but if it's a celebrity author of the great American novel you're expecting forget it. I'm afraid I'm just a hack free-lancer and budding pulp novelist. But it keeps me busy and sober and always researching for new material."

"That's cool, hey if you ever need a pizza delivery character in one of your stories I'm your man," Steve said laughing.

"I'll keep you in mind, Steve, you never know."

"Well I need to get back to work, maybe we'll bump into each other again Danie, nice meeting you, sir."

"This was quite a surprise to see you Steve. I really enjoyed our little chat and if things work out for me like I hope I'll be spending a lot more time here. Say hi to Liz for me and give the kids a big hug," said Danielle as he walked towards the door.

"Will do Danie, she'll be tickled that you're back in town. Get ready to get caught up on all the gossip in Beaumont. Maybe she'll even convince you to stay; I know she'll certainly try."

"Take care Steve, don't work too hard," said Geoff.

"Yeah, with two kids and a wife I don't have much choice. I have to hustle. See you, bye."

After he closed the door Geoff turned to Danielle. "Sorry I broke into your conversation so abruptly, sometimes I overreact. I didn't mean to spoil any reunion for you."

"Please Geoff; you have nothing to apologize for, you didn't spoil anything. And thanks for being so protective. It's nice to feel safe."

"Ah you're welcome Danielle it's just that I think it's important for you to reconnect. I don't want to interfere."

"Geoff, if you ever do I'll tell you. Anyway, I already have reconnected. Steve's been here forever. He was the first guy in our graduation class to get married. Liz and he were sweethearts all the way through high school and they are still going strong. It's great to see a couple like that. I should be so lucky. Maybe it's a good omen that he's the first person I've met since I'm back and he's an old friend. He knows my dad and says he still sees him around town every now and then."

"Well hey, that's great! Sounds like you're making very quick progress."

"Yeah, I think I'm going to be just fine, Geoff – and I've got you to thank for giving me the motivation, nerve and chance to come back home."

"I didn't give you anything you didn't already have, Danielle. I just reminded you of how strong a person you really are."

"And for that, I thank you – sincerely. You've given me back something I lost."

"Nah you didn't lose it Danielle; I think you just sort of misplaced it a bit. Hey I'm hungry, how about you?"

"I'm Starving! The pizza has probably cooled off a bit. I think I'll nuke a slice. Shall I do yours also?" she asked as she pulled open the box.

"Yes, please, I like it hot," said Geoff as he opened two bottles of beer."

They quickly finished off two slices apiece agreeing that it was really a great pizza - almost as good as they'd had on Bourbon Street. Geoff got up to nuke another slice. "Can you go another slice?"

"No thanks, I want to make a phone call before it gets too late." She got up and went into the bedroom. "Sorry I think I need a little privacy on this one," she said as she closed the door.

"It's okay, I understand perfectly. Good luck."

Geoff settled down on the sofa turning on the television to catch some evening news. In a few minutes Danielle came back out of the bedroom looking a little deflated.

"Anything wrong," he asked.

"My old home number is not in service; it has been disconnected. I guess I'm overreacting but everything seemed to be coming together. Maybe it was all just too easy."

"Hey, hold on Danielle. It's only your first shot. You have to expect a setback or two."

"Yeah I'm being a little selfish I guess."

"No, you're just over-anxious. Let's see if we can find a good movie to get your mind off things for a while. You've made great progress in a short time. Give it a rest. Here, you drive," he said as he handed her the remote.

As she turned up the volume she heard the local news reporter announce the latest news item about a local councilman that made her sit bolt upright.

Councilman Doug Porter is here with us to discuss his pending new ordinance to curtail the proliferation of rave parties and nightclubs which he alleges have led to a serious rise in illicit drug use, mayhem and vandalism by teens and young adults.

The camera cut to a picture of Councilman Doug Porter at his office.

"Oh my God… Geoff, that's my dad. Oh my God!"

Five years of bottled up emotions came cascading out as the tears welled up in her eyes and streamed down her face. She choked back a few sobs until she shook uncontrollably. Geoff gently pulled her close in a comforting hug.

"It's okay, Danielle. It's okay! Things are going to work out for you. This looks like the silver lining of a big break in the clouds for you. Your dad is obviously a high profile responsible community leader. He should be very easy to find and contact. I think fortune has finally turned around with a big smile to brighten your life. It's been long overdue."

"Where do I start looking?"

"Why not try the phone book under local government listings. They should have a number for city councilmen."

She retrieved the phone book from the nightstand checked the index and in a minute or so she had the listing for a Councilman Doug Porter with his office number.

"Got it, she said with a bright smile. Why didn't I think of the old phone book, what would I do without you?"

"You would have thought of it if you were thinking clearly. Give yourself a break, you're just stressed out."

She called the number and heard her father's voice for the first time in five long years even if it was just his voice mail… *Hi this is Councilman Doug Porter; I'm either away from my desk…*

"Hi Dad, this is Danielle. I'm back in town. I'd really like to see you – if you want to see me." She left the number for the motel. "Dad, I love you, please call me, bye."

Early the next morning they went out for breakfast. Afterward they did some food shopping for essentials, mostly breakfast and lunch items. Dinner they agreed would be either take-out or casual dining restaurants whenever they developed cabin fever and needed a change of atmosphere. They returned to the motel room to put away the groceries and check for phone messages – there weren't any.

Geoff sat down and turned on the TV to channel surf for some news. He preferred national or international but today maybe even local coverage would do. He was beginning to get as anxious as Danielle was for something to happen. He hoped that when something finally broke it would be positive. Danielle sat reading the local newspaper. She gave the classified section a once over but was too preoccupied to really focus on anything.

"Danielle, these walls are beginning to close in on me, I need some air. How about you; feel like taking a ride?"

"You read my mind, Geoff."

They hadn't driven more than a mile or so when Danielle broke the silence that was slowly building to a roar like a waterfall in his ears. He had begun to feel a little inadequate.

"I think I'm ready for the next step. Let's drive by my old neighborhood."

"That's my girl; take the bull by the horns. You've got nothing to lose, so stare destiny right back in the eyes."

"I wish I felt that confident."

"It's easier for me Danielle, this is your rodeo. I'm just along for the ride. Well, the ride and maybe a little moral suasion, to try to keep you on track."

Topaz Drive ran along a canal, just west of the interstate. He guessed they probably called them bayous down in these parts. The roadway curved away from the canal and up over a culvert. Just up ahead on the left was a neat brick ranch style house with a white shingled hip roof set back off the road about fifty yards and surrounded by a canopy of trees. A long curved driveway leading up to an attached two-car garage on the side broke the expanse of a split rail fence enclosing what he guessed were several acres of land – this was Texas after all. Geoff heard her audible inhalation and looked over to see her with her hands cupped over her nose and both cheeks of her face.

"Oh Geoff – there it is! That's...well, that was my home. It still looks in great condition. Dad always was a stickler for maintenance."

"There's a truck parked in the driveway – looks like someone's home," said Geoff.

"Oh God, Geoff, what do I do?"

"Follow your heart, honey – just tell me what you feel." He slowed down as they approached the driveway downshifting all the way to second gear. They rolled past the drive and gradually picked up speed. A quarter mile ahead was a gas station with a convenience store on the left side of the road.

"Geoff, I'm sorry I need to stop."

"Me too Danielle, if I were a smoker this would be a smoking moment," he said as he pulled into the parking lot and shut off the engine. Danielle went to the ladies' room and Geoff went inside.

When she came out Geoff was waiting by the passenger side of the truck with his elbows hooked over the bed rail.

"Hey want to share half of my candy bar? It's guaranteed to make you feel better," he said holding out an unopened Baby Ruth bar.

"If I thought that were true I'd eat the whole thing," she said.

"Oh no you wouldn't, I only offered half!"

"I was only kidding."

"I know... so was I."

He split the candy bar, wrapper and all, in half and handed half to her. They stood there leaning against his truck munching silently on their candy.

"Wow, I guess we both needed that," Geoff said after they had finished.

"You were right; it does make you feel better."

"Of course, it's a Ruth bar, Danielle! Takes you back to your childhood when the whole world seemed innocent and life was simple and easy."

"Was it ever that way?"

"Sure it was, Danielle, you've just forgotten all the good parts. Maybe it's time you settled down and got back to living life for yourself and started making pleasant future memories to bury all the pain from your past. …Hey, I'm sorry Danielle; I'm the last one who should preach about settling down and not holding onto or trying to rewrite the past."

"No, it's okay Geoff, thanks for reminding me. I can learn a lot from someone who has been there. Sometimes I need a little shove in the right direction."

"We all do now and then Danielle; it takes a wise person to realize that. So, do we make a return run by the old homestead?" he asked.

"Yeah, let's go!"

They drove back slowly. When they reached the driveway they saw the truck was gone.

Chapter thirty

When they returned to the motel there was a message waiting for Danielle. It was from her dad. He said to please get in touch as soon as possible no matter the time. He also provided his home and cell phone numbers. Danielle went into the bedroom and closed the door. She decided to try his office number again.

Hi this is Councilman Doug Porter; I'm either away from my desk...

Next she tried his cell phone.

The party you have dialed, Doug Porter, does not answer; you may leave a message...

Finally, she rang the home phone. It rang three times, four, five six...no answering machine picked up. She hung up the phone.

"Shit, daddy where are you?"

Just as her frustration was beginning to peak the phone rang.

"Hello?"

"Hello, is this Danielle?"

"Yes it is...uh, daddy... is that you?" she asked her voice beginning to crack as she recognized his voice.

"Yes it is honey, oh my God; my prayers have been answered after all these years. How have you been? Where have you been? Are you all right?"

"Oh I'm fine daddy. It's so good to hear your voice again."

"Well when do I get to see you again? How long are you in town for?"

"I have no plans daddy, whenever is good for you, I guess."

"Well shoot, come on over now! We can have dinner together. We can either go out or throw some steaks on the grill, whatever you want to do. We have a lot to talk about; a lot of things have changed."

"Uh... is stepmom there?"

"No, honey we got divorced about two years ago, that's one of the things we need to talk about."

"Well I came here with a friend. In fact, he's the reason I came back to try to reconnect. He's been like another dad to me."

"So bring him along, I'd love to meet him. Look I'll be home in about a half hour. Just come on over, okay?"

"Okay daddy, I'll see you in a bit. I love you."

"I love you too Danielle."

"Oh wait! Daddy?"

"Yes honey, what is it?"

"I tried to call you at the old number but it was disconnected. Are you still at our old house over on Topaz?"

"Yes I am, I had the number changed when Karen and I were divorcing and she was bombarding me with a lot of obnoxious calls. But I'm still here at your old home."

"Okay great, I can't wait to see you, daddy, love you, bye"

"Love you too honey, bye."

She burst out of the bedroom and ran over to where Geoff was seated on the couch reading the newspaper.

"Geoff that was my daddy on the phone," she said with a shriek as she jumped on the couch and hugged Geoff. "He invited us over for dinner. Uh...I hope you don't mind that I took the liberty to mention you."

"Not at all, Danielle; I'd really love to meet your dad. I am so happy for you."

"He said to come on over as soon as we can. I need to freshen up a bit; I'll just be a minute."

"Take your time, I'll finish reading the sports section."

Her dad's truck was back in the driveway as they pulled up. Geoff pulled in and parked next to it. They walked around to the front of the house. Two stone steps led up to a slate porch enclosed with wrought iron railing. The front door behind the outer screen door was open. Danielle rang the bell.

"Daddy it's me, Danielle," she called out through the screen door.

"Come on in honey, its open."

Danielle walked quickly inside as Geoff hesitated behind to close the screen door. Her dad came into the foyer and they rushed into each other's arms in a tight embrace.

"Oh daddy, it's so good to see you again. I...and then the tears came and she shook with sobs."

"It's okay sweetheart. You're home now. Things are going to be different."

"Daddy, it's been so long. I didn't..., I didn't know if..."

"Danielle, you have been constantly in my thoughts. I prayed to your mom to watch over you from her place in heaven and asked her if there was any chance at all that she would help to give you the will to return to me. I didn't know if she would listen to me after the way I treated you and Tammy after she passed away. I'm so sorry Danielle; I thought Karen would be a much better step mom."

"She was a witch, daddy. She never gave a damn about us, just had her own agenda and wanted you all to herself."

"Yes I know that now, I'm sorry it took me so long to realize. I guess I got caught on a rebound and just wanted what was good for me. It was really selfish of me; I can see that now."

"I had to work through some bad times daddy. I was angry, sad, guilty...so I just took off to give myself some space and put my head back together. Things went from bad to worse. I almost got to a point where I didn't give a damn anymore if I didn't wake up."

"Why didn't you call me honey? Give me a chance to try to be a better father, to make up for what happened to Tammy."

"I just didn't think you cared."

Her dad glanced over at Geoff who stood off at a discrete distance. "Please excuse us sir. We don't mean to ignore you."

"Oh, I'm sorry," said Danielle wiping her eyes as she clung to her dad. "Daddy this is Geoff McEwen. Geoff, this is...well I guess it's pretty obvious...he's my dad," she said giving him another hug.

Her dad held out his hand as Geoff walked over and shook hands.

"I'm very pleased to meet you, sir," said Geoff.

"He has been a godsend, daddy. I really think mama sent him to rescue me and get us back together."

"It's a pleasure to meet you too, Geoff."

"He restored my faith in the goodness of some men and convinced me that I should give life another chance. I'm really here because of his influence. For the first time I met a man who didn't want to take advantage of me. He reminded me of you, daddy and what it was like before mom got sick."

"My daughter doesn't pass out praise lightly Geoff, you have my undying gratitude. It is indeed a pleasure to make your acquaintance. Please - call me Doug."

"Doug you are a very lucky man; you have a great daughter there. I'm glad I was able to play a small part in getting you guys back together. But she deserves the major portion of the credit. She has a great moral compass; you did a fantastic job rearing her."

"Uh, guys could we eat soon; I think we've passed around enough accolades," said Danielle rolling her eyes with a sudden hearty chuckle.

"That's my little girl, she's back," said Doug. "Listen, I bought some steaks we can throw on the grill. Maybe I can twist Danielle's arm into making mom's old potato salad, toss up a green salad and we can just sit and talk."

"That sounds terrific to me," said Geoff, "how about you Danielle?"

"Yeah, I'll do it for both of you. The two best men in my life."

Her dad grilled the filets; Danielle steamed some new potatoes, sliced them, diced some celery and mixed up her mom's special mayonnaise vinaigrette dressing with parsley and her mom's special herbs and spices for the potato salad. Then she mixed up a green salad with tomatoes, carrots, radishes and hot peppers. Geoff opened the wine they selected. While he grilled the steaks Danielle and her dad filled each other in on their lives.

"After you left we had a lot of arguments over you. I began to see the real Karen. She started to drink a lot more frequently getting drunk three or four times a week. She wanted her own children but she had only a very small probability of conceiving. Then she blamed it on me and got more possessive and demanding until I finally just had had enough. One evening at dinner she got really drunk and began loudly berating me at one of my favorite restaurants and then got up and walked out. I was so embarrassed; I paid the tab and went to look for her, driving around the parking lot and the surrounding area but she was nowhere around. Early the next morning she called on the phone - sounding still a little drunk from the night before – to ask if she could come home. I told her don't bother; just stay wherever you are! The next day I filed divorce papers."

"Oh daddy, I'm so sorry for you. You didn't deserve that."

"If only I had been more involved as a father with you two after mom passed maybe I would have recognized the signs and made a difference. I could have intervened. Tammy might still be with us today."

"Daddy, please don't do that to yourself. We were all grieving over mom in our own ways. Tammy unfortunately lost her way to peer pressure. You can't take all the blame. We both could have tried harder. But she's up there in heaven with mom now and they are probably both looking down and smiling now that you and I are back together."

"Well what are you going to do now that you're back? What are your plans? Where are you staying?"

"I'm staying at the extended-stay motel just off the interstate with Geoff. We got a small two room suite. I'm really kind of putting him out since he insisted I take the bedroom while he sleeps on the couch."

"Well, look I'm not telling you what to do, but this is still your home. I've remodeled and made the two smaller bedrooms into one large guest master bedroom. You're welcome to come back home as soon as you feel comfortable. You can stay here indefinitely or until you find something more permanent. That is if you want to stick around and work here in Beaumont."

"I had a wild fantasy dream last night that I went back to my old paralegal job at Barclay Rogers Williams and Clay. I wonder if they still remember me."

"Maybe I can help you with that honey, they are the primary legal counsel for the city and I've got some connections from my work on the council."

"Yes, daddy I saw you on the television news the other night, it was quite a surprise. It made me feel so proud to be your daughter."

"And I'm very proud to have you as my daughter," he said as he reached over and gave her a hug and kiss on the cheek.

"So it's settled then, you want to stay here tonight? You'll just have to make up the bed."

"I really need to discuss it with Geoff. He feels like a stepdad to me, actually even closer. I don't want to walk away and leave him cold after all he has done for me."

"I understand Danielle; you do whatever you feel is best, I want you to be comfortable."

Doug carried the steaks inside to the table and Danielle brought over the potato and tossed green salads.

"Geoff, please pardon the delay; Danielle and I got carried away with family history," Doug said when they finally sat down to dinner.

"It's okay, Doug I understand; It's been a long time. It's nice to see you and your daughter enjoying each other again. If I were in your shoes I don't know that I would even attempt to make dinner."

The steaks and potato salad got raves all around. They finished the wine to pleasant conversation. Doug asked Geoff about his travels and how he had wound up in New Orleans at the right place and right time to meet his daughter. Danielle made coffee and the night slipped into the early morning.

"It's getting late or rather early I think it's time I head on out; Danielle, are you staying here tonight or...," Geoff asked as he stood up.

"Ah yeah, I think so. Dad said I could move into my old room if I wanted. I..."

"Great, I think that's the right thing for you. Tell you what, give me a call tomorrow and we can get together and pack up your stuff and bring it all over. Just don't make it too early."

"It won't be early Geoff, I promise. I'm ready for a sleep in after all this," said Danielle.

Geoff turned to Doug, "I'll probably hang around town for a few days and then maybe head up to Austin. I haven't been there for a few years. It's about time for a revisit."

"Be sure to stop by before you leave, Geoff; you have my phone numbers, right?"

"I'll make a point of it Doug, don't worry. I can get the numbers from Danielle. Goodnight all."

"Goodnight, Geoff," Danielle and Doug said in unison.

Chapter thirty-one

Geoff stayed in Beaumont another five nights although he didn't spend much time in the room. Just went back there to sleep. It felt a little empty now that Danielle was reunited with her dad. Well, actually it felt a lot empty. Try as he might he just could not get over goodbyes easily. Danielle had made him feel necessary again. But it was good to see her get her life back so that was at least some consolation for his emptiness.

Her dad used his contacts and got her an interview with Barclay Rogers Williams and Clay. As luck would have it they had been searching for a reliable paralegal to add to their staff so the timing again was right. Danielle was on a fortunate roll. Who knows one day it could be Barclay Rogers Williams Clay and Porter. He got to spend a few nights with the Porter's celebrating Danielle's new job and her next big step in reconnecting with life and the promise of a bright future.

The final goodbye of course was the hardest. He and Danielle shared a long hug. She kissed him on the cheek and he returned it on hers. Even her dad got into the act and gave Geoff a hug thanking him profusely for all he'd done.

"Geoff my house is yours anytime you are in town. I honestly hope we see you again," he said.

Back out on the interstate Geoff, as was his custom, decided on the long way taking the I-10 interstate all the way to San Antonio where he transitioned onto I-35 up to Austin. The drive slowly exhausted his feelings of melancholy. He arrived in Austin in the late afternoon and got a room at a motel on the south side near the blues bars – some that he remembered and some others of which he would still need to make an acquaintance. Yes, sir Texas - especially Austin - was high on his list of places that were good for his soul.

He got a loaded turkey sub sandwich and a quart container of grapefruit juice and took it back to the room. Watching the early evening news while lying on the bed he fell asleep. He awoke about an hour later but just couldn't summon the will to get up and go back out so he decided to call it a night. Flicking the channel selector on the remote he caught the beginning of an old classic movie, *Watch on the Rhine*. Halfway through it he fell back asleep.

Early the next morning he went out for a jog at a park he had found on his way into town then returned to the room for a shave and shower and went back out to hunt up a café for breakfast.

After driving around for a bit in concentric circles from the motel trying whatever streets looked interesting to him he found just what he was looking for. The Borderline Blues Café on a wide dusty side street off the interstate service road with a median lined with old growth Live Oak festooned with layers of Spanish moss. They had a breakfast lunch and dinner menu on display in the side windows of the wooden double door entrance. It was a venerated old three story brick building which stood between two vacant lots that separated it from the surrounding deeper lots containing the usual assortment of newer food stores, dry cleaners, Laundromats, banks and the ubiquitous drug store chains. It was a testament to solid construction and a simpler more relaxed lifestyle. The upper two stories looked vacant. Large windows nearly two-thirds of the height of the first floor ran almost completely around three sides of the building and were capped by what were once vent windows which had been replaced by panes of stained-glass. Parking was ample marked by railroad ties throughout the two vacant lots. There were a few cars scattered in both lots.

Once inside he was greeted by a cheery young blonde at the hostess stand holding a handful of menus.

"Good morning sir, welcome to the Borderline Blues Café; table for one for breakfast?"

"Good morning miss, yes please; how about one of those round hi-tops."

"Sure, you can have your choice, sit wherever you'd like. May I get you some water?"

"Water sounds like a good start; yes, please!"

She came back with a pitcher of ice water, filled his glass and left the pitcher. "Dakota will be your server today, have a nice breakfast!"

The inside was fascinating with a high ceiling that enhanced the openness giving off a feeling of being in a large hall. The ceiling had to be sixteen feet or so he guessed. Exposed heating ventilation and air conditioning ductwork wound its way throughout the room. Several large five bladed fans kept the air circulating. The hardwood floor must have been the original he suspected, from its worn, weathered and well trafficked appearance which exuded a warm comfy atmosphere to the cafe. Against the far wall facing the entrance was a long restored antique oak back bar with arches and fancy scroll work around three huge mirrors. On either side of the mirrors were columns of small shelves. Stained glass inlay ran along the arches and over the valance which connected the arches and columns into one huge monolith giving the impression of an altar. The front bar had a wide old-fashion wooden bar rail with a dark slate bar top. A brass foot rest ran the length of both legs of the L-shaped bar. High back stools lined the front of the bar, the shorter leg of which ran into the service bar and server station. Round hi-top tables were set in the bar area with four stools each of the same type stools that lined the bar. Formal dining tables formed a perimeter raised one step up from the bar area. Several patrons sat at window tables along the raised perimeter.

As soon as he sat down another cheerful blonde approached his table. "Good morning, my name is Dakota, I'll be your server today; have you decided or do you need a little more time?"

"Good morning Dakota, I'm sorry I haven't really looked at the menu yet. I was just soaking in the atmosphere. This is a very interesting place."

"That's the most common reaction we get when people walk in here for their first visit. We have only been open about three months but business has really been fantastic. It's exciting to work at the newest in-place in south Austin. And to think this used to be a vacant building for as long as I can remember. May I get you some coffee while you decide?"

"Yes, thank you Dakota; oh and make it decafe please."

He glanced down at the menu. It had a choice of six entrées and a chef's special on an insert. Today it was a *Laredo frittata* - three eggs folded in with pepper jack, Swiss and provolone cheese, green chili with pork, green and red peppers, black olives, jalapenos and salsa on the side. It came of course with Texas breakfast fries and seasonal fresh fruit. It was no contest. When Dakota came back with the coffee he ordered the Laredo frittata.

"That's my favorite; if you like spicy you'll love it. It's our most popular special."

As she went off to put in his order a tall slender woman came in and took a seat at the hi-top across from him. She was well dressed in a tailored light gray pin-striped pants suit with a ribbed white silk blouse and black string bowtie. She glanced up from the newspaper she had started to read and they made eye contact. Geoff looked away not wanting to be rude. A few seconds later when he thought it safe he looked over again and got caught in her return look.

"Oh, good morning, sorry, I don't mean to stare...," he said feeling a little embarrassed for getting caught.

"Good morning... don't worry it's okay, I think I'm guilty of the same," she said with a bright sunny smile and an easy chuckle. Are you alone?"

"Why yes, yes I am; and you?"

"Alone," she said as she gave a little shrug of the shoulder.

"Would you care to share my table, I'd welcome some company," said Geoff.

"Thanks I'd like that very much; I hate being conspicuous even more than eating alone."

Geoff got up and pulled out the chair for her. "My name's Geoff," he said as she came over.

"I'm Karen," she said offering her hand. "It's nice to meet you."

"The pleasure is all mine," said Geoff as he took her hand.

Dakota came over with a place setting and brought over the water. Karen ordered the healthy yogurt with fresh fruit.

"Do you live here in Austin, Geoff?"

"No, I just got in late yesterday from Beaumont but I'm not from there either."

"So where is home?"

"Home is usually my last address. I move around the country a lot."

"Really; what do you do that takes you all over?"

"I'm a freelance writer; magazine articles, short story collections and vignettes. I've been on a road trip researching for what I hope to make my first full length novel. What do you do Karen?"

"I work as a victims' advocate for the Austin DA's office. I handle a lot of domestic violence, rape and abuse cases."

"That has to be tough. I would imagine it gets pretty depressing with the increasing level of violence these days."

"Yes it does Geoff; but I don't know that the level is necessarily increasing. I think it's just much more reported by the victims and sensationalized in the 24/7 media."

"Boy I have to agree with you there as far as the media is concerned."

Just as the conversation paused Dakota brought out the food.

"Oh, that looks good, but it would be way too much for me," Karen said looking over at the frittata.

"I'm afraid I'm a bit of a glutton when it comes to breakfast; it's my favorite meal," said Geoff.

"Can I get you anything else?" asked the server

"No thank you, I'm all set, how about you, Karen?"

"I'm fine, thanks."

"Enjoy it, I'll be back to check on you in a bit," said Dakota.

"Are you originally from Austin," he asked as he dug into his frittata.

"No, I grew up in Beaumont; still have some relatives down there. I'm curious, how did you happen to pick this place for breakfast today, since you just got into town yesterday?"

"I'm a real fan of blues music so south Austin was a natural since I've been through here before. This morning I was just out driving around looking for a good spot for breakfast when I noticed this place. It looked inviting and the name piqued my interest."

"It was a fortunate find then, they have some great blues jams here on Friday and Saturday nights. On Monday nights they do a Blue Monday special that starts at the four o'clock happy hour and goes until the crowd leaves."

"It sounds like you have spent some time here," said Geoff.

"Oh I sure have; I'm a big blues fan also. Look if you're still in town this Friday you have to check it out."

"I'm sure I'll still be here and I've got nothing on my calendar so I'll probably come by; how about you?"

"I've been here every Friday since this place opened; I wouldn't miss it for anything." Just then her cell phone rang. She checked the number and then switched it off. "Work is calling; I need to get going. Thanks for inviting me to share your table I really enjoyed the conversation. I'll look for you Friday."

"You're welcome Karen, thanks for accepting so graciously."

As she stood up Dakota came by with coffee for refills. "I just need my tab Dakota; I've got to run." Dakota fished it out of her apron. Karen paid her tab and with a wave goodbye, walked out.

"How did you like the frittata?" asked Dakota turning her attention back to him.

"It was excellent - a little bit of heaven."

"Would you like more coffee?"

"Yes, please...thank you."

"I'll leave your tab. Have a nice day and come back and see us again."

He felt a deep sense of contentment, maybe it was the sense of relief that his self-imposed responsibility for Danielle had a positive ending. Or maybe it was just the letdown from the tension of the last few weeks or the fact that he was just back in his comfort zone.

He became aware of the music playing on the background sound system and he recognized the strains from *Red Headed Stranger* an old Willie Nelson album. He had played the tape in his truck until it had worn out. As he listened to the music his mind began to wander, to take inventory of where he was and where he had come from...

He was running again; he was always running – running away. Wherever he was he needed desperately to be somewhere else.

It was, he mused, a search for a place to call home, a search for a life, a search for...yes, for his own identity. He had to find out who he was. Oh, he knew all right – with respect to the usual assorted identification of driver's licenses, birth certificates, credit cards and the whole gamut of audit trails the system forced upon him. But he really didn't know – who he was. It was a feeling he could never quite articulate yet it was there, always just under the surface.

There was a burning gnawing emptiness deep down inside of him, deep down in his very soul, a place that he dared not explore. He supposed it was the seat of his sensitive nature and a place to which he forbade even himself access lest it become trampled into insensitivity. He was staunchly independent and he would always remain so. He believed that it was his right to do whatever he chose as long as it did not impinge upon the aspirations or rights of others or infringe upon their enjoyment of those pursuits.

He was not a competitor. Competition to him was wasteful of energy and too often taken to harmful extremes. The cliché that number two was the first loser was to him uncharacteristic and unacceptable. He did not play games and he had little regard for those who did.

The vivid recollection of a recurring dream he had had took control of his consciousness...it was a dream of death, his death. He realized with his final breath that he hadn't wanted to die. He still had things he needed to accomplish. He was being taken away from those whom he loved, from all that he cherished.

Somehow a spectral part of him was being levitated ever higher into the sky and up into the clouds that at first dissipated and then engulfed him. He could still clearly see those below from whom he did not wish to be separated. He called out to them but they could not see or hear him. He shouted at the limit of his lungs but it was as if he couldn't make a sound. They did not respond. He felt a deep suffocating sense of loneliness. Slowly he was propelled away. The sunset faded out into deep purple and then to blackness. The day surrendered its innocence and we, each of us, became a little older. And always when it faded, he would awaken with a quick short muscle spasm.

He guessed it was some kind of symbolism of his view of loneliness and the despair of not ever knowing the fulfillment of one's most intimate and cherished dreams. He was momentarily startled as he suddenly became aware of Dakota standing there at his table. She was asking something but he hadn't been listening. He shook his head as though to clear his senses.

"Pardon me, did you say something? I must have been off the planet there for a bit," he said a little sheepishly.

"I just wanted to know if I could get you anything else; maybe more coffee?"

"No thank you, I need to get my butt in gear. Enjoy your day, Dakota."

"Thanks, you too, come back and see us again."

He paid the tab and stepped out into the brilliant sun of the gorgeous Austin mid-morning.

Chapter thirty-two

That Friday afternoon Geoff went back to the Borderline Blues Café. The parking lot was much fuller than it had been when he'd stopped in for breakfast on Tuesday. It had been a relaxing week for him. He'd managed to do a little writing but for the most part just drove around reacquainting himself with the city where he had often thought he could see himself settling down.

The happy hour crowd was already beginning to swell. He barely managed a seat at the bar. Most of the high-top tables in the bar area were occupied. Many had even been pushed together to provide seating for a larger group. And of course extra seats had been commandeered from empty tables as well as the bar. One table had even been left with a solitary seat.

The cacophony of the occasional loud voice, ringing cell phones and the ever present background of laughter and conversation had begun to rise in volume creating a dynamic that fed on itself. Everyone including the staff raised their voices to be heard over the din of the crowd which collectively responded by unconsciously and automatically raising their volume in a continuing spiral.

But it was after all Friday. The week's work was done, for most. The office political battles had all been fought. The winners gloated while the losers licked their wounds and plotted next week's revenge. Friends were updating each other on their respective lives and sports fans were arguing statistics on their particular sport. The season for most sports seemed to last all year long these days rather than being restricted to a unique period of just a few months. The women gossiped with each other about other women or lamented about their former relationships.

It was a scene repeated over and over in all the cafes, bars, taverns, saloons and pubs across the entire globe. He'd seen it on a business trip to a half dozen European cities and on a ski vacation in Austria. Socializing after all is what made the fortunes, misfortunes and uncertainties of life a little more bearable.

He was on his second drink of tequila grapefruit when he heard a female voice call out his name. He glanced around to see Karen standing just behind him with a drink in her hand.

"Hi Geoff, I see you took my advice. Quite different from Tuesday morning isn't it?"

"It sure is Karen, here why don't you have a seat," he said as he got up.

"Oh thank you, you're a real gentleman. I got here a little later than I had planned. I had some last minute issues to take care of. How was your week?" she asked as she slipped into the seat he offered.

Karen looked even more attractive then she had on Tuesday. She had natural looking wavy blond hair that she wore in a short layered style that enhanced its radiance with a soft look. The pale blue silk blouse with a ruffled front panel and covered buttons that she wore had a plunging v-neckline that revealed her soft feminine curves along with a fitness that required regular hours in the gym. A cream colored skirt with a rear slit came to just above her knees. She had on a pair of strapped white slides with medium heels to complete her outfit and accentuate her sculpted calves. She wore a delicate gold chain necklace with a string of amethyst stones as an accessory.

"Karen, you look resplendent this afternoon. You even outdid last Tuesday - when I thought you looked really terrific," said Geoff looking into her sparkling blue-gray eyes as he spoke.

"Oh, thank you Geoff! I love when my fashion sense gets rewarded with compliments. Tuesday was my business attire; these are my play clothes. I love getting dressed up."

"You do it very well Karen."

The bartender came over and pointed at her glass, "Are you ready?"

"Yes please."

"Bartender put that on my tab please," said Geoff.

"Oh thank you, sweetie," she said rubbing her hand softly over his forearm.

"Do you have plans for dinner or would you care to share a table and dine with me?" Geoff asked.

"I have no plans, and yes, I would love to dine with you. I don't want to drink too much on an empty stomach."

"Great, I'll go queue up with the hostess now; there'll probably be a bit of a wait," he said.

He came back with a small pager they used to signal a ready table, "She said it would be about thirty-five or forty minutes."

"That's fine with me; it'll give me time to unwind. You didn't tell me how your week was," Karen said.

"Oh I'm sorry; guess I was distracted by your charms."

"Umm well that's okay I like being appreciated," she said with an amused chuckle as she softly ran her hand around his neck gently pulling him towards her. She gazed into his eyes switching her focus momentarily to his lips and then back to his eyes as she angled her lips towards his. There was a moment of hesitation and then their lips met brushing for an instant in an ephemeral kiss.

"You're excused," she said with a nod of her head as she picked up her drink and looked intently into his eyes from over the rim of her glass as she sipped her drink.

"Whew," was all he could manage. "You have quite a knack for stimulating disconcertment."

"Whatever," she said with a coquettish blink of her eyes. "Anyway Geoff, so how was your week?"

"Oh it was nothing to write home about, although I did get in a little writing. I just relaxed and drove around taking in the sights and letting my mind wander. I'm afraid I'm addicted to daydreaming."

"Well if that's all you're addicted to you're a very lucky man."

"You know, at this moment in time I am. I'm feeling very lucky, sitting here enjoying a drink with a very pretty lady with whom I'm waiting to share dinner. Now it's your turn Karen, tell me about your week?"

"Oh please Geoff. I don't even want to think about it anymore. It was very traumatic and emotional. It took me back to my situation from years ago in Beaumont."

"Hey, I'm a pretty good listener Karen and I like stories. If you need to get something off your chest that will make you feel better go right ahead. Sometimes it helps to talk about it."

"It's kind of a sick story. The beginning of it goes back about eight years ago. I met this guy at work who transferred into our department. He was super nice and very attractive. He had just lost his wife to a long battle with cancer and was pretty strung out. He had two teenage daughters to take care of by himself.

We started going to lunch together and became close friends. He began to confide in me. After a few weeks he asked me out to dinner. We began dating and frequent dates almost immediately turned into a whirlwind romance. We went away together for weekends. He was the first to broach the subject of marriage. He didn't want just a relationship he wanted commitment."

"Isn't that what women are always looking for?"

"Most of us do; but this was just a little too quick for my taste. He hadn't even introduced me to his daughters yet."

"Yeah I see your point. How can you step into the role of stepmom if you haven't even met your perspective stepdaughters?"

"Exactly! But anyhow he kept pressing and said I was everything he was looking for and he knew I'd make an excellent stepmom and get along great with them."

"Oh, boy!"

"Umm, right; that should have been my red flag. But I guess I was naïve enough to believe him. I finally got to meet his daughters at his oldest daughter's high school graduation. We did have dinner with his daughters on a few occasions after that but there was always a lot of tension, you know - forced conversation and remote politeness; at least that was my sense of it."

"Whew…that sounds pretty cold," he said.

"Yes it was, anyway to make a long story short - we did get married but it was just he and I. His daughters put up a wall that I just could not breach. I even suggested to him that we have a baby and try to involve them in building a family as half-sisters; but he would have none of that."

"So he really didn't see a problem?" Geoff asked.

"Stranger than that, one night I woke up alone in bed. He wasn't in the bathroom or anywhere around the house. I found him curled up in his younger daughter's bed. The next day I asked him what that was all about. He claimed she was having a nightmare and he was sleeping with her to comfort her."

"I don't think I like where this is going," Geoff said with a disgusted look on his face.

"Over the next few weeks this activity continued sporadically. We started arguing about it. I demanded to know what was going on. He as much told me to mind my own business and not interfere with his parental discretions where they concerned his daughters."

"Wow, that doesn't seem like the same guy you began to describe."

"No, you're right! It sure doesn't and he wasn't. It's like he had this charming façade masking a heinous secret dark side of himself. I tried to get his younger daughter to confide in me but I suspect she was so freaked out that she was suspicious of both of us. She probably thought I would side with him. She must have felt like she didn't have a friend in the world. Her older sister was much closer to her dad and had assumed the position of mother over her. I think she probably felt alienated from her also."

"Karen, that's a recipe for tragedy."

"Yes, it is and that was the result. His younger daughter started hanging out with a fast crowd until all hours of the morning. She became remote and avoided the whole family. I tried to intervene again but I did it in front of him and it triggered an ugly confrontation between the three of us. She stormed out of the house and was gone for a week solid."

"That's so sad," he said.

"One night after she came back I came home early from work and surprised her in our bedroom. I sat down and tried to talk with her. She was high on something. She said something so nasty to me and so disrespectful to her father that I had to bite my tongue to restrain myself from slapping her face. She ran out of the house, jumped into her car and took off."

"You were fighting a losing battle with no help."

"That was the last time I saw her. A few days later on a Sunday morning we awoke to an insistent knock on the front door. It was the county sheriff who came by to inform us that she had overdosed on some club drugs at one of those rave parties."

Geoff had a sick feeling in the pit of his stomach as her story unfolded and became more and more familiar to him. It felt like a sucker punch that had knocked the wind out of him. He struggled to regain his composure, his mind reeling to make sense of all this; to collate it with his experience.

"Karen, do these people have names?"

"I'd rather not reveal their names Geoff; I just want to forget about the whole experience. The crazy twist is my ex is now a councilman in Beaumont."

"Yeah, I would have guessed that."

"Oh really… what are you saying?"

"Oh nothing…the book is never the same as the cover I guess."

The red lights on the pager began flashing and it vibrated on the bar. "Hey, let's go eat, Karen, I'm hungry," he said thankful for the interruption.

The dinner special was halibut steak with rice and asparagus; one of Geoff's favorites and as it turned out also one of Karen's. They shared a bottle of Sauvignon Blanc.

"So what are your plans, Geoff? How long do you think you'll stay in Austin?"

"I don't make plans. I'll probably stay until life tells me it's time to move on."

"What if you find a reason to stay?"

"I'm open-minded, Karen. I've been down a lot of roads. I prefer to think of them as lives. As one ends or is ending, another begins. I've come to realize that life is a journey and in a lot of ways I'm just a passenger along for the ride."

"Hasn't there ever been anyone special, someone that you wanted to hold onto forever?"

"Forever hasn't seemed to work out for me. It's always been an interlude rather than a destination. What about you Karen? What are your plans?"

"Plans for what, Geoff?"

"For the future…the rest of your life; after your marriage disaster in Beaumont."

"That was actually my second marriage. The first was almost as bad but thank goodness there weren't any children to suffer a broken home," she said.

"Well, we are even there. I've been married and divorced twice myself," he said.

"Do you have any children?"

"No," he said anticipating her next question.

"Did you want children?"

"With the right person, yes."

"Well we're even there also," she said.

Geoff poured the last of the wine. He raised his glass for a toast. "Here's to life, may we both find what it is we are looking for."

"Umm hmm, and may we recognize it when we do," she said as she reached across and took his hand in hers. "Geoff, may I impose on you for a ride home? I don't have my car with me."

"That's no imposition, are you ready to leave now or shall we have another drink?"

"I'm ready, I just need to use the ladies room first; I'll meet you at the door."

Chapter thirty-three

Twenty minutes later they were pulling into the driveway at her place a nicely landscaped townhouse complex.

"Geoff, do you like old classic movies?"

"Oh yeah, absolutely - I like them much better than the current crop that passes for entertainment these days."

"Why don't you come in? I'll put one on and we can relax and forget about the world's troubles."

"That sounds like a nice ending to a very enjoyable evening."

As they walked up to the door Karen slid her hand into his and gave a little squeeze. Stopping at the door she slipped her arms around his neck her face close to his.

"Thank you for dinner, Geoff; I really enjoyed it along with your company," she said looking back and forth between his lips and his eyes.

"The pleasure was all mine," he said as he answered her unspoken message and their lips met for a long tender kiss.

Once inside Geoff was impressed with the plush furnishing and décor of the main floor of the townhouse. A tiled open foyer joined an oversize living room which was probably meant for a combination living and dining room. It was comfortably furnished with an oversize plush sofa, love seat, side chair and a rocker recliner all arranged along the border of a large aquamarine toned oriental rug which lay atop of the plush silver gray wall-to-wall carpeting.

A large oval shaped slate coffee table set on the rug near the sofa; smaller matching end tables set between the sofa and love seat on one side and the sofa and side chair on the opposite side. Large oriental table lamps on the end tables gave off a warm glow.

A home theatre setup enclosed in a modular cabinet with glass doors included a large wall-hung flat panel television monitor; probably a fifty-five inch Geoff guessed.

The kitchen was open with a cooking island, a breakfast bar and a dining area off to the back. Double doors led he guessed to a den. Stairs ascended to a balcony with a short hallway between two bedrooms separated by a bathroom. Live plants were scattered throughout the first floor and the balcony. Tasteful artwork hung in all the strategic places. The bow window had an Austrian valance treatment with sheers.

The whole place was elegant, but not gaudy or ostentatious; it had a subtle and relaxing quality with a feeling of intimacy and comfort.

"This place is gorgeous, Karen; you have wonderful taste and a real talent for decorating."

"Thanks Geoff, decorating is a hobby of mine. Why don't you pick out a movie; I'll go pour a little wine we can sip." She slipped out of her slides and walked to the kitchen.

Taking a cue from Karen, Geoff slipped off his shoes leaving them on the foyer tile next to hers. He walked over to the theatre cabinet and opened the glass doors to scan the movie titles. "Hey you have *Arch of Triumph* with Bergman and Boyer; I haven't seen that in a long time, it's one of my favorites."

"Oh, a great choice, it's one of my favorites also," said Karen as she came over and set the glasses down on the coffee table. She loaded the DVD into the system and led him to the sofa where she sat down on his left side.

"Here's to getting acquainted!" she said as she hoisted her glass of wine.

"To classic movies and classy ladies to share them with," said Geoff as he tapped the lip of her glass with his.

"And handsome, hunky men with good taste," she said looking deeply into his eyes as she ran her tongue slowly over the rim of her glass before taking a sip of her wine. She pressed the remote play button and in seconds the room filled with the sound of the introductory leader announcing the cast and title. After adjusting the sound to a lower volume she placed the remote back on the coffee table tucked her right leg under her and snuggled up against Geoff's shoulder.

"Hmm lady, it's going to be hard to concentrate on the movie," he said as he slipped his arm around her gently rubbing her shoulder.

"Umm we've probably both seen it so many times that we can recite the lines from memory."

"You can recite, I'll listen or maybe I'll just...," the rest of his words were smothered by her lips gently pressing against his, sucking on his lower lip, her tongue slipping along the inside. His passion quickly leapt towards a peak as his hands gently kneaded her back; one kiss ended only to begin again with another one each more passionate than the last. He began to undo the bottom buttons on her blouse and slowly slid his right hand up underneath. She wasn't wearing a brassiere; just what he guessed to be a silk camisole separated his fingers from the mound of her modest firm breast. She moaned softly as he gently brushed her nipple protruding through the soft silk with his forefinger. Then as quickly as their intimacy had begun she pushed him gently but firmly away.

"Okay, that's enough let's watch the movie," she said in a teasing sexy voice, her eyes sparkling with passion her mouth set in a tantalizingly satisfied smirk.

Geoff met her bluff, "It is a great movie; I really want to enjoy it," he said as he lifted his glass for a sip of wine with a pretense of extreme concentration on the screen.

Charles Boyer was playing a Czech physician whose wife had been a victim of Nazi torture. He had escaped to Paris where he joined the French resistance. He was called to the hospital to perform lifesaving surgery on a young girl who had suffered a botched unlicensed abortion. Ingrid Bergman hadn't yet made her appearance.

Karen reached for her glass and lifted it to her lips taking a long slow sip. When she returned the glass to the table she too feigned intense interest in the movie and watched in silence for a few minutes. When her attention span expired she ran her fingers behind his head softly kneading the nape of his neck with her fingertips. With her left hand she undid the buttons on his shirt and slid her hand through the opening.

"Oh phooey, Geoff you're wearing an undershirt. We've got to get rid of that, baby." She gently tugged his t-shirt out of his trousers and ran her hand slowly up through the hair on his chest. "Ooh that's more like it," she said cooing as she planted kisses along his jaw line.

Now it was his turn. He grasped hold of her hand. "Hey, hey, hey; I thought we were going to watch the movie?"

"We are; but it's going to be on my terms," she said with a very self-satisfied chuckle. She hit the stop button on the remote. "I need to go get more comfortable. Be back in two seconds. While I'm gone why don't you make yourself more comfortable?"

When she came back down the stairs several minutes later Geoff caught his breath and exhaled appreciatively through his lips. Karen approached the sofa as if she were walking down the runway at a fashion show. She was enjoying his eyes bathing her in attention.

She was wearing a royal blue silk and lace slip that came just below the top of her beige stockings held up by a black garter belt that peaked through the lacy side flaps of the slip. She watched him watching her all the way as she sauntered into the kitchen to retrieve the bottle of wine. Topping off the glasses she sashayed back to the kitchen in slow deliberate steps.

She returned to the sofa and stood there with her hands on her hips. "Geoff, you're still fully dressed. C'mon baby get comfortable; I know you're not the shy type."

As he slipped out of his trousers she unbuttoned his shirt and gently pulled it off along with his t-shirt. Then she restarted the movie and settled into Geoff's lap wriggling around until she got comfortable and exposed a bit of her sheer black lace string bikini panties. Geoff was down to his boxer shorts; very little cloth separated them both from complete nakedness. The effect was mutually overwhelming.

"You are one very sexy lady. Do you practice that performance or does it come natural?"

"Oh I never plan it; it's just an impromptu response to the moment. It depends on who I'm with, a sexy man feeds my sensual appetite," she said as she leaned her head towards his for a kiss.

The movie played on in the background. Charles Boyer's *Dr. Ravic* was offering Ingrid Bergman's *Joan Madou* another brioche.

Geoff's and Karen's kisses grew more passionate. Their hands explored each other as far as position would allow although Geoff definitely had the advantage. They would stop occasionally for a sip of wine. Karen ran the tip of her finger lightly around the rim of her glass and then looking into his eyes she delicately traced the outline of his lips with the same finger and then kissed him softly.

"Do you want to stay with me tonight?"

Geoff inhaled deeply and then forcibly exhaled to regain his composure.

"Karen you'd have to bodily throw me out of here to get rid of me at this point. I want you so much I ache on both a physical as well as mental and emotional level. But I have to admit that I'm a little conflicted right now. I'm trying to fight it on one hand and wondering what the hell I'm doing on the other."

"What are you saying Geoff?"

"There's a little voice inside my head yelling 'slow down'. That old nagging question keeps tormenting me; where do we go from here? What do we do after the mood passes; we hardly know each other?"

"Do you believe in playing games Geoff?"

"No Karen, I don't like games."

"Well I don't either. So let's forget about that little voice. I'm not thinking about tomorrow or next week. I'm not testing or judging you. I just want to make love with you tonight. I need you as much as you said you needed me; physically, mentally and emotionally."

She sat up twisting around until her knees straddled his lap as she sat on his thighs. With her forearms resting against his shoulders, her hands softly cradled his head as she brought her lips close to his.

He met her open mouth with his in a deep passionate kiss. Her fingers ran through the hair on his neckline. He ran his hands along the outside of her thighs. She raised herself up on her knees, slipped the straps of her slip off her shoulders and pulled his head towards her chest until his face was buried between her breasts inside the plunging V-neck of her slip.

He brushed his lips over her breasts planting soft kisses while watching her chest heave with her heavy breathing accompanied by her moans and squeals of delight. Then he ran his fingers up the backside of her thighs and gently massaged her derriere. With the tips of his fingers he began to probe under the edge of her panties until she at last offered token resistance grasping his wrist with her hand in a weak effort at blocking his advance. Her head was on his shoulder nibbling on his neck; her breathing audible in his ear.

"Ohhh umm …," she said drawing it out in a long low sensual moan. "Geoff, please don't tease me, baby; don't start anything that you don't want to finish," she said in a low husky voice as she ran her tongue lightly along his earlobe.

"I've never yet started anything that I didn't want to finish Karen, let's take it upstairs and stop time while we enjoy each other's company." He stood up lifting her gently into his arms and as she slipped her arms around his neck he carried her up the stairs to the master bedroom.

Chapter thirty-four

Saturday morning had already faded into the early afternoon by the time they had showered - together again - as they had last night before the love making. It had gone on well into the early morning hours. Karen resisted his invitation to go out for something to eat insisting instead on making brunch at home.

Dressed in her long flowing silk Japanese kimono, she whipped up French toast with sausage links, cooking them well done and butterflied as he liked them. Geoff helped out with the preparations slicing up fresh fruit for a salad. Karen kept bringing out more fruit until he had sliced up a pineapple, honeydew and cantaloupe melons, several kiwis, pears, two papayas, a mango and a banana and mixed them all up into a large bowl along with orange slices and a few slices of lime. Karen apparently was as big a fan of fresh fruit as he.

"What kind of coffee do you prefer? I have fully-leaded or decaffeinated French Roast."

"The French Roast decafe, it's my favorite."

"Oh good, it's my favorite also we seem to have a lot in common, even in our taste for food."

"Um hmm, it seems that way," he said as he came up behind her and slipped his arms around her waist as she stood by the stove draining the grease from the sausage. He kissed her neck and nuzzled her ear.

"Ooh now don't you start Geoff, we'll never get to eat," she said with a squeal. She put the plate of sausage down on the counter then turned around and reached out to him drawing him close to her and resting the palms of her hands along the sides of his face.

"Come here lover," she said as she slipped her arms around his neck. Their lips met teasing each other with soft kisses. "Okay that's enough," she said turning it off as quickly as she could manage and moving her lips quickly away from his. "It's time to eat."

She brought over the plate of French toast and sausage and Geoff popped the cork on a bottle of champagne she said she had saved for just such an occasion.

"If we sit at the bar we can watch a movie as we eat; I've got another Charles Boyer movie I think you'll like."

"A movie in the background would be nice but I warn you, remember what happened watching the last Charles Boyer movie."

"Umm hmm; maybe we can reprise our roles," she said with a wink as she walked over to the cabinet took out a movie and inserted it into the DVD drive. Charles Boyer and Hedy Lamarr starring in *Algiers* came on the screen.

"Excellent, Karen, you have me figured out, perfectly."

She came back to the bar and slipped her arms around his neck from behind kissing him softly on his right cheek, "It's just synchronicity honey; don't fight it. And to think I might not have ever met you if I didn't go to the Borderline last Tuesday for breakfast. I was driving past the place and thinking about just getting a quick breakfast burrito at Pedro's Tex-Mex-2-GO when something told me to take some extra time and get something healthy."

"And so you did Karen, I am pretty healthy."

"Um hmm...and I'm still amazed that you invited me to your table and I accepted. It felt so natural, so spontaneous. It must be destiny. It's like we are meant for each other."

They finished their brunch after many interruptions, lots of touching and not a few kisses. They rinsed the dishes loaded the dishwasher and brought the coffee and champagne into the living room. Karen snuggled up to Geoff, her legs drawn up and her head on his shoulder.

"It's nice having you close to me Geoff. I'd forgotten how good the feeling is. How does it feel to you?"

"If you have to ask I guess I'm not communicating my feelings as well as I should. I might not get to heaven Karen but close time with you will make a nice consolation; I'll take any and all you have to offer, and still come back begging for more."

"I really didn't have to ask; my intuition tells me all I need to know. But sometimes confirmation is nice," she said pulling him close to her until their lips met. After a few minutes their passion began to rise and Karen squirmed away giggling. "Hold those thoughts for later, honey. I need to run a few errands. You need to go get your things from your motel. As long as you're in Austin you can stay here with me."

"Karen, there's nothing I'd like better, but…"

"No buts, Geoff; just go get your stuff. I'll pick up some pork chops for dinner tonight. You can do the grilling. You do like pork chops?"

"Sweetheart you are amazing. I grew up on pork chops and roast pork, with dumplings and sauerkraut; they were a staple at home with my mom who was Czech."

"Well I don't know if I can match your mom's cooking; but I'm willing to give it a try."

She stood up and undid the waistband of her kimono. Geoff caught his breath as he watched it fall open to reveal that underneath she was naked.

"Just something to think about while we're apart," she said with a sexy flutter of her eyelashes as she slipped into his arms for a parting passionate kiss, "I shouldn't be too long. I'll give you a key; you can let yourself in if I'm not back before you."

Geoff went back to the motel and packed his things. It was way past check-out time but they let him slide since he had spent the whole week with them.

As he drove back to her townhouse he tried as best he could to keep the nagging thoughts running through his mind at bay. Was he going down the same old road yet again? He thought back briefly of Amy and Jennifer and yes Sonni too but then did his best to banish those thoughts of her firmly from his mind. Perhaps this time he needed to forget the feelings in his heart and move on. It would do no good to compare. There was no comparison the circumstances were totally different. He had pursued the acquaintance of Karen that first morning at the Borderline. He didn't need to justify anything. Just accept things as they are. Wasn't that his creed after all? Hadn't he learned anything from all those failed encounters?

He realized that he was unconsciously holding back this time. He hadn't uttered the L-word yet. Had he become jaded? Was he taking and not giving back? Karen seemed to be making more effort than he and she was certainly doing remarkably well in that regard. She had been the one to take the initiative and had been consistently very open and receptive from their first introduction.

He slowly became conscious of the concentration of his thoughts. They were all about Karen. I wonder what she doing? Should I have insisted on helping with her errands? No that would have been a bad move. You need to let her have her space and the solitary time to enjoy it.

What are these feelings that are beginning to stir?

I want to be with her right now. I can't wait to see her again.

Oh lord, it's happening again. I think I'm falling in love with this lady.

He spotted a florist and found a close parking spot. They had a dozen long stem red roses that had been reserved but since it was after five o'clock in the afternoon they let him have them. His next stop was a liquor store for a bottle of champagne. They had Moet Chandon White Star Brut in the cold case.

When he pulled into the driveway of her townhouse he didn't see her car. Seconds later she pulled in alongside. He got out and walked around to open her car door.

"Thanks for being such a sweetheart, Karen," he said as he presented her with the roses.

"Roses! Oh Geoff... thank you so much sweetie! That's so nice of you, I love flowers, especially roses they are so beautiful."

Karen unlocked and opened the garage door and Geoff carried in the packages. Geoff brought them into the kitchen and put them on the bar. Karen rummaged through a cabinet and brought out two vases. She split the roses putting six in each vase and setting one on top of the breakfast bar and the other on the living room sofa table.

"I bought some champagne for tonight if you're so inclined," he said holding up the bottle.

"Oh Moet, that's my favorite!"

"And I bought you a little something to relax in," she said handing him a package with a Nordstrom wrapper.

Geoff opened it and took out a very expensive looking navy blue satin robe with fancy embroidery lined with red silk and trimmed with black velvet on the lapels and the cuffs of the sleeves. The matching belt had black tassels on the ends.

"Oh honey, thank you sweetheart; it's gorgeous but you're spoiling me I've never owned one of these before."

"I'd love to spoil you even more. I can't wait to see you model it for me commando style - wearing just the robe over your hot hard naked body," she said with a mischievous chuckle.

Geoff gathered her in his arms, "I missed you Karen, even in that short time while we were apart... I really missed you. It felt like I had awoken from a dream and everything was gone. I'm sure glad to find out that I wasn't just dreaming."

"Really Geoff...Ooh honey, how sweet; that's so nice to hear. I missed you too sweetie." She met his lips and they shared a long kiss that ended in an extended hug. "You are really getting to me mister."

"I feel the same way about you, lady."

"Well we'd better get busy with dinner. We don't want to waste Saturday night just eating. I can't wait, I want to see you in that robe."

Geoff prepared the pork chops for grilling. He checked her spice rack and found what he was looking for. "Karen have you ever had caraway seeds on your pork chops?"

"Uh, I don't think so, if I did I don't remember but that sounds like a great addition."

Geoff did the grilling on the outdoor patio barbeque. Karen was cooking up something special she said. Geoff made the salad while he waited on Karen's okay to start grilling so everything would be done together. They sat down to a dinner of grilled pork chops with caraway seeds, Karen's special dumplings, sauerkraut and steamed corn on the cob.

"I hope the dumplings are okay, I rushed them a little. Let's save the champagne for dessert; I have some peach mango frozen yogurt we can put on the rest of the fruit salad from this afternoon."

"Everything is fantastic. You're a great cook, Karen."

"No; we are great cooks. Thanks to your help, everything is perfect."

After they finished dinner they cleaned up and loaded the dishwasher. It was fun working together as a team and it seemed so natural.

"Okay, honey now it's time to get comfy, let's go upstairs take a quick shower and get changed into our robes. Then we can watch a movie, sip champagne and munch on fruit salad and..."

"And share lots of hugs and kisses," said Geoff.

"Umm hmm, of course lover; hugs and kisses and...I'm in a very sharing mood."

After a quick shower, which Karen insisted that they take separately this time to keep their libidos at peak, they went back downstairs and watched *Breakfast at Tiffany's* as Karen's movie choice, sipped champagne and fed each other the fruit salad with peach mango frozen yogurt - both wearing their robes and nothing else.

Chapter thirty-five

They slept in Sunday morning, or to be more precise they slept through the morning. Although even when they got up they hadn't spent many hours actually sleeping. They were still getting to know how to satisfy each other. It was, they agreed, something that was going to take a while... a long, pleasant, exciting while.

Champagne and a classic movie had proved once again last night to be a perfect aphrodisiac. Karen couldn't wait for the bedroom. Careful not to soil their robes they had discarded them and wrestled playfully until Karen had prevailed pushing Geoff down recumbently and sliding into his arms. Lying naked on a beach towel spread over the sofa they made love slowly and passionately and then dozed off in each other's arms.

"Today is play day Karen. No cooking, no cleaning, no errands - let's go out to someplace nice for brunch," said Geoff as they cuddled in bed before their shower.

"Oh I'm ready for that, how about downtown. There's a huge new upscale hotel, it's one of those large chains, I forget which one; anyway it has a wonderful view of Town Lake. Rumor has it they have the best brunch in town and the atmosphere is absolutely regal; I've wanted to check it out for a while but I've been waiting to find the right someone to share it with. And here you are."

"I'm certainly glad that I was fortunate enough to be in the right place at the right time to be chosen," he said

"Umm hmm so am I."

"We better get a move on or we'll miss the party," he said kicking the covers off.

They had to hurry a bit but still managed to get there in time. The main brunch crowd had already dissipated. It was perfect. A musician played at a concert grand piano in the atrium. His soft classical and jazz sounds carried across the dining area.

The brunch was a buffet boasting over seventy-five items. Along with the usual waffles, French toast and omelets made to order there were three varieties of potatoes, scrambled eggs, Eggs Benedict, thin and thick bacon, sausage links and patties, broiled grouper, salmon, cheese blintzes, strawberry crepes, an assortment of steamed and raw vegetables, chicken wings, a variety of pasta salads, a huge fresh fruit platter, beef Stroganoff with noodles and a carving board and condiments with London broil, pork loin and turkey breast sliced on request.

Another table had assorted breads, breakfast rolls, muffins, croissants and even brioche. Behind all that was another long dessert table with assorted pastries, cakes and pies including a Black Forest cake, and seven different flavors of ice cream.

They took a seat at the bar and ordered tall mimosas on the rocks. Between the two of them they tried a fair sampling of all the items except for all the pastries. They feed each other samples of the different choices they made. By the time they were ready for the pastries they were both so contentedly full that they agreed to just share a chocolate mousse. Afterwards they walked hand in hand around the atrium and stopped at the waterfall to make a wish and throw a coin into the stream that flowed through the lounge.

"Let's throw one together," Karen said taking two pennies from her purse.

Geoff had taken out a quarter, it was all the change he had with him.

"You can't throw a quarter," she said looking at the coin he held, "you won't get your wish."

"What, I've never heard that," said Geoff.

"It'll bring bad karma; you'll piss off the wish fairy because of ostentation."

"Oh my gosh, really," he said as straight-faced as he could.

"Sure, pennies are special, they make everyone equal."

"So you're saying the wish fairy is a democrat?"

"You're making a big thing out of this, just accept it," Karen said trying to stifle the giggles and failing badly. After they threw the pennies Karen asked, "What did you wish for?"

"I can't tell you that! It won't come true."

"Just give me a hint, I'll tell you what I wished for," she said fluttering her eyelashes.

"No!"

"You're being a brat," she said wrinkling up her nose.

"And you're being a tease." He took her in his arms and brought his head close for a kiss. She turned hers away with a squeal.

"Nope...you called me a tease; say you're sorry."

"Hey, you called me a brat."

She couldn't continue she was laughing uncontrollably; she slipped her arms around his neck leaning her head back and shaking her hair free until at last she got control of her laughter. She gently pulled his head closer until their foreheads rested together for a few brief moments and then their lips met in a passionate kiss.

"Geoff...honey, you are really getting to me."

"I'm way ahead of you with respect to that aspect of our relationship lady; you have already gotten to me in a very big way."

"Oh my I'm going to hate going to work tomorrow."

"I'll be waiting for you when you get home," he said kissing her softly.

"Umm just knowing that will get me through the day."

They strolled through the lobby and browsed the gift shops not wanting to end the day; finally, they headed to the parking garage to retrieve Geoff's truck.

"Oh gosh, my sunglasses; I must have left them at the restaurant," he said as he climbed behind the wheel. He drove over to the portico by the lobby and left the engine running to keep the truck cool for Karen; "I'll just be a minute honey". He climbed back in minutes later without the glasses. "Someone must have taken a shine to them, they're gone. Would you check the glove box for me, please; I think I have a spare pair in there."

She rummaged through the glove box and found an extra pair; as she took them out a small envelope dropped out. When she retrieved it from the floor the inscription caught her eye: *To Geoff, Love Always Danielle.* It had not been opened.

"Oh what's this; a love letter from one of your girlfriends?"

"What! Where'd that come from?"

"The writing on it says 'To Geoff, Love Always Danielle' and it's still sealed."

"Well open it and read it to me," he said as he pulled the truck out of the portico and down the hotel drive.

"Do you really want me to?"

"Sure, babe, I've got no secrets to keep."

"Okay," she tore it open and read aloud – "*Dear Geoff: Thank you so much for all you have done for me and given me. I owe you a very great debt of gratitude. You will always be special to me. If you ever get back to Beaumont, PLEASE look me up. Love Forever, Danielle.*"

"So who is Danielle, from Beaumont?"

"Remember that story you told me about your ex-husband in Beaumont, last Friday night?"

She looked at him with a puzzled expression that slowly turned to dread, "You don't mean to tell me…It couldn't be…"

"I met her in New Orleans; she's young enough to be my daughter. She was in a bad situation and had been through some rotten experiences. I guess I had a lot of influence with her I pretty much convinced her that she ought to try to get back home and reconnect with her dad. I drove her back to Beaumont for the reunion. I thought it worked out perfectly, until I heard your story. She had a sister Tammy who died of an overdose of Ecstasy. Her dad is Councilman Doug Porter. That's why I asked you the names of those people. It was so much of a coincidence I assumed you were talking about the same family."

"Oh my God! Geoff, I've got the shivers, I can't believe what I'm hearing."

"Then I'm right, you were married to Doug?"

"Yes, yes I was."

"Geoff, why didn't you say something? Why didn't you tell me this Friday night?"

"I held off because I don't want to prejudge anyone. I don't know the whole story and I need to reconcile the parts I do know. But I guess I really held off because I wanted to get to know you for myself. Doug and Danielle both did quite a bit of character assassination in their allegations regarding you."

"That doesn't surprise me," she said, "I just couldn't get through to Danielle. She wouldn't let me into her life."

"That's understandable, she's is a very strong young woman. But the wife and stepmother they described don't seem to square with my own impression, of the lady who I'm beginning to get very fond of. I've been through two divorces Karen; I'm very much acquainted with the acrimony, the lies, and the vicious personal attacks."

"Does that mean I get a chance to redeem myself?"

"That's not necessary. Our relationship here and now doesn't have anything to do with the past. I just need to know that Danielle is okay and not in any danger. As for Doug, well perhaps the fact that he is a politician speaks for itself."

He held her hand as traffic allowed gently squeezing and glancing over at her from time to time. Sometimes she returned his squeeze but most times she sat motionless just staring out the side window. He fought back thoughts and feelings of grim foreboding trying to drive it from his mind lest it establish itself as reality. They rode the rest of the way back to her townhouse in an uneasy silence. Geoff parked the truck in the driveway.

"I need to rearrange the garage so you can fit your truck in," she said breaking the tension a little.

"That'd be nice, you feel like doing that today?"

"Oh, I don't know. It's too hot."

"Come on now don't wimp out on me, let's just get it done."

He opened the garage door in front of his truck. There was plenty of room in the garage. He moved some things to the rear and the sides of the garage and then broke down some empty boxes and stacked them neatly on the side held in place by some five-gallon paint cans. She watched him for a few minutes and then pitched in moving some stuff around. The whole project took maybe twenty minutes.

"That's good enough to get the truck in, we can sort through this stuff later," he said. I just need to keep her involved, he thought to himself; try to make a bridge to the future.

"I should probably get rid of a lot of this stuff," she said.

"Whew! It sure is hot out here, let's get inside. I need to take a quick shower, honey. How about you, care to join me?" he asked.

"Oh I ..."

"Come on, you'll feel much better. I'll give you a really nice back rub."

She joined him reluctantly as if only to please him. Once in the shower standing behind her he gently rubbed her neck and shoulders; he could feel the tension.

"Karen I meant what I said earlier," he said softly into her ear. "Whatever went on between you and Doug in your marriage has no bearing whatsoever on our relationship. Your marriage to Doug is over; it was in another life. You can't change anything about that. But we can build a beautiful life together, something really special starting today – starting right now."

She turned around and embraced him her arms wrapped tightly around his chest her head nestled between his neck and shoulder. "Geoff... honey thank you; thank you so much, I really needed to hear you say that. You are so good for me, and I need you so much."

"We need each other babe," he said softly as he cradled the sides of her face with his hands. He brought his own head close to hers and looked deeply into her eyes. Then he closed the distance between his lips and hers until their open lips met in a long passionate kiss.

Chapter thirty-six

M onday morning came early, too early. Karen was up at six o'clock with her efficient career face on.

"I like to work out before I start my business day. I've gotten into a three day a week workout routine. I don't want to break the habit. How about coming with me? I can get you in on a guest pass."

"Uh can I have a bye for today; maybe I'll go with you Wednesday."

"Nothing doing get your butt up and get ready."

"Were you ever a military drill instructor?"

"Do I look like a drill instructor?"

"No you don't, certainly none that I've ever known. If the military had had drill instructors like you I probably would have made the military a career."

"Flattery will get you nowhere, quit stalling…come on, I'll go start breakfast. We're having oatmeal."

"Aye aye, Ma'am," he said as he bounded out of bed, came to attention and gave her a hand salute.

"You're out of uniform, sailor," she said as she eyed him up and down trying to keep a stern face.

By a little after seven o'clock they were sitting at the breakfast bar eating oatmeal and picking apple and banana slices out of a bowl.

Geoff was dressed casually in slacks and a tee shirt; Karen was in a navy blue pants suit with a pale blue silk top. She wore little make-up.

"Karen, you look fantastic. It's the same look you had the day we met at the Borderline; what was that last Wednesday?"

"Tuesday, Geoff - maybe we should go there tomorrow morning for our one-week anniversary."

"You're on, darling; may I have a kiss?"

"Umm hmm, of course, but just a little one, I know how you are and we don't have time to get aroused and mess around."

"Too late, I'm already aroused."

"Oh too bad…you'll just have to work it off at the club," she said pushing out her lower lip in a sexy pout.

"How about I just save it for tonight?"

"Umm that'll work, I'll make sure to get home early."

Geoff gave her two quick kisses and then a third which lasted until she pulled away.

"Umm…enough, lover, c'mon it's time to go."

They cleaned up the dishes, Geoff grabbed the gym bags and they headed out to the garage.

"We'll have to drive separately so I can leave right for work," she said.

In the next hour and a half or so they got through cardio, two rows of resistance machines and lots of abdominal work and ended with a stretching session.

"Time to hit the showers. I'm sorry honey, we won't be able to take one together in here, although it would create quite a stir," she said with a snicker. "If you get done first don't wait around for me, just go ahead and leave, because that's what I'll do," she said as she disappeared into the ladies' locker room.

The shower after a good workout always felt great to Geoff but today it felt even better. Karen was back to her self-assured independent self. Whatever had been bothering her about her former husband and that whole situation was resolved; at least it looked that way to Geoff. He hoped it wouldn't come back to haunt them.

Of course he still needed to satisfy himself that Danielle was okay. He needed to call her, he probably should have done that already but his concern for Karen had pushed it to a back burner. Besides, he consoled himself; Danielle was a pretty savvy young lady who had demonstrated that she knew how to take care of herself. But then again he still needed to make certain, he felt responsible for her safety.

By the time he finished dressing and headed out to the parking lot he noticed Karen's car was already gone. There was a note stuck in the driver's side window of his truck. *Honey, I left my gym bag with you so you can launder my things along with yours. Thanks sweetie, Karen.* Her bag was in the truck bed. It made him chuckle to himself. Wow, I'm beginning to feel like the stay-at-home spouse. I could get used to this.

He headed back to the townhouse to do the laundry and make a few calls. He needed to get in touch with his agent. He had a manuscript he had submitted advising that they contact his agent with any requested revisions while he was on the road. His credit cards - he only owned three - were setup for automatic payment and he could access his lines and bank account online. A mail-box service took care of any extraneous mail that he might get holding it for his pick-up or forwarding it to him if need be by General Delivery. It all worked well he could remain incommunicado without a permanent address for the most part yet still stay in the loop and manage his affairs on his own terms.

He made some coffee, started the laundry and then began to review the raw notes in his journals transcribing and editing them into scene segments on his laptop for possible future inclusion into story lines. It amazed him how a story would evolve from the seeds of a few lines and take on its own form and direction. Once you had a feeling for a character's personality you could give him free rein and watch the story unfold; sometimes the twists and turns took you to places you hadn't dreamed of when you began. If you took a misstep your character would let you know. Oftentimes he had found himself writing well into the early morning hours. If he tried to abandon the story too early it would not let him sleep.

When he got up to get a refill of coffee and put another load into the dryer he glanced at the clock and was surprised to find it was well into the afternoon; he had skipped lunch. The phone rang. He hesitated initially wondering if he should answer it and then picked it up.

"Hi hon, it's me; I just called to check and see how your day was going."

"Hi, babe, I'm doing fine, got the laundry done and I'm making great progress transcribing my old journals; How's your day going?"

"Oh it's busy, a lot of phone calls and case follow-ups, the usual stuff. I was thinking, how about pizza and beer for dinner tonight?"

"That sounds good to me; do you want me to run out for anything?"

"No don't bother sweetie, I can order it right before I leave work and pick up some beer on the way home. I'll be leaving work about four-thirty at the latest. Do you have a favorite beer preference?"

"You seem to be pretty tuned into my preferences, just surprise me."

"Okay, I'll see you later, bye."

A little after five o'clock Geoff heard the garage door opening. He went out through the laundry room garage door to find Karen juggling a pizza and trying to open her car door at the same time.

"Hey, great timing honey, here let me get that," he said opening the door and grabbing the pizza.

Karen reached into the car and retrieved a six-pack of beer. Geoff leaned over for a kiss and glanced down at the beer.

"Umm, Moosehead; lady you are still batting a thousand. You are almost beginning to scare me with your intuitive powers, or am I that predictable?"

"No, I'm just very in tune with you; it's my female sixth sense working in high gear." Karen stowed the beer in the refrigerator and turned around to wrap her arms around Geoff's neck.

"That little hello kiss I got outside was nice but now I want a real one," she said as their lips met in a long much more passionate kiss and ended with them trading soft kisses until Karen pulled away brushing her forefinger softly over Geoff's lips. "That's enough for now," she said with a quick coy chuckle.

"You're teasing me again."

"It's just balance hon, knowing when to give in and when to hold back to keep you interested."

"You're an unbelievable expert at it."

"Okay, let me go upstairs and change," she said as she picked up the television remote and toggled to the news channel. "Here watch the news and give me a report then we can watch a movie with our pizza if you want."

Geoff set out two place settings on the bar, walked over to pick out a movie from the cabinet and then sat down on the sofa to watch the news.

The international scene was full of news and pictures of two airplane crashes - one in Athens, Greece and the other just outside Paris, France - that were being investigated as suspicious.

Then they switched to the national scene, more senate subcommittee hearings into the out of control insurance industry. The economy was up, unemployment was down, Wall Street was its usual schizophrenic self, and mortgage rates were climbing higher. Then the network cut away for a commercial break before the local news. A few minutes later Karen came down looking refreshed and exquisite in a short lavender dressing gown just above her knees.

"Did you miss me honey?"

"Huh… oh yeah," he said as nonchalantly as he could manage trying to keep his eyes on the television.

"Geoff?" Karen walked around crisscrossing in front of the screen feigning annoyance as he stared intently at the screen. Finally, determined to get to him, she stood still in front of the screen and loosened the waistband of her gown and let it fall open to reveal nothing more than just a matching lavender garter belt holding up her white stockings and a pair of white string bikini panties.

"Oowwweee! Babe you got away from me this morning but not this time; no more teasing. Bring your body over here lady."

Now it was her turn. She came over exaggerating the swivel in her hips and drew her gown tightly closed around her as she sat down next to him, her arms folded across her chest with her hands grasping her upper arms.

"So what was on the news, honey," she asked as calmly and collectedly as she could evince, feigning detachment.

"Well the local news was really racy it featured a short segment about a local couple who sat down to cold pizza after a very steamy session of lovemaking."

"Oh… really, goodness there must be a lot of that going around these days," she said as she reached over and ran her hand over his thigh. She planted soft kisses near his ear and along his jaw line and down his neck as she began to loosen the belt of his shorts.

She pulled off his tee shirt and then began to pull down his shorts as he slipped his hand under her gown to divest her of her panties.

As he gathered her in his arms she tugged off his boxers and they tumbled down on the sofa, their arms wrapped around each other laughing, giggling and reacting to each other's touch with alternating moans and squeals of delight and pleasure.

Their foreplay grew in intensity with touching, fondling, kissing and caressing until they could hold back no longer.

Then they surrendered to their desires and consummated their love, slowly, passionately and in perfect harmony with each other's needs and desires until at last they lay totally spent and supremely satisfied in each other's embrace basking in the slowly ebbing glow of their lovemaking.

"Geoff…oh honey, I…I love you."

He stared deeply into her eyes, running his fingers through the hair on the sides of her head and lightly along the ridge of her jaw. He leaned over and kissed her tenderly.

"And I love you, Karen more and more each day," he said in a gentle low voice.

Chapter thirty-seven

Tuesday morning Karen awoke again at six o'clock but she was in a far more playful and passionate mood than she had been a day earlier. Maybe it was a carry-over from their love making of last night.

"Happy anniversary honey; and to think only one week ago today we met as total strangers and today here we are as lovers. I had a premonition it would be more than just a passing occurrence," she said in a whisper letting her eyes roam over his body as she rested on her elbow while she ran the fingers of her other hand over his chest watching him wake up. She kissed his lips lightly and then his jaw and slowly began moving her lips down along his neck to his chest. They were both sleeping naked and the sensation of her soft flesh lightly touching him as she leaned over to plant soft kisses over his body combined with the fragrant scent of her to work him up into an intense state of arousal.

"Umm yes, happy anniversary darling," he said a little hoarse as he woke up with a start to reach out and gather her into his arms. "What a wonderful wake-up call that was," he said tracing a trail with the fingers of his right hand softly up her arm, over her neck, down her backbone to the flesh of her derrière and along the back of her thigh.

He nuzzled the warm soft fragrant flesh of her breasts trying his best not to irritate them with his rough morning growth of beard as he planted soft kisses to the accompaniment of her moans of delight.

"The Borderline doesn't open for breakfast until eight o'clock. We'll have to find something to occupy our time until then," she said in a conspiratorial tone as she softly rubbed her leg bent at the knee over his legs and ran her toes along his calves and ankles.

"Umm yes, but that shouldn't be a problem it will give us a chance for a little romantic improvisation. Let's see, oh I think I need a quick shave for what I have in mind," he said rubbing his fingers over his beard as he let his eyes roam over her soft curves.

"Umm hmm, well I have a little romantic improvisation of my own and I don't need to shave," she said as she ran her fingers slowly down his chest and over his lower abdomen. She planted kisses on his chin, neck and chest then slowly inched her way lower along his torso to his pubis. She made love to him, her tongue teasing him to extreme until he could no longer hold back. After he finished she slid back into his arms her head against his chest listening to his breathing recover as he gently stroked her hair.

"Whew... Karen that was quite an improvisation and a great improvisation deserves a fitting answer in-kind. But before I give you my performance I really do need to shave. I'll be back before you miss me," he said as he kissed her and then swung his legs over the side of the bed and shuffled off to the bathroom.

When he returned he found her snoozing looking content and peaceful. He lifted the sheet and treated his eyes to an entire view of her body lying in its alluring nakedness, enjoying the stolen opportunity to intimately watch her without being discovered.

He bent over her kissing her forehead, cheeks, lips and neck with quick gentle brushes of his lips. Then he slowly moved down along her arms, her chest and then to her hips and abdomen. She stirred and squirmed a little as he worked his way lower planting soft kisses along the inside of her thighs.

As she woke up he made love to her, his tongue arousing and coaxing her higher and higher while he brushed the tips of his fingers lightly over her abdomen until she surrendered her relatively calm composure to the heat and frenzy of her passion.

Collapsing back in each other's arms they held each other tightly, softly caressing each other as her breathing gradually returned to normal and their passion slowly subsided.

"Oh I do love you, Karen; I love you so very much."

"Umm...I love you too Geoff, even more as each day passes."

They took a shower together sharing more love with the water beating down on them. Then they dressed and left for breakfast. They got to the Borderline just after eight-thirty.

Karen looked stunning in a light peach pants suit with a silk scarf of pink, peach and orange flowers lining the inside of the low-cut v-neckline of her jacket. She wore white strapped slides with heels to complete her outfit.

They ordered the chef's special of the day which today was Crepes a L'orange with a petite breakfast filet mignon and diced new potatoes.

They were just starting to eat when Karen reached down to the cell phone clipped at her waist. Pulling it out she checked the number and put it back.

"They'll just have to wait I'm not ready yet; this is still my time." When she was with someone in a restaurant she customarily switched her cell phone to vibrate. She made it a practice to never interrupt a meal and take a cell phone call. Nothing was that urgent. After all she was not a Physician.

When they had finished their breakfast she reached across the table to take his hand in hers, "I'm sorry honey - I've really got to run."

Geoff got up and they shared a hug and a quick kiss. "Have a nice day Hon, call me if you can."

"I'll make a point of it, love you," she said.

"Love you too babe."

Geoff didn't go back to the townhouse as had been his custom since he had been staying with Karen. He put off checking his email and decided on the spur of the moment, for some reason that today was a good day for a trip to the University of Texas campus. He hadn't been there yet and wanted to check it out – maybe even look into graduate programs, although it did occur to him that maybe he was getting a little ahead of himself, taking things for granted and actually planning a future...maybe that was being a bit presumptuous.

Well looking at the options was not like committing to them even though in his experience just imagining what life could hold in store was usually enough to jinx it and ensure it would never come to fruition, he told himself.

Traffic was unusually light and he got to the campus in twenty minutes. He followed the signs for the library and had just pulled into the parking lot and found a space for visitors when his cell phone rang. He picked it up and flipped the cover open, "Hello," he said expecting to hear Karen's voice on the other end.

"Hello, Geoff?"

The question was posed by a familiar voice. It took a brief second or two for his voice recognition to register and retrieve a name to go along with it.

"Danielle?"

"Yeah, it's me, how are you?"

"Well this is a pleasant surprise, I'm fine. How are you doing? What's going on in your life?"

"Oh Geoff my life is just fantastic and getting better each day and I've got you to thank for it."

"Hey now young lady you've got your own tenacity to thank, not me. I just helped point you in the right direction – you did all the heavy lifting. You need to congratulate yourself on some good choices. So what have you been up to?"

"Well at the moment I'm in Austin, at the University of Texas administration office. I'm going to register for classes. I don't know why, but I just got this feeling that I needed to call you. I've wanted to talk with you for a while and something just told me to call you now."

"Wow, Danielle do you believe in synchronicity?"

"Oh, I think so, but I don't think it has ever happened to me."

"Well then this is your first experience with it. I am right now sitting in my truck at the library parking lot here at the Austin UT campus. I saw signs for the admin building so I can't be very far away from you."

"Oh my goodness Geoff, I don't believe it. I've got chills. Please tell me you're not kidding me."

"I'm not kidding; I really am here. Let's get together somewhere and exchange stories."

"Oh yes, that would be great, give me ten minutes and I'll drive over there. There's a student café right around the corner from the library, we can walk over there and spend some time together. I can't believe this. I'll

meet you right outside of the library main entrance. If you don't see me in ten minutes please call me back on this number, okay?"

"I'll be waiting Danielle and I've got your number if I need it. See you in ten."

Geoff walked over to the library entrance and went in to check it out. Computer screens had replaced all the old card catalogs. There was a staffed information desk that also handled reference inquiries and computer assignments for online internet access. The periodicals section which caught his eye had a very impressive collection of political science and international affairs journals - many that were completely new to him. He would definitely have to spend some time here.

He was just getting into a journal on International Geopolitics when he glanced at his watch and realized he'd better head back outside so he wouldn't miss Danielle.

No sooner had he gotten out the door when he caught sight of a familiar figure walking toward the building. Danielle recognized him and sprinted over to him. When she was about three feet away she let out a yelp and scrambled into his arms.

"Oh Geoff, it's so good to see you again. I can't tell you how many times I've wanted to just call and say hi."

"So what was stopping you, Danielle? Look, anytime you want to talk, just give me a ring, okay? Please, anytime, don't hesitate, call me."

"I guess I just didn't want to become a pest."

"Nonsense Danielle, I'll always have time for you... always. So don't give it a second thought, if there's ever something on your mind that you think I can help out with, or if you just need to talk, I'll be there for you, just call me. So how's life back in Beaumont? How are you and your dad getting along?"

"Oh we're doing fine. I decided to get my own place for a little more privacy... well to be honest after I settled in it brought back too many memories."

As they talked they walked over to the student union café. They ordered mocha coffees, just another taste they found they had in common and found a place to sit outside under an umbrella.

"So tell me about your plans, what classes are you signing up for."

"Oh I've had some fantastic good fortune in that regard. Let me tell you the story. The partners at the law firm like my work so much that they decided they would chip in for my tuition if I wanted to get a degree and go on to law school. Can you believe it; I'm going to be a lawyer one day?"

"Hey now Danielle that's fantastic, I'm really glad to hear that. You deserve it for being such a good person."

"Oh thanks for the flattery, but it's not like I'm some kind of a saint."

"Hey, look you've come through some really tough times for someone your age and you've done it pretty selflessly. It's time you got a break in life as payback."

"I'm going to have to settle down and really concentrate on my studies. It's all based on my grades. I'll get full reimbursement for an A, half reimbursement for a B and a quarter for a C."

"That's great, that's some very good incentive to do well."

"Yeah, I'm really thrilled about the opportunity."

"How's everything else? Have you been reconnecting with any of your old friends?"

"Well yeah, some…"

"Wow that was pretty lukewarm, is there more to it that you're not telling me?"

"You can read me like a book, huh?"

"It's just genuine concern, Danielle. I want to see you take advantage of all the opportunities you can to succeed."

"Well ah… I really wasn't going to say anything; I don't want to bother you with my soap opera but you're the one person I feel like I can trust."

"What's up, Danielle? It sounds serious."

"You remember my friend Steve who delivered the pizza that night in Beaumont?"

"Yeah, sure."

"Well his wife Liz filled me in on a lot of rumors going around since I left town. It seems she also knows a few of Tammy's old friends. And lately they have been spreading around a lot of dark stories about my dad…about things he allegedly did to Tammy.

It makes me sick just to hear it, but then when I seriously think about it…I just can't believe it. I never saw anything, not ever, nothing and Tammy never told me anything like that or even hinted about it. It's just not him. My daddy would never do anything like that. He… he couldn't, he's not capable of that. He was always a wonderful dad to both of us."

"What kind of stories are they spreading, Danielle?"

Danielle turned away unable to continue. Tears welled up in her eyes. "Oh God, Geoff I just can't believe it." She covered her face with her hands and rocked back and forth stifling a sob.

Geoff put his arm around her comforting her wishing they were in a more private spot. "Look, you can tell me later, after you've had some time to put things into perspective."

"No, it's okay, I can tell you now. I need to get it out of my system."

And then she blurted out the words Geoff knew were coming.

"Tammy allegedly told them that she was being sexually abused by my dad, and that she was terrified and had n…no one to turn to," the last words came out garbled as her lower lip quivered and she buried her face in his shoulder to cover her sobs.

Holding her tight, Geoff was silent for a long moment, searching for the right words to comfort her and trying to keep his own calm demeanor. The words disgusted him, even more than when he had heard them from Karen. The thought of something like that happening was repugnant to him. He fought the rage building in him and the urge to rush to judgment.

"Danielle, let's get out of here and take a walk."

There was a slight breeze blowing which kept it comfortable even with the strong rays of the bright sun beating down on them as they walked in silence along the wide concrete pathways. There were a few groups of students on their way to class or appointments and even several groups playing Frisbee on the grass of the large open quadrangle just up ahead.

"Danielle, for what it's worth I've heard a corroborating story about the situation between Tammy and your dad from another source."

"You heard it… from who?"

"Karen, your former stepmom told me."

"What? How in the world did you get in contact with her?"

"It's sort of a long story and it's actually pretty bizarre but it shows how small this world is. When I first got to Austin I decided to stay on the south side near the blues bars since I had been there before and was familiar with the locale.

I found a great place for breakfast and I met this really attractive lady there who came in one morning just after I had sat down. We hit it off and she told me the place had a blues band on Fridays that made it the new crowd favorite. I met her again at the place on Friday and gave her a ride home.

We started dating and we've been hanging out together ever since. During one of our conversations she told me the story of her former marriage that was uncannily familiar. I asked her to fill in the names but I really didn't need to hear them. I knew it had to be about your dad and you and Tammy."

"That is so totally unbelievable. Did you tell her about your connection with me?"

"No, I wanted to check out the facts first but I wasn't sure how to proceed so I just put it aside figuring that I'd try to call you and check on how things were going in your life. But a few days later Karen accidentally found the note you left in my glove box and I told her the story of how I met you."

"So what was her reaction?"

"She got very silent, sort of went into a cocoon. I got the feeling that she didn't see any point in continuing our relationship."

"But you convinced her otherwise, right?"

"Well I didn't think any unfortunate experiences in her past should dictate her future. And she is a very attractive woman; I really wanted to get to know her."

"You are such a sweet caring man. I hope I'm lucky enough to meet someone like you someday when I'm ready for a relationship."

"Take your time Danielle; you've got a great future ahead of you, focus on that. Don't rush into anything that will sidetrack you or keep you from realizing your full potential."

"You don't have to worry about that, Geoff. I think I've gotten all the wild times out of my system. I feel like I'm really ready to settle down and get through my studies. It's much too good of an opportunity to let slip away."

"You'll do fine, Danielle, you're wise beyond your years. How are you going to handle the commute between here and Beaumont?"

"That's another gift from my bosses. They have several company apartments that they keep for attorneys working on cases here in Austin. They are going to let me stay there during the semester and I can go back to Beaumont during breaks or on weekends whenever they need me for something."

"Fantastic, they must really like you."

"It probably has to do with my daddy's influence."

"Don't sell yourself short, Danielle. His influence may have gotten you the opportunity for an interview but your character and performance are what's making the real impression."

"Thank you Geoff, you are so good for my ego. So are you going to be staying here in Austin for a while?"

"Time will tell, Danielle. Things are getting pretty serious between Karen and me."

"Oh, Geoff I just hope it's for real. I don't want to see you get hurt."

"Hey now that's a switch. You're looking out for me?"

"I care a whole lot about you. And I know Karen better than you do, or at least I've seen another side of her from an objective viewpoint that you might be blind to because of your feelings for her. I hope I'm wrong about her, but my instincts tell me she's trouble and my instincts have always been pretty reliable."

"Don't worry honey, I'll be fine. I'm a long way from my first rodeo. Listen, we'll have to stay in touch. When are you coming back up to Austin?"

"My first semester starts in about three weeks."

"Great, maybe we can arrange to have dinner a few times, if you want."

"Oh sure, that would be wonderful, I'd really like that. I'll have daddy down in Beaumont and you my other dad up here in Austin for support. I'm a very lucky gal."

"You deserve it. Who knows maybe we can even get things patched up between you and Karen," said Geoff with a wink.

"Well, maybe...we'll just have to see how things work out with regards to that."

"I won't force the issue Danielle, it's your call."

Chapter thirty-eight

On his way back to the townhouse Geoff did a mental reality check; he was on his way home. He had begun thinking of Karen's townhouse as home. When had this transition occurred? And what had triggered the change from just another chance at a relationship to one of acceptance of permanence or maybe hoped for permanence. His cell phone rang and brought him back to here and now.

"Hello."

"Hi lover, what are you doing?"

"Hi, hon. Oh I'm just working on the computer going through some material for my latest project," he said not knowing why he was lying and feeling a little foolish because of it.

"What's all that noise, it sounds like you're in your truck?"

"Uh…yeah," he said reflexively and then regretted it. "I just went out and got my oil changed and now I'm on the way back," he said feeling forced to continue the deception and hoping that Karen wouldn't detect it.

"I'm afraid I'm going to be working late tonight. I had to reschedule an appointment later than I'd like, but I really need to get it done, I don't want to postpone it for another day. I'm sorry baby."

"That's okay, honey I know how that is. So shall we plan on having a late dinner together?"

"I have an interview to conduct. It might take a long time. Why don't you just go ahead and eat when you get hungry. I'll get something quick before I get home.

"I'd rather just wait for you and then we can eat together when you get home."

"Geoff I don't know how late I'll be - no sense in both of us eating late."

"Are you sure? I don't mind waiting."

"Yes I'm sure, Geoff. Please just go ahead and eat. Don't wait for me," there was the slightest bit of edge in her voice that Geoff hadn't heard from her before but he decided it was just job stress.

"Okay honey, don't work too hard, I'll see you when you get home."

"Umm, bye."

Geoff hit the remote button to open the garage door and pulled in his truck. As he settled into the den and started to go through his email his concentration just wasn't there.

He got up and made a pot of coffee. Then he got the newspapers and absentmindedly scanned through the business and sports sections barely reading the columns. He switched on the television and channel surfed to the news networks. Nothing worked. His mind kept returning to the short cell phone conversation with Karen. He had aggravated her. He was sure of that now. Just a simple thing - like she had to work late - and he was still pushing for her attention. He began to mentally recollect episodes from his past romantic dalliances and reconstruct the dialogue to correct what he was sure were his mistakes and shortcomings in the old what-if game.

Finally cursing himself out for pondering hypothetical scenarios and dwelling on what he could never change he switched the television back on and toggled to the 24-hour News Headlines. He watched for about a half hour until he realized he was hungry. He decided on his old familiar bachelor favorite – a bowl of soup with a can of tuna. A half hour later he was back watching the news and then the History Channel.

The conversation with Karen came flashing back once more in his thoughts only this time with more clarity. He had told her he was working on his computer but when she said it sounded like he was in his truck he had as much as admitted that he had lied and then compounded it by telling yet another fib about getting an oil change.

Women were perceptive enough to pick up those little subtleties yet she hadn't said anything, just finessed the whole moment. But maybe that was the reason she had gotten a little edgy. He realized now that on some deeper level he was covering up the fact that he had been to the UT campus and had by chance met with Danielle. Was he feeling guilty of doing something behind her back or was he was somehow less than confident in their relationship because of their conflicting roles with Danielle?

Sometime near midnight he heard the garage door open. A minute or so later Karen came walking in through the laundry room door.

"Oh you're still up. I thought you'd be asleep by now."

"Hi Hon, no I thought I'd wait up for you - I'd rather not sleep alone when I know there's an option."

"Oh Geoff, what am I going to do with you?"

"Ah well, we could reprise our morning wake-up calls from this morning."

"Oh goodness, aren't you tired?"

"I'm never too tired for you Karen."

"Well I'm afraid it will have to wait for tomorrow I'm really pooped out."

"Did you have dinner tonight?" he asked.

"Yeah, I stopped at a little fast food place and had a quick chicken sandwich and salad."

"Shall we call it a night then and go to bed?" he asked.

"Why don't you go ahead? I need to unwind a bit."

"Is there something bothering you, Karen?"

"No, I'm just mentally drained and emotionally exhausted I just want to relax. I'm not ready to go to bed yet."

"Karen…uh… I didn't want to get into a long conversation today when you called that's why I said I was working on the computer. Actually I was just getting back from a visit to the UT campus. I went there on a whim to see about graduate courses. When I got there I got a call from Danielle. She happened to be there registering for classes."

"Oh really… and how is she doing?" she asked a bit icily.

"She's doing very well; she got her old job back at Barclay Rogers Williams and Clay and they are offering her tuition assistance."

"Oh how nice. So where did you get your oil changed?"

"Ah… I really… didn't that was just a parenthetical device I…"

"You mean a lie."

"Ah, yeah… okay it was a bit of a fib."

"First you lie to me about working on your computer then when you get caught you tell another lie about a bogus oil change that you call a fib. And now you admit that you actually took a trip to the UT campus and had a rendezvous with Danielle. We'll get to that little omission later! So what's the difference between a lie and a fib," she asked with a bit of annoyance.

"Well men don't lie, we sometimes engage in the occasional dissemination of FIBS which is an acronym for Factual Information Bereft of Substantiation, let's see there's fabrication, embellishment, equivocation, prevarication, mendacity, paltering, subterfuge…"

"Oh stop it, don't try to cover it up with humor, you men are all alike… you might have cute names for different degrees of your lying but they're all just lies."

"No we aren't all the same, that's an intellectually vacant generalization," he said still trying to inject a little levity.

"No it isn't, the only intellectual vacancy is your weak defense of the male propensity to obfuscate."

"Whoa…wait a minute here, Karen we're not all…,"

"And what about this rendezvous with Danielle? Was it prearranged or really happenstance like you claim?" she asked interrupting his objection.

"It was total coincidence, Danielle happened to be at UT registering for classes and called when I was there to check the campus out. I've been thinking about going back to school for my Master's."

"She leaves you a love letter in your truck and then you go and hook-up with her on the UT campus… some coincidence. And what else have you been fibbing to me about? I should probably rephrase that and ask what you have been truthful about."

"Geez, I knew that was coming, you're not going to let me off are you?"

"I'm just trying to determine your credibility and establish where the foundation of truth ends and the lies take over. Or if there even is a foundation of truth," she said in a slightly mocking tone.

"Look if I weren't being truthful I would not have brought up this whole subject which now seems to have me mired in muck up to my butt," he said still carefully pleading his case.

"I'm actually getting quite a kick out of watching you squirm from my vantage point on the high moral ground...but I'm getting tired. I'm going to bed; you can sleep down here on the couch tonight."

"Ah Karen, now there's..."

"Oh all right, at least your guilt exposed the lies even though you tried to make light of the whole subject. You can come up to bed, but don't you dare touch me."

The next morning Karen was up early and back to her routine. They had an early breakfast and went off together to a workout. There was no further discussion of the previous evening. The rest of the week flew by and Karen seemed content to let any missteps in their relationship lie dormant. And Geoff was content to let sleeping dogs lie. If she still had any reservations she hid them well. She seemed to be her old affectionate romantic self and their lovemaking certainly did not suffer.

Chapter thirty-nine

A couple of weeks later Geoff was working on his computer in the early afternoon when he heard the garage door open. A minute or so later Karen came walking in.

"Hey great, honey - you're home early. Why don't we take advantage of the extra time and go out for drinks and an early dinner?"

"I'm sorry Geoff, I don't think I'm going to be very good company for you tonight. I got some bad news tonight right after I spoke with you." She came over and gave him a perfunctory kiss as she sat down next to him and drew her legs up under her.

"What's up, anything I can help out with?" he said as he ran his hand lightly over her back.

"It's my aunt back in Beaumont; she is in very critical shape. She survived breast cancer but I guess they didn't get it all. She had a relapse and it has spread throughout her whole body. They don't expect her to live more than a month. She is two years older than my mom and they are very close. My mom is just devastated."

"Oh Lord Karen I'm so sorry to hear that. How can I help?"

"I don't know, Geoff. I have to go spend some time with my mom...I don't know what to tell you."

"Well would you like for me to tag along and lend whatever support I can or do you just want some space and time to get through it on your own?"

"I don't know Geoff; I just don't know. I'm going to have to spend some time back in Beaumont and it's probably not the best circumstances to introduce you to my mom."

"Look Karen, let's just take it a step at a time. You go do what you have to do and don't worry about me. If you need me for anything, just call me and I'll be there, meanwhile I can stay here and house-sit for you or if you prefer I can find other accommodations and you can close the place up."

"Geoff I...I'm sorry I just can't think straight right now."

"I can understand that Karen. You're stressed out. Why don't you take a warm bath and relax? I can grill something up for dinner."

"I'm not even hungry."

"Maybe by the time you're finished with your bath you'll have worked up an appetite. I'll make something light."

Karen went upstairs and Geoff started preparations for a tossed garden salad, a bowl of fresh fruit, rice pilaf and some grouper fillets they had bought a few days ago and stuck in the freezer. About forty-five minutes later he went up to check on Karen. She was just toweling off.

"How does grilled grouper with rice pilaf and a tossed salad sound, hon?"

"You're going to insist that I have dinner right?"

"I won't insist; the final decision is still yours to make but I will make a strong recommendation."

"Okay, grouper does sound really good, I'll be down in a few minutes."

Karen came down in her robe. The sight of her dressed like that brought back pleasant memories of exciting times when their relationship was in its infancy and their passion was limitless. Tonight the mood was somber; they ate mostly in silence with only the perfunctory kudos for the dinner prep. She drank the chardonnay much quicker than usual and even had a second glass.

"What would you like for dessert hon?" he asked after they finished.

"I don't feel like having any dessert."

"Are you sure? How about if I slice up an apple and add some frozen yogurt?"

"Yes I'm sure, I don't want dessert… I think I'll have another glass of wine."

"Uh…okay…look hon, why don't you go relax on the couch, maybe watch some television to take your mind off things. I can clean up the kitchen."

Karen poured herself another full glass of wine and took it into the living room setting it down on the coffee table. She stretched out on the couch in silence. After he finished cleaning up he came over to the couch to find her sitting with her legs tucked up under her and her arms folded tightly over her robe. Her glass was empty. "How are you doing hon?" he asked tentatively, aware of her body language that screamed *leave me alone.*

"I'd like more wine."

"Uh…don't you think you've had enough?"

"I'm a big girl; I'll be the judge of that."

"Okay…uh…I think I'll go grab a shower and maybe turn in early. How about you?"

"Just go do what you want…I'll be up later after I finish my wine."

The next morning Karen was awake as soon as the sky began to lighten. It was still maybe a half hour before the sun would cast its first rays of the infant day. Geoff had been aware of her tossing and turning all night long. He had tried to comfort her but she had gotten distant. He decided not to push things and alienate her more than she already was.

Shortly after the sun shone brightly through the slivered opening of the blinds he got up to see her busy packing a rather large suitcase.

"Good morning hon, did you get any sleep last night?" he asked.

"Mmm good morning Geoff…yeah, some…it'll be enough I don't need a lot when I'm stressed out."

"How about I go make us some oatmeal for breakfast, or would you prefer something else?"

"I'm not really hungry Geoff, maybe I'll skip it. Just make it for yourself."

"Karen you can't drive all the way back to Beaumont without eating, and breakfast is the most important meal. I know you're stressed out but taking some time to eat a decent breakfast might help to calm your nerves."

"You're not going to let me have my way are you?" she said with resignation in a slightly exasperated tone of voice.

"No I'm not. Not where your well-being is concerned."

She put the last few items of clothing in the suitcase and closed the lid.

"Okay, you win, I'll have breakfast with you," she said as she shuffled over into his arms.

He held her close gently rubbing her back. "I love you Karen," he whispered as he ran his fingers through the ends of her hair that fell along her neck.

"You must, to be able to put up with my moods. I'm sorry; I'm just so self-consumed right now. It's not fair to you, I know."

He met her lips with his but he found no passion; barely even a response barren of any feeling beyond obligation.

Geoff went downstairs and put on the coffee and started the oatmeal. He had set up two places on the counter and poured out two servings of juice when she came down lugging the suitcase along with her. He almost scolded her for not asking him to help her with the suitcase but he held back biting his tongue.

It was back to this again. He was once again walking on eggs trying to force a relationship rather than letting the chips fall where they might. The pangs of old feelings of insecurity began to lap at his consciousness. He fought back as best he could.

"Would you like toast or an English muffin?" he asked.

"Oh I'll split a muffin with you, if you want; I don't think I can eat the whole thing," she said as she took a seat at the counter.

"Good, that will work for me also," he said as he poured the coffee. A few minutes later the oatmeal was done and he portioned it into two bowls.

"Thanks for being so understanding Geoff."

They ate in strained silence. Karen was finished first and as soon as she was done she cleaned off her spot and put the dishes in the sink.

"I'm sorry to leave you with a mess but I really need to get out on the interstate before the traffic gets unbearable."

"Don't worry about it. Just drive safely, please." He got up and grabbed her suitcase and took it into the garage to load in her car. She followed with a smaller accessory bag, her briefcase and pocketbook. When it was all loaded into her car she turned to him for a hug and a quick kiss.

"Call me when you get there," he said as she climbed behind the wheel. "I love you."

"I will; you take care of yourself, love you too." she said as she backed the car out and pulled away.

He was left standing there in the early morning chill with a puzzled look on his face, a gnawing empty feeling in his gut and fighting off thoughts of another woman walking out of his life.

Chapter forty

Right around eleven o'clock in the late morning Geoff was browsing through his e-mail when his cell phone rang. It was Karen calling to say she had just pulled into her mother's drive in Beaumont.

"Wow, you made great time," said Geoff.

"I know all the shortcuts and back roads. I've taken this trip enough times."

"Well hon, keep me advised of how things are going; I'll try not to call you unless it's something important. I'll just wait for your calls."

"Thanks Geoff, I'm going to need some space until I get things sorted out."

"You've got it hon. I won't interfere. I'll look after things up here for you."

"Thanks... oh one more thing, please don't bother taking any calls for me, just let them forward to my voice mail, I can pick them up here."

"Sure thing, I'm really good at ignoring phones."

"I'll talk to you later I have to go check on my mom."

"Take care, I love you, Karen."

"Mmm, love you too Geoff bye."

The weekend came and went with no further communication from Karen. Every so often he would pick up his cell phone and check the battery level and then check for missed messages or voice mail. The battery was at max but all the message queues were empty.

The following week dragged by. He found another gym to work out in not wanting to return to the place he had gone with Karen and stir up his empty feelings. It took his mind off things for at least as long as the workout lasted.

That Friday Geoff picked up his cell phone and once more checked for messages. Nothing! He closed the phone and tossed it on the couch. The cynical side of him took control of his feelings. Once again he saw the familiar landmarks of the same old road he'd gone down many too many times in past lives – as he referred to them.

A relationship shouldn't be this hard, he said under his breath. If you have to work this hard for so little reward maybe you need to find a new line of work. His thoughts were swimming with other times and places… snippets of his past relationships that had somehow turned sour bombarded him reinforcing his melancholy.

Damn, they couldn't all be dysfunctional; he was the one constant in all the equations it had to be him. Was this to be the latest chapter in his book of heartache…or was he prejudging…jumping to a premature conclusion…or maybe once more running away.

He put it all out of his mind, at least that's what he told himself to do and went back to reading his e-mail. A cyber from his agent caught his eye and he opened it to find that John, his agent, expected to get a publication date for his book within a month. He wanted to know his availability for a book tour. Well that was good news. He was as available as he could be, the sooner the better, it would be a great excuse to get back out on the interstate – not that he needed one.

He was getting hungry. He thought about making a sandwich, maybe some soup. Then he decided he needed to get out and get some air. In a few minutes he was cruising past the Borderline Blues Café and a moment of indecision hammered away at him. Familiar scenes of Karen and him flashed through his mind until he tossed them all aside.

Damn looking in the rearview mirror again - trying to change the past. Stay in the moment, deal with today Jack, it's all you have, he told himself. He continued on, made a few aimless turns and finally came upon a deli restaurant with a sidewalk patio. It looked busy with the Austin lunch crowd, a reliable measure of reasonable prices, good quality of food and great service. Even the parking wasn't a problem.

In fifteen minutes he had a small table under an umbrella. A pastrami Reuben on the menu caught his eye.

"Welcome to Schultz's, just one today?" asked the server.

"Yeah, unless I get lucky."

"Well you're in the right spot. Lots of pretty ladies come here. You shouldn't have a problem." She was pretty, petite, blonde and very married as evidenced by a well-worn wedding band. "In the meantime, while you're waiting for your luck to change, what can I get for you?" she said with a bright smile.

"I'll have the pastrami Reuben with extra sauerkraut, no fries."

"Would you like fruit instead?"

"Sure, that'd be great."

"Anything to drink?"

"How about a cold mug of Warsteiner's"

"You got it; I'll bring that out first."

It was a gorgeous day. The temperature was in the mid to upper seventies and absent any noticeable humidity. His mood was brightening already as his server brought out a tall frosted mug of the German import beer and set it on a coaster. "Enjoy it; your Reuben should be out shortly."

By the time she brought out the Reuben he had finished three quarters of the brew and it hadn't even been ten minutes.

"Hey you were thirsty, would you like another?"

"I sure would please; I'll need more than this to wash down the Reuben. Guess I was pretty thirsty."

He finished the sandwich and the second brew and thought about ordering another but then talked himself out of it reasoning that he didn't want to get trashed by early afternoon. But he didn't want to go back to the townhouse either. Once back at his truck he climbed in and picked up the cell phone out of habit from the center console cup holder where he usually left it. There was one missed message. He fumbled with it feeling his anticipation rising and finally getting his voice mail. It wasn't Karen.

"Hi Geoff... it's Danielle, I'm going to be on campus tomorrow. If you're around and not busy, maybe we can get together. I have some really

interesting news to share with you. Give me a call to confirm if you can. Talk to you later – bye."

He punched in her number.

"Hello?"

"Hi Danielle, its Geoff."

"Oh hi Geoff thanks for calling back so soon. Are you going to be around tomorrow?"

"Tomorrow is wide open for me. What time and where can I meet you?"

"How about at the student union café about eleven thirty?"

"That sounds good, I'll see you then. I'm looking forward to it."

"Umm hmm, I am too, see you – bye."

He spent the rest of the day aimlessly driving around then went back to the townhouse and tried to write some scenes in his latest project. It was like pulling teeth. He gave up early and switched on the television to the classic movie channel. The movie *Passage to Marseille* came back on following the commercial interruption. It was an old Humphrey Bogart World War Two studio propaganda movie to support the war effort in the European theater. They had tried to reprise the success of Casablanca but it somehow came out bland and quite a bit short of the mark. He lost interest and decided to call it a night and turn in.

Traffic was heavy the next day as he drove to the UT campus and the café was crowded as he got there about twenty after eleven but he caught sight of Danielle waving him over to her outside umbrella table. She stood up and gave him a nice welcoming hug.

"Hi Geoff, thanks for making time for me." She already had a coffee and a small dish of fruit with yogurt.

"Nice to see you again Danielle…oh that looks good," he said glancing at her fruit and yogurt. "I think I'll go treat myself to the same."

A few minutes later he was back with his plate and a large mocha latte. "You'll be starting your first semester pretty soon right?"

"Yes, next week. I can hardly wait. I even got a bonus; UT is accepting the credits I accumulated at junior college down in Beaumont before I left home and hit the road."

"Hey now, that's great that'll put you a little closer to your degree and law school if you decide to pursue that career."

"Yes I'll be starting as a second semester sophomore and law school is a definite goal. I'm sold on that aspect after the breaks I've gotten. I'm moving into the company apartment this weekend."

"Do you need any help with that?"

"No, but thanks for asking. It's fully furnished, so I just have to move in my clothes and a few odd and ends. I'm really getting excited about this new turn in my life."

"You have a lot of people in your corner rooting for you Danielle. I'm sure you'll do very well. Before long I'll be calling you counselor."

"Oh no, we are much too close for that. I should be calling you dad for all you've done for me. My daddy talks about you quite often and wants to stay in touch. Anyway not to change the subject but as I said on the phone I have some news to share with you."

"You sound pretty upbeat, so it must be good."

"Oh it is…it's a big relief. I've been doing some detective work investigating all those dark stories about my dad and Tammy. I found out that the friends that Tammy used to hang with have kind of a vendetta against my dad because he has a lot of influence on the council and it seems that he has been stepping on some toes to get a lot of the questionable nightclubs cleaned up or closed. So they have been spreading rumors about him being abusive to Tammy to trash his credibility and moral values and to try to get him kicked off the council."

"Oh boy, nice friends" said Geoff shaking his head with disgust.

"Pretty neat huh? Tammy's not around to contradict their story. And to add yet another wrinkle I found out that Karen was their assigned social worker when a couple of them got into trouble. So…"

"Don't tell me…, so you think Karen may be orchestrating this whole conspiracy?"

"Hold on, let me tell you the rest of the story," she said very animatedly. "I finally got the nerve to go and have a heart to heart with my dad. He told me that the divorce action had been very acrimonious and that Karen threatened to ruin his reputation unless he agreed to her favorable terms in the divorce and alimony. They finally compromised but Karen still felt she had gotten short shrift."

"That adds up...motive for revenge," he said nodding his head.

"Yes, I'm pretty sure that Karen concocted the whole contemptible story, she can be very vindictive," said Danielle.

"It begins to look like Karen has a dark side that I guess I was just blind to."

"Oh but wait, you haven't heard the clincher," she said motioning at him with her open palms.

"This past Monday Karen came storming into the law offices of Barclay Rogers Williams and Clay and demanded to see me. She made a big commotion in the reception area, called me a tart and told me to stay away from you. Mr. Barclay, the senior partner, who is a very good longtime friend of my dad and who pressed for my tuition assistance and free apartment benefits overheard her tirade and told her to leave. When she refused and resisted, he finally threw her out telling her not to ever step foot in the office again or he would have her arrested and prosecuted for trespass.

Later on that day he told me he would be drawing up a restraining order requiring her to keep away from me. I politely objected saying I could take care of myself. He answered that he had a very contentious history with Karen during my dad's divorce and while he had great confidence that I could take care of myself I was too great an asset to the firm to be in any way intimidated or distracted from my studies."

"That's great, you've got a friend in high places. I'm glad to hear that Mr. Barclay is watching out for you and protecting his future associate. As for Karen, whew...I can't believe what I'm hearing. It doesn't sound like the same Karen I thought I knew. She told me she had to spend some time with her mom because her mom's sister is terminally ill with a recurrence of breast cancer and her mom is taking it very hard."

"What! Oh my God...did she tell you that?"

"Yes, that was her reason for going down to Beaumont."

"That is a despicable lie Geoff, her mom's sister passed away years ago, even before Tammy."

"Whoa... really? ...Geez that's...that's really bizarre."

"I hate to rain on your parade. I know you have some deep feelings for Karen but the Karen you know and her alter ego who I know and who is arguably the real Karen are a real dichotomy. The one I know is an actress and a schemer and it's obvious to me that she is extremely jealous of our relationship not to mention afraid that I will expose her pathetic contemptible lies and drive you away from her – she can get very nasty, you need to be careful Geoff and watch your back."

"Wow Danielle you've done some pretty impressive investigating, I think it bodes well for your future success both in law school and beyond."

"Thanks, I can't wait to get into law school. I'm going to attend classes year round to accelerate getting my undergraduate degree. This is such an exciting time for me."

"You deserve it all Danielle. Keep in touch; I'd like to follow your progress."

"Oh I will Geoff, I promise. And you have to come visit us back in Beaumont, dad and I consider you as family."

"Thank you Danielle, that makes me very happy to feel appreciated."

"I don't want to but I have to go. I need to get a lot of loose ends tied up before the semester starts."

"Study hard, but also try to enjoy yourself...catch you later," said Geoff as they stood up and hugged each other.

"Take care Geoff, let me know what happens...I love you."

"I love you too Danielle."

On the drive back from the UT campus Geoff's head was swimming. Had he been taken in by Karen's physical charms and ignored other character flaws and personality traits? Had he only seen what he wanted to see? Had he accepted what fit his criteria of a perfect mate and rejected anything that didn't? It was hard to defend Karen against the case that Danielle had built. There was just too much disconnect for him to process.

He was still trying to square what he had heard from Danielle with his own intimate experience with Karen as he drove around the curve in her neighborhood and the townhouse complex came into view. Up ahead he saw a car in what he was sure was Karen's driveway. As he got closer he recognized it as Karen's car parked at a haphazard angle with the front passenger side wheel over on the grass. As he pulled into the driveway alongside her he saw Karen slumped over behind the wheel with her head down. It looked as though she was asleep.

He kept looking over at Karen but she didn't look up to acknowledge him. He could feel the tension building as he got out of his truck and walked around to her door. When she still didn't look up he tapped his key on the window. That got her attention and she looked up at him with a scowling expression he had never seen before on her face. She rolled down the window and glared at him through bloodshot eyes, her head bobbing from the effects of the alcohol which he could now smell reeking out of her car.

"I guess you've talked with your little tart of a girl toy, huh?" her speech was heavily slurred.

"Karen how long have you been driving in this condition?"

"What the fuck do you care?" the words came out slurred but the meaning was perfectly clear.

"I do care, Karen. I care about the Karen I thought I knew."

"Sorry I didn't live up to your expectations in your fucking wet dreams."

"Yeah, well life's like that sometimes, look Karen I'm going inside to pack up my stuff. I'll clear out of here. There's no sense in getting into a knock down drag out, let's just try to remember the good times."

"So I got derailed by a young tart?"

"Don't start Karen; I don't want to remember you that way. You have no one to blame except your own foibles and devices."

"Go fuck yourself," the venom behind the words was unmistakable. She fumbled with the key in the ignition trying to start the engine. Geoff reached in and grabbed the keys away from her.

"You bastard! Give me my fucking keys."

"You'll get them back when you're sober."

"I should live that long."

"It's the only way you will live long. C'mon on let's go inside."

He opened the car door and reached for her.

"Leave me alone you fucking bastard," she screamed as she resisted and grabbed onto the steering wheel.

He gently but firmly tried to pry her hands off using his elbow to ward off her repeated attempts to bite his fingers until she reluctantly gave in. He toggled the garage door open and walked her slowly inside steadying her staggering gait and left her lying on the sofa.

Twenty minutes later he was packed and had everything stowed in his truck. Karen had dozed off on the couch. He left the house keys and garage remote on the sofa table, took a last look at Karen in her drunken slumber and shook his head with disgusted compassion as he let himself out locking the door behind him.

During times like this he would play four or five CDs by Emmylou Harris and get lost in the sound of her voice and the poignant lyrics she mostly sang. But some scoundrel had broken into his truck back in Colorado and stolen his whole collection. Damn, well at least the swine had good taste in music. The inimitable Miss Emmylou Harris to him was the goddess priest of the high lonesome sound – an evocative Emmylou fusion of Folk and Country – the kind that made the hair stand up on the back of your neck and tears cascade down your cheeks like a waterfall. Her songs and her pensive delivery of them connected directly to your soul. He needed to get to another of her concerts. It had been far too long since he had last seen her at the Concord Pavilion in California, many lives ago.

He spent the next few nights and early mornings in the blues bars of South Austin until during one sober moment he answered a call from John his literary agent – his book had been published. It was time once again to hit the interstate.

Chapter forty-one

Well that was then...this is now - another damned cliché he thought to himself chuckling derisively as he sat back in his motel room after a late breakfast. It's time to deal with the here and now; time to stop looking back on the past and dwelling on all your mistakes and poor choices. His life had been on autopilot far too long – it's time I re-engaged the controls, and got back in the game, he mused to himself.

He was back in Montana; just like he'd promised himself he'd one day be. The completion of yet another figure eight in his escapades had left him a little older, a little wiser - he hoped - but still playing solitaire. He had been too long living in the rear view while life flashed bye (*sic*) the windshield.

The reason for this, his latest return, as if there had to be a reason for anything that transpired in his life, was simple enough, he was here to kick off the book tour and advertising campaign for his first full length novel. He had insisted that he begin his tour in Montana. He hadn't known why, he just knew he needed to follow his feelings and his feelings told him that he needed to be back in Montana.

His agent had argued strongly against it of course but he couldn't argue with fait accompli and Geoff had already scheduled a string of book signings in cities across the Big Sky Country of Montana from Billings to Missoula. Since he'd gotten here yesterday, less than twenty-four hours ago it had been a surreal experience topping anything he'd encountered in a long time as well as anything he could imagine, and he had a pretty damned wild imagination.

It began yesterday evening with dinner at Southside Johnnie's a bar that he had become acquainted with in a past life a long time ago and decided to revisit as was his custom. But what occurred last night had been worlds apart from any experience he'd ever had in this bar or for that matter any bar he'd ever visited - in all the bars, in all the nights, in all of his past lives.

It was full of irony, strange twists and a chance reunion with his old teammate Brian from his Navy days during the war in Vietnam. He had been served by a very attractive young gal, Tara, who it turned out was Brian's daughter-in-law.

Then there was the incredible disclosure by Brian that she was also the daughter of Frank Robbins the CIA control operative who had responsibility for their forays into Cambodia and who was responsible for his decision against reenlisting all those years ago.

Finally, by an ironic twist of fate he had been drawn into the vortex as a possible candidate for organ donation by virtue of his blood type to ameliorate the terminal condition of this person whom he despised.

It wasn't definite of course, he'd still have to formally declare his intention to volunteer and have the necessary tests to ascertain that he indeed was a viable match but in his own mind there was already a mountain of moral justification for it that he couldn't ignore, at least not if he ever hoped to stand and look at himself in the mirror again and feel good about who he was.

His teammate Brian had saved his life in combat at the risk of his own without the slightest hesitation. Brian's life now revolved around his love for his son and his daughter-in-law. And Tara's immeasurable love for her dad, Frank Robbins, who had touched and influenced all of their lives, was the wellspring of happiness for their entire family.

He conceivably held in his hand the trump card that could make a difference. He could make it possible that her dad would live to see his grandchildren and they would get to know their granddad. Surely human compassion out trumped the banal feelings of contempt and misunderstanding of so long ago.

His thoughts were bombarded with the scenes and conflicting emotions of experiences dredged up from so long ago.

Geoff what are you going to do? Frank Robbins needs a kidney to survive. You've got a spare one and you're a match in blood type. You need to find out if this could be your chance to make a difference.

But you can't stand the bastard. He threatened you with a court-martial or even civilian charges trying to cover his own butt. He doesn't deserve your kidney, even if he is Tara's dad.

But Tara is your teammate's daughter-in-law. He adores her like the daughter he wished he had. And you owe him. You would not be here today - wouldn't have made it back from that last op - without Brian. Teammates once are teammates for life. And now you have a chance to pay back the debt and save the life of another, albeit of the one person whose funeral you would have gleefully danced at so many years ago. Maybe it's fate's circular method of squaring old animosities. Perhaps it's time you had a meeting with Robbins and cleared the air. You need to go see the doctor and let him know you want to test to see if you can donate a kidney.

He dug out the scrap of paper that Brian had given him with his phone number and punched it up on his cell phone. They had closed the place last night and afterwards Brian had offered to put him up in his spare bedroom. Geoff thanked him but declined saying he was already settled in at the motel. Brian sensed his independent nature as driving his reluctance and didn't press the issue.

The phone rang twice and Brian answered, *"This is Brian."*

"Hey buddy, Geoff. Have you sobered up from last night?"

"Aw come on now Geoff, I'm better than that, maybe a bit off my game but I can still tip them with the best."

"Listen Brian I've been thinking about last night…about the deal with Robbins. I've decided I want to go see if I can qualify as a donor."

"Whoa, hey buddy look I didn't mean for you to feel any obligation to get involved in my problems. Sometimes I run off at the mouth too much."

"We're teammates Brian, to me that bond is as strong as family."

"Sure we'll always be teammates Geoff but that doesn't mean you…"

You've done it for me Brian, now it's my chance to return the favor."

"HOOYAH, bud... I guess you understand the gravity of what you're about to do."

"Yeah, it's nothing more than you would have done if you had the chance. So how can I get in touch with the doctor handling his case?"

"I'm pretty sure it's Dr. Riker over at County General Hospital but let me call Chip and verify that. You're still coming over for dinner tonight, right?"

"Looking forward to it buddy."

"Good, I'll call you right back."

A few minutes later Brian called back with the confirmation and Geoff put in a call to Dr. Riker's office. He was transferred to his nurse who upon consultation with Dr. Riker set up an appointment for him for 07:00 the next day. Dr. Riker was the head of the renal care unit and had a sense of urgency for his patient Frank Robbins. He said he would personally handle the donor match test procedures to escalate the process.

Geoff spent the rest of the day researching contacts for book signings. He got to Brian's place, a brick bungalow off Seventh Street, about ten minutes after five. Chip and Tara were already there as well as Marianne, Brian's steady lady. After the introductions Chip was the first one to speak up.

"Dad tells me you're interested in testing as a possible kidney donor for Tara's dad. I think that's a fantastic gesture of selfless humanity."

"I go in for the work-up tomorrow morning. The doc says he wants to accelerate the process by keeping it all in the hospital laboratory."

"Yeah her dad doesn't have much time he suffered some complications last night. That's why Tara took off from the restaurant. I still can't believe the coincidence; my wife was your server just when her dad had this medical emergency. My dad meets us there and he walks into you, someone he and her dad served with in Vietnam all those years ago. And now there's a chance you can save her dad's life."

"Sometimes life gets it right Chip, it's what helps us all get through the bad times. The older you get the more you realize that, but it still never ceases to amaze you."

"It's more than coincidence Chip, I've been saying extra prayers for daddy since I found out we are going to have a baby," said Tara.

"Well congratulations Tara, that's great. Let's hope everything goes positive tomorrow so I can qualify as a donor and your dad ultimately makes a quick recovery to get ready for his role as granddad," said Geoff.

"What do you do for work Geoff?" asked Marianne trying to lighten up the emotionally charged atmosphere.

"It's all creative these days, I'm a writer. My first full length novel just got published and I'm here on a promotional tour."

"Oh that sounds exciting, how long are you going to be in town?"

"I've got three or four book signings scheduled here in Billings and then it's on to Bozeman, Butte and up to Missoula. After that I'll probably head down to Sheridan, Casper, Cheyenne and Laramie Wyoming. But if I qualify as a donor I'll be around a little longer and probably have to postpone some of that."

"Oh my, you must love to travel."

"Yeah I do; I think it's what I do best. It keeps me from getting stale."

"That sounds like something Brian would say. But I've become his chain and anchor and I like having him close by."

"Well Marianne, if I were in your shoes I would too, Brian's good people," said Geoff.

"Ah thanks bud; see that Marianne an unsolicited testimonial," said Brian catching the last bit of conversation as he came in from the patio.

"Whew, it's getting deep in here, is anyone hungry?" asked Chip in a mocking tone as he rolled his eyes.

It was a family dinner. Brian did the steaks on the grill, Marianne and Tara worked up the baked potatoes and veggies and Chip tossed the salad.

"Hey Geoff you're not a guest here you are family, go get the iced tea and glasses and set the table," said Brian.

"Aye-aye, commander," said Geoff with a snappy salute at Brian who was now dressed in a white apron and chef's hat while he worked over the grill.

"Ah thank you, mate, after all these years I finally get my field commission," said Brian as he returned the salute.

After dinner Tara had to go in to work. Chip hung around to help clean up and then headed home to do some homework. He was finishing up his Master's in Finance at Montana State in Bozeman.

Brian, Marianne and Geoff had a few after dinner drinks out on the patio and some easy conversation as they watched the sunset over the Rockies in the distance. Marianne taught senior and AP English at the local high school. Brian was building up a business in electrical contracting. He had five people working for him and was looking for several more to expand into commercial work.

As the light faded into dusk it was time for Geoff to head out. "Well buddy I need to get back to my place and study up for my test tomorrow. Thanks for having me over, I really enjoyed dinner and being able to share it in a family atmosphere. Nice meeting you Marianne, I'm sure I'll see you again. You guys make a nice couple, I'm really happy he's met someone like you."

"Uh hmm, wherever Brian is I'll be close by, nice meeting you too."

"Don't be a stranger Geoff. You know where we live now. My house is your house buddy. Good luck for tomorrow and no matter which way it goes thanks for being a teammate."

Chapter forty-two

Very early the next morning Geoff was sitting at a table having breakfast at a truck-stop restaurant off the same interstate exit as the hospital. It was the same one he had eaten at many times before on his road-trips up here from Colorado Springs. He arrived at the hospital by 06:30 expecting to have to fill out the usual voluminous forms and releases. Admissions had been alerted to expect his arrival and to contact Dr. Riker directly. Within five minutes a nurse had shown up with a wheelchair.

"Hey I'm perfectly ambulatory, I can make it anywhere without one of those things."

"Sorry it's hospital rules our liability insurance requires it. I get this reaction all the time," she said shrugging her shoulders.

They went up to the fourth floor with Geoff reluctantly riding in the wheelchair. Three corridors in different directions led away from the bank of elevators which were situated in a lobby. The nurse wheeled him straight ahead past a large nursing station desk and into an office with a placard on the door marked Dr. Riker Chief of Nephrology. The doctor, who had been waiting, got out of his chair and came around from behind his desk to greet Geoff.

"Good morning Mr. McEwen I'm Dr. Riker," he said holding out his hand. We just need your John Hancock on three forms and then we can start the process. You will have to fill out some additional forms but that can wait until later. I want to get this moving as quickly as possible."

"Good morning Dr. Riker," said Geoff as he shook hands. "That suits me fine. Let's get on with it, where do I sign?"

"Oh extremely cooperative; I like that. Nurse Sanders do we have the special forms for the irrevocable trust? You know… the one that transfers over all his assets to County General?"

"Uh there's a limit to my cooperation Doc."

"Just kidding Mr. McEwen," Dr. Riker said with a deep chuckle. "I was testing your cognitive function. That was a good reaction."

"You can just call me Geoff, Doc; it'll make me feel more comfortable."

"As you wish, Geoff, we aim to make you as comfortable as possible."

Geoff signed the consent and release forms and then they wheeled him into an exam room replete with all kinds of medical test equipment where they had him strip down to his boxer shorts. Dr. Riker checked all his vital signs, measured his height and weight, ran a stress test EKG and gave him a rather complete physical while Nurse Sanders recorded the metrics. Then Dr. Riker drew the blood and harvested the tissue samples himself. During the spare moments Nurse Sanders questioned him on his medical history and began filling out the forms.

"Geoff you appear to be a very healthy specimen. You obviously take very good care of yourself," said the doctor with a satisfied expression on his face.

"I like to stay in shape it's a habit I developed in the Navy."

"Well I'd say you do quite a bit more than average. You're probably in the top one percentile of the profile for your age bracket, that's pretty impressive. We're all done here. After you finish up whatever paperwork is left I'll send you down for a chest x-ray, renal scan and CT scan of your kidneys just to make sure you have two kidneys. You shouldn't have much left to fill out; Nurse Sanders has pretty much covered it all. There's probably just the psychological profile and you're done."

"You'll get my bill in the mail," said Nurse Sanders trying to keep a straight face but failing miserably.

"Don't tell him that yet, wait until he signs the rest of the forms," said Dr. Riker looking at her with a feigned expression of reproach.

"I'm recording all this for my lawyer," said Geoff with a deadpan expression.

"Uh oh, there goes my new Mercedes," said Dr. Riker with a chuckle. Anyway after you're done with the lab work downstairs you're free to go. Any questions?"

"When do I find out if I passed?"

"As soon as I've reviewed all the tests I'll give you a call, probably by tomorrow evening if not sooner."

"Thank you doctor; I'll be waiting on the call."

"Very good, Geoff. It was a pleasure meeting you. I hope to see you back here as a viable donor. I think you'll do well."

After he finished the paperwork in Nurse Sander's office she took him down to the Radiology lab for his donor screening workup.

A little over two and a half hours later he was ready for lunch. That evening he found a nice local steakhouse and treated himself to a filet with a couple glasses of Merlot convincing himself that he needed to replace the blood he'd lost for the test. He made an early night of it and turned in right after he returned to the motel.

The next day the sun was just beginning to turn the pre-dawn sky a light gray in preparation for announcing the new day as he finished his morning PT and headed out for an early breakfast. Afterwards feeling motivated by Dr. Riker's positive assessment of his physical condition he decided to look into options for additional exercise. There was no beach in Billings for a morning jog so he dug out his swim trucks and settled for the local YMCA where he took out a membership so he could use the lap pool. He killed the rest of the morning doing laps alternating between the breast stroke, the butterfly and the back stroke. It felt good to get back in the water again even at an inside pool.

He was on his way back to the motel and thinking about a light lunch when his cell phone rang.

"Hello, this is Geoff."

"Hello Geoff this is Dr. Riker. How are you doing today?"

"Fine doctor, any news?"

"Yes, it's all good - you're a perfect match; couldn't be closer if you were brothers. I'd like you to come in for a short consultation and I would like you to meet Mr. Robbins. Is that something you're prepared to do?"

"Just tell me when you want to see me."

"I'd like to see you as soon as possible."

"Fine, I'm on my way then."

"Very good Geoff thanks, I'll be waiting."

When he got to the hospital he was sent right up to see Dr. Riker. The door to Dr. Riker's office was open and the doctor was seated at his desk going over a stack of papers. Geoff knocked lightly on the door to get his attention.

"Well hello there Geoff. Please, come on in and have a seat. Any concerns, feelings of remorse or anything you want to talk about?"

"No doctor, I've made up my mind."

"Very well, let me explain the procedure. We're going to do a minimally invasive laparoscopic nephrectomy to harvest your kidney. It involves making three one-half inch incisions for the laparoscope and instruments. We'll extract the kidney through another two to three-inch incision just below your navel.

Now there is a second companion procedure that we use as an alternative called open surgery which is much more invasive. I mention that because you will have to sign a consent form for it so I have that option if I deem it necessary should there be an onset of any LP complications during surgery. However, let me just add parenthetically that I came here from the San Francisco Bay area where I taught the laparoscopic technique at UCSF. I performed oh probably eight or nine-hundred of these LPs as we call them and only had two cases where I had to resort to open surgery. Generally, the health and physical condition of the donor dictates the ease of the procedure. In your case because of your excellent conditioning I am 99.9 percent certain of not encountering any complications.

Have I told you anything that has given you any pause about going through with this procedure?"

"No doctor, with your background and experience you've given me complete confidence in your skills and ability."

"Very good, and thank you... now it is still major surgery and it carries all the attendant risks including that of general anesthesia but again in your case I don't anticipate any problems. If I schedule it for next Thursday, you'll be getting out of the hospital on Saturday. You'll be a little sore, maybe have some constipation or abdominal swelling from the carbon dioxide we use to dilate your abdominal cavity. It gets absorbed into your intestines and can create some discomfort. But no need to worry, a suppository will correct that and get rid of the flatulence. You will have to take it easy on the exercise for the first week."

"I have a membership at the YMCA so I'll probably just do laps in the pool," said Geoff.

"Excellent, you can do that as soon as you're released. Any questions?"

"No, I'm confident I'm in good hands."

"Thank you, Geoff...now let's go see Frank Robbins. Are you ready?"

"I'm ready, let's go Doc."

Dr. Riker led Geoff down the corridor to a private room a few doors down on the left. He knocked on the open door and as he went in he called out,

"Mr. Robbins I have someone here you need to speak with. He's your kidney donor. He passed the pre-op work-up with flying colors - a positive match on blood type, antigens and tissue. I'll leave you two gentlemen alone to discuss things," he said as he let himself out and closed the door behind him.

"Frank Robbins...I'm Geoff McEwen, how are you doing?" he said approaching the bedside where Robbins was sitting up.

"Your name sounds familiar; do I know you?" asked Robbins staring as he searched his memory for some recognition.

"You should, thirty years ago you threatened to have me court-martialed. I was detached from U. S. Navy SEAL Team One and assigned as one of your henchmen running through the jungles of Cambodia in 1967."

"Oh Geez Geoff - that was a long time ago. Let's see, ah... then you had to be teammates with Brian, my son-in-law's dad?"

"You've got it covered Frank. You know, I've always wanted to know why."

"Why what...Geoff?"

"Why you were so damned obnoxious, back then? Why did you pull that shit with us?"

"What are you asking, Geoff?"

"You know - the cover-up, the sanitized reports, and the threats of court martial and prosecution."

"It wasn't what you thought. I had a lot of pressure from above. It was just business as usual with the bureaucracy, I was just doing my job Geoff; I needed to keep a lid on things. I was looking after the interests of the company."

"This sailor left the service because of you."

"I'm sorry to hear that."

"We were on the same side. We carried the same government ID except yours was the Agency mine was Defense," said Geoff still pushing his point.

"Geoff it was a covert op, we weren't supposed to be there and as far as most people know we never were. There are a lot of things you don't know and I can't tell you, it's still classified."

"Here we go again, the same old song and dance."

"No Geoff, it was a management decision. I had to send a message that we were in control. State was all over my ass giving me shit about everything. The company even left me out on a limb. Defense wouldn't acknowledge anything; they didn't want to hear about you guys. Nobody wanted to take responsibility or be accountable."

"So you passed it on down to us?"

"Path of least resistance…I knew you guys could take it. You're a tough bunch. You got a Presidential Unit Citation over that. As the field agent-in-charge I wrote the recommendation."

"We lost a lot of good men in that war."

"Yes we did - the cream of the crop."

"They cared enough about our country to fight for it and then we turned our backs on them and walked away. Why did we do that?"

"You're asking me? Those decisions were way above my pay grade, nobody asked my opinion."

"How do you get over something like that… the feeling of betrayal?"

"You don't Geoff. You accept it for what it was and move on. You did your part. That's all anyone can ask – hell, a lot of them never earned the right to ask anyway. I know that's cold but that's all you or Brian or I or anyone who went through it can do."

"Yeah, you're right. I just have to learn to live with it, I guess."

"No that's bullshit! Savor those feelings Geoff, they're what makes you human, what connects you to everybody else on this planet; and that's what matters."

How do you summon the anger smoldering for over thirty years? Try as you might the anger towards Frank just doesn't come. It surprises you. It was what was eating you up inside wasn't it?

You tell yourself the war is over. The war we didn't win - the war we didn't lose - the war we walked away from. More than 58,000 names on the wall, names of heroes lost in vain, stare back at you with a haunting question you can never answer – 'Hey… where *were* you, buddy, I thought you had my back?'

You will do what you must do. You'll do it for Brian, for Tara, for her husband Chip and for the grandchildren to come. But you will also do it for yourself and yes, for Frank too. He will live to see his grandchildren and you will have made it possible.

"So anyway, why are you willing to give me your kidney?"

"I'm a human being Frank, a fellow American, and a veteran I won't let you die not when I have the means to make a difference."

"You don't have to do it for me, I'm not asking," he said brusquely.

"To hell with you Frank, I'm doing it for Tara, Chip and the grandchild and maybe even for Brian so he doesn't have to shoulder the granddad responsibilities all by himself."

"You're a hard case Geoff. Are you through?" he asked rolling his eyes.

"No, I'll be through next Thursday after the operation just like you. And I'll expect you to get your butt up out of bed and get your sorry ass back in shape."

"I don't suppose you'll accept my sincere thanks," Frank said gazing steadily at Geoff.

"Aw shit, I don't suppose you'll tell me to shut the hell up and get over it."

"No I won't do that Geoff."

"You're welcome Frank," Geoff said as he leaned over the bed with open arms. As they embraced and he fought back the tears beginning to well up in his eyes.

"It's over Geoff," he said softly.

"What...what's over, Frank?"

"The war, Vietnam...it's over. Just let it go...let it go and move on," he said his own eyes beginning to mist.

"Yeah... I know."

Chapter forty-three

The next day - Saturday, Geoff was sitting at the bar in Southside Johnnie's absentmindedly watching an early afternoon hockey game from somewhere back east when some guy took a seat next to his. Engrossed in his thoughts he didn't bother to look over, but this guy was crowding him; then he felt a nudge on his shoulder which he ignored as unintentional and then another unmistakably intentional nudge more like a shove. Geoff was about to register his disapproval when he heard a familiar voice.

"Is that you Jackson?"

An old nickname from his Navy days in the teams brought back a flood of memories from times past. Shaking his head, he turned to face Brian who was wearing a shit-eating grin.

"Willie you almost got yourself popped, you son-of-a-bitch," he said using Brian's old nickname from the teams.

"Aw, I was ready for you, I haven't kicked butt in a long time," Brian said with a hearty laugh.

"Shit…where are you going to get ten big men in a hurry?"

Brian brushed him off with a chuckle, "I knew I'd find you in here, but what the hell are you doing watching hockey, you were never into sports?"

"It happened after my second divorce - there didn't seem to be anything else. It filled the empty hours and afforded some camaraderie."

"You know Geoff, if you don't mind... well hell, even if you do mind I'm going to tell you anyway. You really do need to settle down, let some roots grow. You're going to have a real connection to my family. Chip and Tara look at you as an uncle. It's time you put away the roadmaps."

"Well I do like this old coal town, Brian. It does begin to feel like home."

"So then it's settled, I'll have my old teammate back and right here in town where I can keep an eye on him."

"But I can't promise I'll never ship out to another duty station."

"Well I can promise that if you do I'll hunt you down and haul your butt back here. By the way, Tara told me they scheduled the surgery for this Thursday."

"Yeah that's why I'm here giving the old kidney a workout. The doc told me he gave strict orders to Robbins to cut out all spirits for at least six months. I told him I thought that would be a hell of a shock to my kidney. He even suggested I cut back. I told him kidneys are like muscles you have to exercise them or they atrophy."

"Hmm I'm sure he bought that argument."

"Yeah, you know how those medical types are; he gave me some shit about my cavalier attitude and said he hadn't seen any studies in the medical journals to support such an irrational fatuous hypothesis."

"You know Geoff I'm just amazed at how things have worked out. We haven't seen each other in over thirty years. Then one day you show up to pay the band and the dance goes on. What brought you back to Montana?"

"I guess it's like that old saying – things happen for a reason – something told me, probably on some unconscious level that I needed to be here in Billings Montana."

"You're going to need a ride to the hospital Thursday, I'll..."

"Nah, I can drive myself, I don't want to put you out."

"Now quit being so damned independent, you're going to need a ride and I'm going to take you. I need to be there for the surgery anyway."

"Why do you want to waste a couple hours or more sitting around a hospital waiting room?"

"I feel responsible, if I hadn't told you about Robbins you wouldn't be donating a kidney. Besides if anybody's going to be cutting on my teammate and removing organs I damn well want to be there to make certain you're okay."

"Still got my back huh bud…hey maybe you can sneak in a pint of tequila so we can have a toast with Robbins and get that kidney primed and working for him."

"Geez…you haven't changed one bit in all these years, still testing the boundaries. It's a good thing I'm here to keep you in line. So what time do you have to be at the hospital Thursday?"

"Doc said he wants me there by 06:00."

"Shoot we can get in some morning PT then," said Brian grinning from ear to ear.

"Sure, why not? The YMCA opens at 05:00 we can do about forty-five minutes in the lap pool."

"I haven't done laps in a long while but I know I can still whip your butt," said Brian.

"Heh, heh…yeah, you keep thinking that buddy-boy; Geez, I can't wait for Thursday, I'm really going to enjoy this upcoming workout," said Geoff.

Chapter forty-four

E arly Thursday morning Geoff was lying on a gurney in pre-op - dressed or undressed as the case may be in a traditional hospital gown. Through the doors came Dr. Riker with another doctor who Geoff supposed was his assistant since he carried a clipboard and had the requisite stethoscope draped around his neck.

"Good morning, Geoff. This is Dr. Barnes he'll be assisting me in OR this morning. How are you doing today?"

"I'm doing fine, doc - but I'm more concerned with how you're doing. Did you get enough sleep last night?"

"Ah, not to worry - let's see we are doing a Liver harvest today, right?"

"Liver? Hell no, it was a coronary bypass, doc."

"Geoff, it's not nice to one-up your physician."

"Sorry Doc, you left yourself open."

"Well, just remember who has the scalpel."

"Yeah, I guess it's a good thing I'm not here for a vasectomy."

"Vasectomy? I don't do those. Just enlargements, are you a candidate?"

"Oh Geez...touché doc, I concede. I know when I'm beaten; you've got me at a gross disadvantage."

"Disadvantage, oh tut-tut; you're a military man. Verbal banter is a lot like war which is really just an acronym for wholesale annihilation of resistance."

"Hmm, maybe you should have been a pathologist."

"My brother is one, he critiques all my mistakes."

"Yeah and I'll bet your dad is a mortician."

"How did you guess, Geoff? Make a note Dr. Barnes - use the extra-large square needles. I might add that Dr. Barnes here is a military veteran also; Marine Corps, right Pete?"

"Yes, sir!"

"Oh boy, 'Semper Fi' doc."

"You're in good hands, squid."

"Okay, Geoff in about a half hour you'll be going into the OR. We'll give you a 'feel good' shot in a few minutes that will make you drowsy. You probably won't even see the OR. I'll check in on you in recovery around noon. Any questions?"

"Why is it so damned cold in here?"

"We don't want you to fall asleep before it's time Geoff. See you in a few hours."

As they walked out together Dr. Riker turned to his colleague, "He's got a great attitude Pete. He'll do very well. He could probably even make it to happy hour tonight if I'd let him. I really don't see any evidence that he drinks as much as he likes to pretend. His physical work-up belies any substance abuse. Great BP, cholesterol, BMI, trim athletic build, obviously no stranger to the gym."

"Um yes, I agree with you as far as his physical constitution, however I've gone over his psychological workup and his mental health profile gives me a little pause Vince."

"Really, how so doctor?"

"Two divorces, no children, no family, an arm's length of forwarding addresses. Very unsettled lifestyle - lists Brian Wilkins, an old Navy buddy as his next-of-kin."

"From what I understand, Brian, Geoff and Frank were in Vietnam together although I don't know the circumstances Pete. What do you make of it doctor?"

"I see the possibility for a lot of repressed issues; most likely bitterness, maybe anger and disconnect - it's common among vets of that era. For his sake as well as those around him I hope he has worked through these things. If not there could be latent hostility waiting for an excuse to erupt."

"Hmm - you think he's unstable?"

"No - not that extreme; he was in a Naval Special Warfare unit; they're a tough bunch both physically and mentally and they go through constant screening for fatigue issues. To couch it in clinical military terms - this is a guy who doesn't give a rats-ass about what's over the next bridge. He'll cross it in its time, stare it square in the eye and deal with it on his own terms. Perhaps this organ donation may prove therapeutic."

"Agreed Pete, a win-win situation - Frank gets a life extension and Geoff gets a new lease on life. See you in scrub in twenty-minutes doctor."

"Wake up Geoff."

He heard the words and even understood the meaning. Off in the distant shadows he could see someone leaning over him.

"Wake up Geoff, come on open your eyes."

It took a few minutes, it was a long way from where he was to where he was trying to get to and he just couldn't get his body to respond to his commands. He fought it. Finally, Dr. Riker came into focus leaning over his gurney.

"Hey doc," he said in a voice that sounded even to him a little out-of-body.

"The operation went exceptionally well. It was one of my fastest. Frank's new kidney is fully functional and producing urine. He looks almost as good as you now. How are you feeling?"

"Well I'd feel better if I had a pepperoni pizza with jalapeños and an ice cold beer."

"Sorry, I'm afraid that'll have to wait. You'll have to make do with some ice chips when you get thirsty. You'll get a light breakfast tomorrow morning."

"Umm...you didn't disclose that little caveat."

"Yeah we like to keep that as a surprise. Get some sleep. I'll check on you tomorrow morning."

A few hours later an orderly took him back to his room. He dozed most of the rest of the day sucking on some ice chips whenever he got thirsty.

The next morning, he awoke at about 05:00 anxious to get out of bed so he decided to try for a little walk. He chose the wrong way and got as far as the nurses station.

"Oh no Mr. McEwen why are you out of bed? You are not supposed to be up and around yet," said the nurse in her best scolding voice. "You get right back to bed now," she said trying to look her meanest as she attempted to assist him.

Breakfast came at 07:00. An orderly came in pushing a cart with two trays. She placed the first one with juice, gelatin and some bland farina on his tray table. Then she pushed open the privacy curtain dividing the two beds and Geoff realized he had a roommate. He looked over to see Robbins in the bed next to his.

"Hey… good morning Frank, how are you doing? You're looking better than when I saw you last week."

"Good Morning…I'm doing fantastic Geoff; I haven't felt this well in a long time. I'm just lying here thinking about all the extra time I'll have now that I won't have to go for dialysis treatments. How are you doing?"

"I'm ready to get the hell out of here and go get some real food… oh…uh… by the way Frank, I…I'm sorry about all that shit I gave you the other day."

"Forget it Geoff - I have, its bygones. You needed to get it off your chest. It was a small price to pay for a new kidney. I can't find the words to thank you enough."

"You don't have to Frank, you already have. Just seeing you looking so much better and knowing you'll improve and get to enjoy your grandchild is a real high for me."

"I'm really looking forward to it, I'll need to get my golf clubs back out and polish up my game, while I'm waiting for the baby to arrive."

"Hey we better quit talking and eat. Farina is bad enough warm, don't let it cool off," said Geoff.

About an hour later Tara and Chip with Brian close behind them walked into the room.

"Hey guys - how are you both doing?"

"We're doing fantastic," said Frank.

"Couldn't be better except if I were at happy hour," said Geoff with a hearty laugh.

"Your old teammate has that covered," said Brian as he whipped out three miniature bottles – one of Jose Cuervo, one of Jim Beam and one of Jack Daniels and held them up with his usual mile wide grin."

"Dad! They can't have that stuff in here," said Chip with a frown.

"That's one of the prerogatives of age son. You get to push the boundaries to their limit. When you've been through what we have you're entitled to live life large."

He passed the Cuervo over to Geoff, the Daniels to Frank and kept the Beam for himself. They broke open the bottles in unison.

"Here's to faster horses, younger women and older whiskey," said Brian.

"I'll trade you a young horse for a fast woman," said Geoff.

"I'll stick with the old whiskey," said Frank as they each took a swig from their bottles.

Right at that moment Dr. Riker showed up at the door and walked into the room.

"Hey… hey, what's going on here? Where'd you guys get that stuff?" he said standing there with his hands on his hips and using his best authoritative voice as he glanced over at Brian.

"We're just breaking in Frank's new kidney and trying to keep his heart healthy; purely a therapeutic dose," said Geoff with a shrug of his shoulders.

"The therapeutic value of that is questionable and if he keeps that up he'll need a new liver," said Dr. Riker shaking his head. "All right, look I'm going to turn my back, now you guys make that contraband disappear or I'll have to confiscate it. If Nurse Hastings catches you, we'll all be in deep trouble."

They each drained their bottles and passed the empties to Brian who quickly stuffed them in his pocket with his best pantomime of complete innocence.

"I guess I don't really need to ask how you guys are doing, do I?" asked Dr. Riker. "Are you having any problems that you want to ask me about other than a complete lapse of common sense?"

"No, everything is fine with me," said Geoff, "how about you Frank?"

"I'm feeling better than I have for far longer than I can remember," said Frank.

"Glad to hear that. Unless there are any contraindications I'll be discharging you both after breakfast tomorrow. You can both get out of bed this afternoon and go wander the halls and get a little exercise. Just don't overdo it, go slow. Listen to your body. And make sure you drink plenty of water to filter out that poison you've been chugging," said Dr. Riker as he walked out shaking his head and chuckling to himself.

Chapter forty-five

Over the next two weeks Geoff was at the YMCA daily doing laps in the pool, although not at his usual pace. He listened to his body and gradually increased the workout as he felt his strength return. He even got Frank to start going and shamed Brian into joining them on occasion. Within three days of his release from the hospital his appetite had returned to normal and he resumed most of his normal daily functions except for abdominal workouts. He'd let the pool laps work their magic for a while longer on the abdominals.

Frank was doing terrific. He had lost some weight, the jaundice in his eyes had disappeared and the color of his complexion had returned to a normal healthy look. He looked years younger. He claimed to now have the same energy level as he had had five or maybe ten years ago. On the weekends they all got together at Brian's house for a barbeque and then wound up playing Hearts.

Geoff called Danielle to touch base and let her know he was out of town on his book tour. He told her that it was all over between Karen and him and how he had found her drunk and obnoxious when he returned from the UT campus after their last visit.

"I guess I don't have to tell you to be on guard against any reprisals from Karen. You were right Karen does have a very combative ugly side," he said.

"I'm glad you're through with her; let's just forget about her now that she's out of our lives. If she's smart she'll go get some therapy."

"So how's your first UT semester going?"

"Fantastic I signed up for fifteen credit hours and I'm already loaded down with reading lists and term paper assignments but I'm loving every minute."

"That's great, you're going to do well. Keep in touch and I'll do the same. Take care Danielle...I love you."

"Oh I will Geoff, and thanks for everything...I love you too, bye."

Then he returned his attention to his book promotion. He had postponed the tour for the operation and now had to go back over his schedule and reset the dates. Luckily he hadn't set any fixed dates for any signings except in the local bookshops here in Billings.

The local signings all went well. Most bookshops these days have coffee concessions which just increase the possibilities for schmoozing. They were in no hurry to get rid of him and he was in no hurry to leave. He wound up overstaying his scheduled time at each venue. It was good for business and he got to sign more books than he expected.

Once he had finished his book signing engagements in Billings he turned his attention to Bozeman. The first one he had scheduled was at a cozy independent bookshop on the downtown Main street corner. It was in a wonderful old renovated building that must have stood there since the turn of the last century. It was called the Wine & Book Cellar and was a favorite of the coeds attending nearby Montana State University. It was popular as well with a good representation of the faculty and staff of MSU.

The inside had a hardwood floor and high ceiling. The floor had been refinished but it was obviously the original from its worn look. The heating and ventilation ductwork was all exposed with several five bladed fans spaced evenly throughout for air circulation.

Besides the usual coffee concession which was off to the side of the main room there was a full wine bar in a rear room accessed through a wide archway with a good selection of local and regional domestic wines as well as South American, Australian and European varieties many of which were even offered by the glass. They also hosted wine tasting parties scheduled on happy hour Fridays.

There were several vintage wine barrels that served as tables and a few couches as well as seats at the bar. Over on the side was a small platform that he guessed served as the stage for a solo guitar player or even a small combo of several musicians. As luck would have it today was Friday. So he figured he would probably stay for the tasting party.

The staff at the bookshop had set up a special table for him with a display of his book and a placard that read 'BOOKSIGNING: Geoff McEwen – Guest Author' in the main room near the coffee concession.

Along with the coffee the concession had a nice assortment of pastries. He spotted some old fashioned crumb cake, the kind that was loaded with crumbs that made up nearly half the thickness of the cake. It was the only sweet indulgence that he absolutely could not resist.

Not wanting to miss any potential customers he penned a sign that read: 'Author on break at the coffee concession – the guy by himself with the large latte munching on crumb cake...Geoff' and left it on his table. He got a large decaffeinated latte, a slice of the crumb cake and sat down at one of the tables not wanting to sit at his signing table just yet. It was still early afternoon and he wanted to people watch a little and get a feel for the crowd.

After a few minutes he saw several ladies go over to his table, pick up a book and peruse the jacket. Oops, Showtime... he thought to himself. One of them looked around and spotted him. As she made eye contact she held up a book making a signing motion on it with her hand. He motioned her over to his table in the concession area. They each picked up a book and came over.

"Sorry ladies, I don't want to get crumbs all over the place but if you're in a hurry I'll sign it here. This crumb cake is great stuff, I couldn't resist."

"You don't look like the crumb cake type," said one of them chuckling.

"Ah well to use a very apropos cliché – never judge a book by its cover," he said with a wink and a chuckle.

He asked their names and in turn personalized a brief note on the flyleaf of each book along with his signature then handed it back to each one saying thank you very much for the purchase as he looked each of them in the eye.

After they left he finished his latte and took a seat behind his table. Whenever a line formed he would sit down and sign away trying to strike a balance between being personal and not allowing a long wait, otherwise he would get up and walk around to engage in brief personal conversations.

He had been there nearly three hours when two ladies came up to the table together one walking slightly behind the other. The lady in front was very attractive, the one walking behind her and slightly hidden had on a white ribbed turtle-neck sweater under an open ski jacket with a broad brimmed western hat pulled down low over her eyes concealing her features and covering long blond hair with the back flowing down to just touch her shoulders. She had her head tilted down further obscuring her face.

"Good afternoon, would you like an autographed copy of my book?"

"Yes we both would like a copy please."

"And your name is?"

"Meier...Dr. Kirsten Meier."

"Do you spell that M e i e r?"

"Yes that's correct; that was a good guess, there is more than one way to spell Meier," she said with a pleasant laugh.

"Yes I know, I'm very familiar with the name and with that particular spelling, someone very dear to me spells her name that way."

"Oh really, by any chance would you be referring to my sister, Sonni?"

Geoff looked up startled as Kirsten stepped aside and the lady behind her stepped up and removed her hat.

"Sonni...Sonni! Oh my God Sonni wha...what...are you doing here, how are you, how have you been?" the words came tumbling out in a stammer as he leapt to his feet.

"Hello Geoff," she said flashing a bright smile as he bolted from behind the table.

She stood still for an instant her green eyes wide open and doe-eyed sparkling like a deer caught in a car's head beams, then with open arms they threw themselves together in a tight embrace.

"Sonni, oh Sonni, Sonni... I can't believe it..." Geoff choked out over and over as his eyes moistened with emotion.

"I couldn't find your doorstep so this will have to do... I love you, Geoff," she said in a hoarse whisper, "and I missed you so very much. I've been on pins and needles wondering what your reaction would be."

"And I love you Sonni...I never stopped loving you, I just began to doubt that I'd ever see you again."

"I always knew that I wanted with all my heart to one-day return to you Geoff. I just hoped I'd get the chance. But first I had to settle some issues and take back control of my life."

"You mean your ex-boyfriend, what was his name, Keith?"

"Yes, he truly is an ex now. He was shot and killed by the DEA in an altercation of some kind during a drug raid."

"I would have been there for you Sonni, through anything if you had let me."

"I know that Geoff, but I didn't want to drag you into any of that mess."

"Hey guys," said Kirsten, "I don't want to interrupt. You probably need some time alone. I'll be back at my house Sonni. Come on over and bring Geoff along so I can get to know him."

"Oh I'm sorry Kirs. Thanks so much for everything you've done. I'll call you later. And you will get to know Geoff. He's going to be family if I have my way."

Geoff held out his hand, "Allow me to introduce myself Dr. Meier, I'm Geoff McEwen."

"Oh please Geoff just call me Kirs or put the 't' on it if you like, I'm a PhD not an MD."

"Do you still want my book, Kirs?"

"Why yes, of course, I'm in the writer's group here in Bozeman, that's how I found out about your book signing."

"Thank goodness for writer's groups. How about you Sonni, do you want a copy of my book?"

"Oh I think I'll just settle for the author," she said wrinkling up her nose as she rubbed her hand softly over his back and gazed deeply into his eyes.

"Sonni let's get out of here and go find a quiet place where we can get re-acquainted," he said as he pulled her closer within his arms.

They walked a few blocks in the chilly late afternoon air and found a restaurant called the San Marino Underground situated to the side and below the wide front stone entrance steps to an old corner hotel. A menu featuring northern Italian cuisine was displayed in a side window.

The front entrance of the restaurant was through an archway a few steps down from the sidewalk. Inside, the motif was a romanticized version of a World War Two bomb shelter dimly lit with faux candles on the tables and along the bar. Several faux gas lamps hung on the walls near framed photos of scenes from World War Two.

The bar was quiet with one couple at the bar and two others at tables. A long bench seat ran the length of the rear of the bar and provided seating for three tables spaced discreetly for privacy. They took one of the end ones both sitting on the bench facing the bar. Geoff ordered a bottle of chardonnay.

"So what have you been doing since I last saw you? Let's see it was during the harvest moon – although to me, it seems quite a while longer." said Geoff as he looked into her eyes and held her hand between his, caressing it softly.

"I've been a busy girl, I completed and defended my dissertation and received my PhD; so I'm professionally Dr. Meier now just like my sister."

"Hey now that's great Sonni, congratulations, that must be a terrific feeling."

"Oh it is, believe me. I feel so much more credible and independent now. I can command a lot more respect in my field and earn much higher financial compensation. I applied for a position at the Marine Institute of San Diego as a post-doctoral fellow and I'll also be doing some research work at UCSD. So I guess we're a lot alike we just keep repeating past venues."

"Wow that sounds like you're going to have a full plate."

"I had to keep busy Geoff, or thoughts of you and us together would totally consume me driving me off track and I had to complete my agenda. All the while I kept thinking about you and us and Key West."

"How did you happen to be in Bozeman and pick today to come to the Wine & Book Cellar?"

"With a good bit of luck and a lot of help from my sister; I knew your book had to be close to publication so I asked Kirs to keep an eye on the latest releases in fiction and to let me know if she found anything by you. She's pretty tuned in to the literary world as an avocation even though her doctorate is in Biochemistry. She found some advanced notices for new releases on the internet and your book was listed. At her urging her writer's group managed to obtain a preliminary schedule of book signings from your publisher. She was so excited she called me up at two o'clock in the morning to tell me about it."

"That must have gone over well with you," he said chuckling.

"Yeah, I think I was a little rude to her until I heard what she had found. After that I shifted into high gear and even managed to push up my date for the research grant at UCSD. It was just amazing... everything just fell into place like it was meant to be."

"Well it was Sonni; I've been working overtime trying to build up good karma. Remember when I told you if we made a wish on the Harvest moon it would come true before the next Blue moon?"

"How could I forget honey? That was the night I knew that I was irrevocably in love with you."

"Well there's a Blue moon coming up this month on New Year's Eve. I made a wish back then that we would always be together."

"And I wished that my personal problems would all be resolved so that I could be with you. And here I am, no strings attached. I've sold off my business and the house in Daytona, paid off my loans and I'm all set to embark on a new career back on the west coast."

"That's fantastic; you are such an organized and intelligent lady besides being so gorgeous that you take my breath away."

"Now there's just one burning question left that I need to make certain of Geoff, and only one answer that will make this the best New Year's Eve of my life," she said looking deeply into his eyes as she reached over to take his hands in hers.

"I'm hoping it's the same question I have for you Sonni."

"Geoff, will you come with me to San Diego?"

"Sonni I set you free against my will back in Daytona, now that you've returned to me I don't intend to ever let it happen again. There's no way I'll ever leave you again or give you any reason to leave me."

He slid his arm around her and drew her close. "And I think San Diego would be a wonderful place to settle - close enough that we can get back to Montana frequently for visits with family yet it'll be our own little corner of the world," he said. "Say, why don't we take a train?"

"Ohhh yeah, we could. We could fly up to Vancouver B.C. and take it all the way down the coast. It would be a fun trip, very scenic and very romantic," she said squeezing his forearm.

"Do we get married in San Diego or is that too far ahead to plan?" he asked continuing the parody.

"Oh I don't know, what about the engineer on the train, maybe he can perform the ceremony," said Sonni flashing that same zany expression Geoff had seen on the beach in Daytona the first day they met. "Do you think we'll ever get to Paris?"

"I'll never say never Sonni, but if not we can always go back to Key West and maybe stay at the same place."

"Oow I'd like that," she said. "It would make a great anniversary destination. Oh listen to me we're not even married yet and I'm already planning our anniversary."

They burst out laughing together and smothered their laughter with a long passionate kiss.

"I love you Sonni," he said, their faces only inches apart.

"I'll never get tired of hearing you say that, please don't ever get tired of telling me. I love you too Geoff with all my heart."

"And don't you ever stop either Sonni."

"I won't... not until the shore breakers cease their assault on the sands of time..."

"Oh, I like that; it sounds like a good ending for my next book. May I use it?"

"Honey, you can plagiarize me all you want, just never take your love away."

"I won't... not until the shore breakers cease their assault on the sands of time...," he said trying to mimic her voice as best he could.

"Hey...you haven't written the book yet," she said drawing back and wrinkling her brow and pursing her lips in mock consternation.

"We're going to write this one together Sonni and our book won't have an ending..." their lips met and time stood still.

Author's Note

The inspiration for Wannabe dawned on 7-Jun-1994 at the Coffee Cottage in Metarie, Louisiana (a suburb of New Orleans) where I was scribbling thoughts in my ubiquitous steno pad while en route back to my then current address of Venice, Florida after completing a contract position in Mechanicsburg, Pennsylvania.

More than a year later, after relocating to Colorado Springs, Colorado I took a road trip to Montana where I wrote the opening lines for Chapter one on 4-Oct-1995 at Jake's Good Time Bar, an eclectic libation and eating emporium in Billings which became the setting for Chapter one, albeit with a name change.

The writing of Wannabe fraught with many interruptions as life got in the way has been a fond and comfortable companion over many hours in countless bars and through several address changes as my choices in life's journey took me down many subsequent forks.

Author Biography

I was born and reared in a small northern New Jersey town on the west bank of the Hackensack River seven miles west of New York City. Subsequent to graduation from Ridgefield Park high school and a four-year stint in the U.S. Navy I attended computer school and began a career as an IBM mainframe systems programmer.

Determined to pursue a college education and I graduated with a BA in Economics from Rutgers University in New Brunswick, New Jersey.

An avid reader of geo-politics, history and science, I've had a passion for writing since sixth grade where I volunteered to write a novel. It didn't get very far. Some of my best inspirations occur while sitting in bars sipping a drink and absorbing the ambiance as I scribble thoughts and scenes in a steno pad.

Anton K Vyborny

Printed in the United States
By Bookmasters